Hat Trick

ICECATS SERIES

TONI ALEO

Copyright © 2023 by Toni Aleo

All rights reserved.

No part of this book may be reproduced in any form or by any electronic or mechanical means, including information storage and retrieval systems, without written permission from the author, except for the use of brief quotations in a book review.

Editing: Silently Correcting Your Grammar: Lisa Hollett - AS ALWAYS, THANK YOU!

Proofer: Jenny RaRden - THANK YOU!

Cover: Lori Jackson - THANK YOU!!

Cover photo: Wander - thank you!

❀ Created with Vellum

Fear: Face Everything and Rise.
*This book is for **you**, the person fighting daily.*

And for the naughty side of you that wants to be called a "greedy girl," Dart
is yours.

CHAPTER

One

Dart

I will always be Owen Adler's best friend.

Nothing can or will ever change that. From the moment we met at training camp for the Carolina IceCats hockey team, I knew he was my dude. Best part, he has a twin, and Evan became a close friend too. Though, nothing could touch Owen's and my relationship. He's the brother I never had and always wanted. Someone I know will have my back to the end. On the ice, we know where the other is at all times, and we score because of it. His pass is butter, and my shot lethal. We're a dynamic duo, on and off the ice.

I had wingmen growing up, but nothing compares to Owen. We had some fun with the ladies, but that ended when he linked back up with Angela Paxton, an old childhood friend of his. I would say I was upset to see her come along and take my best friend, but I don't think even I could have resisted her. She's a force to be reckoned with and has become an extra sister I didn't know I needed.

One of the greatest honors of my life was being asked to be one of Owen's groomsmen when he and Angie get married, and I was ready. I was ready to support him, party, and do my duty to sleep with any bridesmaid who showed she was down. But that all changed the moment Angie set her eyes on me one afternoon.

"I don't have friends. I've got my sister, and that's it. I don't feel right asking any of the wives here because I'm not really close to them yet. And I mean, I love Owen's siblings, but I'm not close to them yet either. This is a lot to ask, but I'm closer to you than my sister or anyone else but Owen. Will you be my dude of honor, so it'll be even on both sides?"

The answer was easy.

Fuck yes.

When I say I have loved Angie since the moment she and Owen hooked up, I'm not lying. My dude was in love the moment she set her eyes on him, and I know why. She's easy to love. She may not realize that, but for me, it's always been effortless. She's funny, she's a badass, and she's smart. She may have a bit of a plant obsession, and I'm a little tired of being yelled at for accidentally hitting said plants, but she's still one of my favorite people. To have the honor of standing beside her as she proclaims her love for my best friend…man, it's even better than being Owen's groomsman.

I've been waiting for a while, but finally, the big day is here.

And I'm ready for it to be over.

My phone rings as I step off the elevator of the hotel I'm staying at for the weekend. It's fucking packed to the brim since there is a country music festival happening at the same time, but I'd rather stay here than in Owen's family home. I truly care for him, but let me tell you, he and his family are fucking nuts. They are loud, and something is always happening. Always. Some kind of drama, and I don't have it in me to be involved.

For some reason, I'm super fucking nervous to be Angie's dude of honor.

It's stupid, but man, I'm keyed up. I just want to do right by her, and it's hard when she stresses me the hell out. I really didn't know what I was signing up for. As the dude of honor, I had to plan a bridal shower. My idea of beers and strippers was not good enough, so I had to hire someone to throw a girlie shindig. The only good thing was I

HAT TRICK

hooked up with one of Angie's assistants in the bathroom while she opened presents.

Good times.

But as I pause before looking at my phone, hoping it's not Angie bitching about what dress to wear, I close my eyes. The whole dress thing is stressing me, and I'm about to send her down the aisle in a paper bag.

Lord knows she'll still be fine as hell.

I look at my phone to see that, thankfully, it's my baby sister. "Sabine, look at you. I love your hair!"

Her sweet face grins back at me as she brings the phone way too close to her face. Her blond ringlets fall around her cheeks while the top is in an intricate braid. "Thanks! I miss you!"

I smile, my heart doing a flip in my chest. "I miss you. How is everything going?"

She makes a face. "The only good thing about the new babysitter is she does my hair cool."

My stomach falls at her words. I was so close to having her near me, but of course, my mom found a new man and stayed in Arizona. I had the house ready for them, and I was prepared to move them here, but once more, my mom broke my heart. I still have hope, though; my mom doesn't keep a man for long. "I'm sorry, sunshine. Hopefully I'll get to see you soon."

"You have a game out here for preseason?"

I nod. "I do, and if I don't see you before that, I'll definitely see you then."

She smiles widely at me, her eyes the color of the sky. Since the moment she was born, I've called her sunshine because of her eyes. They're so blue, so bright, and remind me of a perfect day. She favors my mom, which means we look a lot alike. And even though there are sixteen years between us, I love her more than I can ever put into words.

"Awesome. I miss you."

My heart snags in my chest as I gaze into her eyes. I have just flown in from Arizona to Nashville for the wedding, but I understand her

TONI ALEO

missing me. I miss her the same. "I know, Sabine. I know. I miss you too, but it won't be long."

She makes a face of distress, and it guts me. I know I should head to where my car is waiting to take me to the wedding, but instead, I go to the bar. "Can't I live with you?"

This isn't the first time she has asked. The only reason she has a babysitter is because I pay the girl. My mom is busy, all the time, and can find no real reason to be a mom anymore. To her, Sabine isn't a reason.

It's frustrating as fuck. "I wish, sunshine. I do. But I'm never home during the season."

"Yeah, but at least you'd want to see me."

It's hard not to hate my mom; it really is. I head for the bar and lay my suit over the back of a chair. The bartender looks at me as I lean on the bar. I hold up a finger for a moment as I look down at my sister's face on the phone. "I love you, Sabine. I do. You know I do."

"I know. I love you too."

"Good. Listen, I gotta get to Owen and Angie's wedding, but I'll call you tomorrow, okay?"

"Okay. Bye, Dart."

"Love you, Sab."

"Love you."

I hang up, my shoulders falling, and I try not to allow my worry for my sister to ruin my day. She's just a kid—a baby, even. Fuck. I wish I could take her and have her live here, but it wouldn't be fair. I'm gone all the time, and I couldn't be a good parental figure. Hell, I'm not even really an adult. I'm still a horny teenager in a man's body.

"Can I get you something?"

I nod to the bartender. "Two shots of tequila."

"Lordy, is it even ten?"

I hadn't even noticed the girl beside me until she spoke, which is unlike me. Our gazes meet, and the grin I start to give her doesn't materialize. I'm stunned by her breathtaking eyes. One is the lightest of blues, almost crystal-like, while the other is a stunning mossy green color. I barely stop myself from muttering a curse at how breathless they leave me. But that isn't the only breath-stealing thing about her.

HAT TRICK

Full lips, glossed to perfection, and the cutest little button nose. Her face is round, her cheeks pink, while her blond hair is in a heap of a topknot on her head. She's wearing a bright-orange Tennessee Volunteers shirt and the shortest shorts, showing off thick thighs that I can tell are sticking to the barstool she's sitting on.

Now, the grin comes.

"One is for you, of course," I say, sliding it to her.

Her brow perks above her blue eye. "Smooth."

I wink at her as I hold up my glass to her, and she takes it, tapping hers to mine before we both down the drink. She takes a pull of the orange juice she has in front of her, while I suffer the burn. The burn being the reason for the shot before ten a.m.

"What are we drinking to?"

"Survival, at this point," I joke as I ask for another round. "Am I drinking this round alone?"

"Of course not," she says, her lips curving, and once more, we tap our glasses before downing the liquor. "Survival, you say? I can feel that."

I nod, wiping my mouth, my beard rough against my fingertips. I hope Angie doesn't bitch at me for not shaving. "Yeah. I have a wedding to be in. I'm the dude of the bride."

She grins. "That's really cool," she says, her twang sending chills down my spine.

"It is. So let's drink to their happiness, eh?" I ask, and she nods as I order another round. I'm going to regret this choice, but then again, I'm not. She takes hers and I take mine before we tap our glasses and down the shots once more. I move the glass up before digging into my pocket for my wallet. I lay my keycard on the bar and then my wallet before getting my card out to pay. "What are you drinking to?"

She bites into her lip, and she squeezes her thighs together as she gazes at me. Any other day, I'd be on the girl like white on rice, trying my hardest to get between those thighs. So thick, fuck me, I want to suffocate between them. "I got a new job, and my friends are taking me out to celebrate."

"Congratulations," I say, handing the bartender my card. "I'm lucky to have gotten you started."

5

TONI ALEO

Her cheeks redden. "Yeah. This is a great start, for sure. My room's not even ready."

I sign the tab, leaving a nice tip before handing the receipt and my card back to the bartender. "Put her tab on me."

She protests almost immediately. "No, you don't have to do that."

"I want to," I tell her, and her words trail off. I sign another receipt and grin at her as I tap my card to the bar. "Congratulations."

"Thank you," she says, her eyes bright and mesmerizing.

I reach for my wallet as I stay locked in her gaze. Unable to control myself, I ask, "Are your eyes real?"

She pauses for a second and shakes her head. "No. I got them off some dead guy on the side of the road." I grin and she laughs. "Yeah, they're real. My momma calls me husky, not only 'cause I'm chunky, but because my eyes remind her of a dog's."

Ooh, cock be still. The word *chunky* coming from those lips in that twang has my cock throbbing. I shake my head, chuckling. "They're insanely gorgeous," I tell her, and her lips turn up into the widest, most stunning smile. "And just know, if I didn't have a wedding, and my sister hadn't upset me, I would totally be hitting on you right now."

Her eyes darken a bit, striking me square in the chest. "And here I thought you *were* hitting on me."

I chuckle at that, and her lips curve again, leaving me breathless. I tap my wallet to the bar. "You live here?"

"Knoxville."

I nod. "I'm not from here, and I don't think one time would be enough with you."

Her eyes flash with heat. "It'd be a damn good time."

"Yeah, yeah, it would," I agree, holding her gaze. "We'll leave it to fate."

Her brows knit. "Fate?"

"Yeah, if I see you again before I fly out, we'll know. And nothing will stop me from truly hitting on you."

"So, you weren't hitting on me?"

I grin. "Maybe just a bit."

"Then God help me when you decide to fully hit on me." Everything goes tight as her eyes hood a bit, her lips part, and she leans in, her shoulder pressing into mine. She holds her fingers up, showing me they're crossed as her eyes dance with mine. "But until then, here's to hoping."

Her confidence is intoxicating, and I exhale heavily. I find myself fighting the urge to skip the wedding and get lost with this gorgeous girl. I grab my suit bag and give her one last grin, which is a huge mistake. Those eyes are bewitching. "Have a good time celebrating."

"You too," she says softly, and then she holds her hand out. "Tennessee, but I usually go by Tennie."

"Your parents must love this state."

She nods. "Oh, they do. They both grew up here, met at University of Tennessee, and since I failed them by being a girl who couldn't play Volunteers football and they couldn't name me Neyland, they named me Tennessee instead."

"Impressive. I think it's a perfectly unique name for a girl with unique eyes," I say, taking her hand. It's soft, warm, and the touch has blood pumping right to my cock. I have to force myself to ignore my need, and I somehow get out, "Dart."

"Dart?"

"D'Artagnan, but no one calls me that."

"Don't know why. It's a badass name," she says, cupping her face with the hand I just shook. "There has to be a story behind that name."

I nod. "Not as great as your story, but I'm named after *The Three Musketeers*. My mom is obsessed with the movie since I don't think she's read a book in her life."

She grins. "I've never seen it."

I chuckle. "Oh, the pickup line is on the tip of my tongue, Tennie," I say, meeting her gaze. "If I didn't have somewhere to be, I'd tell you to come on upstairs and I'd find the movie for us."

She grins. "Damn your friends for falling in love."

"Rude, right?"

"Super rude," she agrees as I back away from the bar.

I tip my chin to her. "See ya, Tennie."

"I sure am hoping so," she says as I start to walk away. "D'Artagnan."

I stop midstep and look over my shoulder at her. She leans on her hand, her eyes playful and full of lust as blond tendrils fall on either side of her round face. She kicks the leg she had crossed over her other, causing those thighs to call to me like a zapper to a bug. I have to remind myself that Angie is waiting for me. She's gonna bitch I didn't shave, and she is depending on me to be a buffer between her and her sister. Plus, I don't think she knows what dress she is wearing yet. I gotta go. Angie needs me, and I'll always be there for the people who want me around. The fact that I am choosing Angie and her wedding over getting lost between Tennie's thighs says a lot.

A whole fucking lot.

Growth. I'm growing. Maybe I am an adult?

With a wink and a wave, I turn and walk away.

Nope. Still a horny teenager, because the only thing I can think is that there better be someone at this wedding with whom I can ease the regret of walking away from Tennessee.

CHAPTER
Two

TENNESSEE

"Why didn't you give him your Snap?"

I shrug as I put on my eyeliner, and I hate how her simple question makes me feel inadequate. I meet Josie's gaze as I press my lips together. "I don't know. I mean, it was line after line. If he was interested, he would have asked for it."

Lindy stands beside me, curling her long blond hair. "Tennie, men aren't dumb. Men don't chase women anymore, and a guy sure as hell won't make a move unless he knows you want him."

"For real. And are you sure he was talking to you?" Josie asks, and Lindy makes a face.

Anger sparks inside me, but I swallow it before acting like I'm looking for something in my makeup bag. I was hesitant to go out with them, but I knew I really didn't have any choice. When my mom suggested she'd get a hotel room for me to celebrate, I knew that she meant for *us*.

I grew up with Lindy and Josie. Our moms were sorority sisters, they all bought houses on the same cul-de-sac, and bam, I had two instant best friends. We did everything together; our families were always together, and everyone just assumed we were three peas in a pod.

I love them. I do. Yeah, kids can be cruel and I wasn't built like Lindy and Josie, but they never made me feel different for it.

But then college happened. Things really changed. We were no longer in our small town, where everyone knew everyone.

Like our moms, we went to UT, and we got into the sorority together. The only difference—I was now the fat one. For the first time in my life, I felt like I was on the outside. I was the one to drive everyone home when they were drunk because I didn't need the calories from the drinks. Since guys were never interested in me and they always saw me as a friend, I was the one sent to find out if a guy was interested in either of them. We shared a room, but I never felt like I was a part of anything. They shared the bunk bed, and I had a full-size bed in the corner. I knew the only reason I was even in the sorority was because of who my mom was. She had been the president of the sorority and sent a lot of money to the school. Too bad I was a disgrace to her legacy, and too bad I didn't give two shits.

I love my mom. I love her with all my heart—as well as my dad—and while they'd never say I didn't live up to what they wanted for me, I know I didn't. They wanted me to go into finance like they did, but I wanted to go into medicine. I wanted to help people. I also carry weight, unlike them, and sometimes I felt like they had an issue with that when I was growing up. But I have to think that was my own insecurities.

Now, though, I don't care what they think. I am happy with how I look, and I refuse to let anyone make me feel less for it. Since everyone at home tends to do just that, this new job of mine is my ticket out of this fucking state that I share a name with and everything in it.

I glance over Josie as I unclip my hair. "Well, he was looking right at me and no one else was around, so I assume so."

She shrugs. "I'm just saying, that's real forward for someone who didn't even ask for your Snap."

"For sure," Lindy adds. "I feel like if he wanted to take you upstairs, he'd have asked for your number at least, even if it was just to lose it later."

HAT TRICK

Why am I here? I shouldn't have come; I should have just started packing, even though I don't leave for another two weeks. "Well, that's real fucking rude, asshole," I say, meeting Josie's gaze, and she waves me off, laughing.

"I'm only joking."

Which is always her response. That's the thing about Southern folks; we can be real passive-aggressive. I ignore her as I comb out my hair, and Lindy says, "We should have done your roots before we left."

I sigh deeply. "Y'all are starting to piss me off."

Josie snickers. "Oh my. Tennie gets a big-girl job and has a hot guy hit on her, and now she's too big for her britches."

I know she doesn't mean it the way she says it, but it still pisses me off. Maybe I'm about to start, or maybe they are just being bitches today. I reach for the curling iron and start on my hair as they do what they do best. Ignore me.

"Did you see that Amy was saying she might meet up with us?" Josie asks, and I roll my eyes.

Great.

"Why would she? She doesn't even like Tennie! It's her night," Lindy asks, visibly confused.

I have to hold back from asking if they really even like me.

"That's what I said. I was like, um, we're good," Josie agrees before finishing her hair.

Lindy takes the curling iron from me. "Let me do it. We are celebrating you."

I allow her to curl my hair as Josie asks, "Have you told your parents you took the out-of-town job?"

"Not yet," I admit. "Don't be telling y'all's mommas."

"We won't," they promise, and I hope they don't. I really do want to tell my parents myself, but I made the mistake of being drunk when I got the email that I had been hired, and I blurted it out to them.

"They're gonna be proud, Tennie. Even if they don't want you to leave, you're going to be so involved with all kinds of sports, which is what they wanted," Lindy reminds me.

Too bad I'm not doing it for them.

I've always found the way the body moves during sports fascinating. I used to watch my dad play football, and my mom softball. I played softball my whole life, and I even had the chance to play for UT. It's always amazed me how our bodies can do what they do when it comes to sports. I wanted to know everything, and I wanted to help people when they had goals that felt unattainable.

When I got my master's degree in kinesiology with a concentration in biomechanics, I had every intention of working for the University of Tennessee in their sports programs, but I also knew I needed to get the hell out of here.

I almost feel like I don't know who I am. Like, I love who I am, but I haven't had time to discover *me* because I'm constantly under the influence of Lindy and Josie. Just looking at us three, it's obvious the only difference is I'm the bigger one. We wear our makeup the same, we wear our hair the same, all three of us are bleach blondes, but I'm the darkest of us three. Oh, I have two different-colored eyes, but Lindy has blue eyes, and Josie has green. Our parents have always said that half of them made me, and I have always hated it. I struggle with how I feel because these girls are my sisters in every sense of the word, but I don't care for them much anymore.

It makes me feel fake. It makes me feel like my whole life is a lie.

And I've got to go. I've got to get the hell out of here.

I know it will be hard for my parents, my grandparents, and even my great-grandparents. No one from our families has ever left Tennessee. Some may have moved from Knoxville, but for the most part, everyone is still there. I'll be the first to leave, and while the fear has me on edge and the unknown makes it hard to breathe, I know I've gotta go. And I have to go alone.

"Did you by chance check social media for him?" Lindy asks, yanking me from my thoughts. Josie picks up her phone then as Lindy pulls my hair up halfway, putting it in a hair tie before tying a bright-orange ribbon around it. Just like hers and Josie's. Our UT pride is on full display. I don't doubt they have UT pride, but sometimes I think they do it because it draws in guys. For me, I just love the team.

"I did. Couldn't find anything." Which is a lie. I didn't look for him at all. I didn't want to fawn over someone I'll probably never see again. I kind of like the idea of leaving it to fate. While I can't get his

HAT TRICK

lips or his eyes out of my mind, I know this way is for the best. I'm on my way out, and he isn't even from here. So, what's the point? A night of passion may sound like a damn good idea, but I'm sure when we walked away, I'd have a hard time filling the void he'd leave.

"Yeah. I can't find anything for Dart. Who names their kid Dart?" Josie asks, her face all scrunched up.

I meet her gaze. "Hi, my name is Tennessee."

She snorts. "Which is badass," she says, smacking my arm. "Maybe he was a drug dealer, and that's why he had tattoos along his neck."

I almost feel embarrassed for how easy it was for me to describe him. The moment he walked up, I was taken by how attractive he was. Dark-blondish hair in a heap of a mess, falling into his eyes, and blondish-brown hair along his jaw and lip. He had full-sleeved arms, and even his hands were tattooed. Along his neck was the word sunshine, and his grin was so easy and blinding. He had hard lines to his jaw, but full lips and even fuller cheeks. Even in his tee and shorts, I could see the lines of muscles, and I was curious as to what he did for a living.

"And the fact that he bought three rounds of shots before ten a.m. and paid for your breakfast," Lindy adds, but I shake my head.

"I think he is an athlete. He was super buff."

Josie makes a face. "And he was hitting on you? That's odd. Usually athletes want super-skinny supermodels."

I blow out a breath as I meet her gaze. "Thanks for the reminder that I don't ever need."

She meets my gaze. "What is wrong with you? You are being really testy today."

Maybe she's right. Maybe I have let her comments about my size slide a lot before. But fuck, I'm over it. "I'm tired of you constantly pointing it out. Yes, I am bigger than you. It is what it is. Do me a solid and recognize I'm more than my weight."

Lindy meets my gaze and nods, but no way in hell will she say anything. Lindy is the soft-spoken, easygoing one of us. Josie is the loud bitch, and me... Hell, I don't even know.

"I never said you weren't more than your weight, Tennessee, and

I'm highly offended right now." The way she draws out my name, in her holier-than-thou manner, has my blood boiling.

"Oh, are you?" I ask, holding her gaze, and Lindy clears her throat. "How the hell do you think I feel?"

"I don't mean anything by it, though. I'm only stating what I see."

"Which is that I'm fat?"

"Tennessee, what the hell?"

"That's what you're stating, correct?" And that has Josie pressing her lips together tightly, her eyes wild.

"I think emotions are high and we need to move on," Lindy suggests. But my gaze stays locked with Josie's in a heated glare. Once more, Lindy clears her throat. "Okay, so I'm done. We ready to head to dinner?"

I tear my gaze away first, mostly for Lindy's sake. I smile at her. "Thanks for doing my hair."

She leans in, squeezing my shoulders. "You're beautiful, Tennie."

"Thank you," I say before I get up and go to grab my purse. My shorts have rhinestones dangling from them, and my orange tank, which is adorned with rhinestones too, hugs my boobs, showing a little bit of my stomach. My custom UT cowboy boots glitter, and I could be one hell of a UT version of a country Winnie the Pooh.

Lindy is right; I am beautiful. And I know the words Dart said to me were true. He was interested—hell, I was too—but leaving it to fate is probably for the best.

Even if it's painful to know that no matter how tightly I cross my fingers, I'll never see that guy again.

CHAPTER
Three

Dart

Angie is pacing.

So much that I want to pace with her from the nerves that are eating me alive. Back and forth, over and over again. To the point I'm pretty sure she's going to make a rut underneath her feet in the carpet of the private room of the Parthenon.

I figured they'd go for a rustic venue since they both grew up here in the Nashville area, but Owen said that since Angie is a goddess to him, he wanted to marry her where she belongs. In the Parthenon. Yes, I truly gagged when he told me that sticky-sweet shit. But for Owen, it's his truth. He is very vocal about it, but right now, I think Angie is forgetting who the hell she is.

As she paces, I lie across the chaise, watching her stop at each wedding dress that hangs before her and then staring at it. My friend has lost a bit of weight, but she doesn't see that. In her head, she should be the size of her sister and mother, who are both very thin. While they are beautiful women, Angie has always caught my eye. She is stunning, with her blondish-brown hair and blazing green eyes, full

TONI ALEO

cheeks, and Cupid's bow lips. As Owen says, she could be a goddess for sure.

I hate that she is struggling, and I really hate the silence in the room. I figured maybe her mom would do something, or even her sister, but no one is doing shit but sitting here and staring at her. I'm dying. I clear my throat, and I call to her, "So, just so you know, I chose being your dude instead of banging this chick at the hotel."

Without looking at me, Angie scoffs. "I'm surprised you didn't do both."

"The night is still young," I agree, pleased with myself for making her smile. "But that being said, I'm here to be supportive and shit. So, what can I do?"

She exhales hard, her whole body making the motion as she just stares at the dresses. There are four, and each is beautiful in its own right. One is tight on her body, showing every bit of her curves with one hell of a slit. Another is tight right under her boobs before flaring out with flowers and shit all over the skirt. Another is lace that looks like a curtain on her, and the other is really ugly. I don't even know why it's here. It has no straps and hugs her to her thighs before billowing out like a clump of seaweed. I called her a busted-looking Ariel in that one, and the look I got was downright murderous. I actually went and hid in the men's room when that happened. The whole wedding dress thing has been an issue from the beginning. They even pushed back the wedding because of her issues with the dresses. I told her just to go down the aisle in some sweats, but apparently that would be unacceptable.

I watch as Angie's throat works, and I sense that she might cry. I look at her mom, who is watching her, worry apparent on her face, and her sister, who is on her phone, bored. I'm not entirely sure what to do, but I just follow my instincts. "Can I have a moment with her?"

Her mom's eyes widen, and her sister gets up and leaves without a word. I'm not sure how I feel about Charlotte, but she is a teenager. I'm told they're no fun. Mrs. Paxton looks between us. "Angie, can I do anything, honey? You know the carriage will be ready in fifteen."

Angie closes her eyes, and when she doesn't answer, I look back at Mrs. Paxton. "She'll be ready."

I don't even believe that, but Mrs. Paxton leaves the room then. Hesitantly, but she goes, nonetheless. I get up, fixing my suit before buttoning the jacket and going to my girl. I stand beside her, crossing my arms over my chest as I take in all the dresses.

I side-eye Angie, and damn, if she isn't stunning. Her makeup is done in a dramatic yet ethereal way. Her skin shimmers, even though she looks as if she may break out in tears at any moment. Her lips are glossy with only a tiny bit of color on them. Her hair is in an intricate updo that has braids and twists throughout it. Tendrils fall along her face, reminding me of Tennessee from the bar. I can't think of her right now, though, not when my girl needs me.

"Alrighty, Angie, what we thinking?"

She shrugs, gazing at each one. "That I should just call Owen and tell him I can't do this. That we should just cancel the whole thing, and we can head to the airport, get an earlier flight."

I grin. "I thought you were getting cold feet for a second there."

She shakes her head. "Never. I want nothing more than to be married to Owen."

"Okay, so why are you stalling?"

She doesn't answer me at first. "Because I don't want to embarrass him," she admits, her teeth coming down onto her bottom lip to stop it from quivering. "My body doesn't look good enough for any of these dresses, for him."

Oh, the rage that stirs in my chest is real. "Tell me something—"

"I'd rather not."

"I know, but humor me," I say, turning to look at her. She looks up at me, her sweet eyes shining with unshed tears. "Has Owen ever made you feel embarrassed by your body?"

She doesn't look away. "You know that answer, Dart."

"Exactly. I do. As do you," I remind her. "So, why in the fuck would you think you're going to embarrass him today? I'm pretty sure you could walk down that aisle butt-fucking-naked, and he'd be all kinds of things—but not even a bit embarrassed."

She swallows hard.

"It'd be a surefire way to get the wedding canceled, for real. He wouldn't be able to resist taking you on whatever surface he could

TONI ALEO

find," I add with a wink, and that has her grinning from ear to ear. "He loves you, Angie. All of you."

She nods slowly. "I know, but…" Her voice trails off, and I wrap my arm around her shoulders. She cuddles into my side as she looks up at me. "I want to feel beautiful."

"Girl, feel it, because you are," I insist, cupping her jaw. "You've got four dresses, Ang. Each one looks fantastic on you and will leave everyone in the hall breathless at your beauty."

"You said I looked like a busted version of Ariel in that one dress," she says dryly, and I nod.

I reach for the dress, throwing it to the side. "Yeah, I hate that one. So, three." Her grin returns, and I squeeze her to me. "Wanna know my favorite?"

"Sure…"

I point to the one that hugs her curves and falls along her legs like butter. It has a sexy-ass slit that goes to the top of her thigh. The corset bodice is covered in crystals and glitter, and one strap drapes over her arm in a truly goddess-looking way. It's actually the dress that I had helped pick out. She fought me on the slit, but I told her she'd be jaw-dropping in it. "I chose it for a reason."

She swallows hard and then reaches for the dress. "Okay."

"Really?"

"Yeah, I've got to do this. And since I know you and Owen think about the same, if you think I'll look good in it, maybe I will."

I hold her gaze. "You will, Ang. Honestly."

She gives me a small smile before she turns to gather the dress in her hand.

I let my head fall back, silently thanking the good Lord above as she heads to the dressing room.

Before she goes in, she looks back at me. "Thanks for choosing me over getting laid."

"It was an easy choice," I tell her, giving her a bright grin.

She returns the grin, her eyes twinkling. "Liar."

I don't even disagree with her on the accusation because she's completely and utterly right.

HAT TRICK

By the look in Owen's eyes, I know Angie chose the right dress.

She knows, too, the moment she sets her eyes on Owen. The big grin that fills her face, the way her eyes widen with awareness of him, and how the blush creeps down her neck means one thing—she feels gorgeous under her soon-to-be husband's gaze. The way she should.

When Angie hands me her bouquet, she leans in and gives me a kiss on my cheek before whispering, "Thank you."

"Anytime."

It is a promise I intend never to break. As she turns to Owen, my dude cries like a baby, and I can't deny it is hard to keep it together. I swear there isn't a dry eye in the place as Owen and Angie proclaim their love for each other. I watch as Owen's hands shake with hers, how he stumbles over his words, and when they kiss, sealing the deal, even I wipe a tear from my cheek. These two are my bestest of friends, a family I've always wanted, and watching them become one will be a highlight in my life I'll never be able to forget.

I stand against the bar, watching as they move around the floor for their first dance. With the way they gaze into each's other eyes, I'm pretty sure, to them, no one else is here. I feel my lips tip up as I tear my gaze from them to look around the venue. The Parthenon is a beautiful place already, but they made sure to decorate in a regal way, with gold and white throughout the whole space. They didn't have to do much since the Parthenon is so stunning, but what they did really added to it. Huge white flower arrangements fill each table, which is covered with a gold tablecloth. The chairs around the tables are fancy and painted gold, making it feel as if we're in ancient Greece and Angie truly is Athena. In front of a statue of Athena is the table for the wedding party, full of flowers and gold candleholders. Along the front of the table, it reads "Owen and Angela" in elegant gold script.

It is a stunning environment.

One full of love.

I continue to look around the room for something—or, better yet, someone—to capture my attention. Of course, gorgeous women are everywhere, but most are holding on to their spouse's or date's arms. I should have convinced Tennessee to be my date. That would have been a blast, for sure. Man, her eyes are heavy on my mind. I wonder what they'd look like when I'm between her legs and taking her over the edge. Lost in that body that is begging to be held. I may have made a bad choice, picking this wedding over her.

But when Angie's gaze falls on me, her lips tipping up just for me, I know that's not true. I was there for Angie when she needed me, and that's all I've ever wanted to do for her. Remind her how fucking gorgeous and perfect she is. Help her have the confidence that she should never, ever lack. I wasn't sure about my role as dude of the bride, but I gotta say, I killed it. I tip my beer up to my lips, taking a long pull as couples move to the floor, dancing alongside the newlyweds.

"Think I can leave?"

I hadn't even realized Quinn Adler, Owen's baby brother, had come to stand beside me until he spoke. I cup the love-sick fool's shoulder and shake my head. "Sorry, dude. I was told you gotta stay."

He doesn't like that answer, and I don't blame him. Who wants to watch people get married and be happy when you're brokenhearted over a girl who says she loves you but doesn't want to be with you? That shit makes no sense to me, but I hear no one thinks Emery Brooks is making sense. As long as I've known Quinn, he's been smitten with Emery. Told me numerous times—mostly because he didn't want me to hit on her. Not that it would have stopped me if she'd interested me. She's beautiful but not my type.

"I wish she were here."

I just shake my head. I heard at the last wedding, he sang to her and begged her not to leave, but she blew him off. It was completely cringeworthy and awkward, and I'm thankful I missed it. Owen gave me a play-by-play, and even that made me embarrassed for the kid. "Let's be glad she's not so you aren't making a fool of yourself."

He groans, shaking his head. "She makes me foolish."

"Yeah, I've heard."

Quinn looks out at the wedding reception. "I should just find someone to forget with."

HAT TRICK

"Good idea," I agree, nodding to where a couple of ladies are watching us. "There is a gaggle of women right there."

He shakes his head. "I grew up with them. There is no hooking up with them without feelings. On their part, not mine."

"That's unfortunate. Think I got a chance?"

He chuckles at that. "Pretty sure you'd piss someone off if you did."

I laugh with him. "Probably." I turn to order another beer, and then I grab my wallet to leave a tip. When I open it, though, I notice my hotel keycard isn't in there. I curse as I pull some cash out for the tip. "I think I left my room key at the hotel bar."

Quinn makes a face. "That blows."

"It does," I agree, knowing I'll have to swing by the front desk for another one before I crash for the night.

We lean against the bar, watching the party take off, and I smile when I see Owen's twin brother Evan with his arms wrapped around his girl, Callie. I'd go hang out with him since Quinn is making me depressed, but I get tired of being the third wheel with all of my friends. I need to start hanging with some of the single hockey players back home. All my friends are getting locked down quickly, and while I'm happy for them, I'm bored out of my mind socially.

Which has been an ongoing thing lately. Nothing has kept my attention, nor anyone. It's weird, but I blame my friends. If they were out with me, trying to hook up with girls, I'd have more fun. Instead, I've been staying at home with Owen and Angie, watering fucking plants.

I really need new friends.

"I don't think I'm going to get laid tonight," Quinn says, and I let out a long sigh.

I tap my beer to his and nod. "Same, bro. Same."

CHAPTER
Four

TENNESSEE

Tension is still as thick as my ass as I head downstairs with Lindy and Josie to start our night. Josie hasn't really spoken to me since I called her out, and I have no desire to speak to her. Which leaves poor Lindy in the middle, trying to smooth things over. Not that she is trying, really. They are talking about something on social media as I lean on the wall, wishing like hell I could go back to the room and watch some trash TV.

As we get off the elevator, my phone rings. I look to see it's my mom.

"Hey, Mom. What's up?"

"Hey, honey. Are y'all about to head out?"

"Yes, ma'am. We're on our way down to FGL House."

"Well, that sounds like a blast for a night to remember," she says, and while I don't feel the same, maybe I should. Maybe I should let go of what has been said, just enjoy my friends before I leave. I don't know. But then I sense a hesitation in my momma's voice. "Listen, I saw Denis's momma at the Piggly Wiggly." And there it is. Fuck me.

HAT TRICK

"And we were talking. I told her about your new job, and she said that Denis was missing you like crazy. So, I may have meddled a bit."

It takes everything in me not to curse at my momma. "Momma, why?"

"I know, I'm sorry. But he's there." I swear, I feel like I'm in a movie because just as she says that, I see Denis by the sliding doors of the hotel entrance. "He wanted to celebrate with you, and you know I adore him."

And this is another reason I've got to get the hell out of this state. My momma meddles like no other. It's like she's scared I'll never find anyone but Denis, and she is beyond wrong. "I'm going to let you go so I don't yell at you."

"Tennessee, I did it with love."

"As you always say. And sometimes, it makes me question this love of yours. Bye, Mom." I hang up as Lindy's and Josie's gazes fall on me.

"What's wrong?" Josie asks, and I tip my chin toward Denis. All three of us look at him, and I can tell right away he's pretty sure we're seeing and talking about him. Don't get me wrong; Denis is a decent-looking dude. Sandy-brown hair, combed to the side, dark eyes, and a nice line to his jaw. He wears a pressed blue polo with beige golf shorts. Denis is also my height, maybe a bit shorter if I've got my heels or boots on. He is skinny as a rail, and that doesn't do it for me. I'm a big girl; I want a guy who can literally toss me around like a sack of potatoes and fuck me senseless. Denis fucks like he's scared he'll hurt me. Because he's nice. That's it. Nice. He has always treated me with nothing but respect, but he does not make me burn like the fiery depths of hell with desire.

I need more. I deserve more.

"Did you ever get him to choke you that one night?" Josie asks, and I scoff as he starts for us. Since he knows we've been talking about him, I appreciate the confidence he's portraying as he comes toward us. Still, it does nothing for me.

"Girl, he told me he couldn't do it. He didn't feel right cutting off my airway. Said it couldn't be safe."

She snorts. "You should have done it to him."

TONI ALEO

"I tried, and he panicked," I say softly. "It's my fault. I should have known the first time we hooked up."

Lindy makes a face. "You were younger and didn't know what you wanted yet."

"She's right. This on-again, off-again thing has been a problem for a long time," Josie adds, and I nod in complete agreement.

Denis and I have dated on and off since I was sixteen. We were each other's senior prom dates, my first time, and we dated a lot through college, but he never actually fulfilled me. He has done right by me, but I was the one to finally end things. Everyone blamed it on me being the young one since he's two years older than I am, but it wasn't that. He isn't *it*. While I truly care for him—and I know our parents have been planning our wedding since we met—when we broke up, I knew that was it. We were really done, and we *needed* to be done for both of us to move on.

"Why is he here?" Lindy asks, and I shake my head.

"Momma got involved once more."

"I mean, he is nice to you," Josie reminds me, and I flash her a dark look.

"But I want more."

They both sigh deeply as Denis comes toward us, a nice grin on his face. He meets my gaze and then leans in, kissing my lips like we haven't been broken up for three months. "Hey, Tennie."

"Hey, Denis. How are you?"

"Good," he says, grinning. He then hugs and greets Josie and Lindy. "Hope y'all don't mind me crashing y'all's little celebration. I'm in town for a dentists' convention and wanted to celebrate with y'all."

Another thing about him that drove me crazy—his obsession with teeth. I bet right now I can put my hand in his pocket, and he'll have a toothbrush. He always tasted like spearmint to the point I now despise the flavor of it. His mouth is always clean. Always. And I know that should be a good thing, but sometimes I want to taste the beer on a guy's lips. Denis didn't even like to give oral because I'd complain when he'd go to brush his teeth after. God, he's so fucking wrong for me.

HAT TRICK

I almost remind him that we aren't getting back together because he has that gleam in his eyes, but I refrain, not trying to be a bitch.

"No worries. Let's go," Josie says. "Let's see what the night holds."

I go to link arms with Lindy, but Denis threads his fingers through mine. I look up at him, and he kisses my knuckles. "You sure do look gorgeous, Ten. You've slimmed down."

I look at Lindy, and she scowls as she links arms with Josie, walking ahead of us. Instead of responding to his comment, I decide to ignore it and, instead, walk face first into this clusterfuck I call my celebration night.

———

When we get to FGL House, Denis is quick to pay for everything. Our drinks, our food, and of course, Josie and Lindy don't complain. Mostly because it won't fall on them; it'll fall all on me. As I lean on the rail around the rooftop that overlooks the city, I ignore my phone that is going off in my pocket. It's my mom, texting to see how things are going. I'm pretty sure she already has my wedding venue picked out.

With that thought, I can't help but be reminded of Dart. I wonder if he's having fun as the dude of the bride and if he's thought about me like I have him. The look in his eye as I accused him of hitting on me has me grinning from ear to ear.

Fate.

I should have convinced him to take me with him. I can't help but think of those shoulders of his and how great it'd be to dig my nails into them. I bet if we'd gone upstairs to watch that movie, he wouldn't treat me like he'd hurt me. I bet he'd throw all control out the window and leave me begging for more.

And I'd have no issue begging him.

I swallow hard as I look out at the city. I love Nashville. I thought about working here, but it's entirely too close to Knoxville. Plus, I know Lindy and Josie would try to stay with me on the weekends to party, and that doesn't work for me. Like now, they're not hanging out with me. They're at the bar, laughing and flirting with guys. I tried to

25

hang, but it's hard to flirt with guys when I have Denis watching my every move.

I feel a pair of arms move around me, and I freeze at his touch. I smell the spearmint before he even speaks. "I love when you wear shorts."

I roll my eyes, moving out of his arms. He looks hurt that I did so, but surely he didn't think I'd let him hold me when I haven't spoken to him in months. "What are you doing?" I find myself asking, and he shrugs, leaning his hip on the railing.

"Figured it was fate that I was here tonight when you're celebrating the new job."

I shake my head, hoping like hell this isn't the fate Dart was speaking of. "Absolutely not."

"Come on. You know it's true."

"Denis, no. My feelings haven't changed."

He laughs. "Tennie, don't say that. We belong together."

Now I'm laughing. "We certainly do not," I tell him, holding his gaze. "You do absolutely nothing for me."

His eyes darken as he leans in. "That's a really messed-up thing for you to say. We've been doing this almost ten years."

"Exactly," I say, looking at him. "And it doesn't work. We make it work for show, or maybe out of loneliness, but this isn't what I want."

"We're good together, Ten."

"We aren't," I stress, pulling my hand back when he tries to hold it. "I mean, we get along because you're nice and I care for you, but that's it."

"But I love you."

Oh, come on. "Denis, yes, there is love. But it's not a burning love. There is no heat between us."

"I feel heat," he tries, but he must be able to hear in his own voice that there isn't any.

"I don't. I never have. You're familiar, you're safe, but I need more. I need fire, which is why I'm leaving."

"What do you mean, leaving?"

"I took an out-of-state job."

HAT TRICK

"What? Where?"

"It doesn't matter. I need a fresh start."

He just stands there, staring down at me. I don't understand the look on his face. It seems as if I've betrayed him, but how? We haven't even spoken or been together in three months. "I always thought we'd get married once you finished school."

I gawk at him. "I don't know why. I never told you I would."

"I didn't ask."

"Thank God, because I would have said no," I tell him, and anger fills his features. "There is someone out there who is going to be perfect for you, but that's not me."

He doesn't say anything for a moment, and then he clears his throat. "I'm gonna go."

"Okay."

"You're not going to stop me?"

"No," I say, holding his gaze. "I need more."

He's visibly upset, but he doesn't say anything else. His throat works with emotion, but thankfully, he walks off. The relief that runs through me is welcome and needed. I'm on a mission to cut ties and tie up loose ends. I have to start a life that is mine. Not Lindy's, not Josie's, and not my momma's. I head to where the girls are, and when Lindy looks at me, she grins, already a bit tipsy.

She hands me a shot, and I take it eagerly before she asks, "Where is Denis?"

"Gone."

"Over, over?"

"Over, for sure."

She hands me a beer, and we tap the necks before Josie is pulling us onto the dance floor. The drinks flow, and the men are in abundance in Nashville tonight. I dance with a lot of guys, do shots, and dance—oh, I dance so much. With Lindy and Josie, and then by myself. It's a damn good night, one I know I needed, even if I was hesitant about it. The girls find men left and right, and while I've had some interest, we'd promised we wouldn't go home with anyone since our mommas had all thrown in for the hotel as a gift and we are sharing a room. When

TONI ALEO

all three of us are good and drunk, we jump into an Uber and head back to the hotel.

We are laughing about nothing really when we get out and head inside. Lindy is leaning on me since she's about to pass out, while Josie is Snapping a couple of guys she had exchanged her Snap with while we were out. When she looks up at me, I smile as I move Lindy's hair out of her eyes.

"Where's Denis?"

I laugh. "Jo, I got rid of him early."

She scrunches up her face. "Why?"

"What? You know why!"

"But he's nice."

"Then you date him," I throw at her, and she shakes her head. She's drunk, one eye open and the other looking everywhere but me.

"You know he loves you right?"

I stare at her blankly. "And you know he didn't do it for me."

She shrugs. "But you can teach him how to fuck, Ten. It's not like you have a line of guys trying to lock you down."

And there it is. I knew I was having too much fun. "Wow, Josie."

"I say that 'cause I love you," she stresses, trying to grab me, but I move her hands away. "Don't be like that. He really does want to have a life with you."

"Not a life I want," I snap back at her as the elevator dings and the doors open. I'm not drunk enough for this.

"But a good life. He'll love you, and it's not like you're ever going to lose—"

I whip around, and Lindy falls to the floor. I feel awful, but I can't stop myself from going toe-to-toe with Josie. "You bring up my weight, I swear I'll never speak to you again."

"You're my sister, Ten. I only say this because I care. Maybe you should get that gastric done."

I gawk at her. "How big do you really think I am?" I ask, shaking my head. "Maybe I am not a size two like you, and maybe I am a little overweight, but I don't need gastric. I need my friends and family to love me for me. And listen, this is the second time tonight you've made

HAT TRICK

me feel like I'm not enough because of my weight, and you're pissing me the fuck off. Stop it. Like, now."

"But you would be so much prettier if you were skinny like us," she slurs, and I glare. "I know I'm drunk and all, but I feel like you shouldn't just cut him off."

She may as well have hit me. My stomach drops, and my chest burns as I shake my head. "And now, I've cut you off."

As she protests, I turn, picking up Lindy and helping her into our room. I move her to the bed as Josie comes in behind me.

"You don't need to be like that, Ten. I only want what is best for you!"

I ignore her, throwing the keycard at her before grabbing my bag. I hadn't unpacked since I'd had the outfit I'd worn tonight in my purse, just used their stuff to get ready, so my bags are still perfectly leaned on the wall. I grab them and go for the door. I look back at Lindy and then at Josie. "Since you can't be a good friend to me, please make sure Lindy is taken care of."

I stomp out of the room, ignoring her pleas, and head to the elevators. I'm shaking mad as I ride down, ignoring my phone as Josie starts to call over and over again. When I step off the elevator, I turn off my phone since I bet my mom will be next to call. Anytime we get into a fight, Josie is quick to call her mom, who calls mine, and then I'm always coaxed to talk to Josie again. I should have cut her off a long time ago. Oh, I'm pissed.

I head to the front desk and get another room. I take the key and put it in my back pocket before gathering my things and heading back to the elevator. I still can't believe she said that, and I also can't understand why I'm even entertaining her comment. There is someone out there who'll love me, and Denis is not it. Just as there is another friend out there for me; I've just got to find her. Them. I don't know. I have never felt so betrayed in my life. Josie is supposed to be more than my best friend—a sister—but I know I'll never be enough for her.

I trip out of the elevator, and I almost start to cry. I don't know if it's because I'm pissed or because I'm drunk, but I'm feeling all the emotion. I head down the hall, struggling with my bag, but I don't care. I just want to go to bed. I just want to forget this night ever

29

TONI ALEO

happened. I never want to speak to anyone in this godforsaken state again.

As I stop in front of my room, I take the key out of my purse and try to enter the room, but it doesn't work. What the hell? Maybe I have the room number wrong? I look at the key. Pretty sure the front desk guy wrote my room number on the envelope, but I must have lost the envelope in my purse. I move next door and scan the card, and the door blinks green, letting me in.

I am too drunk for this.

I walk inside and start to strip off my clothes as I head to the fridge for a bottle of water. I stand there, naked as the day I was born, as I down the water. As I gasp for breath since I drank the whole bottle quickly, I take in my body in the mirror in front of me. I'm fluffy, but damn it, I'm fuckable for sure. I'd fuck me, and I deserve to be fucked good. Desire hits me then, and man if I don't want to be fucked good by a man who won't hold back with me.

By Dart.

A soft moan leaves my lips at the thought of his big hands and thick fingers. His lips were so full, and I bet he could suck me whole into his mouth. I fall back onto the king bed, gasping at the thought of him between my legs and touching me. It would be glorious and a damn good time. Maybe I should get dressed and go to the bar. Maybe I'll get lucky and he'll show up.

Or I'll get arrested for public intoxication.

I look great in orange, but I'm not made for jail.

I let out a huff as I sit up, knowing I need to get this desire out of me. I stumble to my suitcase and open it to get out my vibrating dildo. I usually wouldn't pack it for an overnight trip, but I didn't take it out of my bag after my last trip two weeks ago, and boy, am I thankful in this moment. I lie back on the bed as I swirl the head of the dildo over my pussy as my blood pounds through my body. I close my eyes, remembering everything about Dart. How he tapped his card to the bar, how he looked at me like he wanted to eat me, and how he wanted to take me to his room for a so-called movie, but we both knew what would really happen.

I slowly move the dildo inside me, breathless and trembling at the

HAT TRICK

instant pleasure it brings me. I'm lost with it, crazed from it, but then I think I hear the door open. But surely I don't. Why would I? Who would have my key? I laugh at my stupidity and start moving the toy into myself faster, my need for a release greater than making sure no one is breaking in to kill me.

But then everything stops when a slow, deep voice envelops me. "Well, hot damn. Fate is being kind to me tonight."

CHAPTER
Five

Dart

Even though my key opens my hotel room door with no issue, I still check to make sure I'm in the right room.

Needy moans met me at the threshold. There is a trail of clothes from the door, clothes that aren't mine, and a bag that doesn't belong to me looks as if it was torn into by a ravenous bear. When I hear a buzzing noise, I check the number on the door once more.

Yeah, it's my room.

I close the door behind me and walk toward the buzzing and the moans. I may have been exhausted when I got to my room, but that's not the case anymore. My body is shaking with awareness, I'm tingling everywhere, and when I turn the corner, nothing could have prepared me for the sight on my bed.

Tennessee.

Wow. I knew she was gorgeous fully clothed. But naked… Fuck me, I wasn't prepared. Her back is arched as her heels dig into the edge of the bed, the dips and curves of her skin making my mouth water. Her thighs are thick, jiggling as she pounds herself with a bright-orange dildo, and I want nothing more than to throw the toy to the side and take over. She holds one full boob in her hand, squeezing her nipple between her thumb and forefinger. Her eyes are closed and her lips parted in a way that has me unable to stop myself from moving closer. I know I should say something, maybe even ask why the hell she is in my room, but I don't give a shit why she's here.

The only thing that matters is that she is.

I watch her, my gaze vibrating just as that dildo does inside her. I swallow hard, my mouth dry as I stare at her, fully engrossed in her body. She is bare between her legs, glistening, and everything inside me wants to taste her. I almost reach out; I almost do what my body wants me to do, but I hold back, taking in a deep, lung-filling breath before letting it out in a hiss.

"Well, hot damn. Fate is being kind to me tonight."

Her eyes shoot open and fall on me. She freezes, her gaze widening as awareness and recognition hit her. Thick, heated silence spreads between us, and I swallow as she gasps for breath. Her eyes are wild, and as I imagined, they are stunning when they're full of lusty goodness. Her mouth moves, but nothing comes out as her gaze burns into mine. My jaw ticks as I ball my hands into fists at my sides, trying to resist touching her. I need her to tell me it's good, that she wants this. That she wants me.

"I should probably ask what the hell you're doing in my room," she says, her voice trembling.

"I should probably ask the same since this is my room."

Her brows come together, but then the sneakiest of grins comes across that naughty mouth of hers. "I don't give two shits whose room this is."

"Nor do I," I say, pressing my knee into the bed between her legs.

The heat of her hits me like a billion frozen pucks to the chest.

I throw my phone to the floor as she says, "I don't have it in me to watch a movie."

My cock strains in my pants as I tear off my suit jacket, throwing it to the floor on top of my phone. "Oh, baby doll, you won't be watching anything but me eating this sweet pussy of yours after I get my fill of looking at you." Her breath catches as I pull at my tie. "Keep fucking yourself," I demand as she gasps. "Now, Tennie." She does as I

TONI ALEO

ask, her sounds of pleasure making it real hard to get my shirt off. "That's good. You like it deep, eh?"

She only nods, a tremble running down her body. Her eyes start to drift shut, but I shake my head. "Absolutely not. Keep those eyes on me. I want to watch them as you fuck yourself."

"I'd rather you fuck me," she insists, and I chuckle as I pull my shirt off.

"We'll get there. But first, I need this pussy in my mouth."

Her gasp is so loud, it makes it hard for me to think. I cover her hand with mine and push the dildo into her as she squirms under my touch. "Do you play with yourself a lot?"

Her voice is strained as I work it in and out of her. "More than I'd care to."

"Don't be embarrassed. I'd play with this pussy all the time if I were given the chance," I tell her, and her eyes darken. It's crazy 'cause one looks like a storm, while the other is like a forest. I swallow thickly, knowing what I said before was true.

One time won't be enough with this girl.

I take the dildo from her. "Open those legs wider, Tennie."

She does as I ask, and I throw the no-longer-needed dildo over my shoulder. My hands shake as I press them into the backs of her legs. Her skin burns against my palm as I squeeze her thighs, my fingers digging into her skin, and I'm rewarded with a strangled moan that sets me in motion. I push her up the bed to give myself room to work before I go for what I want.

Her sweet pussy.

I squeeze her ass in my hands as I run my nose along her slick lips, deeply inhaling her desire. "Fuck, you smell like heaven." I see her fingers dig into the sheets, her knuckles turning white as she arches toward me. I tsk at her. "Greedy girl," I whisper against her lips, softly kissing her wetness and wanting to drown between her legs. "You want me to taste you, don't you?"

"Yes. God. Please," she begs with no hesitation, and it sets everything inside me on fire.

"You don't have to beg, baby doll. I want this as much as you do," I whisper, and she arches against my mouth once more, causing a

HAT TRICK

tremor to run through me. I run my finger along her slit, rewarded with a moan before she squirms under my touch.

"Please," she begs once more, and I can't make her wait.

I don't want to.

I run my tongue along her, pressing her thighs open more so I can really get to the spot I want. I slide my tongue into her, swirling it around her entrance, tasting her need before I run my tongue up her to her clit, and she almost comes off the bed. She cries out, her thighs pressing into my shoulders, but I hold her in place by her ass. I squeeze it as I lick her, slowly and with every intention of driving her crazy. She thrashes, she cries, and I grin against her, loving every fucking sound. I curve my tongue along her clit, but then she starts to grind against my mouth, and gone is the restraint, replaced by the pure drive to make her come on my face.

"Yes, baby doll. Fuck my face," I demand, my voice not my own, before burying myself in her. I cover her pussy with my mouth, sucking her whole as she screams out, her back arching as her heels dig into the bed. I suck her clit between my lips before I flick my tongue against it, loving the sounds she gives me. I move my hand from her ass and slide two fingers into her easily, much to her delight.

"Fuck, you're so wet."

She groans so loudly, I swear I almost come. I love how responsive she is. I fuck her with my fingers and flick my tongue along her clit faster with each moan that leaves her mouth.

When she breaks, her whole body makes the motion, and I'm in awe of her. Her pussy squeezes my fingers as she jerks against my mouth, an uninhibited scream filling the room. I look up at her, still nuzzling her pussy with my mouth, and I can't breathe at the sight. Her body is flushed, her eyes squeezed tightly shut as she fights for air. I kiss her pulsating center, feeling her heartbeat pounding through her whole body. I kiss the insides of her thighs, her hips, then her belly, leaving a trail of kisses as I move up her body.

She takes a deep breath, her eyes meeting mine as I lower myself between her legs, hoping she doesn't mind my weight, but knowing I can't care. I want to feel her against me. Her slick center is hot against my stomach as I hold myself up, my hands on either side of her head.

TONI ALEO

Tennessee's eyes burn into mine as she looks up at me, a lazy smile moving over her lips. She swallows as she glides her hands up my bare sides, along the front of my chest, and then up my neck. I gaze down at her, memorizing everything about her face before she cups my cheeks and brings me down for her lips to meet mine.

And holy fuck, I'm a goner.

Her lips are full, hot, and soon, I'm lost in our eager, sloppy kiss. Our tongues play, and I know instantly she's been drinking. I can taste the beer, and it has me pulling back to look down at her. "Are you drunk?"

She nods. "I am, but I know I want this."

Fuck. I should walk away.

"I want you," she says, and then she grinds her center against my stomach, making it real hard to be a gentleman here. Given who I am, though, I have to be careful. When the regret hits, she could turn this around and say I took advantage of her when she was drunk. But something in her eyes tells me she wouldn't do that. I don't know how or even why, but I trust her.

"I wanted you at the bar," she admits, her eyes burning into mine. "And yeah, I may sound really desperate, but I've thought about you all night. So, I promise I know what I'm doing here."

My body goes taut. "If you're desperate for thinking about me, no telling what that makes me."

"What do you mean?"

"I had to jack off to kill some nerves before the wedding, and all I could think about was you."

Her breath catches as her lips curve slowly into the most devastating grin. "That's hot."

"Not as hot as you," I tell her. I take a deep breath as I move my nose along her lips. "I should be a gentleman, but I don't think I can."

"That's the last fucking thing I want," she scoffs, and everything inside me vibrates at her words. She runs her thumb along my lips, her eyes urging mine. I'm lost in them as she moves her other hand between us, undoing my belt. I don't move as she makes quick work of it, pulling the belt out of the loops and throwing it to the side. She unbuttons my pants then and slides her hand into them for my cock. I

HAT TRICK

arch into her hand, groaning loudly as she squeezes me at my base. "Do you have a condom?"

"I do," I say through my needy haze. "Since this is my room."

She squeezes me. "My key worked."

"How?"

Something shifts in her eyes, almost like she just thought of something. Her lips curve, and then she laughs. "It wasn't my key."

I grin down at her. "Did you realize that when you grabbed ahold of my cock?"

She slides her hand up the length of me, her eyes burning into mine. "I found it at the bar, and I forgot to turn it in. I figured I'd do it later and stuck it in my purse. I bet if we look in my shorts, my key for next door is in the back pocket."

I hiss out a breath as I hover my mouth over hers. "You won't need it tonight, baby doll."

She nips at my bottom lip, and a growl leaves my lips as I kiss her hard. I pull away before I get lost in that kiss and move off her to go to my bag. I push my pants down on the way, toeing out of my shoes as I reach into my bag that is on the luggage rack. I take out the box of condoms I'd bought since I'd hoped I would bring someone back here from the wedding, stepping out of my pants. Thankfully, Tennessee was the only thing on my mind all night. I head back to the bed, loving how she watches me like she wants to gobble me up whole.

"You keep looking at me like that, this is going to be quick."

She purses her lips. "It's hard not to."

I look her over, mouth going dry as I shake my head. "I was thinking the same."

I sheath myself and take her by her ankles, pulling her to the edge of the bed as she cries out in surprise. I grab her hips, flipping her over and then pulling her up onto her knees. She gasps, looking back at me, and I grin at her. "That's right. Keep those eyes on me."

Her lips part as I grip my cock, going to my knees behind her on the bed. I rub her left ass cheek with one hand as I run my cock up and down her pussy, reveling in her desire for me. I guide myself into her, and when she drops her gaze, almost falling onto the bed with a loud groan, I smack that sweet ass hard. My hand stings, and the handprint

37

on her ass makes everything inside me turn molten. Her head whips up, her heated gaze meeting mine. "I told you to keep those eyes on me," I say as I slide out of her slowly before thrusting back into her. "I want you to watch me."

"It's too much," she gasps, white-knuckling the bedsheet. "I can't."

I smack that ass again, the sound music to my ears. "You can," I tell her, caressing the spot I smacked. I withdraw only a bit before thrusting in again, feeling her squeeze around me. She's so fucking snug, and I feel my balls getting tight.

"God, you make me wild," she gasps, her eyes dark and full of everything I'm feeling. I can't even answer her; I smack her again after I thrust hard into her, my hips digging into her cheeks as I still, taking in deep breaths. I angle my hips, moving in and out of her, my hands shaking against her.

"I want you to come again. I want you to come all over my cock."

"I'm almost there," she says as I thrust once more.

Instantly, I'm dazed by her and need more. I reach up, taking her by the front of her neck and drawing her back into my chest. I fall out of her with the change in position, much to her dismay. "Don't make me smack that ass again."

"Please do," she begs, and I do as she wants, the sound filling the room as I soothe my hand over the spot. I lean back on my haunches and guide her down on my cock, holding her around her waist as I fill her. She leans her cheek against mine, and I kiss her jaw before I slide my hand from her waist up to my mouth. She watches as I lick my fingers, getting them wet. "You taste like a drug I want to be addicted to and never recover from."

She sucks in a sharp breath before I slide my fingers between her thighs and find her clit. She cries out, jerking against my hand as I work her clit, angling my hips, gently moving in and out of her. I take ahold of her jaw with my other hand, directing her mouth to mine as I kiss her deeply. She cries into my mouth, and I feel myself falling over the edge. I'm dizzy with need, crazed by her, and I finger her roughly, wanting her to come. I drop my hand from her jaw to her neck, squeezing her tightly as I assault her pussy in the most pleasurable way. She cries out loudly and shatters beneath my hand. She squeezes my cock so hard, I can't hold back, and I fall with her. Light explodes behind my eyes as I roar against her neck, jerking inside her as she squeezes my thighs beneath her hands. Neither of us speaks, both of us fighting for breath as we don't move an inch. I can't breathe, and I sure as hell can't believe this just happened.

I kiss her jaw as I still hold her neck with my hand, her pulse awakening all my desires once more. I replace my hand with kisses along her neck, and then I lick down her shoulder as she leans into me, her head falling back into my shoulder. I make my way down her back, kissing and licking, before I find the red marks along her ass. I kiss them, soothing them with my tongue before I kiss her ribs.

"Fate," I murmur against her heated skin. "Fate was good to us."

She stretches her body, a delicious little noise leaving her lips. "I fucking love fate."

I chuckle against the curve of her shoulder before I nip at her earlobe. I press my lips into her ear and then whisper, "Are you good?"

"So good," she practically moans, and I smile against her ear.

"We aren't done yet."

"Oh God, I hope not."

"Greedy, greedy girl," I taunt, licking the spot below her ear, and she moans ever so softly. "It's okay. I'm greedy too."

She turns her head then, her eyes meeting mine before she captures my lips with a need that has me buzzing all over. She takes over the kiss, and a chill runs down my spine that has me almost breaking the kiss to laugh at the truth of the matter.

Because I knew it. I fucking knew it.

One time won't be nearly enough—probably not even five times—but that might be all I've got, and I'm going to get my fucking fill of Tennessee.

CHAPTER
Six

TENNESSEE

Dart drags his lips along my shoulder and my neck before kissing me at the base of my throat, sending a fluttering feeling through my body. I'm breathless and a little dizzy, but I'm also deliciously spent. My face is flushed, hot, and I know I want more. He kisses me once again and then whispers against the back of my neck, "I'm going to go clean up. Do you need anything?"

"You?" I answer without hesitation, and he chuckles against my neck.

Lord, it's deep and dangerous, and I swear it rocks my soul.

A smile pulls at my lips as he says, "In addition to me, would you like a water?"

"That sounds wonderful. I should stay hydrated."

He squeezes my ass as he snakes his other hand around me. "That would be smart."

His kiss is soft and quick as he pulls out of me before getting off the bed. I fall against the mattress, my body feeling cold the moment he's gone. I watch as he walks toward the fridge, his ass tight, those legs so damn strong, and muscles rippling along his arms. He has a huge

HAT TRICK

black-and-white dragon with its wings spread wide across his back. Its tail curls around to his front, and I have so many questions. I want to know everything, but I realize I can't. This is one night. It doesn't have to be said out loud for me to know the truth. If I start asking questions, if I start caring about anything but the pleasure he can bring me, I'll yearn for him once I go my way and he goes his.

I have to treat this as what it is.

A one-night stand.

Ugh, that doesn't sound right. I really don't care for the term, but I know the truth.

And I can't forget it.

He comes back toward me, that easy grin on his lips as he hands me the bottle of water. "Thank you," I breathe, and he winks at me before heading into the bathroom.

I can see everything he does from where I lie in the bed, and I don't look away. I don't want to waste a moment not taking him in. He pulls off the condom, throwing it in the trash before washing his hands. A grin plays on his face in the mirror, and I can't help but smile. He's so fucking gorgeous. His body is rippled with muscles, and I want to discover each tattoo that adorns his skin. I want to trace the ink with my tongue. I want to get lost in everything that is him. I lick my lips as he looks over at me, drying his hands, beautifully naked. I love that he doesn't rinse his mouth or brush his teeth as he gazes at me. His eyes are darker than they were in the bar. His jaw is tight as he looks me over, that grin unstoppable on his lovely lips.

"That gaze of yours is going to spoil me, Tennie."

My lips quirk. "How so?"

"I love how you look at me," he says, stalking toward me in a way that has my body quivering with delight. "Like you want to devour me."

I lick my lips. "I do."

His chuckle is low, and desire swirls in my stomach as he leans onto the bed with only a knee before he nods toward the bottle. "Are you done?"

"I am," I say, feeling like I'm in a trance caused by him. He takes

TONI ALEO

the water from me, sipping thirstily before he sets it on the nightstand beside us.

He climbs onto the bed and takes my left butt cheek in his hand. He lifts it to examine his handiwork on my ass. "I didn't hurt you, did I?"

I scoff. "Hardly."

Heat flashes in his eyes as his lips curve ever so devilishly. "I have to be honest."

"Yeah?"

"I've never just done that without discussing it first. But, Tennessee, your ass is a thing of beauty, and it needs to be slapped. Hard."

The way he says "hard" should not have heat pooling between my legs, but here we are.

"Why, thank you," I say, my teeth sinking into my bottom lip as he lets go of my ass to prowl over me.

He cages me between his body and the bed, while my hands slide down his delectable swell of muscles. I lean up, licking his nipple, and he hisses out a breath, cupping the back of my head as he tangles his fingers in my hair. I wrap my legs around his waist, feeling him throbbing against my ass. He's not hard yet, but he will be. I run my tongue up his collarbone, his neck, before I catch him off guard and push him to his back. He lies before me, his eyes hooded, and his lips curve as I climb over him, my ass landing on his thighs as I run my hands along his taut skin. I kiss the middle of his chest, his stomach, and then each of his abs before running my tongue along each side of the V that points right where I am headed.

I kiss his thighs as I fall between his legs, and then I run my tongue up his semi-hard cock. I look up to see him watching me. He rises up on his forearm, his lips parting as our gazes lock. He reaches out, dragging his thumb across my bottom lip. "You want my cock in that pretty little mouth, baby doll?"

I capture his thumb between my teeth, biting him as he hisses, shaking his head, a chuckle bubbling in his chest. I then soothe his finger with my tongue, sucking it before I kiss the tip. Against his thumb, I ask, "Does that answer the question?"

His brow perks. "All that did was make me want to consume you."

HAT TRICK

My mouth goes dry as my heart hammers in my chest. "Come here," he says, but I shake my head.

I lean down, running my tongue along the shaft of his cock as he groans deeply with no restraint whatsoever. "I'm where I want to be."

"Fine. Then turn around to sit on my face so I can get my fill too."

"You don't have to tell me twice," I say, climbing up his body, much to his delight.

His chuckle runs down my spine as he says, "Greedy girl, I can't wait to have you fucking my mouth."

Lord, I might be on my way to You. But first, let me commit some sins with this man.

He takes my hips in his hands, guiding me to where he wants me— hovered over his mouth with my thighs touching his cheeks. For two seconds, I'm almost self-conscious with my ass in his face, but when he takes ahold of me and buries his face between my thighs, my insecure thoughts fly out the fucking window. I lean forward with one hand and take his cock in my other hand. I draw him into my mouth, fully to the hilt, gagging myself. He chuckles against my pussy, and my gut clenches with desire. I hold him in place, trying to ignore the intense pleasure he's giving me, and slide him in and out of my mouth with zealous rhythm.

"Fuck yes," he hisses into my center, making me squirm against his lips. "Yes, my greedy girl. Yes."

I start to rock against him, enjoying all the sensations. His beard is rough against my center, and I love it. I crave it. He takes my clit in his mouth, sucking hard, and I hover over his cock as I cry out, unable to move from the extreme pleasure. A smack comes to my ass, hard, and I cry out once more, arching my head back and wiggling my ass at him. His chuckle will be my downfall. He smacks me again, and everything gets tight.

"Tennessee, suck me."

Oh. Oh God. I pull him back in then, trying to ignore what he is doing, but I can't. I sit up, eager and completely lost in the pleasure he is bringing me. I rock against his mouth—the feel of his beard, his mouth, and the bite of his fingers on my ass too much. That only eggs him on as he flicks his tongue along my clit quickly and teasingly.

TONI ALEO

"Dar... Dar... Oh, D'Artagnan!" I scream before I come so damn hard, I'm sure I'm going to pass out from lack of air.

He laps at me as I twitch above him, my head falling back as I gasp for air. I fall off him into the pillows, but he doesn't let me get far. He covers my body with his, pressing himself into me, squeezing my hips and bottom in his hands as his mouth joins with mine. I arch into him, hooking my leg around his waist and moving my wet pussy along his cock. God, he feels so good. He drags his mouth from mine, sucking my jaw, my neck, before kissing the base of my throat.

"I wish I could make the way you screamed my name my ringtone."

I laugh, utterly lost in him. He kisses down my breasts, licking my nipples and sucking them into his mouth. I arch into him, breathless. "Dart, please. I want you inside me."

He drags his lips along my breast. "Shh, you. I'm getting my fill."

I let my eyes fall shut as he trails his tongue down my stomach, tonguing my belly button before kissing it. I open my eyes when I no longer feel his lips, to find him sheathing himself with a condom.

"Thank God."

He flashes me a wide grin, his teeth ever so white as he moves between my legs, his hips biting into my thighs. I feel him everywhere, and still, it's not enough. He takes me by the back of my thigh, opening me for him before guiding himself into me. I groan at how he stretches me, how fucking good it feels to have him inside me. He pushes in until he can't, and everything is set on fire.

"Lift your hips, baby doll. Let me in deeper."

God. Oh God.

I do as he asks, and he sinks into me even more. Breathing isn't even an option. He groans loudly as his eyes fall shut, and my goodness, he's beautiful.

"Look at me," I demand, and his eyes shoot open, a slow, dangerous curve of his lips appearing. He thrusts into me, and the fire in his eyes makes it hard to think. I hold his hips as he slams into me, over and over again, and I get completely lost in his eyes. Soon, the way he looks at me stuns me, and I know we're getting too intimate for a one-night thing.

"I want to ride your cock," I tell him, and his stills, his eyes hooded as they burn into mine.

"Later" is all he says as he continues to thrust into me, his eyes never leaving mine. "Don't think. Just feel, Tennessee," he whispers, his lips capturing mine and driving me absolutely out of my mind. I cup his face in my hands, squeezing my eyes shut as he hammers into me in every single way I could ever ask for. When he pulls back, it's only slightly as his hand moves between us, finding my clit.

Out of breath, I say, "I can't."

"You fucking can," he insists as he thumbs my clit in circles that have me almost coming off the bed.

"I've never come this much," I protest, the sensation overwhelming.

He stills inside me, but not that thumb; it still moves along my nub, his eyes burning into mine. "By yourself, or with someone else?"

"Either."

The way his lips curve ever so slowly leaves me knowing I'm about to come without him even saying a word. "Let me tell you something," he says, licking my bottom lip. "I play hockey."

I just look at him, my gaze hazy, but thankfully, I still have my wits about me. "Really? By the looks of your body, I thought you had a desk job."

He grins, and my soul is set on fire. I need him to stop looking at me like that. He doesn't seem to know what he is doing to me—or maybe he does—but instead, he says, "Do you know anything about hockey?"

"I like how big your stick is," I groan as I close my eyes, arching up, and his laughter almost takes me over the edge. "But yes, I know a thing or two."

His thumb speeds up as I cry out, and when he starts to move into me, my body goes tight. "So, you know what a hat trick is?"

"Oh my God, this is a lot of talking," I whine, licking my lips. "I'm almost there."

He stops completely, and I cry out. "Tell me, Tennie."

"Yes, I know what it is!" I yell, frustrated and throbbing. "A guy scores three times!"

TONI ALEO

"Good girl," he says, and without even a warning, he pulls out of me and covers my pussy with his lips. He sucks me hard into his mouth, my thighs squeezing his face as I cry out, trembling everywhere. He replaces his mouth with his thumb before guiding himself back into me and driving me absolutely insane. He starts to thrust into me, and everything is building again. I feel the heat everywhere; my stomach clenches, and right as I fall over the edge, he says, "Just so you know, I'm known for many hat tricks."

And I fall. Face first into the most glorious release of my life. He groans, his hand on my hip squeezing me to the point of delightful pain. He falls into me then, his body half on me and half on the bed, his mouth right at my jaw. He fights for breath as I do the same, unable to move or even open my eyes. I feel like I may just go to sleep, but before I can, he whispers, "And tonight, my greedy girl, I'm going to get two of them."

Laughter chokes me as I grin widely, still unable to move. I take a deep breath as I ask, "What time is it?"

"Don't know. Don't care," he says, lazily moving his fingers along the bottom of my breast.

"Don't you have a flight tomorrow?"

"I do," he admits, licking my jaw. He lifts his arm then and groans. "It's four."

"And your flight?"

"Ten."

I nod. "Then you have only six hours to make that happen—really only four if you want to be on time for your flight."

He smiles against my jaw. "I'm torn between saying fuck my flight and accepting the challenge."

Oh, that brings me more pleasure than all the orgasms he's given me. "I have family brunch, so I have to leave around the same time you do."

He kisses my jaw. "So, I'm accepting the challenge?"

"You are," I agree, turning to meet his gaze. "If that's what you want."

His eyes soften as his hand spreads across my neck, his thumb

HAT TRICK

stroking against my pulse. "I want it. And then I'll be taking your cowboy hat as my reward for my hat tricks."

I grin as his lips meet mine, and while I love my UT cowboy hat, if that's all I have to give for a night like this, then I'll be just fine.

Or at least, that's what I keep telling myself.

CHAPTER
Seven

Dart

When I wake up to my alarm blaring like a nuisance, I'm instantly reminded what is about to happen. I can't help but regret plugging in my phone in the night. I slap the alarm off somehow, and then I look down at where Tennessee is wrapped around me like a koala bear. Her thick body touches me in all the right ways. I run my hands over the curve of her ass, along her hips, before I cup her full boob. Her pretty little chin is pressed into my chest with her lips parted as she breathes evenly. Her hair is up in a topknot, something she did after round five, I think. I glide my fingers along her jaw and then her lips as I cuddle her closer to me, unable to let go of her yet.

I watch as she sleeps, reliving everything we did and feeling all kinds of things. I have never in my life experienced pleasure like that. I'm pretty sure I have nothing left in me, and I'm completely okay with it. The uncontrollable releases I experienced just kept coming, and it's really hard to accept that this is over. I know she knows it, and I know I do, but fuck if I don't like it one bit. When my alarm sounds again, I reach for it, shutting it off the correct way before throwing my phone

HAT TRICK

down on the bed. I lean in, kissing her cheek, her nose, and then the corner of her lips.

"Tennessee?"

Her lids flutter open, and her eyes meet mine. Her lips curve, and she says, "Good morning, gorgeous."

Pain hits me in the chest. "Hey there, beautiful."

She stretches against me, that hot body so soft against mine, leaving me completely breathless. I pick up my phone and groan.

"Time to go?"

"I've got a solid thirty minutes, and I have to shower."

"That takes how long?"

"Five minutes, tops."

"Okay, so don't move. I'm comfy."

I feel myself growing harder against my thigh.

"And apparently your cock doesn't listen."

I grin against her lips. "Nor do I," I say, and then I get up, taking her by her ankles and pulling her to me.

She laughs loudly. "What in the world?"

I tug her up and to her feet.

"What are you doing?"

"You're showering with me so I can fuck you at the same time," I say, pulling her into my arms and cupping her ass in my hands. "One more time."

Something moves in her eyes, and it causes my breath to catch. Her voice is unsteady as she wraps her arms around my neck, and I feel like she's sad. "One more time."

I take her by the backs of her thighs and lift her into my arms. She wraps her legs around me while I carry her to the bathroom and into the glass shower. I press her into the smooth tile, and she hisses in response. "It's cold," she laughs, and I wink.

"I'll warm you up, baby doll."

As I turn on the shower, she takes my lips with hers, and our mouths move together desperately. Or, at least, that's how I feel. I taste every inch of her mouth, my tongue playing with hers as the water runs over our bodies. Our hands are wild, touching and squeezing each other. I don't know about her, but I don't want to forget this. The way she feels, how thick her ass is, and how fucking perfect her pussy is. I drag my lips from hers as I let one of her legs fall so I can have a free hand. I slip my hand between her legs, cupping her, and she arches into me in response, only one word leaving her lips.

"D'Artagnan."

Fuck, my name on her lips has the potential to undo me.

I slide two fingers into her wetness and capture her mouth as I start to pound her sweet pussy. She cries into my mouth, arching her hip into my hand so that my thumb comes down on her nub each time. I'm crazy for her, and I go faster, harder, as I get lost in watching myself fuck her with my hand.

"Be a good girl, Tennie. Tell me when you're almost there."

She only groans, her back arching off the tile as she meets my gaze. Her body shakes against mine, and I see the heat creep up her neck and along her chest. I bend forward, sucking her nipple into my mouth as my cock throbs for her. I then suck on the other one before I kiss and lick her chest, her moans urging me on. I bury my face between her shoulder and suck her neck, just wanting to taste her. I rake my teeth over her, and she shrieks in the most erotic way.

"I'm almost there. Please, please, D'Artagnan."

I kiss her neck as my hand stills, and I slowly free it from the vise grip her pussy has on it. I guide myself into her and then stop. "Fuck, I didn't plan this well."

"Ugh."

"My bad. Play with yourself," I say, and she laughs as I run naked and wet to where I left the condoms. I look back at her, and she's watching me, her eyes dark. I can see all the spots I've touched on her. Red marks along her neck, her chest, and hips. Fuck, it does something to my heart as I quickly open the condom. "I thought I told you to play with yourself."

She shakes her head. "I want to come on your cock, Dart."

"Touché," I say as I sheathe myself and head back toward her. I bend down, capturing her lips with mine as I lift her up by the backs of her knees against the slick tile. Once I have her in place, I guide myself into her and groan as I fill her. Her nails bite into my shoulders, as do her

HAT TRICK

heels into the backs of my thighs, and she throbs around my cock. Gone is any control. I thrust into her feverishly, and I still can't get enough. Her moans and mine mingle in a way I never want to forget. I never want to stop, but when she comes, shaking against me, my release comes next, racing through me and fulfilling me, but also...leaving me feeling empty.

Because this is the last time.

I drop my face into the spot between her shoulder and her neck and inhale deeply. She smells like me and like sex and more. I don't want to forget this scent. Ever. I kiss her neck and then her jaw before exhaling against her flushed skin. She runs her hands up my back, along my shoulders, and down the backs of my arms. She moves her lips to my ear and whispers, "I'll never forget you."

Emotion slaps me in the face as I hold her tighter, kissing her jaw. I don't know what to say, and that overwhelms me. I kiss her bottom lip as our eyes meet. "I couldn't forget you if I tried."

And that's the fucking truth.

———

We shower in silence, stolen kisses here and there. We brush our teeth together, and while she fusses with her hair, I wash my face. It's easy and feels normal to me. As she moves out of the bathroom to get dressed, that's when it hits me. This is almost over. I walk out and follow suit. I pull on my dark-blue shorts with a thin white tee before packing up my suit that I had thrown to the side with no cares last night. I gather my things, or at least, I act like I am so that she doesn't know I can't stay still.

If I do, I'll start thinking. And when I start thinking, I'll beg her to come home with me.

I swallow hard as I sit on the edge of the bed and look over at where she's sitting in front of her bag. She's wearing the flirtiest little green summer dress. It has thin straps and dips wonderfully so that I can see the tops of those gorgeous tits. Her hair is back in a sleek pony-tail, and on her feet are a pair of flip-flops that show off her cute orange-painted toes. She folds her clothes from the night before, and

TONI ALEO

when she reaches into the pocket of her shorts, she holds up the envelope with her room key in it.

"I did have the right room number, just the wrong key," she laughs, and I shrug.

"Eh, I think you had the right key and the right room." We share a smile that warms me everywhere. I have a lump in my throat as I ask, "So, you have a family brunch?"

She nods. "I do. It's something we do every Sunday."

"That's nice."

"Do you live near family?"

I shake my head. "No, my mom and sister are in Arizona. I don't know my dad."

"I'm sorry."

"Don't be. I don't need him," I say simply, licking my lips.

"So, you play hockey?"

I nod. "I do."

"Professional?"

"Yeah, I play for the Carolina IceCats."

Her eyes meet mine. "That's amazing. Are you good?"

I shrug, a grin pulling at my lips. "I score a decent amount."

"I'm sure you do," she says naughtily. With a gleam in her eye, she adds, "I only follow the Nashville Assassins, of course." She rises up on her knees, and I don't know what gets into me, but I reach for her, bringing her between my legs.

I stroke my hands along her face. "Well, you better start following the IceCats, just so you know when I'm playing here."

Her lips curve. "I'm moving."

That's right. "Where?"

"Virginia."

My stomach drops. "There's no hockey there."

She shakes her head. "No, there is not."

I run my thumb along her lips, and her head tips back, giving me free rein, and I take her mouth to ease my disappointment. My hands tangle in her hair as I deepen the kiss, unable to accept that this is it. I lick along her bottom lip, then her top, before I pull back, pressing my nose into hers. Her eyes are closed as she holds me, her

HAT TRICK

grip on my neck tight as she inhales hard and lets it out just as hard.

I move my thumb along her lip again, meeting her gaze as my heart slams into my chest. "This sucks."

She nods. "It does."

I try to find the right words, but I don't know them. "Should we exchange numbers?"

She swallows as she shrugs. "I would love to, but it might be hard to keep in contact."

"Yeah, I'm sure you're busy."

She shakes her head. "That's not how I mean."

"No?"

"No," she says, her eyes searching mine. "It'd be hard because of the distance."

My chest aches as I nod. "Yeah, you're right."

"I feel like we'd get to know each other, and we already know how great this is, so it'd only set us up for failure."

Or set us up for life.

"We could see how it goes."

The sorrow in her eyes hits me in my chest. "I think we should just accept this for what it is."

I only nod, knowing good and well she's right. There are too many moving parts. I live in South Carolina; she's moving to Virginia. She's starting a new job, and I've got a lot going on with my sister and my mom. I don't know if I can even commit to a relationship right now. As soon as I think that, I feel dumb. A relationship? *Slow your roll, Dart. This was a hookup, plain and simple.* But why does it feel like more?

Unable to answer her or even add to what she said, I lean in and kiss her once more. She kisses me back, circling her arms around my neck and pulling me closer. I wrap my arms around her middle and hug her back as our mouths play.

When we part, we're both breathless and our eyes meet once more.

"Can I walk you out?" I ask, and she nods.

"I'd appreciate that."

But neither of us moves. I sigh and kiss her forehead before I let her go. She gets up, and I do the same. In silence, we grab our things, and I

TONI ALEO

roll her bag out with mine. Together, we walk to the elevator, and I try to figure out what to say. What I want to tell her. Or even ask of her. But I can't think of anything, so I just take her in. The curve of her cheeks, the fullness of her lips. God, she's gorgeous.

"Oh!" she gasps, reaching for her UT cowboy hat that is strapped to her bag. "I forgot." She removes it and then steps toward me to put it on my head. "Your hat for your hat tricks."

My heart pounds in my chest as I grin down at her. "I don't think scoring a hat trick will ever be the same."

A flush spreads over her face. "Good."

God, her confidence is irresistible.

I can't end this yet.

I hit the stop button on the elevator, and it jerks to a stop as she cries out, "What in the hell?"

I take her wrist in my hand and pull her to me, kissing her once more. She melts into me, and I do the same to her. I kiss her three more times, short, sweet kisses, before I press my forehead to hers. "I didn't want it to be over yet."

Her eyes soften from the panic as she nods. "You're making this so hard for me."

I smile against her lips. "You? I'm struggling, and I don't even know you."

She sighs. "Same."

I pull out my phone, but I don't break our embrace as I hold it up to snap a photo of us without her knowing. Then I say, "Look."

She does, and the brightest grin comes over her face.

I snap another photo, and my heart does a dance.

"I want that," she says, pulling out her phone. "Give me your number."

My lips curve, and she smacks my chest playfully. "I know, but maybe we can just keep in touch. Maybe we can link up if we're ever in the same place."

"Maybe fate will be kind to us again," I say as she types in her number and sends herself the photo.

"Don't threaten me with a good time," she says, handing me back my phone.

HAT TRICK

I cup her jaw and hit the button for the elevator to start once more, breaking our gazes. "I'm gonna act as if I hadn't asked for a picture so you'd want it and then give me your number."

"I'm gonna act as if it's easy to walk away from you."

Her words hit me hard as the door opens, but neither of us moves. I gaze into those unique eyes and pray I never forget them. If the day comes and I do, hopefully we can find a way to see each other again.

"Tennessee! What the hell!"

She looks away first at the sound of her name, and I follow her gaze to two very angry-looking girls. "We've been calling and looking for you for hours. Your momma is about to call the police!"

She doesn't react or even answer them. She just looks back up at me. "Thank you."

I bring in my brows. "Surely you aren't thanking me for what we did. It was a team effort, baby doll."

She grins. "No, you made me forget about those two. Thanks for that," she laughs as we step off the elevator. We walk past the girls, both of them watching her with anger and surprise, to the front doors of the hotel. She puts her hand on mine where it rests on her bag, and we thread our fingers together as our gazes meet.

Her lips tip up a bit. "You're gonna have to run to your flight."

I shrug. "Even though I got a lot of cardio last night, I'm good to do more."

A smile fills her features, and I return it as I step closer, taking her hip in my other hand. I bring our clasped hands to my lips, kissing her knuckles as I get lost in those eyes. She pulls her hand from mine and wraps her arms around my neck. Our bodies press together, and I lower my forehead to hers. I'm fighting for more time, begging the clock to stop and just let us be, but I know that won't happen. I really don't get it. I've had plenty of one-night hookups, but something about this one is making it difficult to walk away. I just want to know more about her. I want to know *her*.

My words are nowhere to be found, and I think she feels the same as she goes up on her toes and presses her lips to mine. I squeeze her to me, lifting her off her feet and devouring her mouth for what I know *has* to be the last time.

TONI ALEO

Unless fate decides to be kind once more.

She's the one to break the kiss, and when she does, I gasp against her lips as my eyes search hers. I place her on her feet, kissing her nose again, and she says, "Till next time, D'Artagnan."

I kiss her top lip. "Hopefully it comes sooner rather than later, Tennessee."

She kisses me once more and then pulls out of my arms. She steps back, rolling the suitcase between us, and exhales heavily. I don't know how she is this strong. How it seems easy for her to watch me walk away, because I'm on the verge of moving to Virginia. But I can't. I blow out a breath and turn then. I start for the door, trying not to look back. I check my phone to see where my car is, but the text she sent herself of the photo of us is still up. Then I notice her contact name.

The Only Ten You'll Ever See.

A full grin fills my lips as I look back at her, and she's grinning just as big, watching me with those intense eyes. She lifts her hand and waves, and I do the same, fighting the urge to go back inside. But then her friends are there, blocking her from my view, and my phone rings, telling me my driver is here.

I look up to see if Tennessee is still there, but she's not.

And I fear that fate won't ever be as kind as it was last night.

CHAPTER
Eight

TENNESSEE

I'm thankful for the solitude of my car once I hit the road.

I knew driving in by myself was a great idea, because when I don't want to speak to Lindy and Josie, I don't have to after a whole-ass night with them. I had no desire to interact with them when they approached Dart and me in the hotel, so I walked right away from them, heading for my car. I didn't even turn on my phone because I knew the texts and calls would come one after another. From them and my parents. While I know there is a text I do want, I'm not willing to turn my phone on for it yet.

Not when I'm barely holding it together.

Instead, I turn on my favorite brokenhearted playlist, and I sob the whole way home.

The pain chokes me, and not in a good way. My tears feel like fire sliding down my face, and my chest aches in a way I've never experienced before. I knew. God, I knew that I was supposed to keep it at just the orgasms Dart could bring me. That I had to keep my feelings at bay and call what we did what it was—a one-night stand. But I failed, damn it. I failed.

I enjoyed his laugh, his teasing grin, and how he made me feel. Like I was worthy of being worshipped. He held me, he laughed with me, and he brought on the most unbelievable pleasure I've ever felt in my life. He thoroughly satisfied me and never stopped. It was as if he couldn't get enough, and Lord knows I couldn't. He had me begging for his touch, his lips, his quick grins. Him… Fucking him… I would beg for him over and over again. When he held me, I felt completely and totally safe, and when he looked into my eyes, truly into my eyes, I felt my soul burn for him.

It's terrifying how deeply I feel, but surely it's just lust.

Or, better yet, infatuation.

But then, why am I crying about a future I won't ever have with him?

It just won't work. He is not the kind of guy I can be in a long-distance relationship with. I could fall deeply, madly for him, and knowing I couldn't touch him or feel him whenever I wanted because of the distance would shatter me to pieces. I've only known him a day, and my body craves him in a way I don't understand. And I'm supposed to put space between us? I would get jealous, knowing he could have anyone he wants. Even if I felt like he saw only me. Even when we walked by Josie and Lindy, his eyes never left mine.

Yeah, I know the pain of missing him would be too great.

Hell, it's too great now, and I don't even know his last name.

What in the hell am I going to do?

―――――

Even though I told Dart I had family brunch, I decide to skip it when I arrive at my apartment. Once I'm upstairs, in my space that will no longer be mine in a couple weeks, I decide I don't want to be around anyone. It means I need to call my mom and let her know, but I just don't have it in me to do so.

My heart hurts.

I put my phone on the charger, but I still don't turn it on. I lean on the counter, resting my head on my arm as I think about what Dart is doing. He's probably already boarded the plane and landed. I wonder if he's thinking of me and if he misses me...

Damn it, I can't stand here and do this to myself.

I push myself off the counter, ignoring how deliciously spent I am and how badly I wish Dart were here, and I move through my apartment, picking up and trying to keep busy. Thankfully, I stopped crying when I got here, but when I look at my bare walls, a new round of tears starts. I've been in this apartment for two years, and seeing the emptiness, after experiencing last night, the realization that I'm leaving hits me hard. I push past my tears and start to pack all my textbooks and then my favorite recreational books that I haven't even had time to read. I still buy them, no matter. Will I have time to read when I get to Virginia?

The company I work for will have me traveling all over to different colleges and professional sports teams to help with all different kinds of players' goals. I don't know if reading will happen when I'll be knee-deep in scans, formulas, and making plans to help our clients improve from injury or to help them succeed in their sport. I'm excited to work with pitchers, because while I couldn't pitch softball for shit, I still loved doing it, and I want to help the next great one out there.

I move to the next bookshelf, taking down photos of my family and then one of Lindy, Josie, and me at a UT game when we were kids. We look so happy, attached at the hip, and it's crazy how quickly things change. Just thinking of what Josie said, wanting me to settle for Denis, has a laugh bubbling in my chest. Settle for him? When a man like Dart exists? A man who consumed my body like it was his last meal. A man who made me feel things I thought I could only dream of. Things I had never experienced in my life.

I drop my hands holding the photo into my lap and look at where my phone is lying on the counter. I work my upper lip between my teeth and then go to get it. I lean on the counter and turn it on. As I assumed, it dings and dings with voice mails and texts. I open my texts and find Dart's thread. The photo of us truly pains me to see. Both of us flushed and grinning from ear to ear. His hair had fallen into his face, and his lips were swollen from the many kisses I pulled from him. My gaze shifts to my face, how bright it was, and I notice how red my

TONI ALEO

neck is in the photo. I press my hand to my neck and swear I can still feel him there. I close my eyes as my heart pounds like a jackhammer ready to break through my chest. Heat pools between my legs, and God, I wish he were here.

A knock at the door snatches me from my thoughts, and my brows come together. The stupid and irrational part of me prays it's him, but I know it's not. I go to the door, opening it to find my mom on the other side. She looks distraught with worry, and I sigh in annoyance. "Mom, I don't have it in me."

"Tennessee Lynn, do you know how worried I've been?"

I turn as I nod. "Yeah, I'm sorry. It was a long night."

A deliciously long night.

"So I heard!" she yells, slamming the door behind her. "You blew Denis off, his momma is pissed at me, and now she's saying she won't donate to the softball field anymore."

"Mom," I say, turning to look at her. I could pass for her twin if I were half my size and had my natural wheat-colored hair. "I don't give a shit about Denis or the softball field. I don't. I freaking don't. He is nothing to me."

It's as if she didn't know this. As if this is the first time I've said it. It's not.

With her brow furrowed, she wails, "Lordy, Tennessee. How can you be like that? He's been in your life for so long."

"Good riddance is what I say," I tell her, sitting on the stool in front of my kitchen island.

Her eyes widen as anger sets in. "And what about Josie? She said you said you'd never speak to her ever again."

I run my hands down my face. "Did she tell you she told me I would never be thin enough to pull a guy better than Denis?"

I look up at her then, and her eyes soften. "Well, that is unkind and untrue," she says tensely. "And she sure did not tell me that."

"She always says sly shit like that, and I'm tired of it."

She nods. "I'd feel the same. And I don't appreciate that at all, but you can't stop being her friend. You guys have known each other since you were babies."

"I can," I tell her simply. "I don't deserve that."

HAT TRICK

"No, but she loves you."

"I don't want that kind of love. Especially when she then runs and tells you a version that makes her the victim. She's always done that and has always painted me as the bad guy, when, really, it's her."

"Tennie, it's not that bad."

"It feels that way," I insist. "And Lindy may not twist stories, but she sure doesn't support or defend me against Josie."

She gives me a pitiful look. "I think maybe y'all have just grown apart a bit. You should talk. Maybe a girls' trip."

"Absolutely not."

"Tennie, don't be like that. It's not kind."

"Maybe I don't want to be kind to her. Lord knows she's not to me."

She eyes me. "I really think you should talk to her. She was so worried about you when she couldn't find you."

"I was just fine."

"So I heard," she says, giving me a stern look. "It's not very lady-like to sleep with men you don't know."

Kill me now. "Mom, see? She's supposed to be my best friend, but she tells my mom I had a one-night stand?"

She winces since perfect Marcy Dent would never do such a thing. "That's beside the point. You don't know what you could have caught."

She has me there. Though, I feel she means an STI rather than feelings.

"I was just fine, Mom. I'm not stupid."

Though, I probably am.

"I raised you better than that," she reminds me, and I roll my eyes.

"You raised me to enjoy life. And believe me, I was enjoying myself immensely last night," I say, and her gaze is dark when it meets mine.

"That toes the line of vulgar, Tennessee Lynn. Act like a lady, please."

If only she knew how much of a lady I did not act like last night with Dart slapping the hell out of my ass.

I sigh as I look away, shaking my head. When I look back, her eyes are glancing around the room, and dread fills me. I watch as her

TONI ALEO

brows knit when she takes in the apartment. "Why is everything in boxes?"

My shoulders fall, but I won't look away. I respect her too much for that. "That job I got is in Virginia."

Her eyes widen as her mouth falls open. "Virginia?"

"Yeah," I say, threading my fingers together. "I leave in two weeks."

"For Virginia, the state?"

"Yes, Momma," I say softly. "I need a change."

"But that's so far away."

Not far enough, in my opinion, but I shrug instead of admitting that. "Not too bad. Only ten hours' drive."

She looks as if I've smacked her upside the head. "But you've never left home."

"I know," I agree, nodding. "And I've got to. I need a new start, Mom. I've gotta do this. For myself. To do what I want. To find who I am."

"Tennie, what are you saying? You're wonderful."

"Thank you, Mom. Truly. But I'm not happy here. Haven't been since I went to college, and I think it has a lot to do with the fact that I can't be myself. You just told me I was unladylike for a one-night stand—"

"Tennie!"

"It's true, and maybe I like one-night stands. Maybe that's what I want to do and not have someone constantly telling me how I should act or have my friends tattling to my mom what I am up to. If I want to get rammed through by the whole Vols baseball team, screaming 'Yes, Daddy' the entire time, I should be able to, without fear that my mom will scold me for it!"

"Lord Almighty, Tennessee!"

"I want to live, Mom! I don't want to stay in the box all y'all have put me in."

Her frown deepens as she shakes her head. "I can't believe this."

After this conversation, I can. I may have been sad earlier, but now, I can't wait to leave. I look down at my phone, the photo of Dart and me staring back at me. I swallow and ask, "You fell in love with Daddy instantly, didn't you?"

HAT TRICK

"Yes, but we met at church and not during a one-night stand."

I groan loudly, rolling my eyes as I stand up.

"So please don't try to tell me you've fallen for someone who only wanted you for sex. I mean, my God, does he even know your name, Tennessee?"

I look over my shoulder at her, and without hesitation, I say, "Yup, he was screaming it all night."

Oh, that ruffles her feathers as a flush quickly fills her face. "That is disgusting."

I shrug. "I beg to differ." I am completely done with this conversation. "I've got things to do. Can you let yourself out?"

"Have you lost every bit of your manners, Tennessee Lynn?"

I whip around. "No, Mom. Will you please leave so I can not deal with you anymore?"

She vibrates with anger, but I ignore it as I reach for my phone and head into the bathroom, praying that when I come out, she'll be gone. I shut the door and sit on the toilet, opening my phone to look at Dart and me. When a text comes through, I hold my breath since it's from a number I don't have saved.

Hey, I landed, and I wanted you to know I haven't stopped thinking about you.

Oh, the thrill that fills me is overwhelming as I read the text over and over. Tears burn my eyes, and my heart aches. My fingers hover over the words, knowing what I want to say, but also knowing if I do, I'm bound to fall for him completely. My eyes drift shut, and I set my phone to the side before covering my face as the tears start to fall.

I know it would never work with Dart.

CHAPTER
Nine

Dart

A month later...

Man, I love preseason hockey.

My lungs are burning as I head up the ice, puck on my blade, with my eyes on where my wingers are. The ice crunches under my skates, and the crowd is going wild. For the Coyotes, not the IceCats, but still, I love the noise. I carry the puck over the blue line as Adler and Anderson rush the goal. I pass it to Litman at the blue line and head to the net as they set up, everyone doing their part to get the puck into the back of the net. My eyes shift quickly to where Adler is set up in the right circle, and I find Anderson toward the left of the net. The puck moves to Adler, who deflects it into the boards, and it pops onto Anderson's stick, but it's knocked away by the defenseman with more force than I think he anticipated.

I watch as it hits the glass, coming back to Adler, who slides it back to Moon, who shoots with all his glory. His stick snaps, but that's not what I watch. I watch the puck ricochet off the goalie's shoulder pad

HAT TRICK

and land right in front of me. I react before I even realize I'm moving, wristing the puck into the back of the net over the shoulder it just hit. The goalie's shoulders fall as I throw my hands up instinctively, and the red light shines.

Goal.

My third, a hat trick.

Out of nowhere, I'm thrown back into that hotel room. Her clothes all over the floor, her ransacked suitcase, and that damn orange dildo, sliding in and out of that mouthwatering pussy. The way my heart slammed in my chest as I found her on my bed. The deep red of her cheeks as that orange ribbon fell into her eyes. Her thighs... Oh, those glorious thighs against my fingers. The taste of her when she came on my mouth. The sounds she made, more fulfilling than the ones in this arena. How she felt when I sank into her and wanted nothing more than to get lost in her. The ache of walking away, her taste on my lips.

Her.

Tennessee.

The guys wrap their arms around me, hugging me in celebration as a few hats fly onto the ice. None of them matters, though. The only one that does is the UT cowboy hat back at my house.

Fuck me.

Because just like I knew she would, Tennessee ruined any future hat tricks for me.

––––––––

I lie with my arm behind my head against my pillows, my fingers sprawled across my stomach. I wear only a pair of boxers as I watch her move around the room to gather her things. Samantha. The girl I found at the bar to spend the night with. She's tall, almost my height, with long black hair and dark-brown eyes. Long, thin legs, no ass, and no tummy. Not my usual type, but she did the job. She pulls her shirt over her head and looks back at me as she rubs her ass. The marks where my hands and teeth played, and it brings me no joy whatsoever.

"My ass still hurts," she accuses, shaking her head. "I like it," she says, sashaying to me, crawling over me, and straddling me. I move

TONI ALEO

one hand up and over the spot, rubbing my thumb along it. If I'm honest, I wish she'd just leave. "I love that I have your mark on me." I force a grin and kiss her when she drops her lips to my mouth. "When will you be back this way?"

"I think November."

"Okay. So, hit me up?"

"We'll see. I usually come in earlier so I can see my sister."

"Great. Sounds good. Don't be a stranger," she says, kissing me again, and I feel almost like I'm on autopilot. As she crawls off me, I wipe my mouth free of her taste and watch as she grabs her purse. Before I'd even gotten her in the elevator to come up, I'd told her she had to be gone by eight that morning. With a glance at the time on my phone, I'm surprised she doesn't try to linger. "Bye, D."

I swallow. "Bye."

When I hear the door click, I close my eyes as I cuddle deeper into the pillows. That did absolutely nothing for me. My phone burns in my hand, and even though I know I shouldn't, I check our text thread. As I've been doing for weeks. Or better yet, my one-sided conversation with her.

Me: Hey, I landed, and I wanted you to know I haven't stopped thinking about you.

Me: I can still taste you.

Me: When do you start your new job?

Me: Just check in?

Me: I think you just declined my call.

Me: Are you ghosting me?

Me: I've never been ghosted. I'm usually the ghost.

Me: Well…fuck.

Me: I mean, shit. I guess, have a good fucking life, Tennessee.

I sent that final one last night, before Samantha came up to my room. I scroll through the texts and hit the picture, gazing at her sweet, round face. Those unique, intoxicating eyes and that smile that has the power to bring me to my knees. I go to the first photo where we're kissing, and I swear I can still feel her lips on mine. I sigh as I close my eyes, and I allow the ache in my chest to grow.

I'm not sure what happened. I don't know what changed from our hours in that hotel room to when I walked away. I know she felt what I felt, I know she enjoyed herself, and I know...God, I know she thinks of me. She has to. How can she not? I was incredible—and fuck, she was even better. I can't accept that it was a one-time thing. Nothing is a one-time thing. There is always some contact until everything fizzles out and dies, but this wouldn't have.

We wouldn't have.

When a knock comes to the door, interrupting my pity party, I sit up and grab a pair of shorts before throwing them on. I go to the door and open it just as my sister runs through it. She's like lightning, striking her small body into me, and I catch her with ease. I hold her close, and she hugs me just as tightly as I turn, hoping my mom can find her way in. I kiss Sabine's cheek as she pulls back to look at me.

Her face scrunches up. "Ew, are you wearing lipstick?"

I laugh as I wipe my mouth, slightly embarrassed as I drop her onto the couch. "Maybe. Does it bring out the color of my eyes?"

She laughs as I go to clean it off and to fix the bed so neither of them knows someone was here. I reach for a shirt, pulling it over my head. "I hadn't expected you two yet. I thought we said nine?"

Sabine bounces happily as I look at my mom, who is holding up Samantha's green lace thong. "Someone wanted as much time with you as she could get. Sorry if we crashed your party."

I snag them away from her, throwing them in the trash. "No apology needed. Where is Cliff?"

"Jason," Mom corrects me, and I roll my eyes. "Had other plans."

"Oh, that's too bad," I say, putting on some deodorant as I take in my mom.

She had me early, around fourteen, so she doesn't look old enough to have a twenty-four-year-old. With dirty-blond hair in a short bob, she has blue eyes that are as striking as Sabine's and mine. She wears a simple baby-blue dress that's a wee bit short for a mom of an eight-year-old, but who am I to judge? She has her priorities—which are only what bring her happiness.

TONI ALEO

And not a priority of making sure my sister is happy.

That's my job.

Sabine grins up at me, and I tap her nose as I go to the sink. I get ready quickly, and then I show them out of the room since the embarrassment lingers, knowing that I hadn't had time to clean up whatever was left behind from Samantha and me. Once we're in the hotel restaurant, we order drinks and then food as Sabine tells me all about the new violin she wants.

"What's wrong with the one you have?"

"Nothing. I just want another. So when I'm in a blue mood, I play my blue one, and then when I'm in a classic mood, I play my black one," she gushes, grinning at me with two bottom teeth missing.

"Seems a bit excessive."

She gives me a look that clearly tells me she doesn't agree. "Don't you have, like, eight sticks?"

I return her look. "I'm an adult with adult money."

"And I'm your favorite sister."

I eye her. "I don't know that. I may have some more out there," I tease, and she giggles as I wrap my arms around her, kissing her temple. "When I come to this recital, if I'm impressed, I'll get it for you, okay?"

She beams, her little cherub-like cheeks turning red. "Okay!"

I kiss her temple and find that my mom is watching me. I swallow apprehensively because I have a feeling I know what she's about to ask. "Yes, Mother?"

"Can I have the teacher call you, and you pay her? I always forget to bring the money, and then I'm having to wait for you, and it's just a pain."

How do you forget to pay for your kid's lessons? Man, I'm so glad this isn't the person who raised me, but then the grief I feel over my grandpa's loss is real. He'd never forget to pay for my sports—or anything, for that matter. "That's fine."

"I also need some help with the rent. Jason is between jobs—"

I put up my hand to stop her. "I told you, I don't pay your rent for your boyfriend to live there too. If he's gonna live there, he's gonna pay." I look to Sabine. "Earmuffs." She drops her fork and covers her

HAT TRICK

ears. "And if I find out he's mistreating her, you'll never get a cent from me."

"D'Artagnan, it isn't like that." I don't know how I can hate the way she says my name, but I do. It drives me insane; it's almost like a curse on her lips. I don't know why she even speaks to me. I feel more like a burden than someone she loves. "I only need help this month."

That's what she says every other month, reminding me exactly why she speaks to me.

"Mom, why don't you guys just move in with me? I have the space."

"Yes!" Sabine begs. "I hate it here."

But Mom is already shaking her head. "I don't like South Carolina. I like it out here."

I blow out a breath, meeting Sabine's sad gaze. I pinch her chin before she goes back to eating, and I look at my mom. "I think you could like it."

She makes a face. "I don't know. Let me see how things go out here. I'm starting a new job, and Jason is lovely. Also, I need to know your break for Christmas. Jason wants to take me home to meet his family for Christmas, and I need someone to keep her."

I just blink at her. "You don't want to spend Christmas with us?" I ask, and she shrugs.

"And do what? We aren't holiday people."

No, *she's* not, but I don't say that. I don't want to get into a fight with Sabine right here, and I know that's what'll happen. "I'll get those dates to you," I say, hating how I try everything to make her happy. How I want so fucking badly to please my mom. Maybe then she'll love me. I lean into Sabine, and she rests her sweet head on my shoulder. She looks up at me, those blue eyes shining as she asks, "Can I play on your phone?"

"Sure," I say, handing it over. "Games only."

"Yeah, I know," she laughs, but when she turns on the screen, the photo of Tennessee and me stares up at us, taking my breath away in one swift swoop. "Who's this?"

I feel my mouth go dry, even though I just downed a cup of orange juice. I lick my lips, and I wrap my arm around her, holding the phone with her. "That's a friend of mine."

She side-eyes me. "Like your friend who left lipstick on your mouth and her panties on the floor?"

I chuckle. "No. She's something entirely different."

She's more.

Sabine takes her in and then smiles. "She sure is pretty."

"Yeah, she is."

I feel my mom looking over, and even she smiles. "Look how happy you two are. Is this a girlfriend?"

I shake my head, leaning it in Sabine's. "Nope, just a girl I know."

I feel my mom's gaze on mine as Sabine asks, "Can I meet her?"

The emotion constricting in my throat makes it real hard to breathe. I can't answer her at first and only shrug. "We'll see."

Which is a lie. There is nothing to see. Because in a perfect reality, Tennessee would have met Sabine by now. She wouldn't be ignoring my calls and texts. She'd be telling me how much she loved me and asking me what I wanted to do once I got home from my road trip. She'd tell me how lonely that bed is without me in it. We'd have a dog. Or a cat. Shit, might as well add a damn white picket fence to the yard too. A fantasy, that's all my thoughts are. All she was.

Because none of that is my reality.

Instead, I'm being ghosted by a girl who rocked my world, and I am still thinking about her daily. Which is fucking pathetic. I can have anyone I want. Anyone.

But I want Tennessee.

CHAPTER
Ten

TENNESSEE

Another month later...

"You see this spot right here?" I say, pointing to Leann's scan, where it shows the reason for the weakness in her ankle. "This is your posterior tibial tendon, and it's weak, which is hindering your jump." I swipe to the next slide that illustrates how she jumps for a block, and the spot turns deep red. "Your jump is already the highest on the team, but it can be even higher—a solid two inches, according to my calculations." I swipe to the next slide, showing my calculations and then a simulation of how, if the weakness is fixed, the AI figure of her could clear the net with ease.

"Wow," Leann says, watching as the AI version of herself jumps with ease and blocks like a brick wall when the other AI team tries to spike the volleyball down. "What can I do?"

I swipe to the next slide with a nod. "Rehab. We need to get you a good brace that will support that tendon until it's stronger. You need to

TONI ALEO

up your calories, and you need to up your strength training on weight days."

"Did you already make a plan?" Coach Rey asks, and I smile at him since he already knows the answer.

"Yes, sir." I swipe one more slide, and together, we go over everything Leann needs to do to achieve her goal.

The Olympics.

I know she'll get there, too, especially with my plan.

As I explain it all, going over the science and the formulation that are the basis of my strategy, a giddy feeling fills me from head to toe, as it always does when I get to this part of my job. The confidence of trusting my knowledge, my plan, and knowing it will work.

I have a very high success rate, the highest in the company, especially for someone who has only been working for them for two months. The only two people I've worked with who didn't succeed had that happen because they quit the sport. I was devastated since a lot goes into these simulations and the formulations I use, but at the end of the day, I still love my job.

As I start to pack up my equipment, they thank me over and over, and I smile proudly at them. "Just let me know if I can help with anything. I've emailed everything to both of you, and if you have questions, call me."

"I will. Thank you, Tennessee," Leann says, and the gratitude in her eyes is overwhelming. I give her a wide grin as I slide my computer into its sleeve and then start wrapping up cords.

They've left, and I'm almost done when my phone rings. I pull it from my pocket to see that it's my dad.

My grin widens as I answer. "Hey, Daddy."

"Hey, darling. Was missing ya. Thought I'd check in."

My heart sings for him. While my mom is still upset I left, Daddy has been nothing but supportive. He helped me move in to my apartment, filled my fridge, and even left money on the counter. *Just in case*, he said. He has driven up to see me twice since I left, and I can't appreciate him enough. "I miss you too, Daddy. How's everything?"

"Good, busy. We got the softball fields ready for fall ball. Mom is coaching the bigger girls, and I'm handling the smaller ones."

HAT TRICK

"Right where you belong, setting the foundation," I say, and he chuckles on the other end.

"And dealing with crazy-ass mommas. Man, these women are a lot."

I laugh at that. "I bet. Everyone wants their kid to succeed."

He scoffs. "Darling, I had this lady offer me sex, and I bet you can figure out how that went down."

I almost drop my computer from laughing. "Oh my. I bet Momma lost her damn mind."

"Like a fool. Kicked her out, kicked the kid out, and made sure everyone knew that I was off-limits—since apparently that wasn't a well-known thing. Through no fault of my own."

"Of course not."

He laughs. "Now all the women give me a wide berth."

I snort. My mom is the personification of a country song about not touching her man. "Not surprised at all."

"Right? Lord Almighty, that woman. Anyway, how's work?"

A delighted smile fills my face as I tell him about Leann and her goals. I go on about the baseball players I've been working with and how, with football season coming up, I'm about to get even busier.

"Did that contract go through with the college hockey team?"

I shake my head. "No. It wasn't in the budget, but we got hired by some travel teams. And I have been helping some high schoolers, potential D1 kids, and it's been awesome."

"That's pretty damn cool."

"Yeah. I think I'm a hockey fan."

He scoffs. "Hockey is fun, but you best remember, you are a Tennessee sports team fan. Don't be wearing any navy and orange. You know your colors."

I snort. "I mean, my name speaks for itself. Which, by the way, people make fun of me here."

"They're jealous that Tennessee has the best sports in the USA." God, he bleeds orange. "Which reminds me, Coach Vitello called from the Vols. He was wondering how to contract with you."

"Daddy, are you trying to pull me back there?"

He doesn't even hesitate. "Yes. I miss you."

TONI ALEO

My face warms as I sit in the lobby to wait for my coworker. "I don't know if we're contracting that way. I heard we're moving into the Carolinas next."

Which has my stomach clenching since a certain someone lives there.

Someone who accused me of ghosting him, which I guess I did—not that I allow myself to dwell on that.

Much.

"Will you go down that way?"

"I don't know. Everyone likes me here, and I have a great success rate so far. But I am training coworkers with my formulas so we can help more people."

"Giving away your secrets? They paying you for that?"

"Yeah, Daddy. I'm doing mighty well."

"Good. Listen, I need a weeklong vacation, so get on that," he teases, and I laugh.

"Sure will," I tell him, leaning back and crossing my legs. "How's Momma?"

"She's all right. Missing you. It doesn't help that Lindy and Josie are always calling and asking her about you."

"Really? That's surprising," I say. I haven't spoken to them since I left. I thought I would miss them, but I don't. I feel good, I love my job, and I love my apartment. I enjoy my coworkers, and I'm good with how everything is going.

Somewhat.

"Yeah. Maybe give them a call?"

"I'm just fine not doing that," I tell him, and his laughter is booming.

"Whatever you wanna do, darling, I'm good with."

"I love you, Daddy."

"Oh, darling. I love you, miss you."

My heart aches from missing him. I look up just as Troy, my coworker, comes out of the side court where he was working with more clients. His athletic pants are loose along his legs, but I know he is strong beneath them. His shoulders are wide and his arms thick. He's an ex-baseball player and has the body to show for it. His red hair

HAT TRICK

is combed to the side, and he's clean-shaven with nice lines to his jaw. His lips are thin, and his eyes are the color of moss. He strolls toward me with that look in his eyes he always has when he sees me. It isn't a secret that he's into me, but I just can't seem to pull the trigger and let myself enjoy him. We've been hanging out a lot, but nothing has happened.

"Miss you, but let me let you go. Troy is finally done with his client, and we're heading out."

"Troy? How's that going?"

I roll my eyes. "It's nothing, Daddy. We're just friends."

"Mmm-hmm," he draws out. "Momma said you were dating."

"Hardly. We're getting to know each other. That's all."

Considering the last time I slept with someone before knowing anything about them, I caught feelings I didn't know I could.

"Well, make sure he looks good in orange, or I won't like him."

I laugh at that, shaking my head. "Bye, Daddy. Love you."

"Love you, darling."

I hang up as I stand, my grin still in place, and Troy comes to a stop in front of me. He's my height, and while he smells wonderful, it's not the spiciness that I find I miss. "I like it when you smile like that."

I sigh deeply as I meet his mossy gaze, ignoring his comment. "You ready?"

"Yeah," he says, grabbing my bag for me. "Are we doing dinner tonight?"

I swallow and force myself to nod. "Sure. Where do you want to go?"

He holds the door for me as I go through it, and then he falls into step with me. "I was thinking I could cook for you. At my house."

My heart constricts in my chest. My mind tells me to say yes, but that heart of mine can't do it. I know I should pull the trigger and enter into whatever this is, but I can't. I know why, but giving it a voice means I really did ghost him. Even if it was out of fear, it may be the biggest regret of my life.

When Troy steps in front of me, I almost run into him, my eyes widening in confusion. "Whoa."

His mossy eyes are dark as he looks into my eyes. He's not a big

TONI ALEO

guy, but he's a good guy. Another fucking nice guy. "Tennessee, tell me something." I'd rather not, but instead, I press my lips together as he asks, "What are we doing?"

I swallow as I gaze into his eyes. "Honestly, I don't know."

"I feel like there is something here," he says.

I mean, I sense it, but I don't know how to allow myself to feel it.

"I like you—a lot." He reaches out, cupping my cheek in his hand. "I find you incredibly gorgeous and so damn smart it makes me wild. I love coming to work because I know I'll see you."

I don't know what to say to him. I do care for him; he's been so nice to me since I moved here. He's always there for a laugh, we work out together, and he's shown me around. We work great together, and we go to sports games together.

The problem is, I want what Dart did for me. I want that all-consuming feeling. But how can I have that when Dart is in South Carolina and I'm here?

While Dart is nowhere near me, Troy is right here, looking at me.

"I enjoy your company a lot," I tell him. "I just don't know if I'm emotionally available right now. I'm still adjusting to all these life changes I've made."

And because, emotionally, I'm still in Nashville.

He searches my gaze, and I don't like how he only looks at one of my eyes. I know that's silly, but I feel like he doesn't even see my other eye, which makes me feel like a freak. I look away and blow out a breath.

"Maybe if we take this to the next level, you'll find you *are* emotionally available."

I meet his gaze again and sigh deeply. It all sounds like a good idea; it all sounds like he could be onto something, but deep inside, I know he's missing a bunch of tattoos. He doesn't have dark-blond hair and blue eyes that stop me dead in my tracks. He doesn't have the word "Sunshine" along his neck and a badass dragon covering his back. He doesn't call me baby doll, and I bet if he called me a greedy girl, I wouldn't come at the sound. No, his voice is missing a lot of the depth that only Dart had.

But I ghosted him. I didn't respond. I didn't try, and that's on me. I know the truth, though. I knew that I would fall so deeply for him that nothing would ever matter. I wouldn't have taken this job, I would have gone wherever the hell he is, and I would have given my whole self to him. I wouldn't have done what I needed to do. Found out who I am. That's what these last couple months have been, and it's refreshing to know I wasn't faking it.

I am spunky, loud, smart, and I am beautiful. Yeah, I'm thick, but it doesn't matter because it's who I am. Here in Virginia, I have drawn so much attention from guys, and I wish that Josie could see it. That it doesn't matter about my size—it matters who I am, and I'm awesome. I no longer look tired and unsure of myself. I look and feel the confidence I knew I had inside me. I am doing what I love and what I needed to, but my heart yearns for that night in Nashville.

Lordy, it hurts so badly.

I miss him deeply, but I know nothing will ever come of it.

It can't. It was one night.

One night I'll hold in my heart forever, but I gotta move on.

I swallow, my heart aching as I say, "I think dinner at your house would be fun."

The smile that fills his face doesn't leave me breathless, but I smile back just the same.

The words that have just left my mouth don't feel right. I know I don't believe them in the slightest, and I may just as well call him Denis to the second power, because once more, I'm listening to my mind instead of my heart.

But how can I listen to my heart when I haven't had it since Nashville?

CHAPTER
Eleven

Dart

Another month later...

Celeste sits on my shoulders, putting my hair in different ponytails while *Paw Patrol* plays on the TV, and Raine lies in my lap, holding her feet and rocking back and forth.

"Sissy, look," Celeste cheers, but her sister doesn't even know what is going on. Raine's too engrossed in these weird-ass dogs. And I still don't know why there is a group of cats if the show is called *Paw Patrol*...well, I guess cats do have paws. But why is the mayor mean? He's the damn mayor!

I hate this show.

"Dart, you pretty," Celeste says then, and I laugh 'cause I'm sure I am anything but pretty. Laughter fills the room as I glance over at the girls' parents. Jaylin and Kirby Litman sit on the love seat, limbs tangled as they look through a baby name book. Finally, we have a boy coming. I was damn sure it would be a girl again since apparently Kirby shoots nothing but girls, but thankfully, it's a boy. Jaylin snaps a photo of me, and I'm sure that'll be brought up at practice tomorrow.

"Thanks, Celeste," I gush as I tickle her toes. She laughs happily as Raine looks up at me, her dark eyes full of wonder and looking just like her momma. Her black curls are wild and shiny, just like Jaylin's. I tickle her thigh, and she giggles before turning her attention back to the TV. A text sounds on my phone, and I glance down to see it's my mom, asking for money.

I groan loudly as Jaylin asks, "Do I need to take them?"

"No," I say simply, ignoring my phone. "My mom is asking for money again."

Kirby rolls his eyes as Jaylin gives me a gloomy look. "I'm sorry."

"Why doesn't she just move here or at least let you take Sabine?" Kirby asks, annoyed by now. They know all about my family woes.

I shrug. "I don't know. She's driving me crazy. She and that dude broke up, and now I'm paying her rent every month."

"Don't," Jaylin urges me. "You don't owe her anything."

"But if I don't, she will keep Sabine from me," I tell them, picking up Raine and cuddling her to my chest. I kiss her temple, enjoying the sweet lavender smell of her. "And I can't have that."

"But she knows that, and that's why she does this," Jaylin reminds me, and I know she's right.

"What do I do, then?"

"I mean, I'll represent you to get custody of Sabine. But I don't know that we'll win, especially with you being a single hockey player."

"I know," I say, meeting her gaze. Jaylin has been offering since I started having issues with my mom and the money demands. My mom hasn't said she'd keep Sabine from me, but it's almost as if she doesn't have to say it. I feel like it'd just happen as a way to get the money out of me. She knows I have it; her father didn't leave her a penny. It all went to me, and she knows my weakness.

Sabine.

"Ignore her," Kirby suggests, but I know that won't help anything. She'll just keep trying to contact me, and then she'll have Sabine call me. "I know it's easier said than done."

I don't react as Raine turns in my arms and leans her head on me. I love these kids. I feel Jaylin watching me, and when I look over, she is lowering her phone. "Stop taking pictures of me, woman! I'm gonna start charging you."

She snorts at that, her dark eyes full of love. Jaylin has always been very special to me. I tried hitting on her when I first met her, but then Kirby threatened to murder me, and I ran away quickly. "I love how great you are with the girls."

I lay my head on Celeste's stomach. "Celeste, does Uncle Dart love you?"

She gives me an exasperated look. "Duh, you love me most."

I look back at Jaylin, and she's grinning from ear to ear. "We all do, don't we?"

"I don't. He's a pain in my ass," Kirby announces, and I scoff at that. "I like the name Gerald."

I make a face. "I told you guys to name him D'Artagnan. I get all the ass."

I'm met with dry looks. "Because that's what we want for our child," Jaylin reminds me, and I point to Kirby.

"He does," I accuse, and Kirby laughs.

"Not at all, because then he'll knock up some dumbass and have to deal with her until he gets custody of his kid," he says, reminding me of his own story.

"Hey, it worked out great for you," I say, and his eyes fall on his wife. He gives her a wide grin, kissing her nose, and I hate how jealous I am of them.

Of their perfect life.

"It did, but we still aren't naming him that," he says just as the back door slides open.

We all look over as Sawyer Anderson enters without knocking. He never does. He's about my height, built like a truck, but he looks like a surfer. Long blond hair and ice-blue eyes. His brother plays for the Nashville Assassins, and he's been friends with Owen Adler his whole life. I had no choice but to like him when he came to the team.

Everyone else does.

HAT TRICK

"Hey, bro," I call to him as he goes right for the fridge.

"Please help yourself," Jaylin says to him, and he sends her a toothy grin. He's missing his front teeth after getting hit with a puck right in the mouth during his first preseason game. "Are your teeth still not in?"

He shakes his head. "Nope, and I'm starting to get used to the whistling noise when I talk, so I don't know if I'll wear them when they show up."

"I love the whistling noise," I tell him, and he laughs as he comes toward us with a beer and three pouches of applesauce. He sits beside me, handing one to each girl before opening his. "Where is mine?"

His blue eyes settle on me. "In the fridge."

"Jackass," I say, and Celeste leans forward, giving me a squirt of her applesauce. "That's why you're my girl, huh?"

She nods. "Yup."

"What are you doing tonight?" Sawyer asks me. "I was gonna hit the beach bar. They're having a blowout since they're closing down for the winter."

I sigh deeply. I could go. We don't have practice tomorrow, and Lord knows I could use a night of drinking and bringing someone home. But I like where I am, too. "I don't know."

I feel Jaylin watching me, but I ignore her as Sawyer says, "Bro, I need a wingman."

"Maybe," I say, and then I glance over to Jaylin. "Yes, Jay?"

She shakes her head. "Nothing."

"You sure?"

"Yes," she says, but I know she's lying.

Just then, the back door opens once more, and Owen strolls in. He looks at all of us and then throws his hands up. "So, I guess my invite to hang wasn't extended?"

Sawyer shrugs. "I had no food."

"I came to play with the girls," I say, and Celeste hugs my head.

"They weren't invited," Kirby tells him, and Jaylin laughs.

Usually, this is the hang-out spot. Everyone comes to Kirby and Jaylin's. For one, there is always food, and for two, the kids are cute.

81

TONI ALEO

We play video games, eat, and even play cards together. Well, we haven't played cards for a long time. The last time we played was before I slept with my teammate's best friend and ruined all that. Now, we don't see Thatcher or Audrina socially anymore. It's all my fault and something I'm not proud of. The night wasn't even that great, nothing like how it was with Tennessee.

Great. Now I'm thinking of Tennessee.

Not that that's a new thing or whatever…

"I figured. Hey Jay, do you have Angie's neem oil? There is a bug on Angie's plant, and she's currently on the porch screaming and crying that she can't find her oil," Owen whines, sounding every bit how I know Angie is sounding right now. I laugh at him, thankful for the distraction.

Jaylin nods. "Oh, I do. Hold on."

She gets up, and Owen leans on the counter. "What're y'all doing tonight?"

I shrug as Sawyer says, "Trying to get Dart out, but he's being difficult."

Owen snorts at that, and I set him with a look that has him pressing his lips together. He's the only one who knows about Tennessee. Though, I suspect he told Angie, who told Jaylin, given the way she was looking at me. "Why don't you want to go out? You still talking to Andie?"

I make a face. "God, no. That was a one-and-done."

Which is what Tennessee was supposed to be, but I forgot that in the middle of hat trick number two.

"Didn't you date her for like a week?" Sawyer asks me, and I shrug.

"Okay, it was a week thing."

Jaylin rolls her eyes as she hands Owen the bottle of oil. "Have you called her?" she asks me, and I snap my gaze to Owen, but he is running out the back door without even saying goodbye.

"Jackass," I mutter, and Celeste echoes me. I would laugh, but by the looks on her parents' faces, they aren't happy. "Sorry."

She echoes that too, and I have to fight my lips not to grin. "But, no. I haven't."

"You should. It's been, what, a couple months now?"

I swallow hard. Eleven weeks. It's been eleven fucking long-ass weeks.

I shrug. "She ghosted me. It's cool."

"Wow, you aren't a very good liar," Kirby says, and I set him with a glower. "Just saying."

"Who are we talking about?" Sawyer asks.

"No one," I say quickly.

Thankfully, the front door opens, and the girls squeal in delight as Jean, their nanny, enters. Celeste climbs off me and runs to her as Raine rolls to her stomach to get off me. I set her on the floor, and she army crawls to Jean as I'm left alone without my girls.

"I'm wounded, girls!" I call to them, but they ignore me as Jean picks them up and kisses them all over.

Man, I remember a time when I'd look at Jean and want to eat her whole. She is thick in all the right spots, a round face, thin lips, and a wide nose. Her cheekbones are high and beautiful. She has long dark hair and even darker eyes. She's beautiful, stunning, but she has never had any interest in me at all. After Tennessee, I find that I no longer have any interest either.

Which is tragic, really.

"You'll be fine," she calls to me as she walks into the living room, carrying the girls before throwing her stuff down on the floor. "Are we having a party?"

"No, they just show up and don't leave," Kirby says, and I laugh at that.

"I told you two to stop buying all that food. That's why they come," she reminds him, and I set her with a pointed look.

"Excuse you. I come for the girls."

She smiles at me, and I return it. "I apologize. You usually do."

I gaze into her eyes, and then my grin widens. "What're you doing tonight?"

"Sleeping?" she answers and then laughs as Raine kisses her cheek. "I have to be up early to go see my family."

"Wanna go out with Sawyer and me tonight?"

Sawyer nods. "Yeah. I'll take you out all night, Jean."

TONI ALEO

She laughs at that. "Hard pass, Sawyer," she says, and then she looks to me. "And I won't be your second string to who you're really pining over."

I glare at Jaylin then, and she holds up her hands. "She was here when Angie told me."

"You women talk too much."

Kirby scoffs in agreement. "You have no clue."

I glance back at Jean, hoping I'm knocking down some walls with my intense gaze and quick grin. "But Jean, baby, you've always been my first string."

She rolls her eyes. "I'm not interested, Dart."

"Come on now. We both feel this heat."

It's really more like Antarctica between us, but some heat moves through her eyes. Which is great, because I refuse to let my friends think I'm weak and shit, still pining over some girl who doesn't fucking want me. I could kill Owen. But whatever. It is what it is.

Jean drags her gaze from mine and exhales. "Fine, but I'm not sleeping with you."

"We'll see about that," I say with a wink.

I feel Jaylin watching me, and even she knows the truth.

There is nothing about it to see. I won't be losing myself in Jean.

She reminds me way too much of Tennessee.

I get up. "I'll swing through at nine to grab you."

She makes a face. "Nine? That's late."

"Jean, baby—" I pause then, shaking my head when I can't say what I wanted. I clear my throat. "Be ready to stay out well past your bedtime."

I kiss the girls and then head to the door. I've gotta get out of here. I don't like that Jaylin knows. Because if she knows, then Kirby knows, and that means everyone thinks I'm ridiculous. It was bad enough I knew; I didn't need anyone else to know. I'm known for my love-'em-and-leave-'em reputation, but now that I was loved and left, it fucking hurts.

I reach my truck, getting in and then turning it on. Music blasts through the speakers. It's a slow song, something country, and I look to see who it is.

"Tennessee Orange," by Megan Moroney.

Within seconds, it all comes crashing back into me.

I lay my head back on the headrest, closing my eyes, knowing good and well I'd wear Tennessee Orange for that gorgeous girl with eyes as unique as her soul.

CHAPTER
Twelve

TENNESSEE

Until now, Momma hasn't been to visit me.

"What do you mean, you don't have sweet tea?" she asks, confused, as she looks up at the waiter. I fight back my grin as I push the little packets of sugar toward her. "I don't want that. It does nothing. You have to boil the sugar in the tea. What the hell are y'all drinking unsweet for? Are y'all even alive inside?"

I snort at that as Dad rolls his eyes. He pats my mom's hand. "Marcy, please."

"Thomas! No sweet tea," she stresses then looks at me. "How have you been living here?"

I beam at her, loving how ridiculous she sounds. I've missed her so much. "I don't come out to eat much," I tell her, and she groans loudly.

"Just let me get a Coke."

"We have Pepsi," the waiter says with a wince, and I know he knows it's coming.

"For the love of God!" she complains, and then she sets him with a look. "Do you have water? Or is it that sparkling crap?"

Dad's booming laugh only makes me laugh harder as the waiter

HAT TRICK

basically runs in the other direction, promising the water is not sparkling.

"I hate it here," she tells us, and I can't stop laughing. She's absolutely insane, and I've missed her so much.

"Good thing I'm going farther down, huh?"

I just got word that I am being transferred to North Carolina for a new contract with three teams I haven't gotten the names of yet. Troy thinks they are professional teams, but I think that would be too good to be true. I've been doing great and bringing in more money with my success rate, but I haven't gotten to work in professional sports yet. I'm excited and hopeful. This could really elevate my career, even though I'm already the best in my field in the short time I've been in it.

Troy has worked for the company for years, and his success rate is nowhere near mine. When I mentioned my dissertation during the interview process, I told them I had formulas and a program that I have scientific proof is effective. That's why UT and Vandy wanted me, but I chose to come here. Sometimes I feel guilty, but then I'm also excited.

Troy knows how much I offer because he has mentioned branching off from his uncle's company and starting our own. Each time I do a study on an athlete, I find new ways, new formulas, to help with the athlete's range. Daddy doesn't want me to go into business with Troy, but I don't know. The work I'm doing is exciting, and if I do decide to go on my own, I can accept contracts anywhere and still return home to help with Mom's and Dad's athletes. Sometimes I miss home a lot, but at the same time, I am ready to see where this career will take me.

"Thank God. I bet they have sweet tea."

"I'm sure they do," I say to my mom.

"I'll believe it when I see it."

My upcoming move is why my parents are here. They're helping me pack and are going to travel with me to get me settled. When I told them I was being transferred, of course they were excited—until they found out I would be even farther from them. Dad being Dad, though, he told me to let him know when moving day was, and they'd be here.

I sold all my furniture to the company that I work for so that they can use the furnished apartment for my replacement. They took over

TONI ALEO

the lease and even leased me a place in North Carolina. It'll be furnished, which makes me feel like I may not be there for long. I don't know how I feel about that, but I'm just relieved it's not South Carolina, where I know he plays.

While I'm supposed to be getting over him, taking my relationship with Troy to the next level, I find myself in bed watching the IceCats on ESPN. I zoom in on his face and allow myself to remember how those lips felt on mine, on my body. When he scored his first hat trick of the season the other night, I let myself relish the memory of the two he gave me.

Sometimes I wonder if he still has my hat. I'm sure he set it on fire by now. I follow his stats, and it's becoming a very unhealthy obsession of mine. I've even analyzed him and have ideas for how to help his shot. Not that I'd ever get a chance to help him. I know it's bad for me, but it feels like it's giving me something of him but isn't requiring me to give him anything of myself that I know I'll never get back. I don't know; I could just be a fucking psycho, which is probably the case anyway.

Once we get our drinks, we order some appetizers as Mom tells me all about the fall ball season. As I knew they would, her team won state and even regionals, but they lost the championship by one run. She's obviously still devastated. But proud, nonetheless. "Did Granny call you the other day?"

I nod. "Yeah, we talked for a bit. Is her foot okay?"

Dad makes a face. "They may have to take it. That damn diabetes is a bitch."

I make a face. "That sucks."

"It does, but she wants to come see you when you're settled in," Mom says, and joy fills me.

"I'd love that." Our appetizers arrive then, and we wait to place our dinner order as we snack. Dad asks about my volleyball player, Leann, and pride practically bursts from me. "She's jumping a half inch higher in a month, so we're hoping for a full inch by next month. Troy is actually going to take over for me since I'm leaving."

They both nod, but neither really asks about him. I don't know if that's my fault since I don't talk about him much. Troy wanted to meet my parents before I left, but I'm not ready for that. I like how things are, simple and clean-cut. He may feel things for me, but nothing has changed on my side. I care for him, but I don't think I'm emotionally attached enough to ever love him.

"Oh, so he isn't going with you?"

I shake my head. "Not at first. He is going to finish contracts here and then meet me there in a couple weeks."

Mom holds my gaze. "Will you two live together?"

"No. He has his own place—same building, but his own place."

"I'm surprised. Haven't y'all been dating for a couple months now?"

"Not quite that long, but I don't want to live with him."

"Good," Dad says, holding me with a look. "I saw that photo you posted, him in that damn Cavaliers shirt. I told you, Tennessee Lynn," he warns, and I laugh. "Orange is the only color I'll accept."

"I know, Daddy."

"Maybe that ugly purple the Assassins wear or that blue the Titans wear." I roll my eyes as he points his finger at me. "But I'm iffy about the gold and black of Vandy."

"Which is why I'd never date a Vanderbilt man," I say with a teasing grin, much to Mom's dismay.

"I don't know. Those Vanderbilt men are usually doctors, and that means money."

Dad lets out a booming laugh. "Marcy, our baby doesn't need a man. She has her own money."

"Damn right, Marcy," I throw at her, and she snorts gently before she laughs softly.

"Just as we raised her," she says, cupping my jaw in her hand. I share a smile with her as I lean into her touch.

"Thank you for being here."

She squeezes my jaw. "My love, I wouldn't want to be anywhere else—even if they have no sweet tea. Because I miss you more than words could ever express." I wrap my arms around her, hugging her tightly as she kisses my cheek. In my ear, she whispers, "I'm sorry I was such a bitch."

I laugh, squeezing her hard. "It's okay. I am too."

TONI ALEO

"I know. You're my daughter."

"I am," I laugh, kissing her again, but as we part, I see Troy at the front of the restaurant.

What. The. Fuck.

His eyes fall on mine, and I let my mom go, standing up straight as I eye him. He's with some guys from his gym, but why did they come here? I'm pretty sure I told him I was coming here. He points to me, and the guys I've gotten to know wave. I wave back as he comes toward me. My heart is in my throat.

"Darling, you okay?" Dad asks, and I nod, unable to fathom what the hell he is doing. I told him I wasn't ready for him to meet my parents. Even though he was ready for me to meet his on day two of my being in his bed.

Troy strolls toward me like this isn't fucking weird. "Hey, baby."

He leans in, kissing the side of my mouth.

"What are you doing here?"

"We came to eat after our workout. I thought you said y'all were going to the one on the west side?"

I shake my head. "Why would we, when we can walk here?"

He doesn't seem embarrassed or even concerned that he's invading my privacy. "True. I'm sorry. You look upset."

"Because I am," I say, but I feel my mom and dad watching me. I take a deep breath. "I wasn't ready for this."

"I understand. I can go back with the guys."

"Nonsense," my dad booms, standing up to his full six-foot-four height and holding out his hand. Troy takes it happily, while I fume with anger. "Troy, is it? I'm Thomas Dent. It's great to meet you."

"You too. Thank you." He holds his hand out to my mom. "Mrs. Dent."

Mom looks back at me before taking his hand. "We've heard a lot about you."

From whom, I want to ask, but I just look back at Troy as he meets my gaze. "I guess I'll return to my friends. I just wanted to say hi."

"You should join us," Dad suggests, sitting down. "It's nice to get to know the guy my daughter has been dating, even if he is a Cavaliers fan." I whip my gaze to my dad's, and he shrugs. "What? It's true."

HAT TRICK

Kill me now. Of course, Troy is all for it. "I'd love to, thank you. Let me go back and tell my friends."

He scurries off as I sit down, glaring at my parents. "Thanks, Dad."

"What? I didn't want to be rude," he says innocently.

"Do you even like him?" Mom asks, leaning in. "You seem very upset."

"Because I didn't want him meeting y'all yet. We've only been dating for a month."

She sets me with a look. "Yet you're going to do long-distance with *him*."

I glare at her because I know what she is implying. I know whom she is speaking of. Even though she'd dismissed my feelings, I did tell her what happened and how I felt, so I know what she's getting at. Man, she is a bitch. "Because he's coming in a couple weeks."

"Hmm," she says, shaking her head. Then Troy comes over, sitting between my parents and across from me. "Troy, Tennie tells us you guys work well together."

And just like I knew he would, he charms my parents. He knows what to say, smiles the right way, and is the perfect gentleman. Just as Denis was, and it bores me to tears. I lean on my hand as I pick at the florets of my broccoli, wishing like hell this dinner would end, when my mom's phone rings. I almost cry out in relief.

"Do we need to leave?" I ask, and she waves me off.

"No, it's Venessa." Josie's momma. I bring in my brows as I watch her answer. She covers her mouth and then squeals happily. "Oh! I can't even! Congratulations! I am so excited for y'all! Yeah, no. I am actually with her. No, I'm sure she will. Lordy, I'm so happy! Yes, I'll let you know."

She hangs up the phone and looks at me, tears in her eyes. "Josie is engaged!"

I perk a brow. "How wonderful."

"To him?" Dad asks then, and I look from him to my mom, who is grimacing. "That was fast. He knock her up?"

"Thomas!"

"What? I'm just saying."

"Who?" I ask, just because I'm nosy. "Not that I care, but that is

TONI ALEO

kind of fast. She was single when I left."

"Who are we talking about?" Troy asks, and I groan inwardly. I haven't spoken about my life back home.

"Josie, Tennie's best friend."

"Ex-best friend," I correct her, and she gives me a look.

"She wants to speak to you."

"Well, I don't want to talk to her."

"I think you need to," she urges, and I laugh.

"Hard pass on that, for sure," I say, giving my dad a look that says *What in the hell?* But even he looks concerned. "What…?"

"Tennie, darling, she's marrying Denis," he tells me.

My smile fades and my jaw drops. "Denis," I echo. "The Denis I dated for almost ten years?"

"Just the same," Mom says slowly.

"The same fucking Denis she said I would never find better than?" I ask, and Mom winces at my words.

I look between them, ignoring Troy completely as I snort with laughter. "What in the world!" I laugh so hard, I start to cry. "Man, karma don't play."

"He loves her."

I choke at that, unable to hold in my laughter. "Mom, he told me he loved me the night in Nashville when I told him I'd never love him. Good Lord. That's funny."

"Not the reaction I thought she'd have," Mom says to Dad, but he doesn't seem surprised.

"I told you she never loved him," he says, and I point back at my dad.

"I told you the same. I have never felt anything like love until…" I let my words trail off, and I press my lips together, closing my eyes as I turn my head to regain my composure. I clench my jaw. "I'm ready to go."

I look for the waiter as Troy asks, "When is the wedding?"

I snap my gaze to his. "Why? You going?"

"I was just wondering," he says slowly. "Which was obviously the wrong thing to ask."

"Exactly," I say, shaking my head.

HAT TRICK

"In a couple months."

I laugh at that as I wave down our waiter. "Yeah, she's knocked up."

"Has to be," Dad agrees as Mom scolds us with a tsk.

Once we get the check, Dad pays and we leave, thank God. Outside, Troy takes my hand and pulls me to the side. "Are you mad at me?"

I look up at him and shrug. "Now is not the time. I'm frustrated, and I'm ready to go home and load the truck."

He eyes me, cupping my jaw in his hand. "Let me help you—to make up for my unannounced visit and then assuming we'd go to the wedding together."

I scrunch up my face as I gawk at him. "*I'm* not even going to the wedding."

"Oh," he says, and then he swallows hard. "The guys will come help too."

"Fine, but I'm still upset."

"I'm sorry. Let me make it up to you," he says, wrapping his arms around me and kissing my neck. "Start you a bath, rub you in all the right spots."

I sigh. "Okay."

"Okay." He grins against my neck before kissing it. I wish he'd grow a beard.

———

While everyone is putting stuff in the truck, I head into my room for a breather. I sit on my bed and then fall back, exhaling heavily. I can't believe Josie is marrying Denis. I'm not hurt or upset, but I do find it pretty funny. I wonder if she liked him the whole time he was with me? I wonder if that's why she was always saying something about my weight, because the guy she liked picked me. The biggest one of the three of us. With thoughts of Josie and Denis come thoughts of Dart. A grin pulls at my mouth, remembering the way he looked at Lindy and Josie, like he was about to step between us to protect me from them in the lobby.

TONI ALEO

Ugh, I miss him.

I sit up and walk over to my dresser. I open the top drawer, where the photo of Dart and me sits in a frame from the dollar store. I figured if I bought the frame there, it wouldn't be a big deal that I'd framed the photo. But I had been keeping it on the bedside table, just so it'd prompt good dreams before I went to sleep. When I decided to move on with Troy, I felt I needed to put the picture away. But I still see it every morning since it hides in my underwear drawer.

I run my finger along Dart's lips, and the way he smiles takes my breath away still to this moment. Something inside me urges me to text him, tell him I'm coming to North Carolina. But I know that's still too far away for us to see what could happen.

And what about Troy?

Chills run through me at my loss, and the regret burns deep in my chest.

"Is that him?"

I practically jump out of my skin when my mom's voice comes from my left. "Jesus, Mom," I say, pressing the photo to my chest. "What is wrong with you?"

"I called you like six times."

"I wasn't listening!"

"Obviously," she says, setting me with a look before she pulls the frame from my hand. I watch as her brow furrows, and her lips tip up at the side. "Well, lordy me," she whispers. "Look at you two."

Emotion squeezes my throat in a way I wish were Dart's hand instead. "He's a looker, huh?"

"Devastatingly handsome," she says, studying the photo closer. "But it's the two of you together that is breathtaking."

My heart constricts in my chest. "It was the best night of my life."

She leans into me. "Have you talked to him?"

"No, not at all," I whisper, sighing deeply. "Is it pathetic I miss him?"

She laughs. "Baby, I don't even know him, and I wish I did." She gathers my hair in her hand, twisting it gently. "I don't think this thing with Troy will work out."

"It could," I say softly. "It should."

HAT TRICK

She gives me a very motherly look, and I know I'm not about to like what she has to say. "Oh, my sweet girl," she says, wrapping her arms around my neck. "It won't as long as this man has your heart."

My heart burns in my chest as I close my eyes because I know she's right.

"What am I going to do?"

"Tennie, my baby, I don't even know—"

"Tennessee!" My eyes fly open at the sound of Troy's voice, and I stuff the photo back into the drawer as I look toward the door he's standing in. "Baby, did you see the email?"

I bring in my brows, moving out of my mom's arms and picking up my phone. I open the email from my boss and read it quickly.

My whole body goes cold as I read the name of the last of the three professional sports teams we're contracted with.

IceCats.

I look up at Troy, and he's obviously excited. "I thought we were contracted for North Carolina?"

He shakes his head. "No, South. They made a change, also secured different apartments."

Mom looks at me, confused. "Well lordy, Tennie, how long is this drive gonna be!"

But I can't process the drive. Or even the other two teams.

Because all I see is the IceCats.

The very team D'Artagnan Miklas plays for.

My gaze whips to Troy's excited one, but I don't feel his enthusiasm.

No. For me, it's pure fear as I realize that not only is karma not playing around when it comes to the upcoming nuptials of Josie and Denis, but now fate wants to join in by bringing me not only to the same state, but the same arena, as D'Artagnan.

And I'm involved with someone.

Who is not D'Artagnan.

That's cool. Totally fine.

I'm totally fucking fine.

CHAPTER
Thirteen

Dart

"Did you hook up with Jean?"

I take a deep breath in as I hold myself up, rolling my hip out on the foam roller. I don't spare Owen a look as I answer, "I'm not telling you shit. You've got a big mouth."

Owen's laughter fills the stretching room as he rolls his back out. "In my defense, my wife only has to look at me and I'm telling her my darkest secrets."

I side-eye him. "She couldn't have known anything about what happened."

He meets my gaze. "No, but she knew something was up with you. She was worried and said she tried to ask you about it, but you blew her off."

That's nice and all, but damn!

"Still, she told everyone," I remind him, and he winces. I'm not sure if it's from the spot he hit with his foam roller or knowing I'm upset about his big fucking mouth.

"Yeah. I didn't know she'd do that."

"No? 'Cause they don't all love gossip?"

HAT TRICK

He sends me an apologetic look. "I'm sorry, man."

I switch to my other hip. "It's fine. I love when my friends think I'm weak and pathetic."

Owen's blue eyes darken. "No one thinks that."

"Bro, *I* think it," I admit, exhaling hard as I move up and down the foam roller, loving the pain. "I didn't take Jean back to my place. I took her home and didn't even kiss her."

"Because she might have slapped you?"

I snort. "I still would have tried. We had a good time, but it just wasn't what I wanted."

"*Who* you wanted," he corrects, and I cut him a dark look. "Just saying."

I don't want to tell him he's right, so I don't say anything as I continue to stretch.

"Maybe you should just go see her."

I scoff at that. "So she can reject me to my face?"

"But then you'd have closure, ya know?" he says, and I look over at him. "Listen, if I had the best sex of my life and was still thinking of someone three months after the fact, even when there is no contact whatsoever, I would be searching the ends of the earth for her. Thankfully, I just gotta go into the plant room, and Angie's there."

I want to gag. "Well, not everyone has the power of plants to keep a girl in his house," I throw at him, and he laughs.

"It's more than the plants, believe me," he says with a wink, and I chuckle at that. "Really, man, I think you should find out where in Virginia she is, and let's roll up on her. I'll go with you."

My ride-or-die, right here.

"I know where she is," I answer, sighing deeply. "I found her Instagram."

He perks up like a dog when you ask if they want a treat. "Oh? And?"

I shrug. "And, what? She's somewhere near a college, working for CapitalCare, and it looks as if she is seeing someone."

He brings in his brows and hisses out a breath. "Damn, dude. I'm sorry."

"It is what it is," I say, swallowing past the lump in my throat. In

TONI ALEO

the photo of them at the Cavaliers stadium, with the caption, *Go Hoos*, which doesn't make a damn bit of sense, the guy was holding Tennessee tighter than she was him. But fuck if she wasn't gorgeous as all hell. Just how I remembered her. Though, she has lost a bit of weight, much to my dismay.

"When did she post that?"

"I just found her account last night," I admit, and he gives me a look. "Yes, at the party. I finally found it. I don't know why, but I just kept clicking every fucking Tennessee account. Then I switched to searching for Tennie, and that's when I found it under *The Only Ten You'll See*." I say, feeling stupid as fuck since that's what she put in as her contact.

"That's funny," he says, moving the roller down to his calf. "How old was the photo? Maybe she isn't involved with him anymore."

I don't answer him. Instead, I slide my phone over to him. "It's up."

"Jesus, you're crazy."

"I know. Thanks," I say dryly. "I just don't know… I feel like closure would be great, but I'm not sure if it'll help. I think I'll just need some fucking time. I feel stupid."

He gives me an understanding look as he sits cross-legged on the floor, looking through her profile. "She posted that two weeks ago. And if you click on him, he hasn't posted anything about her."

I almost fall off the roller trying to get to him. "You found him?"

Owen nods. "Yeah, look," he says, showing me where TroyTheS-canMan commented with a heart. "She works with him."

That piques my interest. "Think they aren't dating?"

"I don't know. He did put a heart. Hold on," he says, and then he grabs his phone. Soon, Angie is on FaceTime. "Hey, baby."

"Hey. Aren't you supposed to be busy all afternoon and not calling your wife?"

"I am never busy enough not to call my girl, but I need you to do some Instagram digging."

"Sure," she says, and then she smiles at me. "Hey, dude of honor."

I grin. "Hey, bride."

Her eyes are bright as she asks, "Who am I looking up?"

All Owen has to give her is his Instagram name, and she goes to work. "Troy Walsh, thirty-one, born and raised in Charlottesville, Virginia. Works for his uncle, who owns CapitalCare, a company that helps athletes rise to their full potential, according to its mission statement." She reads out the info like a damn FBI agent. "It says he's single, but there is a picture of him at some college event, kissing a very gorgeous blonde on the cheek."

Tennessee.

"Is this her?" Owen asks, holding up Tennessee's profile.

I nod.

"Hold on, let me do some digging on her," she says, and then she comes back. "Tennessee Dent. She's twenty-four, lives in Knoxville—" Her words cut off, and then she looks at the camera. "Is this her? The girl Dart is broken over?"

I flinch at her choice of words. "I mean, I wouldn't say broken."

"I would," Owen supplies, and I side-eye him, which he laughs at. But Angie looks at me compassionately.

"Stop looking at me like that," I demand, feeling foolish.

She fixes her face and quickly says, "Wow, she's the best in the company. She just had a birthday, but I don't know that they're *together*. His profile doesn't have anything of her on it, and hers only has that one photo, which I think she looks pained in."

"I think she's beautiful," I say softly, looking at it and admiring it, but hating it at the same time. I want to break that dude's fingers. I want to smash his face. I want to grab her and never let her go.

"She is that. Very much your type, all thick and ready for the cuddles," she says, grinning from ear to ear.

"Just like you, my gorgeous, hot wife," Owen purrs, and I fall back onto the floor.

"Can you two not be so in love when I'm dying here?"

They laugh at that as I look up at the ceiling, letting my leg dangle over the foam roller. It doesn't really matter if she's dating the dickface; it's not like she is answering my texts or even contacting me. She's moved on. Like I need to do. But for some ungodly reason, I won't.

"I'll call you later, baby."

TONI ALEO

"Okay, love you. Bye, Dart," Angie calls, and I only wave before I cover my face with my arm.

I feel Owen's hand come to the middle of my chest, tapping me there, before he says, "I don't think I thanked you for taking care of Angie at the wedding."

"Bro, I can't do that right now. Thank me later, please."

His laughter is welcome as I sigh. "What the hell am I doing?" I ask, sitting up. "I'm D'Artagnan Miklas. I can walk into any room, point to a girl, and she's naked."

Owen doesn't disagree. "I mean, you may have to speak to her and not point."

"But yet, I'm over here all sad and fucked up over a girl who doesn't want me."

Owen scrunches up his face. "You don't know that, which is why you need closure."

"But what will that do for me?" I ask, holding his gaze. "Will it change how I feel? Will it automatically fix everything and make me move on? Why do I feel like a dumbass?"

"I get that. Girls do that to you."

I couldn't agree more. "What would you do? If it were Angie?"

"I'd track her down," he says, confirming what he said before. "I'd make her tell me to my face she doesn't want me. But like you said, it's not like I'd be instantly over her. And then I think of my stupid brother and how it doesn't matter what the girl he cares for says, how she rejects him to his face in the middle of a wedding. He still loves her."

I hold up a hand. "I just found out her last name. I can't love her yet."

"Crazy. Why would I say that?" he says dryly, rolling his eyes. "If it's not love, what is it?"

I blink a few times. "A mindfuck." He laughs at that, and I shrug. "I'm fully infatuated by her, but I'm not in love with her."

"Yet."

I can't argue with him on that. "If I did have a chance just to date her and get to know her, I know I would. I just know, with her, I could."

"I met Angie when I was nine, I think?"

HAT TRICK

"Fuck me. Here we go," I groan, and he laughs.

"She knocked me on my ass, like plowed right through me on the ice, and I watched her skate off, scoring, and all I could think was, what the hell just happened to me?" he says, and then a soft chuckle leaves his lips. "She's been doing the same thing to me since the moment she came back into my life. Plowing through me. And I still don't know what the hell is happening, but I do know that I don't want to be plowed by anyone but her."

I hold his gaze, my best friend, my brother, and nod. "I'd pay to see her knock you on your ass."

"Shit, she does it with a look. Dude, the right woman...they're dangerous," he tells me, and I slowly nod, agreeing with him completely. I look down at my phone, Tennessee's smiling face staring up at me, and I ignore that dickface beside her. I swallow hard and then glance back at Owen.

"Maybe I will call her."

"I would. One more time."

Before I can muster the balls to do so, Sawyer comes into the stretching room. "Hey, Coach wants us for a moment," he says, and we hop up since Coach says jump, and we ask how high.

"Did we have a meeting?" I ask, because it'd be just like me to miss it.

"No. We've got some exciting news," Coach says as I come toward him. He hands me a piece of paper, and I stop since I can't read and walk. Give me a stick, and I can carry a puck like no other, but don't make me read while trying to do anything else. I only get to the first word before everything around me stops.

Tennessee Dent of CapitalCare is excited for this opportunity to work with the IceCats.

My gaze snaps up at the same time Owen's does, his eyes meeting mine, before I look forward to all the guys standing around Coach. We make our way to where everyone is gathering. And as my gaze falls on her, it's as if I've been knocked into the boards by a six-foot-six, 230-pound dude whose wife I slept with.

Instead, it's by the girl who has starred in my dreams for the last three months.

101

TONI ALEO

In the flesh. Boy, even my dreams haven't done her justice. She wears black athletic pants and a long-sleeved blue CapitalCare tee. Her hair is curled to perfection, half up with a blue ribbon. It takes me back to the orange one that teased my nose when I kissed her hair and held her body to mine.

Holy. Fuck.

"I'd like everyone to meet Tennessee Dent. She is from CapitalCare, and she will be helping us with speed, agility, and improving everyone's shot."

A wide smile is plastered on her face, but I can see the uneasiness in her eyes as she stares straight at Coach, not anywhere else. I can see her hand shaking as she flexes and balls it up over and over again. Does she remember this is the team I play for? I feel like she should; it was a big part of why I spent time explaining what a hat trick was, considering I'm a hockey player from South Carolina. I move slightly to the left and step into her line of sight.

Beside me, Owen murmurs, "Oh, this is about to be awesome."

I ignore him, crossing my arms and standing tall as I stare at her, re-memorizing the curve of her jaw, the tilt of her eyes, and how damn full her lips are. Her unique eyes meet mine, and the room falls away. I don't hear or see anything but her. Her breath catches visibly, her cheeks burn with a flush that travels down that sexy neck of hers. Tennessee's lips part, and such a beautiful look comes over her face. An expression somewhere between pure desire and pure horror, but I don't give a shit about the latter. I'm lost in the desire because I feel it every-fucking-where. My body burns for hers, and as she tears her gaze from mine, pulling in a deep breath, all I can do is tell myself not to grab her and take that naughty mouth with mine.

"You'll need to sign that sheet of paper before you can work with her," Coach says, and I look over, snatching a pen from Sawyer, who is gnawing on it, and sign it quickly. I push past the guys, coming toe-to-toe with Tennessee as she takes in a quick gasp. Her eyes widen and her jaw drops as she looks up at me, and all I can do is think how fucking beautiful she is. Once more, I will myself not to take her into my arms and run to the nearest spot where we can be alone.

"Name the time and place, Ms. Dent. I am excited that *fate* has given me the opportunity to work with you," I announce, my gaze saying one thing, while my words are all business.

She doesn't move, and neither do I. Heat travels from the tips of my toes to the top of my head, and everything inside me vibrates for her. I've waited for this moment; I've dreamed of having her within arm's reach, and I know what I want to do. What I need to do. But I resist. The passion in her eyes burns into mine, and I can see the flush spreading up her neck. Nothing but pure, undeniable desire flows between us, yet I don't move, and I don't know why.

But Owen... Owen is cackling like a damn hyena—not that I care.

Because now that Tennessee and I are in the same place, and she's here to help me with my shot, the hat tricks are about to be happening in abundance.

On and off the ice.

CHAPTER
Fourteen

TENNESSEE

It may sound crazy—or hell, I might be crazy—but I have felt D'Artagnan Miklas's presence in this damn state since I entered it.

When we crossed the border, my neck ached with imaginary beard burn.

When we got to my apartment on the coast, my nips throbbed.

When I entered Malcolm Peterson Practice Compound, my lips felt swollen.

When I walked into the team meeting, not only did my heart go insane in my chest, but my knees felt like they couldn't support me.

But nothing, and I mean not a goddamn thing, could have prepared me for when my eyes meet Dart's.

My hands clench at my sides, burn, and feel like they're not even my hands. My heart is fluttering like a damn hummingbird on twenty Red Bulls. My stomach feels like it's full of bees on crack that are stinging me everywhere. Between my legs? My desire is thick, pulsing, and screaming for him. I feel like it's calling to Dart like how the ocean calls to Moana.

HAT TRICK

Did I really just compare my pussy to a Disney movie? I need fucking help.

No. I need D'Artagnan Miklas.

Even his name feels like sex.

He hasn't changed, not even a bit, and tears sting my eyes with the relief of seeing him. I look up at him, the only thing between us a flimsy piece of fucking paper. I memorized his face; it's seared in my head, and still, I don't want to look away. His dark-blondish hair falls over his forehead, shaved neatly along the sides of his head. The hair on his jaw and over his lip is coarse and lush, and my lips ache to brush against it. His lips mock me, a little tip up because he knows exactly what I am feeling. But it's the eyes that do me in. Usually the color of the sky, they are thunderous storm clouds right now, and my next breath is nowhere to be found.

It's then I realize that in just these few seconds, I have felt more desire than in all of the last three months.

And it's him. D'Artagnan Miklas.

What is this? What is this hold he has on me? Fucking hell, I want him.

I find myself leaning toward him when his eyes fall to my lips. But then loud laughter, much like that of a hyena, reminds me where I am. My eyes widen, and it's as if I'm smacked back to reality. I take a full step back before clearing my throat. I pull my gaze from his, shaking my head free of the lust cloud he has enveloped me in, and clear my throat again, louder. With more determination, to wake myself the fuck up. What the hell am I doing? I am a professional!

But then I meet his gaze again, and all I want to be is his.

No.

Whoa.

Okay.

Tennessee fucking Lynn Dent, get your mind right! You are at work.

You are the face of CapitalCare!

But he's here and… His eyes.

His lips.

Oh, they turn up, sinfully appealing, and I lick my own lips.

No.

TONI ALEO

When he chuckles, low and dangerous, I gasp, and it only makes that smirk grow.

Fuck. My. Life.

I close my eyes for a moment and then open them to look at the paper in my hand. "D'Artagnan Miklas," I say, and when he groans ever so softly, I know no one heard him but me. The sound is music to my ears, and my body wants to dance, but damn it, not now. I am a professional, successful, fantastic girlboss! I do not get gooey over men with "Sunshine" neck tattoos and dragon tattoos and big dicks.

At work.

At home...whole other story.

But you are at work! my brain screams at me, and I clear my throat again.

To no avail.

My fingers bite into the paper, and his chuckle is wicked. Oh, he knows he is driving me crazy. I look up at him. "Quit."

"No fucking way," he mutters, shaking his head. "Months, baby doll. Months."

A chill runs down my spine. "Please," I beg, and God, that grin is sinful. "Phone number," I say louder, and he covers my hand with his, heat creeping up my arm, before taking the pen.

"I don't want you to lose it or write it down incorrectly to where you can't get ahold of me," he says in a way that lets me know he is not happy. He writes down his number and then hands me the pen back. "And the next thing you know, it's three months later."

I yank the paper from him and ask, "What is your availability?"

"I told you, Tennessee—" I didn't forget how wonderful my name sounds on his lips, but hearing it once more has my thighs clamping together "—name the time and the place."

I need to quit. I need to go home and pack and cut my losses here, because there is no way in hell I can work with him and keep my sanity.

"Do you two know each other?" the coach asks, and my breath catches as my gaze slams into his.

I'm ready to lie, but apparently lying isn't Dart's jam.

With nothing but a wicked grin, he says, "I met Ms. Dent in Nash-

HAT TRICK

ville a couple months ago for Adler's wedding. We had some plans to get together for her to work with me, but we lost touch."

"I moved, and I never had a chance to help him with his shot."

"I'm very skilled when it comes to scoring, but I feel I could do a lot better with Ms. Dent's help."

Did I just come? Jesus help me. I clear my throat, for what reason, who knows—it isn't helping with the lump that hasn't gone anywhere since he set his eyes on me. "That being said, I knew I could help with how his back leg seems to move farther out with the power of his shot. I believe he has a bit of weakness in his right knee."

That grin of his is unstoppable. "As you can see, she is a highly efficient and methodical professional whom I am excited to work with."

"He was interested in my work when we discussed it." I try to sound calm, but I think I sound like a foolish high school girl with a crush! I could kill him.

"Very. Interested," he adds, and I silently curse him.

The coach looks between us, and I hear even more chuckles and catcalls that have me wanting to curl up into a ball and die. The coach looks at me and then shakes his head. "I don't know what is happening right now, but leave me out of it."

Kill. Me. Now.

Embarrassment courses through me as I give Dart a pointed look. "That's all I need from you."

"Is it?"

"Yes," I say through tight lips.

He eyes me, his own lips pulling up at the side. He taps the paper I am clutching like it's a life preserver and I'm drowning. "Don't lose my number."

Oh, the warning in his voice has me burning up on the inside. This is bad. Very, very bad. I can't work with him. I'll be naked in seconds, and that's so unprofessional.

Oh my God, I have a boyfriend!

Fuck. How did I forget about Troy?

I squeeze my eyes shut and pray for help.

Jesus. Are you there? It's your favorite Vols fan, and I need you. Please.

When I open my eyes, though, neither God nor Jesus is here to

TONI ALEO

help, but Dart is watching me as he leans against the wall, that smirk on his face and those eyes full of all kinds of naughty things.

Oh, I am so fucked.

———

I somehow survive getting paperwork from the team and answer any questions they have. The coach, whose gaze I can't even meet because I know he knows that something happened between Dart and me, kept me for hours. He had question after question, and I was thankful for the distraction, even if I couldn't look directly at him.

"I should bring my son up here, have you do an assessment of him. I wonder if I can get the GM to pay for it," he jokes, and I grin.

"No fee. I'd be happy to help. I was working with some high schoolers in Virginia. It was refreshing—they're so eager, and it excites me to help."

He nods. "Well, Jax is just that. He wants to play for Michigan or Wisconsin before he tries for the draft. I know he can do it, but I feel something in his wrist isn't right. He broke it a few times."

I open my iPad to make a note, and then I smile up at him. "Just let me know when you can bring him in. I gave you my schedule for the guys, so I'll just fit him in at the end or beginning, or I can even take scans while I eat lunch."

"Thanks a lot, Ms. Dent."

I wave him off. "Call me Tennessee."

He shakes his head. "Vols fan through and through, huh?"

I shrug. "I bleed orange."

"Good to know," he says, patting my back. "See you soon. I'm excited for all you can do for us."

"Me too," I say happily, feeling a lot better about our working relationship. I feared he would think of me in a negative way since Dart basically humped me in front of everyone, but he never even brought it up again.

By the grace of God, really.

And now I'm wondering where Dart is. I lost track of him when I was making the schedule with Coach. I know I need to text him his

HAT TRICK

time slot, but I don't know if I can. There is a reason I didn't text him back, and it's because he makes me feel things that terrify me. If how he makes me feel without even touching me tells me anything, it's that I have to stay away from him.

While every girl dreams of falling in love, I know how I am. I know what he makes me feel, and when it's time for me to move on from here, I wouldn't. I'd stay here with him because I couldn't do long-distance with him. I just couldn't.

But the alternative, the fact that I'll be working with him and unable to touch him, feels as if I'm being ripped apart inside. Why is this so difficult? Why is this so confusing?

Why do I want him more than I want my next breath, but I'm also terrified of him?

I let my head fall back, and a frustrated groan leaves my lips.

What am I going to do?

I tuck my iPad into my bag. I reach into my pocket for my phone, but before I can take it out, I see him in my peripheral. He stalks toward me, his eyes only on me as he rubs his hand over his mouth, leaving me breathless. Tingles run through my body, my heart slams in my chest, and my knees are weak.

He stops and then points to me before gesturing to me. "Come here."

Two words.

Just two.

And my knees are trembling.

I shake my head. "No way."

"Tennie," he demands, his eyes burning into mine and clouding my senses. "Come here."

I don't move, but I watch as he turns the handle on a door and pushes it open. The invitation is right there. I shake my head again, clutching my bag. "I am fine where I am," I tell him, and his lips curve in a way that has my pussy crying.

"I won't ask again."

"Do you. But I'm not coming to you, because if I do, we'll end up in there," I tell him, holding his gaze.

His chuckle is sexy as he nods. "Fine" is all he says before he comes

109

TONI ALEO

toward me, each step making my heart pound harder. I don't think running will help me, especially since I think I'll probably run to him rather than away. Like I should if I weren't a complete idiot. He stalks over to me in all his glory, his smoky smell hitting me, and I just look up at him. "I want to talk to you."

"We can talk here."

"No, we can't," he says, and I notice his hands are in white-knuckled balls beside his thighs.

Jesus. Help. Please?

"You ghosted me."

I press my lips together. "I know."

"And you're okay with that?"

I don't know what to say, and I feel the tears burning in my eyes.

"Stop looking at me like that, Tennie. I can't—" His words cut off, and his eyes set my soul on fire. "I can't handle you looking at me like that."

"Like what?" I ask, my words not my own. Or at least, I didn't mean to say them. Shit, I don't know. I can't think around him.

"Like you want me but think you can't have me." He moves closer; I don't know how that's possible, but he does. "You can have me. Take me. God, Tennessee, take me."

My breath catches as my heart skips, trips, and explodes in my chest. "I can't."

"Oh, but baby doll, you can," he murmurs just as he wraps his arm around me, bringing me into his chest. It all happens so fast; I can't stop him.

"Dart. Please."

His lips come close to mine. "I told you that night, and I'll tell you every night that follows, you don't ever have to beg me," he whispers. And then he strikes. His lips take mine, and I almost cry at the connection. The relief… Oh God, I've missed him. I don't even know we're moving until a door shuts and my back slams into it.

Oh. My. God. What am I doing?

I pull back. "Dart, I can't."

He cups my throat with his hand, his thumb pressing into my pulse, making me fucking crazy. "Tennie, you can. Fuck, I've missed you." He moves his tongue over my bottom lip before biting me in that way I crave. His teeth sink into my bottom lip, and I cry out against his mouth before he sucks my lip between his. His tongue caresses the spot he tasted, leaving me panting. "There isn't a moment when I'm not thinking of these lips, this throat. Fuck," he mutters against my mouth, and I'm lost. Fucking lost. "I dream of your eyes, each one, different and stunning."

He presses his hips into mine, and I feel every inch of him. He drags his lips against mine, making everything melt inside my body. My eyes drift shut as I gasp.

"This body, Tennie... God," he groans, grabbing my ass as I clutch at his chest, and I whimper loudly. "This ass, Tennessee. Why—fuck, how could you not answer me back?"

I open my eyes to find him looking down at me. I see such pain in his eyes, and the guilt of hurting him is overwhelming. I want to make it better; I want to apologize. But then I remember why I can't do this.

I push on his chest, breathless, but he doesn't move. "Dart, I can't do this," I tell him, unable to breathe but forcing the words out. "I'm seeing someone."

The moment the words leave my mouth, his eyes narrow to slits. Heat creeps up his neck, but he doesn't let me go. If anything, his grip on me tightens. I try to push him away, but he doesn't move as his eyes search mine.

"Please, D'Artagnan. Let me go."

"No."

"You have to."

"I don't want to," he tells me, his eyes searching mine. "Because if I do, the statement you just made will be real, and I don't want to believe that you've allowed someone into your life when that's where I belong."

Oh, come on. What am I supposed to say to that! I'm lost in everything that is him, his words, the feel of him. I sure as hell don't want him to let me go, but I am not a cheater. "Please, Dart," I beg, my voice breaking as I gaze up at him. "If you don't let me go, I'll become something I'm not." His eyes soften, and I swear the world around me stops. But he lets me go. "I'm not a cheater."

He takes a step back, and instantly, I feel bare. I wrap my arms around myself to replace his arms as I press my head into the back of the door. I squeeze my eyes shut while I try to find my bearings. Though, I don't know where they are. I never do when he is around. I feel his gaze on me, and I can hear our labored breaths over my heart beating loudly in my ears.

"Tennessee," he whispers. Only my name. I feel the tears slide down the sides of my face. "Why? Just tell me why."

I shake my head. "I don't know." The words sound so cowardly as our gazes meet. The guilt is overwhelming. His eyes, damn it, they're killing me. Unable to handle it, I turn, opening the door with a shaking hand and walking right out of it.

And right into Troy.

Troy's hands steady me, his laughter easy, and I can't look at him.

All I can think is, really, God?

Are you even trying to help me out?

Nope. Because even He knows that fate has a twisted sense of humor.

CHAPTER
Fifteen

Dart

My heart feels like it's been used in place of a puck for a face-off.

I'm seeing someone.

She fucking said that to me. Like this guy has meaning to her. Even with my hands all over her, my lips drinking from hers, she said that. But the words didn't reach her eyes. Those eyes were on me, drunk with the desire that flows between us. Still, she said it. She meant it. She pushed me away. This can't be real; this kind of thing doesn't happen to me.

I break hearts, not the other way around.

I'm not a cheater.

No, she's not. She is a fucking angel without wings, and damn it, she's mine. She has been mine since the moment I set eyes on her. I know why I didn't take anyone home from that wedding. It was her. I was so caught up in her that it was even hard to focus on Angie. If I'm honest, I would have gone down to that bar when I got back from the wedding, looking for Tennessee, but I didn't have to. But here I am, fate having brought her back to me, only to be told she's fucking seeing someone?

113

TONI ALEO

Anger rattles inside me as I look to where she just took off out of this room. My hands are shaking—hell, my whole body is shaking. Not only with anger but hurt. And also, if I'm honest, utter want for her. The rational side of my brain is telling me I knew this could be a possibility. She's too fucking beautiful, too funny, too smart, not to tempt another, but the irrational part that wants Tennessee more than I want anything in this world is saying fuck that rational side.

She's fucking mine, and only mine.

I have to stop her.

I have to tell her that.

I go to the door, but I pause when I hear a male voice. "Tennessee! Baby," he laughs, a comfortable laugh, and everything turns to rage.

She isn't his baby. She's my baby doll.

"You almost took me out. Are you okay?"

"Troy, what are you doing here?" I hear her say, her voice as jittery as I feel.

"I came down for the weekend since CapitalCare is throwing a meet-and-greet with the teams tomorrow night." Silence stretches between them. "What is wrong? You okay? Did you hit your mouth? Your lip is puffy."

You're fucking right it is, I think. And I know I shouldn't, but I come out of the room. Yep, I was right. I shouldn't have come out, because instantly, I'm stopped dead in my tracks when I see them. The fucker holds her, his thumb moving along her bottom lip as he gazes down at her, concern in his gaze. In any other world, any other reality, I'd say they're cute together. He's got orangish hair, Tennessee's favorite color, but I won't allow that to deter me.

His gaze moves to mine, and a blush creeps up into his face as he lets her go. Dumbass. I'd never stop holding her. "Sorry," he laughs and then threads his fingers through hers. Tennessee doesn't dare look up. Instead, she covers her mouth with her hand, guilt-ridden.

I almost feel bad. Almost.

"I haven't seen her in a couple days. You know how it is," he says, holding out his hand to shake.

"I do," I say, but I don't take his hand. "It fucking sucks."

HAT TRICK

He drops his hand, eyeing me and then looking back at Tennessee. "Um, yeah."

His green gaze moves to mine, leaving me three seconds from wanting to piss on her leg.

Mark her, let him know he can try, but there is no point.

I swallow past the rage bubbling in my throat and bite out, "Tennessee, call me."

Troy makes a face at that. "For what?"

"So she can help me score," I say, and her gaze flicks to mine, annoyance swirling deep in those two rare depths.

Troy's brows knit together tightly as he looks between us, but I won't look away from Tennessee first. She'll have to. And unfortunately, she does, looking up to him. "This is D'Artagnan Miklas. He's a forward for the IceCats."

He knows that's not all I am, and that pleases me more than it should. I'm being a real dick right now, but I don't give a fuck. "That's right. I knew I recognized you."

I slowly nod. "Yeah. So hit me up, Tennie."

His eyes narrow as his back goes straight. "I'll probably get in contact with you," he says, stopping me from moving. "I'll be down in a week's time, and we'll be sharing these contracts. I'll more than likely work with the IceCats."

The way Tennessee looks at him tells me she doesn't agree with that.

"I can tell you this right now… Our team wants the best, and she's the best. So, we'll be working with her," I say, even though I have no control over that whatsoever. But I'm going to act like I do.

His eyes darken a bit, and I can see how uncomfortable Tennessee is. She looks as if she is about to come out of her skin. "While she is the best, we are a team. And together, we work best."

Ha. He thinks they're a team? He doesn't know shit. I chuckle deeply but with no humor. "Whatever you say, buddy. Just hit me up, Tennie," I call over my shoulder as I walk away from her once more. I can feel their gazes on me as I stalk down the hall I came from—before I deck him in that mouth of his and take Tennessee back in my arms.

Where she belongs.

TONI ALEO

———

I slam my stick into the puck over and over, almost falling but not giving a shit.

I may be missing the goal, but it's not about that. It's about the rage that's inside me.

I haven't felt this kind of anger since I found out that one of my mom's exes had disciplined Sabine by smacking her across the face when she broke his game controller. She was barely a toddler, probably Raine's age, and I lost it. Blacked out and beat the shit out of the guy. Thankfully, I was only seventeen, and my record was expunged when I turned eighteen. I try not to allow myself to get that bad, to allow that all-consuming anger to come to life, but right now, in this moment, I am livid.

It's almost as if I have no control over my feelings. They're all over the place. I'm happy Tennessee is here, ecstatic, but then I'm miserable that she has apparently moved on. That he touched her. In front of me. But the two of them together doesn't feel right. If she had moved on, she wouldn't have reacted the way she did. She wouldn't have kissed me. She wouldn't have touched me and looked at me the way she did. I know she wants me. I know nothing has changed. But why in the hell, if she knew she was coming here, is she still with that guy?

And why didn't she contact me?

It doesn't make any fucking sense and honestly has me questioning myself. Am I making this up? The way she looked at me, the way her lips pressed to mine, the way her fingers clutched my shirt—did I make it all up in my head? Am I not good enough for her? Does she not want me? Not need me how I need her?

I drop my gloves and stick, letting my head fall back before I let out the loudest, most frustrated roar of my life in the middle of the arena. I don't feel like this. I know who I am. I know what I offer, and I know good and well Tennessee feels the same way. No one experiences what we did and walks away unscathed. My roar echoes throughout the arena as I quake with confusion, and I just don't understand what the hell is happening right now.

"So, I'm guessing the reunion didn't go well?" Angie's voice doesn't even surprise me. I'm sure Owen texted her the moment I set eyes on Tennessee. My bride probably dropped her plants to be here. Okay, I might feel crazy, but I know she set the plant down gently before she rushed here. I look over at her, and she looks worried. "Am I right to assume the guy was her boyfriend?"

I have a lump in my throat. "Yup. She had the audacity to look at me and tell me she was with him."

"At least she was honest," she reminds me, as if that helps the situation.

"Was she, though?" I ask, my gaze burning into hers. "'Cause if she was honest, she would tell him to fuck off and be with me."

Angie sighs. "Dart, I'm sure she is confused."

"Why?" I ask, skating toward her before leaning on the boards in front of her. "That doesn't make sense to me. Bro, it was the best night of my life, and I'm not ashamed to admit that. I know she felt what I felt. I saw the tears in her eyes. So, what the hell?"

"I know," she stresses. "Dart, she ghosted you for a reason, but now she's here, and that night is probably smacking her in the face left and right. And then she has this guy she's been seeing, and I'm sure that's confusing."

"It doesn't need to be, though. Nothing has changed for me."

"But it could have for her."

"That's bullshit," I exclaim, clutching the boards in my hands and wanting to rip them in half. "It didn't. I'm telling you, Ang. Nothing has changed for either of us. I felt it—I felt her."

"I don't doubt that," she agrees, holding my gaze. "But you need to give her some space. Be patient."

"Space? That's the last fucking thing I want," I tell her. "Damn it, Ang. What if I made all this up?"

Sympathy fills her features. "Does it feel made up?"

I shake my head. "No. But then, I have never felt like this."

"And that could be the case for her too, and now she's scared."

"She doesn't need to be," I say, my voice almost a whisper. "I've got her."

Angie's hand covers mine, squeezing it. "Talk to her."

TONI ALEO

"I tried." I meet her gaze, and she gives me a look. "While I tried to make out with her."

"Exactly," she scolds. "Talk to her—with your words, not your mouth."

"I need my mouth to make the words."

"Yes, but keep your mouth to yourself," she says dryly.

"I'd rather not," I admit, shaking my head. "She hasn't answered any of my texts before."

"Before you weren't in the same state as her. Didn't she say she couldn't do long-distance?"

It'd be hard because of the distance.

Man, those words still hurt, and it's been months. With that lump threatening to suffocate me, I somehow get out, "Yeah, she did."

"Okay. But there is no distance now, so try again."

I think that over. "The company she works for is throwing a party for us tomorrow night. I can try to talk to her then."

Angie shakes her head. "The boyfriend will be there. I think you need to call her so there is space between you, because I don't trust you to keep your hands to yourself."

She's got me there. I bite into my cheek before pointing to my phone that sits on the bench she's perched on. "Hand me that, please."

She does as I ask, and I find our text thread. Or better yet, my endless attempts at contact.

Me: We need to talk.

Angie stands to watch, and I don't even try to hide my screen. Minutes pass, and I almost throw my phone. But then to my surprise, a text bubble pops up, followed by an address.

The Only Ten You'll Ever See: Meet me here in an hour.

My heart leaps into my throat as my body trembles with excitement. I look up just as Angie grins at me.

"Good luck."

I scoff, feeling on top of the world. "I don't need luck. I've got fate."

And please, fate, don't let me down now.

CHAPTER
Sixteen

TENNESSEE

Troy doesn't say a word to me as we walk toward our cars. I can tell he's upset, not that I blame him. It doesn't take a rocket scientist to figure out there is history between Dart and me. It's palpable, raw, and I know I'm not the only one feeling it everywhere. I still taste him, and I'm sure I smell like him. That dark, spicy, sinful, smoky scent that only he has. I run my fingers along my mouth, my heart pounding in my chest while I walk down the steps to my car. I know I should say something as I reach for my door handle, ask where Troy is staying, but the guilt is eating me alive.

The guilt from hurting Dart and from kissing him when I'm seeing Troy.

I open the door as Troy asks, "Do you know him or something?"

He doesn't have to say his name for me to know exactly whom he is speaking of. I could play dumb, act like nothing happened back there, but what will that do for me? Buy me time? For what? I don't even know what the hell I am doing right now. What I am feeling. Damn it.

I throw my bag into the back seat and rest my hip on the driver's

TONI ALEO

seat of my truck. "Yeah, I do."

He leans on the door of my truck. His eyes are suspicious and full of concern. "Is he an ex-boyfriend or something?"

My stomach clenches. "No, we were never official. It was a one-time thing. I met him when I was out celebrating getting this job three months ago."

"A one-time thing?"

I swallow. "Yeah. I haven't seen or spoken to him since I left him that next morning."

"Oh, so you were intimate?" he asks, a roughness to his voice.

But intimate isn't the word I'd use for what happened in that hotel room.

Baring of bodies, souls, and hearts.

What am I thinking?

Tears prick my eyes, and I look away from him. My teeth start to chatter, even though I'm not cold as I stand there, unable to answer him.

"What are you not telling me here, Tennessee?"

My heart aches in my chest as I shrug. "A lot, obviously," I answer, meeting his gaze. "I never expected to see him again, and now things are a little spotty for me."

His eyes search mine. "Did something happen in there?" he asks, hooking his thumb behind him toward the practice compound.

"Yes," I admit, unable to lie. I don't want to. "He kissed me, but I stopped him and told him I was involved with you."

Troy's eyes turn to stone, and I don't know how his look makes me feel. "Did you want him to?"

"Huh?" I ask, caught off guard by his question.

"Did you want him to kiss you?"

My mouth goes dry. "I don't know how to answer that."

"Honestly?"

"I am being honest, but I don't want to hurt you."

"Then answer the fucking question, Tennessee," he demands, and I look away, trying to keep my composure. When, really, I want to cuss him out. He has never raised his voice at me, never demanded anything of me, but I probably deserve it.

120

HAT TRICK

"I did," I whisper, closing my eyes and feeling like utter shit for my truth. "And I kissed him back, but then I stopped him."

Silence envelops us. I should have lied, but I won't. I know what I did, and while I'm ashamed for letting it happen when I'm involved with Troy, I couldn't have stopped myself if I'd wanted.

Dart makes me forget reality.

"I came here to be with you," he tells me.

I open my eyes to look into his. "I know, not that I told you to."

"You didn't have to. I want to be with you."

"I know that."

"Do you even care for me?"

"Yes," I admit, and I mean that.

I just care for Dart more.

"So, what are you thinking here?" he asks, his eyes wild.

"I don't know, Troy. I don't," I admit because it's true. "It's all so confusing, and I honestly didn't think I'd ever see him again."

"Is he more than a one-night stand, Tennessee?"

My shoulders fall as my heart screams the answer I'm unable to admit out loud. "I can't answer that because it's complicated. I never expected to see him again, and with me traveling and him a professional hockey player who also travels all the time, it just doesn't seem feasible—"

"But you want it to be," he says, cutting me off.

Chills run down my back because of course I do, and that alone terrifies me. "Don't put words in my mouth. I am trying to talk to you here."

"Tennessee!" he yells, his eyes narrowing on mine. "Do you not know that I am wholeheartedly in love with you?"

Why does that make me feel guilty rather than excited?

He makes a scoffing sound as he looks away, running his hands down his face. "But you don't love me."

I look away as the tears start to fall down my face. "I told you I wasn't emotionally ready to be with you."

"Because of him?" he roars, his eyes dark and full of anger.

"I don't know," I whisper, my lip quivering. "I just don't know."

TONI ALEO

"Well, tell me what you do fucking know," he demands, and I swallow thickly.

"I need to think," I say, holding his gaze.

"To think?"

"Yeah," I say slowly. "I need to clear my head and figure out what the hell I am doing here."

"This is bullshit. I thought I was falling in love with someone who was doing the same."

His words are like knives, and I refuse to look away. "If I made you feel like that, I'm sorry. But I am pretty sure I've been honest since the jump."

"If you were honest, you would have told me about him."

"Why would I do that? I've been trying to get over him."

He scoffs. "So now you tell me you aren't over him?"

I let my head fall back, a frustrated huff leaving my lips. "I'll talk to you tomorrow."

He grabs me then, pulling me into his chest. I try to hold back, but he's stronger, and he holds me close as he gazes down at me. "I love you, Tennessee, and I want to make a life with you. Don't throw away what we have for a one-night thing that was only about sex." His eyes burn into mine. "I saw the way he looked at you. He only wants to fuck you. He doesn't care who you are, how incredible you are, how smart you are. I do, though. I love all of you."

I'm unable to think or even react, and he drops his mouth to mine. It feels all kinds of wrong. His words, his actions, his lips, it's all just utterly befuddling. I pull away, covering my mouth as I shake my head.

"I'll call you tomorrow," I say, stepping out of his arms and climbing into my truck.

I go to shut the door, but he holds it, his words stopping me. "Are you going to see him?"

"Probably not," I admit, because I don't think I will.

"But if he asks, will you?"

I shrug. "Troy, I don't know. I need to think."

He nods. "I'm not going to sit back and just let you go."

I press my lips together. "I don't want to hurt you," I admit to him.

HAT TRICK

"Just give me time to think."

He wants to fight me. I can tell he has a lot to say, but I don't allow him to. I pull on the door, and he reluctantly lets go, allowing me to shut it. I feel him watching me as I start the truck and drive off. I feel like trash, and I hate that I've hurt him, because I do care for him. He has been nothing but good to me, and I know this makes me an asshole. I've known from the beginning that he has felt more for me than I've ever felt for him. Or than I've allowed myself to feel for him. I couldn't. Not when I won't allow myself to feel anything but what Dart brought out in me.

Just his name reminds me of the pain I caused him, and now I feel even more like trash.

I hit my mom's name on the CarPlay, and her voice fills my truck. "How was your first day?" A sob rips from me, and fear laces my mom's voice immediately. "Oh, Tennie. Darling, what's wrong?"

Unable to see, I pull off to the side of the road, throwing the truck into park and letting my head fall to the steering wheel.

"Tennessee Lynn, what is wrong?"

Another sob tears from me, and I feel like I can't breathe as I squeeze my eyes closed. "He was there. I saw him."

I don't have to tell her his name for her to know. Her breath catches. "Oh, Tennie."

I swallow the next sob and tell her everything. She doesn't say a word; she only listens, her breath catching as much as mine had.

"Mom, it was so wonderful, yet so terrifying, because it was as if nothing had changed. As if these last three months didn't even happen. I was thrown back into that room with a vengeance. And then Troy showed up, and now I feel like trash."

"Oh, my darling, you are not trash," she tells me, but she's my mom. She's supposed to say that. In her eyes, I'd never be a cheating whore. "You didn't know that was going to happen, and you were honest with Troy—when most would have lied."

"I'm a cheating whore, aren't I?"

She scoffs. "Hardly, my sweet girl. You got caught up in the moment with someone who obviously has you in knots—and who you still feel something for."

He does have me in knots, and I do feel something for him. But what do I do? Do I break up with Troy and jump into something with Dart? How can I do that to Troy? But how can I not when I don't feel for him even an inkling of what I feel for Dart? Three seconds, I swear that's all it was, and everything I felt totally overshadows the last month with Troy.

I take a deep breath. "What do I do, Momma?"

She doesn't answer as the tears rush down my face, and I wipe them away, hating them. I feel like I'm not in control of who I am, and I don't like feeling that way. "Have you asked Dart what he wants?"

"Huh?"

"Like, is he only wanting to hook up? Or is it more?"

"I don't know," I answer, and I don't think I care. I just want him. But I save that for myself, so I don't toe that cheating whore line. "We didn't really talk."

She chuckles. "Lordy, you can't control yourself with him, can you?"

"No," I admit, and I want to laugh at how pathetic I am. "He... Mom, he does things to me."

"Bless," she coos, and I smack my head on the steering wheel until I can't anymore. "I think you need to sit down and talk to him and see what he is thinking. Be honest with him like you have been with Troy."

I know she's right, but that scares me. When I talk to him, I'll fall harder, and then what? I give up my job because I don't want any distance between us? "Troy is the safer choice."

She sighs. "Absolutely. But is he the choice you want?"

I don't even have to answer for her to know the truth. Just then, a text comes through from a number not in my contacts. I know immediately it's from Dart.

"He just texted that we need to talk."

"Lordy, lordy, lordy," she tsks, and I can't help but laugh. "Y'all do, Tennessee Lynn. For your own sanity."

I know she's right, but that doesn't mean I'm not scared out of my fucking mind.

And excited at the same damn time.

A feeling only D'Artagnan Miklas can make me feel.

CHAPTER
Seventeen

TENNESSEE

I don't have to look for him to know Dart is here.

The moment I enter the Perk Me Up coffee shop by my apartment, I feel him. That buzzing feeling in my bones returns full force. My chest flutters as my gaze meets his in an instant. Breathless isn't even the word to describe what happens to me.

All meaning, all sense, all thoughts, are useless the seconds our eyes meet.

Because on his head is my UT cowboy hat.

And he's sporting an unstoppable smirk that has my insides turning to goo.

Lordy, I'm in so much trouble.

I have no control over my lips as they curve, and the flush creeps up my neck. In seconds, that night slams into me, and God, I've missed him. He tips the hat to me, his smirk dangerous, and every nerve ending in my body tingles. I gulp, and instantly, my thighs tremble, making it real hard to remember how to walk. He leans back in his chair, his legs out in front of him lazily as his fingers dance along the

TONI ALEO

side of the coffee cup he holds. The same fingers that had squeezed my neck. More heat burns my cheeks, and that smirk of his only grows.

Oh, I'm so, so, so very fucked.

I come behind a chair at the table where he's sitting and set my purse down. Neither of us says anything, our gazes locked in a heated embrace, and something as simple as breathing is a struggle. The overwhelming guilt burns my stomach as I look into his eyes. I've missed him so very much. I've missed how it feels to be under that gaze of his. To be utterly devoured by just his eyes. I clear my throat, trying to pull myself away, but I'm unable to.

He licks his lips slowly, tormenting me, before he says, "Can I get you a drink?"

"I can get it," I say, but he's already up and moving in the direction of the counter.

"What do you want?"

"A lemonade spritz."

He steps toward me, brushing his arm along mine, and I take in a quick breath as his eyes consume mine. His scent about knocks me on my ass as he pulls his eyes from mine and goes to the barista. I gulp as I sit down on the other side of the table, hoping the round piece of wood is a good enough barrier.

Though I know for a damn fact it's not.

I cross my legs and try to control my pounding heart as he returns and sits across from me, handing my drink to me. I reach for it, our fingers brushing, and just that touch has me shivering. I don't understand this pull he has on me. This heat between us. With one look at him, I know he feels the same. "Thank you," I say, and he leans back, his eyes moving along me. "Nice hat."

His lips curve. "Best hat I've ever gotten for a hat trick," he says, tipping it toward me again, looking like a naughty cowboy rather than a hockey player.

I look away, taking a deep pull of my lemonade. "So, how are you?"

"Cut it out, Tennie," he says immediately, his voice rough.

I look up at him through my lashes. The unevenness of his voice tickles my stomach.

"I don't want the small talk."

"What do you want?"

"I want you," he says simply, and everything explodes inside me. He crosses his arms over his chest and holds my gaze. "I want to know what the hell happened after we parted in Nashville."

My chest aches, his pain visible on his beautiful face. "I thought it was a one-time thing."

"Bullshit," he says, shaking his head. He moves, leaning on his elbows, his clasped hands beneath his jaw. He may be trying to portray innocence, but I know way better.

There is nothing innocent about D'Artagnan Miklas.

"The texts I sent after that told you otherwise."

I don't dare look away. "I never thought I'd see you again."

"Bullshit again," he throws at me, his eyes wild and gorgeous storm clouds. "I was ready to fly to wherever the hell you were, just for a day, a night, a second with you."

My breath catches at the intensity in his words. I look down, running my fingers along the top of my lemonade.

"Did I make up what happened in that room, Tennessee? Because, for me," he says, leaning in farther, his face so close, all I have to do is move just an inch toward him and our lips would meet, "it was the best night of my life. Nothing could compare to what happened between us."

My eyes briefly drift shut, and his ragged breath sends chills down my spine. "No, D'Artagnan, you didn't make that up."

"Then why? Tell me," he demands, and I open my eyes.

My voice is almost a whisper. "You have to understand, I have never done anything like that before."

"Okay? And? You did it great, in my opinion."

His words are like a drug. "It was easy. With you."

"Exactly, so why the fuck did you ghost me?"

I swallow thickly, the guilt eating me alive. "I was scared," I admit. "And insecure."

"Come on, Tennessee. Don't try to sell that to me, because I'm not buying it."

I hold his gaze. "I spent the night having my best friend put me

TONI ALEO

down, tell me that I should just accept bad sex with a kind guy because it's all I could ever get. Because I'm not thin enough to have anyone better."

The snarl that surrounds me has my eyes widening. "Your body is perfect, Tennessee."

"I know," I say, stronger than I expected. "But she was in my head, and then you happened, and I felt things I never have before. I didn't know how to process what I was feeling. I was moving, I had just cut off my best friends, and I wasn't talking to my mom. I didn't really think you wanted anything more with me than a one-night thing."

"That's trash," he says, shaking his head. "I kept texting you, but nothing came from you."

"Because you scare me." His eyes darken. "One night, D'Artagnan. One. And I was completely taken with you."

He nods thoughtfully. "Was, huh?"

I press my lips together, my heart jackhammering in my chest at the way his eyes hold mine. "I'm pretty sure my actions have shown that nothing has changed. I am still taken by you."

"Yet you ghosted me."

"Because I can't do the distance with you."

His eyes narrow, those blue depths like a dangerous, wild ocean. "But you can do distance with that asshat you told me you're involved with?" he asks, so much bite in his words.

"It's different. He's moving here."

"And I'm here."

I sigh. "I am well aware that you're here, Dart. I feel you everywhere."

His lips tip up at that, and my stomach clenches. "How long have you been with him?" he asks, though I don't think he wants to.

"I've known him for three months, but we've only been together for a month," I admit, unable to look at him when I speak of Troy. The guilt is too great and makes my skin prickle.

"Have you slept with him?" he demands, and my gaze whips to his, gawking at him.

"That is none of your damn business."

"Is it not?" His eyes are challenging, and I give it right on back.

"Have you been sleeping around? 'Cause like you said earlier, three months is a long time."

His eyes darken. "Yes, because I'm trying to forget you!"

I don't know why those words hurt since I've been trying to do the same. "Well, I'm doing what you do when you're in a relationship, and sex is included in that."

His eyes burn with fury. "I wouldn't know anything about that since the person I wanted to have a relationship with ghosted my ass."

I look away, and then I hear the chair groan against the floor before his knees are touching mine, squeezing my leg between his. My gaze slams into his, and his mouth is right there. For the taking. But I hold back. "I bet he doesn't even make you come as well as I do," he accuses, his eyes wicked. "I bet you think of me when you're with him because, Tennessee, that's all I've done since the moment I walked away from you. I tried—fuck, I tried to wait for you. But when I realized you didn't want me, I attempted to find pleasure somewhere else, but I couldn't—unless I was thinking of you."

My teeth chatter as I look down, trying to control my breathing. His knee slides between mine, and I shift my gaze to his. "There wasn't a moment when I didn't want you, D'Artagnan."

His eyes take on a serious look. "Then what the hell, Tennie?"

My hands shake, and I squeeze them together. "Do you know how hard this is for me?"

"For you?" he scoffs. "How do you think I feel?"

"I'm in a relationship," I stress, and he shakes his head.

"No, he's a placeholder for the real deal," he declares, his confidence overwhelmingly sexy. "And I'm right here, Tennessee."

My heart constricts in my chest, trying to remember what my mom said. To find out what he wants with me. "And then what?"

His lips curve. "You'll never walk away from me again."

His eyes are full of all kinds of naughty promises, which does nothing good for the space between my thighs. "This is so complicated."

"It's not."

"Dart, he says he loves me."

TONI ALEO

Oh, he doesn't like that. His nostrils flare as his gaze darkens. "Do I look like I give a fuck?"

"Quite the opposite, actually."

"Then why say it?"

"Because he's the safer choice. He doesn't make me feel the things you do. Like right now, I want nothing more than to kiss you, lose myself in you, and it makes me wild, crazy even, because I'm not a cheater. I wouldn't want it done to me, but I can't deny this pull you have on me. It scares me."

He shakes his head. "You truly feel there is a choice here?"

I hold his gaze. "What do you mean?"

"Tennessee," he breathes, as if that's the only word he was ever meant to say. "There is no choice for me—it's you or no one."

My lip starts to wobble as I close my eyes. "D'Artagnan."

He takes my hand, threading our fingers together. "You ruined me, baby doll."

And I know the truth. He's done the same for me. But do I just blow Troy off? "It's complicated."

"Only because you're making it that way," he says, bringing my hand up under his jaw.

"I work with him."

"That's a him problem, not an us problem." Us. He says it so simply, so positively. "Do you love him?"

I actually laugh at that, which answers the question, but I say, "I told him I wasn't emotionally ready to feel anything for him."

Dart leans in, his nose brushing mine, his lips ever so close and stealing every bit of my air. "Because emotionally, you're mine."

My mouth goes dry, and my eyes fall shut as I inhale deeply. "I can't kiss you."

He inhales just as deeply and then exhales in frustration as time stands still. I can feel the heat of his lips. The brim of my—or really, his —hat brushes against my forehead as I force myself to breathe. "Do you want to?" he whispers, and my center aches. I can only nod. "Then do it."

I swallow hard, and I almost do. God, I almost do, but I pull back and sigh deeply as my body shakes and tingles. "I can't."

HAT TRICK

A frustrated grunt leaves his lips before he leans back, crossing those thick arms over his chest. "I'm having a hard time understanding how you're letting him stand between us."

"I work with him."

"Then quit."

"D'Artagnan."

"What? Dump him, quit, and we'll find you a job around here."

We'll.

Us.

The words come so easy for him. My heart skips because not only is he confirming what he intends for us, but the reason he scares me is on full display. Because I want to say yes. I want to lose myself in him and forget about everything else, but I would be doing exactly what I did back home. I'd be living for him, not for myself. I've worked so hard for my career, and I'm good at it. I watch as he leans on the table with his forearms, and his eyes don't leave mine as he strokes his fingers along my clasped hands, sending warmth up my arms. Without control of my body, I release my hands, and he slides his hand between them, threading our fingers with ease.

"Tennessee," he says, trapping my gaze with his. "We belong together."

That simple sentence rattles my core. "I've missed you," I admit, and his eyes are on fire. "But you scared the shit out of me."

He scoffs. "You have me shaking in my imaginary cowboy boots that match this hat."

I stroke my thumb along the back of his hand.

"But there is nothing or no one in this world I want more than you."

My eyes water, and slowly, a tear moves down my face. His gaze softens as he wipes it away, but when another falls, he moves with a quickness that leaves me breathless. He stands before pulling me up and wrapping his arms around me, holding me close. I press my nose into his chest, and the tears come quick. A sob bubbles in my chest, but I swallow it down as I clutch his shirt with my fingers. I inhale him, his smoky scent urging me to do what I want.

What I need.

TONI ALEO

With one arm around me, he snakes his other up my back to squeeze my neck as he holds me close, his nose gliding along the shell of my ear. Every ounce of my being sings for him, and in his arms, I've never felt safer in my life. His lips brush against my ear as he whispers, "I'd rather be scared of how you could shatter me into a million pieces than live another moment not yours. There is no choice, Tennessee." I can't even remember how to breathe as he nuzzles my ear. "I'm yours, and you're mine."

His words are unnecessary because I've felt them since the moment his eyes caught mine three months ago.

And I can't ignore it any longer.

CHAPTER
Eighteen

Dart

I'm realizing that patience is not my jam.

I should have kissed Tennessee yesterday. Gotten my fill of her before I grudgingly let her go. She left, needing "space." I'm also realizing that space is the last thing I need when it comes to her.

I watch as she brushes her hair off her shoulder, crouching down to fix her camera, and that ass is delectable. She wears a pair of black leggings, those thighs thick and that ass even thicker. Her long-sleeved blue CapitalCare shirt hugs her breasts and is rising in the back as she bends down, showing a very sexy strip of skin.

I've kissed her there. Right there on the small of her back.

"You're drooling," Owen mutters beside me, and I swallow as I look down at the boards, tapping my glove to them. I sigh deeply as his laughter taunts me. "You going to make it?"

"Probably not," I admit, looking back up at her as she explains to Anderson what she is doing. She's here to do our assessments, and I really enjoy watching her work. She's proficient and very detail-oriented, just as she was when she was on her knees in front of me. God, she has me squirming on this bench. Her smiles are quick, her

TONI ALEO

knowledge is vast, and the excitement that covers her face when she gets the right angle does something to my heart. She does this little wiggle. I don't even know if anyone else notices it, but I do.

It blows my mind to smithereens.

"Drooling again."

I swallow again, shaking my head as laughter leaves my lips. But it falls away when I hear the bench door open. I look over just in time to see the jackass who thinks he is dating my girl stepping through it and walking along the rug they have down for the people not wearing skates. The rage I feel is incomparable. He's touched her. He's kissed her. He has tasted her when I wasn't able to. The jealousy inside me is like a caged beast. I want to rip him apart for even looking at her.

"Now you look like you're going to kill someone."

I look toward my best friend. "You're not helping."

He shrugs, his eyes playful, and I know he sympathizes with my pain. I mean, he listened to it all night and even took my phone when I tried to call Tennessee. Angie stressed for me to give her a moment, to let Tennessee get her head on straight, but I'm dying here. Especially when that fucker's hand moves along her shoulder, squeezing it. The only reason I don't get up and kick his ass is because Tennessee steps away from him, giving him a pointed look.

"This is about to get real awkward, isn't it?"

I only shrug. "I mean, we can do awkward, or you can bail me out of jail."

"I pick awkward."

I pick her.

I'm met only with a huff before he says, "Are you going tonight?"

"Yeah," I say, even though I don't want to. The only reason I am is because I know she'll be there. Hopefully on my arm and not his.

"Great. I'll have Angie get cash for bail money."

I laugh as Anderson skates to the bench, entering the door before looking over at us. "You're up, Dart. And also, that girl is hot."

"God help us," Owen says, shaking his head as I just look at my new friend.

"You know we're still deciding if we like you," I remind him, and his brows come in.

HAT TRICK

"I think you're cool as hell," Owen says to Sawyer. "But before my friend can beat you with his stick, that girl is off-limits."

Anderson looks between us, confused. "Because of that guy?" he scoffs. "He asked her to go to dinner before the thing tonight, and she didn't look like she was feeling him."

"Not him. Me," I say, and understanding fills his face.

"Ah, okay. Noted," he says, tipping his chin toward me before disappearing down the hall. I stand up, grabbing my stick, and I look up just as she glances over at me. A blush moves into her full cheeks, and I can't stop the smirk that pulls at my lips.

"I'd say don't do anything stupid, but I know there's no point," Owen says, leaning on the boards.

"Exactly," I agree as I go through the door and skate toward her and the dumbass. I watch as Tennessee brings her lip between her teeth, and crazy prickles run along my body. Her eyes darken, the one on the right a thundercloud, while the one on the left has gone to stone, an emerald.

Man, I should have kissed her yesterday, because now, my lips ache for hers.

I come to stop before them, and my eyes don't leave hers. Her breath quickens as she swallows hard, her throat working and calling out to me to grasp it so I can feel that pulse going crazy under my fingertips. Neither of us says anything, and I feel his eyes on me.

"Tennessee?"

She whips her gaze to his, and mine follows. On my skates, I tower over him, and he has to look up at me. But I'll give it to him... He doesn't cower away. He stands tall, his shoulders back, his eyes dark with vehemence, but he has nothing on me. I move my heated gaze to her, and she takes a deep breath.

"D'Artagnan, come over here, please. And Troy, will you make sure he's in the shot?"

Neither of us answers her; we just move. I follow her to where she wants me, and when she looks up at me, her eyes are pleading. "Please behave."

I chuckle at that. "There is no behaving around you, baby doll," I

135

say softly to her, and her eyes go from pleading for me to behave to begging me not to.

Or maybe I'm believing what I want.

"Lordy me, you're gonna be the death of me," she mutters, that twang doing things to my soul as she sets me with a pointed look. I just grin. "I need a wrister, a slap shot, and just your regular shot. Act as if I'm not here."

"That's not possible," I tell her, and she whimpers in response. All I can do is chuckle as she walks away.

When she tells me to go, I do as she asks, and she captures four takes of each shot. "Okay, one second."

I take a puck, bouncing it on my blade and showing off because I can. I toss the puck up and then smack it into the back of the net with ease. From the bench, Owen yells, "Show-off!"

I snort at that as I skate toward where Tennessee is, and I notice that Jackass is watching me, a glare in his eyes and a tic in his jaw. I stand beside her as she watches the video, unaware of how stupid the dude beside her looks. I lean on my stick, putting my chin on the top of my glove with absolutely no intention but to piss him off with how close I am to her. I can feel the heat coming off her, see the blush creeping up her neck as I stand there. I watch as she presses some buttons, and I enjoy the look on her face. Two little lines sit between her brows as she watches the footage.

"Okay, good," she mutters as she pauses and then moves through the footage again. She nods and looks up at me. "I got it."

My gaze falls to her lips, and they part, wanting me. Goddamn, I love how responsive her body is to mine. "Do you need me…" I say, slowly and with purpose, "for anything else?"

Her eyes widen with desire and a touch of annoyance.

Before she can say anything, Dumbass speaks to me. "Hey, bro—"

"Not your bro," I say, cutting my eyes to his, and he presses his lips together, the tic in his jaw a warning that I'm fucking with him in all the ways I want.

"D'Artagnan, please," she mutters, but Come-Dumpster is speaking.

"Fine, Miklas." He says my name like it's a curse. Which I guess it

HAT TRICK

is, because what he thinks is his is actually mine. "I don't know if you are aware, but Tennessee and I are involved."

"Do I need to call Angie?" Owen calls out, but I ignore him, my lips quirking at the side as I exhale. "I'm calling."

"D'Artagnan," she warns, but once more, I ignore her.

"Involved, eh?" I ask, and Fuckface puffs up his chest. "What was your name? Troy?" He doesn't answer me; he just glares. "Troy, *bro*," I drawl. "We aren't the same." I stand to my full height, towering over him as the fury courses through my body. I feel her hand come to my chest, and I shudder at her touch. "You may be involved with her, but her heart is mine—and only mine."

Her fingers clutch my jersey, and the way his eyes narrow when she does so pleases me way more than it should. I drop my glove and take her hand in mine. I drag my gaze to hers, and she's begging me with those eyes. I bring her hand to my lips, kissing her knuckles before I kiss her palm, and everything around me falls away.

As it always does when her eyes lock with mine.

"I'll see you tonight, baby doll."

She pulls her hand from mine reluctantly, and again, that pleases me to no end. I start to skate off, but I look over my shoulder, my gaze colliding with Tennessee's. Her flushed skin makes my cock strain in my girdle. "Call me when you're ready to go over my scans. I'm excited to work so *closely* with you."

Steam is basically coming out of TicTacDick's ears, but that flush on Tennessee's neck has me grinning even harder. I go through the door just as Owen looks at me, shaking his head while his laughter envelops me. "You're ruthless."

"I am when it comes to what's mine."

CHAPTER
Nineteen

TENNESSEE

I could kill him dead.

I watch as Dart skates off without a care in the world, as if he didn't just flip my world upside down.

"You may be involved with her, but her heart is mine—and only mine."

Good Lord Almighty.

He said that out loud and with so much confidence that my body tingles because I know it's true. I may have been off doing me the last three months, but my heart has been with him the whole time. I've gone through the motions of a relationship, but my heart wasn't available. Not when Dart had already confiscated it.

I ignore the sting along my knuckles where Dart's lips were and flip to the next file, which will be for Owen Adler. I feel Troy watching me, the anger coming off him in waves, but I don't dare say anything. I can't because I don't know what to say. I respect him, care for him, but I worry that if I say anything right now, I'll hurt him. Because in this moment, I want to follow Dart into that locker room. Help him undress and make up for the three months we've been apart.

HAT TRICK

I feel Troy move beside me before he calls out, "Hey, buddy. Give us a minute," to Owen Adler on the bench.

Owen just snorts. "Yeah. You may need it after that."

Lordy, he is not wrong.

I take a deep breath since Troy's anger is substantial. In a low voice, he bites out, "What the hell, Tennessee?"

I let my eyes drift shut. "What?"

"You said you wanted space, and I respected that. But I didn't do that for you to go off and fuck him behind my back."

My brows slam together, and my eyes fly open. "I haven't slept with him."

"I couldn't tell," he snaps, his eyes wild. "Did you hear what he said?"

I can't stop hearing it. It's on a loop in my brain.

Her heart is mine—and only mine. Her heart is mine—and only mine. Her heart is mine—and only mine. Her heart is mine—and only mine. Her heart is mine—and only mine. Her heart is mine—and only mine. Her heart is mine—and only mine. Her heart is mine—and only mine.

Oh lordy.

"He's intense."

"It's not only him. I saw the way you looked at him. You've never looked at me like that."

"We're intense," I admit, crossing my arms over my chest. "I don't know what to say, Troy. I care for you, I do, but—"

"Don't you see he's all talk? He may make you think he's all about you and only you, but I know athletes like him. I've worked with them for years. They have women in every state and are driven only by sex."

I press my lips together. "He's not like that."

"You don't even know him," he stresses, his eyes burning into mine. "You know me, I know you, and Tennie, I love you."

Those three words do nothing for me. Nothing. And that has to mean something. I know good and well Troy is the safer choice. He wouldn't hurt me, he'd be steady and kind, but I would be completely bored out of my mind with him. I refuse to think that's all I am meant for—a boring life—when there is a man like Dart out there who worships my body.

Worships me.

"He is fucking with your head. All he wants is to get in your pants."

"He got in my pants—for twelve hours straight," I tell him, pushing my shoulders back. "He tried to get ahold of me for three months, so I don't think it's only about sex, Troy."

"You're being naïve. Men like that don't want—" He cuts himself off, and I hold his gaze.

"Finish what you were going to say," I demand, my hands shaking at my sides. "Girls like me? Girls of my size?"

"No," he says sternly. "I would never disrespect you by saying that."

"No? Because it feels like you are."

"You are beautiful—"

"I am well aware of my beauty," I tell him, fire in my eyes. "If that wasn't what you were saying, then what were you saying?"

He pauses for a second, and I can feel Owen watching us. I take a quick glance over at him, and his face is red, his lips pressed together tightly. He's visibly upset. Troy clears his throat, watching me as he says, "Men like that don't settle down. He's always traveling, and he won't have time for you the way I do."

His words feed the insecure part of me, but I try to ignore them. The truth is right there, though. I feel it all over. I cover my face with my hands and groan loudly. "Troy. You're exhausting me."

"You're making me crazy, Ten. I don't even know what I am saying, because he kissed you."

My eyes narrow as I drop my hands. "He kissed my hand. It isn't a big deal."

"It looked like a big deal," he throws at me. And in my heart, I know it was. It was intimate, sweet, and crazy-hot. "Are you sleeping with him?"

I sigh in exasperation. "I already told you I wasn't."

"That's hard to believe. You didn't see what I saw."

"Because that's us," I say, throwing my hands up as I meet his gaze, feeling crazy and confused. "It's fire, it's insane, and it's all-consuming.

HAT TRICK

I don't understand it, but Troy, I have never felt anything like that for anyone but him."

He flinches as if I hit him. "There is no heat between us?"

I shake my head. "There never has been. We're friends."

"That's not true. I love you," he insists, and I look away, closing my eyes. "I have loved you since the moment I met you."

"But I don't love you," I admit, my voice small. "I never have, and I never will. I know that hurts you, and I'm sorry, Troy. I am. But I told you from the jump I was emotionally unavailable."

He swallows, his Adam's apple working overtime. I never intended on hurting him. "Because of him."

I nod slowly. "Because of him."

"Someone who will more than likely cheat on you and mistreat you."

I know I should just ignore his comment. I know he's baiting me and he is very upset, but I can't hold back. "He took more care of me in twelve hours, in *every* way possible, than you have in a month."

Anger vibrates his body, and I should have known better than to say anything. "You are a fucking whor—"

His words are cut off when Owen Adler puts his hand on Troy's chest. I hadn't even seen him or heard him coming. Like a silent assassin, he shoves Troy, knocking him off-balance. He falls back onto the carpet with a thud, and I whip my startled gaze to Owen. His face is full of anger, and his eyes are wild as he looks down at Troy. "Be glad I didn't go get Dart like I should have. Instead, I'll issue the warning," he seethes, leaving me wheezing. "Don't ever let me hear you speak to her like that, because not only will I whoop your ass, but Dart will tear you in two."

I am stunned in place as Troy scrambles to his feet, embarrassed and pissed at the same time. "Put your hands on me again, and I'll press charges."

Owen is unfazed. "Watch your mouth, and we won't have an issue."

Troy snaps his gaze to mine. "My uncle will be there tonight. Don't fucking embarrass me."

141

TONI ALEO

I press my lips together as Owen says, "I think you should try not to embarrass yourself. And I hope you enjoy the night—by yourself."

"You don't speak for her," Troy barks at him, and Owen shrugs.

"I know for a fact that she won't be going with you," he says before looking at me. "Am I right?"

"You're right," I agree, crossing my arms over my chest. "We're done, Troy."

The look on his face has me thankful Owen is here. I'm sure Troy wouldn't touch me, and I can hold my own, but I do feel better with Owen standing there. Troy's lips are tight as he says, "Don't embarrass me. Your job depends on it."

I force myself to breathe as he stomps off like a toddler, and I take a deep breath before letting my arms drop. That went *great* and not at all as planned. I wanted to sit down, discuss things with Troy, mainly to protect my career. But Dart had other plans. Damn it.

"I would apologize for jumping in there, but I'm not going to," Owen says. "And I can't tell my wife, because she'll tell Dart, and Dart will kill him."

I snort at that. "You're the best friend?"

He nods. "And you're the one he almost lost."

Almost.

My heart skips as I look away. "You must hate me."

"Not at all," he says simply. "To paraphrase my girl TSwift, you aren't doing it right if love doesn't make you crazy."

Laughter sputters from me, easing the tension that was about to burst inside me. "Did you really just quote Taylor Swift?"

He nods. "My wife forces me to listen to her while she makes me replant her plants."

I try not to laugh. "I have a feeling there is no forcing or making you do anything."

He winks. "Not with her, but I have to be all tough and shit. I'm a hockey player."

"You're a mess," I decide as I shake my head. "But so damn refreshing." I sigh as I hold his gaze. "Thank you."

"Hey, it's easy when I know how important you are to Dart." His words make my heart flutter in my chest. "And all that shit that fucker

HAT TRICK

said isn't true. Was my boy a manwhore? Hell, we all were at one point. I was. And look at me now, so beyond in love with my girl, no one could even come close to her."

"But there is nothing or no one in this world I want more than you."

Dart's promise from the day before comes slamming back into my chest.

Owen speaks again. "But I can promise you this. I have never seen Dart act like this about anyone in the whole time I've known him. You're special, Tennessee. I need you to know that."

Tears sting my eyes as I whisper, "I care for him deeply."

"I know," he tells me with no hesitation. "I've watched you two interact twice now, and we need to keep a fire extinguisher nearby before we all go up in flames."

My lips tip up into a smile as tears escape my eyes. "He's so over the top."

Owen chuckles at that. "Yeah, in all aspects of life. It's the best thing about him."

My lip quivers as I nod, knowing he's absolutely right. Dart's passion, his heart, his everything is overwhelming in all the right ways. Being on the receiving end of all that he is has been the greatest romantic accomplishment of my life, yet I am holding myself back.

From pure happiness.

I look up to Owen as he watches me, and then he smiles. "This is getting really awkward. Do you wanna just make my videos?"

I nod. "That would be great."

"Sorry for making you cry."

I wave him off. "It isn't you. It's me and my dumb self for not doing what I should have from the jump."

I should have texted Dart back; I should have done what my heart wanted and not what my brain told me to do.

"Yeah," he says, and once more, his gaze meets mine. "I get it. But again, to quote the great Pat Benatar, love is a very real battlefield, my friend."

"Wow. You're a lot."

He just flashes me the biggest, cheekiest grin. "I am. That's why Dart and I are friends."

143

I can't help but return that grin and miss Dart terribly.

But my need for him isn't my issue. It's the fact that I have to go to a party tonight with the guy I just dumped.

Who is the nephew of the CEO of the company I work for.

Because my life is easy and all.

CHAPTER
Twenty

Dart

CapitalCare has rented the rooftop of a swanky brewery downtown. I don't usually come here, not my scene, but this IPA that is apparently brewed here is top-notch, and I may have to return. I look around the space, Edison lightbulbs strung above us, twinkling in the night sky. The cityscape is breathtaking from here, and even with all the chatter, I can still hear music. The place is packed with nothing but athletes. Not only are the IceCats here, but our football and baseball teams are here too. Everyone is eager to work with CapitalCare.

To work with Tennessee.

I hadn't realized how popular she was until I listened to everyone around me. She has helped a lot of athletes, and Coach is convinced she'll be the ticket to getting us closer to a return bid to the Cup finals. She apparently developed her own program and has been offered a lot of money for it, but she won't sell. I think it's because she wants to help people personally, not depend on everyone else to do what she does so excellently.

It's impressive.

And fucking hot.

TONI ALEO

I scan the place for her, but she isn't here yet. If she were, I'd know. I take a long pull of my beer as I mess with the button of my suit jacket. I'd wanted to text her or call her when I left this afternoon, mostly because I wanted to know what Dumbfuck said, but I didn't. I'm doing my best to give her space, even though, when we're in the same room, there is no way.

I crave her.

I lean on a bar table, and when the feeling of someone watching me hits me, I look over to see Angie, Amelia Moon, Jaylin, and Aviva Merryweather. The wives of my closest buddies. They all give me cheeky grins, and I groan loudly. I call over to them, "You guys talking about me?"

Angie nods. "Yup."

"With love, of course," Jaylin adds.

"I'm just nosy," Aviva inserts, and Amelia nods.

"I'm just here for the booze and the gossip."

I shake my head as I push off the wall and head toward their table. "Can I ask what the topic of conversation is?"

I can tell Angie's been drinking. Her cheeks are red. "Owen said you had the restraint of a saint and didn't kick her boyfriend's ass."

I scoff. "Boyfriend? Hardly. Just some guy she's passing time with."

Aviva grins. "Ooh, you've got it bad."

"So bad," Jaylin agrees. "I was convinced I was going to have to figure out if I was going to go the route of insanity or crime of passion for my defense of you."

Amelia snorts at that. "Either would fit."

They all agree as I shift my gaze between them. "You guys are a pain."

They laugh at that, and Jaylin leans in. "Is she here?"

"Not yet," I say, doing a scan of the room, and I hate how anxious I feel. I worry she'll show up with him. And then what? Am I just supposed to stand by while she walks around the party with him, acting the happy couple, when I know she wants me? No. I need her to drop him. Now.

"There he is," Angie says, and we all follow the direction of her

HAT TRICK

gaze to see the dweeb walking around, schmoozing the athletes. "I don't see her."

Relief fills me as his eyes move toward where I'm leaning. I stand then, tucking my hand into my pocket and pushing my hips forward, because even if my dick isn't hard, I know it's bigger than his. I tip my chin up at him, and irritation takes over his face.

"Dart, you are just evil," Jaylin says when Dickhead pulls his gaze from me. I'm smirky because I love that he knows she's mine.

"Why did you move your hips like that?" Angie asks and then hiccups. I set her with a very devilish grin, and she shakes her head. "Never mind. I don't want to know."

The girls snicker as I scan the crowd once more. My friends are all playing cornhole. And since I was late, I missed out on being Owen's partner, which is why I'm hanging out in the lionesses' den over here. I could go over where the guys are, but I don't want to miss when Tennessee shows up. I almost pull out my phone, almost text or call her, but I'm still trying to be patient. I'm trying to wait for her. Because that's what I've been doing since the start, and honestly, I don't know how much longer I can wait. And if I do have to wait much longer to kiss those lips, I may go insane. I just need her to blow off that dud.

"When is she going to blow him off?" I find myself asking, and then four pairs of eyes fall on me. "Like, we know she will, right?"

No one says anything for a long moment, until Jaylin asks, "What if she doesn't?"

My heart goes cold in my chest. "Then I'm gonna be a fucking mess, and all of you better be ready to feed me."

Amelia nods. "I'll make you lasagna."

"I'll buy you some ice cream," Jaylin promises.

"I can make you a sub," Aviva tells me, but Angie just holds my gaze.

"If y'all are as explosive as you say you are, we won't have to worry about that," Angie says softly with another small hiccup, and I know she's right. I just need to see Tennessee. I need to know what she is thinking. I need to touch her.

I need her.

I sigh deeply as I take another pull of my beer, and thankfully, I

TONI ALEO

don't have to wait long. I spot her coming up the stairs because of the orange ribbon in her hair. She holds the rail as she climbs the stairs, and when she comes into full view, everything stops. She's wearing an orange silk skirt that's gathered at the top of one thigh but covers her other leg completely and a cropped white lace top that molds to those breasts and has my mouth watering. She has on her UT cowboy boots, a jean jacket hanging from her fingers. Her makeup gives her a cat-eye look with her long lashes, and her lips are glossed as she purses them, her eyes scanning the crowd.

"That's her." I hear Angie, I think. I'm not sure with how loud the drum of my heart is beating in my ears.

"Goodness me," Aviva says.

"Dart, you are in so much trouble," Jaylin tells me, and I already know that.

"So, she must be a Vols fan," Amelia adds, and everyone but me laughs at that.

I lean back, unbuttoning my jacket so I can breathe as I drink her in. "Goddamn, she's gorgeous."

Her gaze meets mine, and that small curve of her lips has me tight as fuck. Everywhere.

"I feel like there should be a song playing for her. Maybe 'Unholy,'" Angie adds, shaking her head. "Because there is nothing holy about the way you two are staring at each other."

"Got that right," Amelia says. "I feel flushed."

"I feel hot," Jaylin murmurs. "Where is my husband?"

"For real. Where is mine?" Aviva asks, and I laugh at them as I push off the table, setting down my beer and going right for her. Her eyes darken with each step I take, and I run my hand over my mouth to hide my ridiculously happy grin as my body vibrates with desire for her.

She came alone. For me.

But then he steps into my view, and I stop midstep.

Gone is the desire, replaced by pure rage.

"Ah! Retreat, Dart! Retreat!" Angie calls to me, and my shoulders fall as Dickface guides her to the left. She looks over her shoulder at me, an apology in her eyes, but it's not enough.

HAT TRICK

What. The. Fuck.

I watch her, my heart pounding in my chest for what seems like days, when it's really only seconds. I try to find my composure, but it's hard when I want to lose my fucking mind. I turn, heading back to the wives before snatching my beer and downing the rest of it. No one speaks to me, and I'm thankful for that. I stand there, watching her like she's the puck and I have to steal it away from that fucker with her.

My body coils and burns as I watch that asshole press his hand into the small of her back. She tries to step away, but he keeps touching her like she's his. I know the truth, she knows the truth—fuck, he knows the truth—but he tries. I drink another beer, the anger too much that I need to drown it.

But then I'm unable to control myself. I take out my phone and text her.

Me: I'm starting to get pissed, baby doll.

I look to where she stands beside him. He still has his hand at the small of her back as she smiles up at a baseball player. I see her glance at her watch, and her brows come in. She looks up at me, and her eyes darken. She holds up a finger to the baseball player and smiles in apology. Then she steps back with her phone in her hand, much to Dick-face's protest. He gives her a look that almost results in my cracking my fist into his nose. Like he's appalled she'd answer her phone. Fuck him. He doesn't need to look at her like that; she does whatever she wants.

As long as it's with me.

I look down just as her text comes through.

The Only Ten You'll Ever See: Relax.

Me: Fuck that. Don't let him touch you.

The Only Ten You'll Ever See: Even if you weren't staring at me, I wouldn't want him to touch me. Give me a second.

Me: No. Blow him off. I can tell you don't even want to be near him.

The Only Ten You'll Ever See: I don't, but I'm working. Relax.

Me: I can't relax when he's touching you.

The Only Ten You'll Ever See: It's nothing, I promise. Give me a second.

Me: One.

TONI ALEO

Her eyes narrow as she glares at me. I know I'm acting like a child, but she is making me act like this. She's driving me fucking crazy.

Me: I'm dying. Lose him, Tennessee. End my misery. Is it him or me?

Her eyes meet mine again, and she blows out a breath, her eyes pleading with mine. She looks back down at her phone, and I do the same as her next texts come through.

The Only Ten You'll Ever See: There is no choice, D'Artagnan.

The Only Ten You'll Ever See: I may be standing beside him at this party, WORKING, but I'll be leaving with you.

The Only Ten You'll Ever See: I can promise you that.

I look up just as she tucks her phone into her purse, ending our conversation and leaving me shifting to relieve the ache in my pants.

That second turns into minutes, and I'm getting madder with every one that passes.

"What'd she say?" Angie asks, and I cut my gaze to her.

"Mind your business. You just want the gossip," I tease, and she grins just as Amelia starts smacking her on the arm.

"I do. What?" she asks Amelia. I watch as Angie turns her head to where Amelia is looking, and then a wide grin spreads over her face. I look in the same direction, and my eyes are instantly captured by Tennessee's. Hers are hooded, dark, and set on just me as she closes the distance between us. I fall under her spell as I watch her hips sway back and forth, showing me a peek of her upper thigh with every step, and once more, everything fades away.

She stops before me, her head tipping back just a bit as she looks deep into my eyes. Even with the chill in the fall air, I'm burning up as I gaze down at her beautiful face. "I broke up with him."

"You're fucking right you did," I growl as my heart skips in my chest, but neither of us moves, leaving entirely too much space between us.

I reach out, but she shakes her head. "You can't touch me here."

"The fuck I can't," I say, taking a step toward her, and her eyes drift shut.

"There are too many people here," she says to me. "Troy's uncle thinks Troy and I are together, and I don't want to piss him off."

HAT TRICK

I tuck my hands into my pockets as anger surrounds me. "Not touching you isn't anywhere in my DNA."

"Jesus. Think if we throw water on them, they'll cool off?" I hear Jaylin ask, and my lips quirk.

"I want you to touch me," Tennessee whispers, her eyes traveling to my lips. "There isn't a moment when I don't want you to touch me."

Angie chuckles as heat swirls in my stomach. "I don't think even throwing them in an ice bath would cool them off."

I drag my trembling hand down over my mouth as I try my best not to snatch her up in my arms and take her right here. Our breaths are labored, and by the grace of God, she takes my hand, pulling me with her, and I follow willingly.

Excitedly.

We round a corner to a spot where no one is, just some boxes and discarded bar stuff. She turns without warning and sets me with a heated look. Our gazes lock as she takes a deep breath. "I'm sorry for hurting you, for ghosting you, and for showing up in this damn state thinking I could go another second without you."

My nerve endings fire off, and my skin tingles under her gaze.

"With you, I'm just so overly exposed. How did I get so close to you in only one night?"

"Fate," I tell her, reaching out and snaking my arm around her waist. She comes willingly, her arms wrapping around my neck as her breath catches. "It was all fate. It's supposed to be this way."

"You live in my head. You are in every thought I have, in every fiber of my being, and I don't know how to be this vulnerable to someone."

I step in closer, pressing my forehead to hers. "You don't have to know how. You already are, baby doll," I answer, my lips so close to hers. I ache everywhere. "Just as I am for you."

"I'm yours, D'Artagnan. Totally yours."

"That has never been up for discussion, Tennessee," I say, my body burning where hers presses into mine. "You've been mine and me yours since we shared three rounds of tequila at ten a.m."

"We had to celebrate," she says, running her fingers along my lips.

TONI ALEO

"You're right. Us meeting," I tell her, and her breath catches as she tugs my lip down with her thumb.

"Why aren't you kissing me yet?" she whimpers. "Dart, I need you."

My jaw goes taut under her touch. "I need you to know something," I say roughly against her lips. "Because you have me fucking salivating, Tennessee."

"What?" she asks, her brows coming in, her eyes widening from the hooded, sexy look she wore only moments ago.

"How dare you look this fucking delicious and make me wait so long to taste you?"

Her breath hitches as she gazes up at me, awareness filling every bit of her being, and that naughty look is back, making me hard everywhere. She runs her tongue along her bottom lip before she whispers against my mouth, "Because I wanted to make you crazy for me."

"Baby doll," I purr, threading my fingers into her hair. "You did just that, and that's totally fine." I slide my hand down her back and grab ahold of her sweet ass, forcing her to press her hips into mine as a sexy whimper leaves those lips of hers. "I'll wait till we get home to punish this sweet ass of mine. I hope you're ready."

She inhales quickly, dragging her thumb along my bottom lip once more. "Not even in the slightest."

I gently bite the tip of her finger between my teeth, and she wheezes in response, sending heat straight to my cock. "Well, get ready."

Unable to wait any longer, I take that mouth with mine and groan at the connection. Her hands clutch my shoulders as she opens her lips, and I invade her mouth with a need only she brings out in me. Like she is the air that I need to survive. In that moment, I know the truth that has been staring me in the face since the moment I met her.

I am head over heels in love with Tennessee.

CHAPTER
Twenty-One

TENNESSEE

Lordy…

His mouth, his hands, his body, Dart's everything completely consumes me as our mouths brawl with each other. We are a tangled mess of tongues and teeth, and I clutch at him, unable to fathom breathing when his mouth is on mine. Gone is all sense of time, of where I am, and even who I am. Because under his mouth, his hands, I am his, utterly his. I grasp the lapels of his jacket, bringing him closer, needing him. And when our hips crash together, his moan vibrates against my mouth, mingling with my own. He drags his teeth down my bottom lip, my jaw, my neck, nipping and sucking my burning skin as I move my hand up over his shoulders.

I grasp him by the back of the neck, holding him in place while he sucks at my neck in the most delicious way. "D'Artagnan," I whimper, the deep rumble coming from his chest sending heat straight between my legs.

"Fuck, baby doll. I can't handle when you say my name," he breathes against my neck. "You're the only one to call me that."

TONI ALEO

"I am? It's your name," I somehow get out as he lifts his gaze to mine.

"But only you take the time to say it," he says, his eyes burning into mine.

A tenderness blossoms in my chest as I cup his jaw. He leans into my hand before turning his face and kissing my palm. With a quickness that impresses me immensely, he spins me in his arms, my body touching the brick wall as my ass collides with his cock. He presses his hand between my face and the wall, nuzzling his nose along my neck and my shoulders as he moves his other hand down my arm, over my stomach, across my hip to the slit in my skirt. I gasp as he strokes his hand along my heated thigh, and my eyes drift shut until he pulls the skirt to the side, up over my love handles, and his hand comes crashing down against the bare skin of my ass.

And it's *glorious*.

I cry out, and his rough chuckle rolls down my spine before he licks the shell of my ear. He slides his hand to the inside of my thigh as my pussy begs for his touch. But then he pauses.

"Tennessee, where are your panties?"

I can't breathe, but my lips curve. "I didn't want anything to be in your way."

His growl is deep, dark, and everything delicious. "Mmmm," he murmurs in my ear, lightly tracing his finger along my pussy. "So, you're saying you want me to touch you?"

I arch into him. "Yes."

"Shh, I am tracing the shape of you," he croons, licking my earlobe. "Fuck, you're so wet, baby doll. So wet for me."

"Yes, only for you," I cry, and I can feel the grin on his lips against my ear.

"God, you feel so good."

I bend toward his fingers, wanting him, needing him.

"Greedy fucking girl. Fuck, you make me so hard." He presses himself into my ass, and I feel every single inch of him. I rock my ass against him, and his breathing is rough, dirty. He slips his finger between my lips slowly, and he finds my clit with ease. But he only brushes it, making me quake everywhere. He slides his finger down and inside me, and then he adds another finger as I moan ever so loudly. He strokes his tongue along my neck. "Stay quiet, because I won't stop if someone comes around that corner."

My heart is slamming against my chest as he moves his fingers in and out of me, his breath so wicked against my ear. "They'll see me fucking you with my fingers, making you come, and I still won't stop."

I squeeze my eyes shut as the pleasure rattles me.

"God, you're pulsating around my fingers, Tennie. Fuck, I love how you feel. I can't wait to bury myself inside you, deep," he murmurs, his fingers going deeper inside me. I moan loudly into the back of his hand, the sound muffled. "Yes, that's my good girl. Keep quiet."

"I can't," I gasp, almost sobbing from the relief of his touch.

"I know where to touch you, how to make you squirm."

"D'Artagnan," I moan against his hand, and he groans in my ear. His breathing is labored, crazed, and I love it. God, I've missed him.

"You are being so good, baby doll. So quiet," he tells me, pumping his fingers into my pussy. "Don't worry. When I get you home, in my bed, you can scream as loud as you want."

"Please—"

"You're so close, aren't you?"

I bring my head back against his shoulder, and Dart's mouth is just as dangerous as his fingers. He pulls them out of me and locates my clit again while his mouth sucks and nips at my burning flesh. He presses his finger to my bundle of nerves, and I jerk against his hand. "I need you to come for me. I can't think of anything but making you come," he demands, and I can't handle him. I can't handle this.

He is merciless, demanding, and just as greedy as me. I lean into his cheek, rocking against his hand as my ass grinds on his cock. His breaths are strangled and match mine in cadence. He circles his finger around my clit, faster and in all the right ways.

He brings his other hand to my cheek, turning my head so our mouths meet. He works my clit, my body quivering as he moves his hand to my shirt, pulling it down so he can grasp my breast. I arch into his hand, my own clutching the pockets of his pants so I don't fall to the ground like I feel as if I could at any moment. He squeezes my nipple, his fingers driving me to the edge as his mouth hovers over

TONI ALEO

mine. Everything is hot, wild, and I feel myself flying over the edge under his hand. "Keep riding my fingers. Yes. Fuck. Right like that."

"Faster. God. Faster," I beg, and just like that, I shatter. His mouth captures my moan of release, and I swear I come again. He squeezes my nipple, pressing his hard cock into my ass, and I am lost.

Disoriented.

Gone. I'm gone.

He slides two fingers into me and groans loudly against my mouth as I contract around him. We rock together, the pure frenzy of us mind-blowing. Our bodies still, and I can feel him throbbing against my ass. He draws a kiss from my lips, pulling his hand out of me, and I whimper against his lips. We part, and I open my eyes to meet his wild ones. He brings his fingers into his mouth, leaving me panting as he licks my desire off them. "You have no idea how badly I've missed you," he says roughly.

"Oh, I think I know a bit," I say, gripping him through his pants, and he growls against my mouth. "I want you so much."

"You have me, Tennessee."

I turn in his arms and take his jaw in my hand, our eyes clashing before I capture his mouth with mine. With my other hand, I undo his belt and his pants before sliding my hand into his boxers. He jerks against my touch, and I drag my mouth from his, a small smile moving along my lips. He licks my smile as I slowly lower to my knees. He stops me, and I look up at him wantonly.

"I want you," I beg, and his eyes flash with such deep desire.

"Kneel on top of my shoes." His voice is so rough, so strained. "I don't want you to hurt your knees."

I swear I almost come once more. I do as he asks and take him in my palm. Our eyes meet, and I run my tongue along his head, his precome salty on my tongue. Before I suck him in, I remind him, "Remember, be quiet."

He presses his hand into the wall and growls deeply before I take him into my mouth. He arches toward me, his cock hitting me in the back of the throat, gagging me. I take his hips in my hands just as he tangles his hand in my hair, and I fuck him with my mouth. Each stroke of my mouth is deeper, faster, and I feel myself getting hotter by

HAT TRICK

the second. His voice is deep and naughty as I continue to suck him into my mouth.

"I love how your boobs bounce, and those thighs... Fuck, baby doll. Take me. Take me deep," he urges, and I do as he asks. "Yes, Tennie. Your mouth is a fucking dream. Keep that up. That mouth... Fuck!" he roars, and then he rises up on his toes, his hips lurching forward, almost knocking me back as he explodes in my mouth. He holds me in place, though, his orgasm racking his body as I suck him dry.

Before I know it, though, he lifts me under my arms and brings me up into his arms. Like I weigh nothing, like it's nothing to toss me around, and I devour him once our lips meet. He has never made me feel anything but desired, and I can't get enough. I spear my fingers through his hair as our tongues play. The taste of him and the taste of me make it real hard to remember that over a hundred people are not far from us.

But as he said, they could find us, and neither of us would have stopped what just happened.

Not even a blizzard could stop us.

We part, but only far enough that our lips brush as we breathe deeply, our eyes locking heatedly. A tender look comes over his face, and my heart sings as he gently glides his fingers along my jaw. He presses his forehead to mine as I move my hands up, clutching the muscles of his back in my fingers, wishing the fabric of his jacket weren't there. He strokes his thumb over my lip, his eyes searching mine, and I feel like he is saying so very much with those blue depths. Promises and more, and I won't look away.

I can't look away.

"You keep looking at me like that, and I'm gonna take you right here."

"Don't threaten me with a good time," I murmur against his lips, and they curve devilishly. "Take me to your bed, D'Artagnan." Heat burns in his eyes as he squeezes his other arm around me. "Now."

I don't have to say it twice.

With only a groan of excitement leaving his lips, we help each other get dressed. Our laughter tickles my stomach as I fumble with his belt, and he waits until the last minute to fix my top. When we're

157

presentable…somewhat…he captures my neck in his hand and brings me in for a long, lusty kiss. I grip his wrist for support since he makes me weak. When he parts from me, his eyes search mine. "Don't tell me I can't touch you as we leave."

Fire burns inside me. "I didn't plan on it."

Though I know that's not smart, I really don't care at the moment. I only want him. I want us. I want those promises that swirled in his eyes. He takes my hand, kissing my wrist, my palm, then my knuckles before threading our fingers together. I grin up at him, and his eyes dance along my skin. "We'll never leave if you keep looking at me like that."

My grin turns into a cheeky one as he pulls me into his side, and we walk around the corner to where the party is still in full swing. I notice that Owen is leaning against a table that no one else is near, and then he holds up his hand. Dart slaps it with his own as Owen winks at me. "Made sure no one went that way."

Embarrassment floods my cheeks, but Dart just flashes him a grin. "Because you're my best friend."

Dart takes my jacket and purse off the table next to Owen. I hadn't even realized I'd dropped those, but then, when do I ever think clearly when it comes to him? The excitement is all-consuming, and I can't wait to get to his bed. I can't wait to rediscover his body, to make sure I didn't forget anything about it, not that I think I did. I couldn't, even if I tried.

And I did try.

We're almost to the stairs when Troy steps in front of us. I feel Dart tense, and when I look up, his eyes are wild with fury.

Well, hell.

Troy ignores Dart and asks me, "What are you doing?"

"Leaving," I say simply, and I swear Dart pulls me closer.

"With him?"

I nod, unable to hide how I feel.

"In front of all these people?"

"You're the only one who cares," I tell him.

"This is absurd," he says, shaking his head, his cheeks matching his hair. "We are supposed to be recruiting more clients."

HAT TRICK

"My work speaks for itself, so I'm not worried."

Troy is livid, his eyes wild. "I leave tomorrow, and I wanted to talk to you."

That's when Dart decides to speak. "There isn't anything to talk about."

"This doesn't concern you," Troy throws at him, but Dart isn't having it.

"Anything that has to do with Tennessee concerns me."

He rolls his eyes, looking back at me. "Please, Ten. Give me another chance."

But I'm already shaking my head. "I can't, Troy."

"But I love you," he declares, and his words tug at my heartstrings. Not because I want to hear them, but because I feel bad for him. "Surely you feel something for me."

Dart stiffens beside me, and I run my fingers along his ribs. "I care for you as a friend, but it has never been anything more."

"Because of him!" he roars, but then he presses his lips together when we see heads turn to look at us. Dart stands like a proud peacock, and I could throttle him. "He won't love you how I do."

Dart holds up his finger, stopping Troy instantly. "You're right. I won't," he says menacingly. "I'll love her more." His words knock out any ounce of air I had in me. "Now, gladly go fuck off, and don't tell my girl that you love her. Next time, I won't use my words."

With that, Dart starts forward, bringing me with him, and Troy immediately moves out of the way. As we head down the stairs, I look up at Dart. Surely he didn't just say what I think he did.

That he loves me?

No, that can't be. He said he'd love me more, which I totally get. The intensity between us is unmatched. This fire of our connection is smoldering, so if he ever did love me, it would be just as intense as that. Which means he didn't claim he loves me. Right? As I gaze up at him, that tic in his jaw needing to be licked, I know one thing for sure.

I have been in trouble since the moment I met him. Because I could love him, with my whole damn heart, and nothing, no one, or no amount of space would ever change that.

And that is absolutely terrifying.

159

CHAPTER
Twenty-Two

Dart

I usually drive, but tonight, I'm thankful I didn't.

I hold Tennessee in the crook of my arm as we walk out to her car. Or what I was assuming to be a car until we approach a jacked-up Ford. The tires are as tall as she is, and the paint is white with orange glitter embedded in it. On the cab, it reads "Rocky Top."

I mean, who else's truck would it be?

"This is yours?"

Her eyes are hooded, and I know she's still reeling from what just transpired between us. "Yeah. Was it the orange glitter or the big Tennessee emblem on the back that gave it away?"

I chuckle as I hold her close. "I think your Vols obsession is terrifyingly cute." She gives me a sneaky grin, and I hold back the many quips bubbling inside me. "Can I have the keys?"

She scoffs. "No."

"You're going to drive? Me? To my own house?"

She runs her fingers over my chest. "No one drives my truck."

"Not even me?"

Her eyes dance with mine, and I think I've got her. "Not even you."

HAT TRICK

She climbs up into the truck with ease, giving me a teasing wink before she shuts the door.

"Wow," I mutter as I walk around the front. The truck roars to life, and I get in as she beams over at me.

"Hey."

I adjust myself since that grin is intoxicating. "Hey."

She does a little wiggle, and I can't even. "You look really hot in the passenger seat of my truck."

I chuckle, shaking my head. "Your ass is so, so mine."

She bites her lip. "Promise?"

I can only groan as she drives off. She hands me her phone, and I put in my address for her. I set her phone on the seat since the directions are on the screen in the dash. Of course, my gaze falls to the slit of her dress, and the fabric strains against the thickness of her thighs. From where I sit, I can see her center, and Jesus, what a sight. I swallow past the boulder in my throat. "Hey." She looks over at me as she sings along with the radio, such beautiful happiness in those eyes of hers. "I can see your pussy, Tennessee."

Desire crashes into her gaze. "Is that a problem?"

When she spreads her legs wider, my cock comes to life. "Not at all."

I unhook my seat belt, and she lets out a strangled giggle. "What are you doing?"

I lie along the seat, pushing her skirt aside to reveal all her goodness. "I can't just sit here with that pussy teasing me and not taste you."

"Dart! I'm driving."

"Then I suggest you keep your eyes on the road," I murmur against her thigh as I drag my tongue over her. "And next time, let me drive." She tries to squeeze her thighs together, but I don't allow her, holding one in my palm so she's open for me. She squirms beneath me as I trace my tongue along the outside of her lips, relishing her sweetness.

"Oh God," she moans as her legs fall open farther, and she scoots down a bit so I have more room. I drag my tongue along her lips, my skin prickling at not only the taste of her, but the sounds she makes.

"That's right, baby doll. Tell me how much you like it."

TONI ALEO

"I do. Please. Oh, Da..." she drags out, her thighs quivering, and she arches up enough that my tongue touches her clit. My cock is instantly hard, throbbing, and aching in my pants as I French-kiss her pussy over and over, unable to get enough of her and knowing I never will. I slide up the hand I'm using to hold her thigh and press my thumb inside her with ease. "Oh. Oh yes."

Her words reward me, and I don't let up a bit. I suck her sweet pussy in my mouth and fuck her with my thumb as she starts to rock against my lips, her sounds becoming more eager, more demanding. "Dart, God yes. I could crash right now, and I wouldn't care."

"I'd rather you didn't," I say against her slit. "Be a good girl and get us home so I can fuck you hard enough to make up for these last three months."

She cries out once more, her body jerking under my tongue, and I'm lost in her. The sounds, the scent of pure sex, the way she tastes, and how fucking in love with her I am. I suck her between my teeth, fucking her faster until she comes undone under my mouth, my name roaring from her lips. I'm breathing just as hard as she is as I kiss her center, her thighs, and then her hip before sitting back in the seat. Her chest is heaving, her fingers white-knuckled on the steering wheel, and undeniable euphoria all over her sweet face.

When we hit a bump, I know she's either hit a curb or has entered my driveway. I grin over at her as I lick my lips for more of her. "Good girl. You got us home."

She throws the truck into park, leaning back and huffing out a deep breath. "Barely." Her hands press to her chest and stomach as she pulls in lungfuls of air, and I'm under the spell that is her.

Tennessee.

I throw open my door and get out before coming around the truck for her. I open her door, and she's still trying to catch her breath. "Shut off the truck, baby doll."

She does as I ask before looking down at me, her eyes wild with lust. "I don't think I can walk. I was trying so hard not to crash."

I snort at that and pull her from the seat into my arms. She laughs as I throw her over my shoulder and slam the door shut before I take a good chunk of her ass in my hand. She squeals, her laughter intoxicat-

HAT TRICK

ing, as I head inside. I barely make it in the door before I am putting her on her feet and stripping off my clothes.

She pulls at my belt and unfastens my pants as I toss my shirt and jacket to the floor, kicking the door shut. I pull at her top and love that she forwent the undergarments. They're useless and get in the way anyway. She pushes my pants down my legs before crouching down to take off my shoes. I watch, amazed by her as I step out of my pants, and they join the rest of our clothes. Except that naughty-ass skirt of hers and those damn UT cowboy boots. She kisses my knees, my thighs, and runs her tongue ever so torturously up my cock, and I rock back on my heels. I take her jaw, tipping her head up so she can look into my eyes.

"I need to be in you, Tennessee."

Her tongue comes out, licking me, and I love that challenge in her eyes. "What are you waiting for?"

I chuckle at that. "The view from here is stellar."

She licks me again. "I was thinking the same thing."

I drop to my knees and slowly lay her back as our lips meet. I sink down onto her body and groan against her mouth at how fucking good she feels. She rocks her center along my throbbing cock, and my control is gone. I sit back on my haunches, grabbing my pants and fishing out my wallet for a condom. I rip the package and sheathe myself as I look down at her. Marks from me are all over her sweet body, and that brings me a whole new round of satisfaction. Her skirt is at her waist, her center glistening for me, and I know there is no way in hell I will be able to make this last. I take her by her thighs, bringing her closer before I fist my cock and run it along her slick, wet lips. "I love how wet you get for me."

Her eyes are hooded, dark, each one making me feel utterly cherished. I push her leg up, pressing it back with my hand as I guide myself into her. The feel of her around my cock, how she squeezes me, how she takes every inch of me, does something real powerful to my heart. I close my eyes, my hips sinking into her, and my name falls softly from her lips. My heart rattles in my chest as I pull out slowly, wanting this to last, before I thrust back in. She angles her hips for me, and if I thought I was going deep before, nothing compares to now.

163

TONI ALEO

She destroys me, and each thrust only makes that more apparent.

My strokes become more urgent, and I watch as she takes me enthusiastically. Her fingers bite into my wrist, and her cries are mind-altering and all-consuming. Her nips are tight buds, and with each thrust, they bounce for me. "I'm gonna spend an hour just sucking those tits of yours."

She lifts her hands to her breasts, gasping, and I notice a new tattoo that wasn't there when I was with her three months ago.

It's the shape of the state of Tennessee, with a heart right where Nashville is.

I stop, and she looks up at me. "Dart?" I poke at the heart on the tattoo, and a breathy laugh leaves her lips. "Like it?"

"Depends, because I thought you lived in Knoxville. So why is Nashville the city with the heart?"

Her eyes lock with mine, searching them and telling me what I already know. "'Cause I left my heart there."

I lean in, capturing her jaw in my hand and shaking my head. "No, baby doll."

"No?" she asks, and my body catches on fire against her.

"Your heart has always been with me."

She sighs ever so sweetly, and I take her mouth. I sink into her, drawing the kisses out of her and getting drunk off her. I go back up on my palms as she drags her boots up the backs of my thighs.

"Oh, I'm almost there. Don't stop."

I couldn't if I tried, but her second release burns through her body like wildfire, and she squeezes me so tightly that I have no control over my need to make this last. I slam into her, lost and not wanting to be found. When I explode inside her, my toes dig into my hardwood floors, and my balls are so tight, breathing isn't an option. I squeeze my eyes shut as the release shakes my body, and I'm met with her little moans of pleasure. I palm her thigh, rubbing her before I fall on her, sliding to the side as I gather her in my arms. I take her mouth with mine and draw luscious kisses from her swollen mouth.

I pull back a bit to fight for breath as she cuddles into my chest, kissing me and licking along my collarbone. She runs her fingers along my jaw, through the coarse hair, and over my lips. I look down then, meeting her gaze, a lazy grin on her lips.

And the words are right there.

She frees a piece of her hair from my mustache and then cups my cheek before kissing me again. I fall into the kiss. I fall into everything that is her. I gather her closer, our noses pressing together as our eyes collide. "Don't do that to me again."

Her brow perks. "What?"

"Three months, Tennessee. Three excruciating months."

Her eyes soften as she runs her thumb along my jaw and whispers, "I missed you, D'Artagnan. So much."

"I was a text away."

"I know. I was dumb," she admits, her eyes searching mine. "I'll never make that mistake again. Three months felt like a lifetime."

I nod. "I felt like I couldn't even breathe."

Tennessee's eyes move with mine as she kisses my top lip. "I'm here now."

"Promise me," I demand, holding her gaze. "Promise me you'll never do that to me again."

"I wouldn't dare," she says without hesitation, her heart in her eyes. "I couldn't if I tried."

Our lips meet, and my pounding heart quiets in my chest somewhat. Because even though I truly trust her and know I'll never love anyone the way I love her, I'm aware if she does disappear again, it'll break me into pieces.

I'd never be the same again.

CHAPTER
Twenty-Three

Dart

Tennessee is only wearing one of my IceCats shirts.

It's tight along her stomach and her breasts, but long enough to keep her naughty bits from showing, even though I complained greatly about that. Once we got up off the floor and cleaned up, I gave her the shirt, and she made a face at it.

"My daddy told me I couldn't wear any color other than orange."

I almost told her I was her daddy now, but I'm pretty sure she doesn't have the daddy issues or the interest in that kink. I'm just thankful she likes the crack of my palm on that sweet ass of hers.

I could punish that ass for hours and still not get enough.

"But, baby doll, you look so good in black and red."

She makes a face. "This shirt is giving Georgia Dawgs vibes, but I'm not going to complain since it does have your name on the back. Plus, we just won't tell my daddy."

I grin at her, and her eyes dance wickedly with mine. "There are a lot of things we won't tell your dad."

"You are absolutely right on that one."

Once she was covered and I had put on a pair of loose-fitting shorts, we both realized we were starving. Thankfully, I had stuff in the fridge to make pizza.

I stand behind her, holding her as she makes our pizza. As she places the mozzarella, I kiss her neck. "I know I could give you some space, but I don't want to."

She snorts at that, leaning her head on mine. "Who says I want space?"

"You did yesterday."

She looks up at me. "I didn't mean it. I just needed to figure out how to cut things off with Troy."

"And how did you?"

Something moves in her eyes, and she says, "He told me you only wanted me for sex, and it pissed me off because I know that's not true."

I press my lips to the tip of her nose. "I mean, it is important, though."

"It is," she agrees, her lips lifting into a smirk. "But I know it's more."

"So fucking much more," I promise as I exhale happily.

She kisses my top lip before she finishes and then claps her hands. "Okay. You put it in the oven."

She moves out of my arms and washes her hands as I do as she said. When she is done, I set the timer while she looks out at the back patio. "Wow. That's one hell of a view, and while I know you're a very successful hockey player, this seems a bit extravagant for a bachelor."

I grin as I lean back into the counter. "I actually bought it from my buddy Kirby. He scored it from another player, and when he started his family, he decided to get a bigger house that was safer for the girls. Instead of selling it for market value, he sold it to me for what he paid."

"It's a huge house," she says, looking around, and I love how good she looks in my place.

It is rather large, which is why I wanted my mom and Sabine to move in. It's four bedrooms with a huge living space, has direct access to the beach, and is elevated off the sand in case of hurricanes or flooding.

TONI ALEO

"I didn't offend you, did I?" she asks, stealing me from my thoughts.

"Not at all. I was just thinking how gorgeous you look here."

She waves me off. "Stop. I'm already wearing your shirt," she says, making a disgusted face as she lifts it from her skin, and that has me laughing.

"You better get used to it, Tennessee. You're going to wear my shirt a lot," I tell her, and her eyes flash with excitement.

"Then I'll need to get you some Vols shirts."

I scoff at that, and she tears her gaze from mine as she looks around the space, taking in the photos and all the sticks that hang on the walls. She runs her fingers along the shelf of pucks that lines the whole wall that leads back to the bedrooms. She raises a brow at me.

"All my goals for the last two years."

Her eyes widen in shock as she looks at them. "Impressive."

"I told you I am very good at scoring."

Her lips quirk as she moves to the other wall, taking in the photo of Sabine and me on the beach from this summer. Jaylin had it blown up for me and professionally framed so it would have a pretty, flashy gold frame and a light that illuminated it.

I told her it was too much, but she said it was the best picture of us she had ever seen. Sabine's blond hair is in ringlets around her face, her blue eyes are shining, and she's showing off her perfect grin. She wears her Miklas IceCats jersey, and so do I. She is sitting on my shoulders, the ocean behind us as we look right at the camera, truly happy. That day, we thought that she and Mom would be living with me. The next day, that changed, though.

"How old is she?"

"Eight going on sixteen."

Her lips turn up more. "She's stunning. Your sister?"

"Yeah," I tell her, coming to stand beside her. "Sabine."

"That's an interesting name."

"As you know, my mom was a huge fan of *The Three Musketeers*."

"We need to watch that," she announces, gazing at the photo. "When did you take this?"

"This summer."

HAT TRICK

"Y'all look so damn happy," she gushes, her twang wreaking havoc on my heart.

"She's my sunshine, for sure."

She leans into my arm and then reaches up, running her finger along my neck. "Sunshine." I nod, and she kisses the spot. "She lives in Arizona with your mom, right?"

"Yeah," I say, my stomach doing a flip because she remembered. Not that I forgot a thing about her family. "I miss her."

"Not your mom?"

I shrug. "Not really," I admit, letting out a long breath. On my phone right now is a text request for money since, apparently, my mom didn't have the money for her water bill. "My mom wasn't the best mom when I was growing up, and you'd think she'd do better the second time."

"She wasn't?"

"She had me young, and my grandpa actually raised me," I tell her, pointing to the photo beside Sabine's. It's of my grandpa and me when I was a junior in college.

"Oh wow. Look at your little baby face," she gushes, rising onto her toes so she can get a quick look. My fingers ache to touch her sweet thighs, but I resist as she traces my face in the photo. "Sabine looks a lot like you when you were younger."

"Yeah, Mom claims we have the same dad. But I feel like if we did, I would have gotten to meet the asshole," I laugh, but there is no humor in her eyes. "Promise, I'm not that damaged—only enough to joke about it."

She snorts at that. "Your granddaddy loves you something fierce, doesn't he? Does he live close?" An ache almost suffocates me, and I guess it's all over my face once she looks back at me. "Oh, Dart, I'm sorry." She comes to me, standing between my legs and wrapping her arms around me. She brings me into her chest and kisses my temple. Her touch is almost as overwhelming as my grief. "When?"

"Right before I was drafted."

Her grip on me tightens, as if she can protect me from the pain. "I'm so sorry. He loved you, my love. You know that," she tells me,

TONI ALEO

and while I nod in agreement, the way she says *my love* in that country twang has me in knots.

"Yeah, I know. He was a great man," I say, my voice strained. "He had an aneurysm in his brain, so it was quick and in his sleep, so he didn't even know." She threads her fingers through my hair. "His girl-friend was the one to tell me. She still calls me weekly to check in."

"How kind."

I move my hands to her thighs, holding her to me as she slides her fingers through my hair. "How are your parents?" I ask, needing to change the subject.

A sweet smile comes over her face. "Crazy as always," she gushes as the oven timer goes off. "Ooh, food is done." She kisses my lips quickly before heading toward the kitchen. "We should eat on the porch."

"We can, though it might be chilly," I say, watching her move around my kitchen. I love her there. It does something to me and urges me to be impulsive.

Like ask her to never leave.

She pulls out the pizza and slides it onto the platter she had laid out. She moves quickly through the kitchen, getting us plates and silverware as I walk to the counter. She opens the back door just as I lean into the counter, and then she shuts the door just as quickly. "Too cold, and I don't feel like putting on pants."

I grin. "I would protest that."

"I know you would," she says, but then I notice something on her thigh. A bruise. I move in closer and notice that it's not a bruise. It's like a burn. She goes to turn and runs right into me. "Lordy, what are you doing!"

I point to the spot. "What is that?"

She looks where I'm pointing and then shrugs. "I don't know."

"Did he do that to you?" I ask, and I don't even know why. I want him to disappear, just go away, so I don't ever have to be reminded that he touched her. "Since I know every curve, dip, and roll of your body, I know for a fact that mark wasn't there. So I can only assume he did it."

Her eyes widen before they go hooded, her lips tipping up. "I have

HAT TRICK

a lot to say to that statement, but I can promise you, he didn't do this to me." She rubs the spot. "I really don't know what that is. Is it a burn?" She bends funny to try to get a good look, and then she pops back up, looking at me. "I sat on my hair straightener, but I didn't think it got me that bad."

I exhale harshly as she reaches out, taking me by the waistband of my shorts. She pulls me to her and then wraps her arms around my waist.

"I hate that he touched you. It'd be different if I hadn't seen you two together," I admit, kissing her top lip.

"I'm with who I want to be with."

"I know that, but he touched you."

She sighs. "I faked orgasms with him, D'Artagnan," she whispers against my lips. "He doesn't even compare, and he never knew how to get me going the way you do."

"You said he was safe," I say, moving my hands up her arms and wrapping them loosely around her.

"Yeah, because nothing would change," she admits, and I can feel her heart beating. "I'd live the same boring life, have the same boring sex, and never ever experience the fear of being destroyed by someone."

I drop my head to hers, kissing her nose. "I won't destroy you."

A small bubble of laughter leaves her lips. "Dart, you already have," she says softly, holding my gaze. "In a really good way that scares me more than anything in the world because I know I am going to fall face first in love with you."

While her words have my lips curving and my heart skipping a beat, they also inform me she doesn't love me yet. I don't know how she doesn't; I'm a damn good time, and she sure as hell loves what I can do between her legs. She couldn't fake an orgasm with me if she tried. I'd know instantly, and I wouldn't let up until she was squealing my name. But she doesn't love me. Interesting. I almost ask, but I don't know if I want the answer. She ghosted me for a reason. Fear. And while I trust she won't do it again, I don't know why she doesn't love me yet. But then, there's that tattoo.

I'm confused as fuck.

TONI ALEO

"You don't love me?" I ask, and I'm not even the least bit surprised. I don't tend to think before I speak.

Something flashes in her eyes as her hands pause at my chest. "What?"

"You said you could fall in love with me, like you haven't, and I don't understand."

Her lips curve. "Dart, we hardly know each other, just that we're explosive."

"That's not true," I say, holding her gaze and not allowing her to look away. "The knowing each other part. The sex part is unquestionably explosive, but you know everything that matters."

She laughs, but then she stops when she realizes I'm serious. Her eyes search mine, and my stomach clenches. Silence stretches between us, and her breath quickens. I don't have to say the words for her to know them. "Dart, really?"

I swallow hard, and talk about being exposed. "Tennessee, I fell in love with you in that hotel room."

Her breath catches as a blush creeps up her neck to her cheeks. "You did?"

"I did," I confess with more confidence. "That's why I kept texting. Usually when I'm ghosted, I don't care. I move on. But I couldn't move on from you."

"But you didn't even know me."

"What else do I need to know?" I ask, meaning it. "You have a very unhealthy obsession with your namesake, which is why you were masturbating with an orange dildo." Laughter bubbles out of her, and I grin widely at her. "You love your mom and dad since you talk about them often. You're great at your job, and I knew that the moment I saw you working earlier. But the most important thing about you that I know is that you make me so unbelievably happy, I couldn't help but fall deeply in love with you."

Tears fill her gaze. "I make you happy?"

I gather her closer. "Yeah, Tennessee. Everything about you makes me happy."

"No one has ever said that to me."

"Because you're mine," I whisper, brushing her hair over her shoulders and cupping her face. My thumb plays along her jaw, and her eyes stay locked with mine as I give her a second to process what I just said. When a minute passes, self-doubt creeps in, and I say, "I understand if you—"

"I do love you, Dart. I do," she says, and I almost cry out in relief. "I think I always have. I just didn't want to admit it because if I did, then the pain of ghosting you would have killed me."

She wraps her arms around my neck, pulling me in, and then presses her lips to mine, kissing me deeply. It almost feels too good to be true, but then I take ahold of that ass of hers, and I know it's real.

That we're real.

CHAPTER
Twenty-Four

TENNESSEE

Oh Lord, Fate, Jesus, whoever the hell is listening, why did I fight my feelings for this man? Why did I torture us both? Why didn't I throw all caution to the wind and just love him how I wanted to?

Because of apprehension.

The distance.

How he makes it so that I can't think clearly.

The way I know I am purely his.

I've never dated anyone like him. Never felt this soul-deep burn for someone until him. I've always picked the easy choice, the stable guy, the one who would constantly be there, but now I've fallen in love with someone who travels, who is currently under contract here in South Carolina but could be traded at any time. What does that mean for my career? The one thing I worked so hard for. I left my parents for myself, but I know I'll leave behind everything for him.

And the truth of that makes me breathless.

Our lips crash together, and the terror that strangled me eases as my lips devour his. I know I'm safe, I know he has me, but the way he

HAT TRICK

kisses me doesn't feel the least bit safe. I can't get enough of him. The feel of his lips, the ripples of muscles on his chest, his abs, the dips that disappear below his low-hanging shorts. I run my fingers down the length of his back, the bumps along his spine, and over his ribs before I shove my hands into the back of his shorts, cupping that hard ass of his. He rocks his hips into mine, and our kisses become even more desperate. He sucks my tongue into his mouth, taking over the kiss and driving me wild.

He pulls his lips away to pick me up, my ass coming down on the counter before he runs his tongue up my neck, over my jaw, and then recaptures my mouth in one swift motion that has me gripping the edge of the counter for dear life. His hips dig into my thighs as he gathers my shirt in his hands, fisting it before pulling it up and over my body as I sit butt-ass naked in front of him. He licks his lips as he looks me over, and his gaze is demanding as he worships me.

"I love you, Tennessee," he murmurs before his fingers wrap around my throat, and everything inside me is set on fire.

"Have you loved anyone else?" I find myself asking, trying to ask questions so that my love for him makes sense.

His eyes flash with something dark. "I have," he says, squeezing my neck as he drags his lips along my nose. "Twice." He kisses the tip of my nose. "Once when I was fifteen, and again when I was in college."

I stroke my fingers along his back slowly, just needing to touch him. "What happened?"

"Amy Yates was my first love. We were young, and it ended because I couldn't keep it in my pants," he admits, brushing his lips over my cheek. "Marley Phillips and I dated our freshman through junior year, and when my grandpa died, she slept with my roommate because I was so fucked up."

My breath catches. "What a bitch."

"Yeah," he agrees, biting my bottom lip. "But it's okay because with them, I never felt how you make me feel."

My lips part as I slide my hands up and along the nape of his neck.

"How about you? Who have you loved?"

His eyes meet mine as his lips hover over my mouth, and tears burn in my eyes. I swallow and whisper, "I didn't really know what love was until you came toe-to-toe with me in the practice lounge." His jaw goes taut, and his lips press tightly together as his gaze scorches mine. "I dated someone for ten years on and off, and many between him. But this, us... This intensity, D'Artagnan... I know I have never loved before." His other hand comes up, cupping my jaw as he runs his thumb along my bottom lip, and I laugh at the pure insanity of my words. I wipe my face free of the tears that are falling against my wishes and meet his gaze once more. "That's crazy, right?"

He doesn't laugh; he only looks deeply into my eyes. Seconds pass, and then he slowly shakes his head, dragging his thumb along my cheek, catching my tears. "What's crazy is that there is not nearly enough time in my lifetime for me to love you the way you deserve."

How am I supposed to think clearly when he says things like that?

A tear rolls once more, and he brushes it away before he lowers his mouth to mine in an intimate, sweet kiss. He has never kissed me like this. So patient, so careful, and it has everything inside turning to goo.

He takes me by the back of the knees and pulls me to him, my ass squeaky against the counter. The laugh bubbles out of me before I can stop it, and his lips curve with mine. He can't hold it in either, and our laughter is our love song. The low tenor of his laugh leaves me throbbing as I wrap my legs around his waist, drawing him in against me. His laughter falls off then, and he lifts me up, holding me close as he carries me to the door.

"What are you doing?"

"Need my wallet," he says, grabbing it with one hand, his other just holding me up under my ass.

"Can I ask how much you lift?" His eyes dance with mine as he takes out the condom and throws his wallet down to the floor. "Also, how many condoms do you have in there?"

His lips turn up in a dirty little grin. "My one rep max is Tennessee Lynn Dent." I giggle at that, breathless and wild for him. "And this is my last, so we might actually make it to the bedroom next."

"Oh, we aren't going that way?"

HAT TRICK

His breath is strangled. "No way. I can't make it."

"Impatient."

"Fuck, only for you," he mutters against my lips as he pushes down his shorts, his cock coming up to press into my center. We both groan as he lowers me to the floor once more. "Ms. Dent."

"Yes, D'Artagnan?"

His lips quirk at that, and I roll him over, straddling him with an ease I didn't know I had in me. He looks up at me, and I can see the awe on his gorgeous face. "You stay fucking wet for me," he says, his words deep, uneven.

"Are you surprised?" I ask, sliding my hand down his arm, his wrist, before taking the condom in my hand. I bring it to my lips, tearing it a bit so I have better leverage to open the package. I discard the wrapping before sheathing him, his hiss of breath making me fumble with the condom. I get it on him, thankfully, but before I can guide him inside me, he takes me by my thighs and squeezes me.

"Sit on my face."

Oh, my insides blow the fuck up. "What?"

"Sit. On. My. Motherfucking. Face. Baby. Doll," he says, making each word its own sentence. But I'm frozen, unable to move, because surely he doesn't want my big self sitting on his face.

"I'll hurt you."

He scoffs. "No, you won't."

"I will. My ass is huge."

To make his point, he slaps both my cheeks, arching into me. "Believe me, I know."

His laughter makes my nipples go rock hard as he slides down, my pussy gliding up his chest, the ridges of his muscle bringing me such pleasure. My stomach clenches and my heart pounds when he runs his tongue along the curve of my ass to the inside of my thighs as he places me right above his mouth. "I could suffocate you," I whimper, but all I'm met with is his laughter.

"Then what a way to go, huh?"

"Dart!"

He slaps my thighs. "Sit down."

TONI ALEO

"Dart," I say, feeling wholly insecure. "I have never been asked to sit on someone's face because it's a death wish."

His eyes meet mine then, his fingers biting into my hips. "Sit."

I shake my head as the blush creeps up my face. "Dart, I don't—"

"Don't make me tell you again," he warns, his eyes dark and dangerous and so full of lust, but they also encourage me, especially that little pull of his lips to one side. "I got you, baby doll." I know he does, and his desire for me is overwhelming. I bite my lip and slowly lower myself just over his lips, the warmth causing a moan to escape. "Lower, baby. Lower. I want to drown in that wet pussy."

Oh, I'm going to fall apart before he even gets his mouth on me. His eyes urge me on, his hands molding my ass as I do as he asks. "Lower," he demands, and I whimper. "When I tell you to sit on my face, Tennessee Lynn, I mean fucking sit. Don't hold yourself up, don't brace yourself. Fucking sit on my face like my mouth is a saddle and. Fucking. Ride. My. Face. Do you hear me?"

I can't even process what he's saying. A frustrated moan leaves his lips, and he pushes my knees out with his elbows. I come down on his mouth with a small scream of surprise. He has me, though; his hands are at my waist as he sucks my pussy wholly into his mouth. I cry out, falling forward onto my palms, which brings on a whole new rush of pleasure. His licks are eager, powerful, and have my thighs trembling as I fight to breathe. His tongue moves from my entrance to my clit, back and forth, and my mind is flooded with hunger. I start to rock against him, slowly because I don't want to suffocate him.

But this dude has a death wish.

"Yes, baby. Ride my mouth. Do what your body wants. I want it—I need it," he demands, his fingers biting into my hips and forcing me against his mouth faster. Soon, I'm so lost, I don't need the guidance. I ride his mouth fast as I groan and cry. I squeeze his cheeks with my thighs as I dance along the edge of my orgasm, and soon, I can't even think. I fuck his mouth with no gentleness, no thought, and nothing holding me back. I grind my pussy against his mouth, his nose hitting me right where I want, and I go faster, needing my release. He spreads my ass cheeks apart, French-kissing my pussy, and everything just explodes.

HAT TRICK

The world.

My mind.

My soul.

I scream his name, my thighs tightening around his face as I jerk and feel as if I might pass out.

Beneath me, Dart chuckles against my hot center like he didn't almost die.

He then takes me by my thighs, and my back hits the hardwood before he's over me. He licks up my body, swirling his tongue over my nipples and drawing the most unthinkable noises from me. When he enters me, he stretches me, and I tangle my legs with his, my toes pressing into his calves as his hips dig into my thighs. His thrusts are demanding, thick, and filling. I arch into him when he sucks my nipples, licking and biting as he continues to thrust into me. He drags his teeth along my collarbone, up my neck, and then bites my chin. "I can't hold off long, my greedy girl," he says against my lips, his voice so rough I almost come undone. "Watching you riding my mouth, those thighs squeezing my face... Fuck me, baby doll, I'm surprised I made it this long."

Each word is a thrust, and I love it.

When he comes, he comes hard, slamming into me to the hilt, and I cry out, loving every bit of the depth. He drops his face to the middle of my chest, gasping for air as I stare up at his ceiling, trying to figure out how I deprived myself of him. I run my fingers along his back, up his spine, until I take his jaw and bring him up for a long, lusty kiss. He responds instantly, and everything inside me is so damn giddy. I kiss his bottom lip, the bridge of his nose, before I say, "I wonder if we'll ever actually make it to the bed?"

His laughter is strained as he continues to fight for his next breath. "Anywhere is our bed, baby doll."

I grin at that, his lips doing the same as my eyes drift shut. "And you say I'm the greedy one."

"I wasn't this greedy until I saw you moving that orange dildo in and out of this perfect pussy of yours."

My breath catches, and my heart just explodes in my chest. I take

TONI ALEO

his mouth once more, unable to get enough, and when I part from his lips, it's not for a breath. It's to tell him, "I love you."

He glides his nose along mine as a smile pulls at that gorgeous mouth. "I love you."

I've heard those three words from a few men, but I never believed them until now.

Until Dart.

CHAPTER
Twenty-Five

TENNESSEE

Dart breathes evenly under my cheek as he makes lazy circles over my ass with his hand. I lie between his legs, my face on his chest, as *The Three Musketeers* plays on the TV. Only one piece of pizza sits on the coffee table, along with the beers we drank with our dinner. I had never seen this movie, and I have to say, I can tell why his mom named him after D'Artagnan. He's an extremely strong character, but for me, not only is Chris O'Donnell hot, but he's very brave and just wants to love.

And I've got the real-life version beneath me.

"I'm a little offended for Sabine to be named after a spy and a murderer."

His chuckles tickle my ear as he grabs hold of my ass. "Yeah, but the only other option she had was D'Artagnan's love interest, and that would have been weird."

"She could have named her after the queen."

"Anne? My name is so epic. Anne isn't."

I snort at that. "Sabine is a beautiful name," I agree as the ending

TONI ALEO

credits start. I rest my chin in the middle of his chest, and he threads his hand in my hair. "You look tired."

"I'm slumped," he agrees, a lazy grin on his face. "Ready to go to bed?"

"Oh, I'm sleeping here?"

His brow perks. "So, you think I'm gonna tell you I love you, make love to you on every surface of this place, and then just want you to leave?"

"I didn't want to assume you'd want me to stay."

"Just assume that anything that has to do with you being around me is a yes." My heart sings at that as I stay trapped in his gaze. "Did you not have a sleepover with Duckfucker?"

I laugh, shaking my head. "You know you call him something different and more degrading each time?" He doesn't seem the least bit ashamed. "What is a duckfucker?"

He laughs. "Pretty self-explanatory. A guy who can't get any ass but a duck."

"I'm dead," I laugh, snorting, which makes him grin even more.

"You seem pretty alive to me," he mutters against my lips.

I bite at his lip, and his eyes burn into mine. "Before things get spicy between us—"

"Baby doll, they stay spicy."

"You're not wrong, but no, I didn't stay with him. I'd always make up an excuse for why he couldn't stay the night."

"Why?"

"I didn't want to stay with him. I just wanted to come, but hardly even got that."

"Not surprised."

I send him a sultry grin. "And with Denis, I had initially thought I wanted to wait till I was married to have sex. But even when that changed, he never really stayed. I think we slept together in a bed a handful of times."

He gives me a look. "You wanted to wait until marriage to have sex?"

I nod. "Yeah, I did. It was how I was raised. My mom and dad

HAT TRICK

waited. Told me I needed to because a real man would want my brain before my body."

Dart presses his lips together, trying to hold in his laughter.

"I lived smack-dab in the middle of the Bible Belt. Shut up."

He swallows his laughter. "What changed?"

"I realized I'm too horny to wait." He sputters with laughter, and my cheeks warm with a flush. "I was actually the last to give in. Josie started a whole year before me, and then Lindy lost hers. I had intense FOMO, so I called Denis and we did it in his dorm room."

"Did you regret it?"

I shrug. "No, I was glad because then I learned what I like and don't like."

Heat shines in his eyes. "I wish I had known you then."

I give him a look. "No, I was boring then."

"Never."

"No, really," I promise, lost in his blue eyes. "I was so attached at the hip to Lindy and Josie that I wasn't confident enough to be me. Josie is a big personality, and Lindy just goes with the flow, so I kinda got lost in the sauce."

"You said they put you down a lot?"

I blow out a breath, feeling that flush move across my cheeks. "Josie more than Lindy. She did it very passive-aggressively, and I never understood why." I look away from him, tracing my finger around his nipple. "Lindy never said anything when Josie would do it either. She'd just let her call me fat or tell me that I couldn't drink because I didn't need the extra calories. That I had to talk to the guys because they only ever saw me as their friend, not as an option. It wasn't that bad growing up, but college was rough."

"I don't like this chick," he says, and I scoff, moving to his other nipple.

"I haven't talked to them in three months."

"Really?"

"Yeah. Josie was trash to me the night we were supposed to be celebrating me, and Lindy said nothing. So I just cut them off."

"Wow, and you three grew up together?"

"Yeah. Our birthdays are days apart. I was first, Josie second, and

183

TONI ALEO

then Lindy."

"I fully support cutting her off. I don't fool with people who don't want me or treat me correctly."

I meet his gaze. "You said your momma isn't good to you, though."

"She isn't," he says simply. "But I have to deal with her to have Sabine in my life."

"She'd keep her from you?"

"I don't know, but I don't want to find out," he says softly, twirling my hair in his hand. "I don't trust her and have tried many times to get them to move here."

"Why won't they? Did y'all grow up in Arizona?"

"Not at all. I grew up in Canada, and my mom had Sabine in Buffalo. Close, but not close enough to raise me."

"I didn't realize you were Canadian."

"It comes out sometimes," he says, pushing my hair off my face. "I say 'eh' just as much as you say 'you all.'"

"It's 'y'all.' One word, not two," I tell him proudly, and he grins. "Y'all."

"I don't care. I just love hearing you say it," he says before he yawns.

"I'm ready for bed when you are."

His eyes hood a bit as he runs his hands down my body, squeezing me to him. "Good. I'm about to fall out."

He kisses me quickly before I push up, getting off him. Together, we pick up the mess, and he shuts off the TV as I go to clean the kitchen. "That can wait," he tells me, and I put the dishes in the sink, turning off the water.

"My mom says you should never leave a dirty kitchen."

"Listen, no offense to your mom, but if I have the choice between doing dishes and doing you in my bed, I'm choosing the latter."

I wipe my hands on the towel. "Same," I agree as I meet him in the hall. He wraps his arm around my waist, and together, we walk to his bedroom. He hits the lights, and I take in the black walls that have black crown molding along the top. On the wall above his bed is a large print of a very fantasy-style photo of a dragon. "So, you're into dragons?"

HAT TRICK

"Are those judgy eyes?"

My lips twitch as I swallow my laughter. "Absolutely not."

"I wouldn't think so since you literally have a Vols dildo." I sputter, and he sets me with a look. "Watch it, baby doll."

His warning only swirls desire deep within me as he heads into the bathroom. I can't help but ask, "So, why dragons?"

He opens the drawer under the sink. "My grandpa was really into them. We read all the great dragon novels, and then when *Game of Thrones* came out, we just became more obsessed. The dragon on my back is actually the art we had made of my grandpa in dragon form."

I press my lips together. "Y'all have dragon forms."

"You drive a white pickup with orange glitter."

"Yes, but I don't identify as a dragon."

That has him laughing as he stands up, setting a toothbrush and washcloth on the sink. He leans out of the bathroom, pointing to the two framed drawings on his wall. I walk over, and immediately, I'm in awe. The dragon on the left, which looks like his tattoo, is visibly older, his scales black with neon-blue eyes and scars along his face. "My grandpa was mauled by a dog when he was younger, so we added that in." The dragon on the right has lighter blue eyes, a strong jaw, sharp teeth, with large horns and reddish-gold scales along his body. "He used to say I was so passionate that I'd go from rage to sunshine in seconds."

"Sunshine," I repeat, his tattoo along his neck calling to me.

He nods. "The word means a lot to me."

My lips curve as I wrap my arms around him, kissing his top lip. "So, what you're telling me is I'm in love with a nerd who thinks he's a dragon?"

His lips twitch, trying not to grin. "Just as I'm totally in love with a girl who is obsessed with the Vols."

"Don't you forget it," I tell him with a wink, and he laughs.

"How can I?" he asks, and I grin as he hooks his thumb over his shoulder. "I got you a toothbrush and washcloth."

"Thank you." I follow him into the bathroom. Together, we brush our teeth and wash up. "You don't have a hairbrush, do you?"

He opens the drawer and moves things around until he finds a

TONI ALEO

Dora one. "It's Sabine's."

"Sure it is… I'm surprised there isn't a dragon on it."

"Is your hairbrush orange?"

"Shut up," I say as I start to brush out my hair, his laughter bringing me joy. We finish up, and as he shuts off the lights, I climb into his massively large bed. He is a big dude, so I'm not surprised. But still, it's rather huge. "Is this a king?"

"Alaskan king," he tells me, and I can fully spread out and still not touch him.

"Why do you need all this bed?"

He takes me by the wrist and pulls me into his chest. "Because I knew one day, I'd have a big-booty babe in my bed, and I'd need the room to love her in all the ways I desire."

His words heat me from the inside out. "Yet we went at it on the floor—twice—when this was in the bedroom. This is nice."

"Hey, hey, hey," he says, gathering my jaw in his palm. "You weren't complaining when you were riding my face."

A deep blush burns my face, and I smack his cheek. "Dart!"

"What? You loved it," he murmurs against my mouth. "You almost broke my nose, you were riding me so hard."

"Oh my God," I groan. "Did I hurt you?"

"Baby doll, I would wear that broken nose as a badge of honor and tell everyone how it happened."

"I would die!" I say, and he just laughs. "That would be embarrassing."

"The hell it would be," he says, squeezing my hip in his hand. "All my friends would be jealous. A fine, sexy, thick woman like you, riding my face until you came all over me. Any man would want that."

"I haven't done that before," I say, feeling bashful.

"Because you were waiting for me," he announces like a promise.

I look up, running my hand along his cheek. "I'm starting to think you might be right, even though I never thought I'd date a nerdy dragon guy."

I bite my lip to keep from laughing until he starts to tickle me, burying his face in my neck as I scream, laughing loudly. He pins me down with his body, and my laughter trails off once I'm under that

HAT TRICK

intense blue gaze. He drags his nose up over my lips then brushes the tip of my nose until I tip up my chin so he can kiss me deeply. We don't have much clothing left to remove, but we do it slowly, taking our time, our gazes staying locked. When he reaches for a condom from the drawer, I kiss up his arm, making it hard for him to put on the condom. We laugh, we grin, and when he sinks into me, our groans mingle like a beautiful love song. He slowly thrusts in and out of me. Each one deeper, slower, and driving me absolutely mad. As he draws kisses from me, my heart flutters in my chest, and I know for a fact that what he said is the ultimate truth. That I was waiting for him to come along.

And now that I have him, letting him go isn't an option.

I hold his jaw as his thrusts get a bit more demanding, and the desire is deep in those blue depths. "I would slay whatever is a dragon's enemy for you."

He stops, and then we both dissolve in laughter. He drops his head to mine, and the joy in his eyes is almost too much to handle. "Why are you ruining our moment?"

I feign confusion. "What? I thought that was super sweet."

He shakes his head, biting my bottom lip. He pushes himself up and flips me onto my stomach before pulling me up on my knees. It all happens so fast that I don't even have my next breath to prepare for him filling me deeply. I reach up, holding the headboard as he thrusts into me, his hand coming down hard on my ass as he wraps his other hand around my hair, pulling it back so I can see him behind me. He kisses my forehead as he thrusts into me wildly, bringing out the most strangled moans I've ever heard from my lips.

I come hard, squeezing him, and his lips are curved against my ear as he whispers, "Now, call me your dragon king."

My eyes fly open to find him grinning at me as he slams into me, his eyes crazed, and I can't even. My laughter mixing with my release is a kind of pleasure I have never felt before, and it only amplifies my climax. I spasm around him, and that does him in. He comes hard inside me, his hand cracking against my ass so hard, it vibrates through my body. I swear, I never thought I could come this hard.

But with Dart, anything is possible.

187

CHAPTER
Twenty-Six

Dart

Even in my huge bed, Tennessee's body is pressed to mine, our legs tangled, her head on my chest. She lost her hair tie sometime in the night, and her long, wavy hair is spread over my chest as the sunshine moves across her face, kissing it ever so softly.

I know I need to get up, get ready to head to the rink, but I really don't want to. I want to stay right here. I've already reset my alarm three times, but I know I can't be late. I kiss her temple before I slide out from underneath her. She cuddles into my bed, the blanket falling to the small of her back, showing a bit of her ass, and making my mouth water like crazy.

And in that moment, I don't ever want to look at that bed and not see her in it.

I swallow that wild impulse of mine and start to get ready. I rush, but even with how quick I am, I come out to find her in the same position. Her hair falls in her face, and her lips are pouted as she snores softly. I climb into the bed, lying on my stomach, and I trail kisses up her back, across her shoulder, before I nuzzle my mouth into her neck.

HAT TRICK

I kiss her there as I draw in a deep breath, her scent overwhelmingly sexy. She smells like me, sex, and that flowery perfume she wears.

I kiss her jaw then the spot by her mouth before I drag my nose along her cheek. "Tennessee?"

She doesn't open her eyes, but she purrs, "Yes, dragon king?"

My laughter comes quick, and I swear I fall for her even more as she smiles lazily up at me, her eyes still shut. I kiss her nose. "You're such a dork."

"Says the dragon king," she mutters, wiping her mouth and cuddling into my chest. I take hold of her willingly, moving her hair to the side so I can kiss her temple. "God, you smell fantastic."

I grin against her hair. "I gotta go in for morning meetings."

"What time is it?"

"Seven."

"Ew," she mutters, cuddling deeper. "Are you leaving now?"

"Yeah, but you don't need to get up."

"I have to go back to my place. I have nothing here." The request is right there, but I hold back. "And the Vols play at one, so I need my special shirt. How long will you be in meetings?"

"Until about twelve. Do you want me to meet you back here or at your place?"

"Just come to mine because I'll start cooking around twelve."

I raise a brow. "You're cooking?"

She opens one eye. "Yes, you have to have tailgating food for a Vols game."

"So, Vols games are a whole thing?"

"Oh, it's a huge thing. I'll have your shirt ready."

I chuckle as I lean down, pressing my lips to her forehead. "Sounds good. I'll see you in a bit."

I kiss her lips and then roll off the bed, but her hand catches my wrist. I look back at her, and she smiles sleepily. "I'll miss you."

I run my thumb along her wrist because if I kiss her, I'll never leave. She just obliterates me. "I love you, baby doll."

Her smile grows as she cuddles into my pillow. "I love you."

I sigh as I make myself get out of bed. I look back at her when I

189

TONI ALEO

reach the door, and her eyes are on me, a flush on that gorgeous face as the sun kisses her skin once more.

And just how I have to force myself from that room, I force myself to keep my fucking mouth shut.

"See you soon," she calls to me, and my heart aches.

"Not soon enough."

———

Me: There is a key on the counter to lock the dead bolt. There is food in the fridge since I ate the last piece of pizza. The coffee machine is a bitch, so tell me your order and I'll put it in down the road at the Dunkin'.

The Only Ten You'll Ever See: You ate my pizza. Rude.

Me: lol. My bad. I was in a rush.

Me: What do you want from Dunkin'?

The Only Ten You'll Ever See: I can order it myself. Aren't you busy?

I am, but Coach can't see me texting under the table.

"Miklas, you know I see you texting, right?"

I laugh at that while the guys razz me, and I lean back, meeting Coach's gaze. "My bad."

"Yeah, sure," he calls to me, and once he turns, I return to texting.

Me: I am, but I want to get you coffee since I didn't have the chance to get it for you this morning.

The Only Ten You'll Ever See: You're lucky my app isn't working. A caramel latte, please. Thank you.

I order it just as Coach turns, and I send her the confirmation, to which she sends me little hearts and kissy faces. My heart does a dance in my chest. I tuck my phone into my pocket and lean back in my seat, listening to our game plan for the game Sunday afternoon. We have morning skate again tomorrow, and I hate the dread that sits in my chest. The season is kicking off, about to be in full swing, and it worries me that Tennessee will hate it. She's made it clear she doesn't want space between us, but hell, this is my career. All of November, I'll be gone. It's one of the pitfalls of what I do. And it's why I don't have custody of Sabine.

HAT TRICK

I swallow thickly, knowing I'll have to see that look in Tennessee's eyes every time I have a road trip. I'll have to sleep without her. Won't be able to touch her. Kiss her. Man, this is gonna suck. As Coach breaks for a moment to take a long for a swig of his water, I lean into Owen.

"How do you handle you and Angie being apart when the season is going on?"

He looks over at me, his brows coming in. "FaceTime, and I'll send you the link on Amazon for a great vibrator for her and some good lube for you."

I just blink at him. He answered that like he was telling me the weather. "Thanks, buddy."

Owen nods, swiveling back and forth in his seat.

It's hard not to laugh, but now, instead of paying attention to the meeting, I'm thinking of all the naughty things I can say as Tennessee gets herself off. Which does nothing good for me since I have no clue what's going on in the meeting. I'll be okay, though; I know how to play hockey pretty well.

It's a long morning, but the reward will be seeing Tennessee and hopefully enjoying the game. I don't watch much football, but I have a feeling that's about to change very quickly. When I come out of my special teams meeting, my phone vibrates.

The Only Ten You'll Ever See: Are you not able to throw your condoms in the trash can?

I snort, and Owen gives me a weird look.

Me: Okay, listen. You drained me, like dead. I yanked it off and rolled over onto you.

The Only Ten You'll Ever See: I stepped on it.

A roar of laughter comes from me, and Owen's look deepens. "What the hell is so funny?"

I shake my head as I write her back, and Sawyer says, "Obviously whoever he is texting."

"Probably his girl. He's smitten."

Me: I'm sorry.

The Only Ten You'll Ever See: Are you laughing?

I laugh harder as Sawyer asks, "The girl who did our scans?"

191

TONI ALEO

"That's her, but keep it on the down-low," Owen says since I can't focus on shit but Tennessee.

Me: Absolutely not.

The Only Ten You'll Ever See: Yes, you are. I know you are.

Me: How?

The Only Ten You'll Ever See: Because I am, and there is obviously something wrong with us.

Me: Depends on who you ask. I am sorry, though. It won't happen again.

The Only Ten You'll Ever See: I don't think you can promise that.

Me: I can't, but I'll get a trash can for beside the bed.

The Only Ten You'll Ever See: Thank you.

The Only Ten You'll Ever See: Not to imply anything, but I have the rod in my arm to prevent little baby dragons. I haven't ever had sex without a condom, and my tests are clear.

My cheek burns as my cock comes alive in my pants, and I snicker.

Me: Don't threaten me with a good time, baby doll.

She sends me the peach emoji, eggplant emoji, and then the water droplets with the kissy face, and I've never loved emojis so much in my life.

"She's absolutely incredible."

"No. Tell me more," Owen deadpans, and Sawyer glances over at me.

"So, you're sprung, huh?"

"Oh, it's more than that," I say as I tuck my phone into my pocket. "I want to ask her to move in."

Sawyer makes a face. "Didn't you just meet her like yesterday?"

I shake my head. "No. We met this summer. We just linked back up."

"She tried to ghost him. It didn't work out well for her," Owen supplies, and Sawyer scoffs.

"I can tell. But still, it's a bit fast, isn't it?"

"Not if I know she's the one."

Sawyer looks between us, but Owen just shrugs. "Listen, when you know, you know. I have loved Angie for a long time, and I just wanted to skip all the middle stuff and jump into the good stuff, which is being her husband."

HAT TRICK

"Yeah, but you've known her our whole lives. He just met this girl," Sawyer says. "She could be a crazy person."

I shake my head as Owen pushes the door open, and we go through it. "The only crazy thing about her is her obsession with the Vols. But even with that, I love every single thing about her."

"Oh wow. Look who finally came around," Owen teases. "I knew you were smitten with her when you were lying on my couch crying—"

"I wasn't crying," I tell Sawyer, but he's laughing at Owen.

"She won't call me. My life is over. What do I dooooo?" he says, mocking me in a whiny voice. "It was the best nut of my life. Owen, how do I get her to answer me?"

"Now we all know you're lying. No one would ask for relationship advice from you," Sawyer teases as we head down the stairs of the practice arena. "I don't know. For me, I gotta know her before I bring her into my bed. I've been stalked, and it's no fun."

"That's doesn't sound ideal. But when you know, you know. And I know what I feel for her is real," I say, but then I see someone standing by my truck. "Who the fuck..." My sentence trails off when I realize who it is. "Come the hell on."

"Man, let me text Angie for bail money," Owen says as Bitchface turns to look at me, tucking his phone into his pocket.

He looks me over and then clears his throat. "Can we talk?"

Uninterested, I sigh. "I don't think we have anything to talk about."

"I'd like to speak to you, man-to-man," he says, his shoulders back and looking like he really thinks he's about to do something here. "Without an audience."

Owen scoffs. "Dude, we're here for your protection."

Sawyer crosses his arms over his chest. "Exactly."

Dipshit looks between all of us and then exhales. "I need to talk to you about Tennessee."

Just hearing her name on his lips makes me cringe. He says her name like the state and not how it's supposed to be said. Like a damn prayer. How did she ever date this fuck? "What about her?"

"I love her," he says simply, and I don't react. I just look down at him. "We are good together."

193

TONI ALEO

I rub my fingers over my mouth, not liking that at all. "I can promise you that the only person she's good with is me," I correct him, my eyes narrowing a bit. "She is mine."

Sawyer lets out a whistle, and Owen blows out a breath. "Yup, intense."

"You don't even know her," Creeper argues, and I scoff.

I hold up a finger for each of my points. "I know how to make her laugh. I know her favorite coffee order. I know she likes to sleep on me like a koala in a tree. And I know how to make her come. So, tell me what I'm missing." I hold up my hand to stop him. "Oh, and I know the lyrics to 'Rocky Top,' so I think I'm set."

Anger radiates off him, and to me, he looks like a pissed-off chicken. His neck is working, and his face is turning red. I'm trying not to be a dick and laugh in his face, but it's really hard. "What the fuck, man? I was with her first."

"Actually, I was," I tell him, and then I scrunch up my face. "Do you know how childish you sound?"

"For real, dude. You can have anyone. Why do you want her?"

Owen leans in. "Angie just texted and she's getting a pedicure, so I'd have to run to the bank."

But I'm not listening to Owen. "Why do I want her? Tennessee Lynn Dent? Why do I want *her*?" I repeat, glaring at him.

"Yeah, dude. You can have anyone, and guys like me can't. I'm a fucking ginger."

"Personal problem, I feel," I tell him, and that only makes him madder.

"Yeah, it is," he sneers. "Which is why I have to date fat girls."

My body goes taut, and Owen casually steps in front of me, whistling. His eyes meet mine, and he shakes his head. Owen then looks to SirFuckUp and says, "As a fellow lover of the Thicker than a Snicker Girl Club, I, for one, don't appreciate you calling my boy's girl fat, or assuming that women with fat on them don't deserve good-looking guys. Looks change. Who a person is doesn't. And you, fucker, are the worst kind of person." He takes a step forward, and Gingerfuck backs up. "And I suggest you get in your car and never show your face

HAT TRICK

around here again. 'Cause when you fuck with my dude, you fuck with me—and our whole team."

"Yeah, go fuck yourself," Sawyer calls to him.

Everything inside me is shaking. "I can't snap him in two, can I?"

Owen shakes his head. "He'll press charges, like the little bitch he is."

"You know she sucks in bed, right?" Momma's Boy calls to me, and Owen closes his eyes in disappointment. Just as he casually walked in front of me, he steps back, and I set Dingleberry with a look.

"Because she was faking every second with you," I say softly.

Sawyer sputters behind me, and Ballsac-Face says, "Whatever. I had her screaming my name—"

I don't even let him finish; my fist connects with his nose, and the crunching noise is wildly satisfying. I watch as he falls back, holding his face, and hits the ground right in front of my truck.

"Well, that's unfortunate you ran into Dart's hand," Owen says, clicking his tongue.

"Yeah, hopefully you didn't break it on his fist," Sawyer agrees, and I grab Gingerbitch's ankle, dragging him from in front of my car.

"Let me move you since you can't see," I say, dropping his leg as he hollers.

"Wow, Dart, you're so considerate," Owen says I walk to my truck. And while popping that dude in the nose isn't nearly enough to make him pay for what he said about my girl, I'll take it.

"It's the least I can do when I feel so awful he ran right into my fist," I say as Sawyer nods.

"I say fuck him," Sawyer calls to me, and I agree.

Owen hangs out his window to call to the walking pimple, "Hey, bro. I wouldn't show my face around here again."

Sawyer hangs out his car window as well and calls out, "Because it's only one fist you ran into today. It could be thirty next time, when the whole team rides up."

I get in my truck and start it. I nod a thanks to Owen and then one to Sawyer before I pull out, knowing good and well there is no other brotherhood I'd want to be a part of than the Carolina IceCats.

195

TONI ALEO

Before I drive away, I roll down the window as Beetledick gets up, holding his gushing nose. "In case it wasn't clear, no, you can't have Tennessee. Not only is she too fucking good for you, but she's mine. So, yeah. Have the day you deserve."

And I drive off, flipping him the bird.

CHAPTER
Twenty-Seven

Dart

The moment the door opens, I step inside her place, taking her in my arms and capturing her mouth instantly.

"Mmm," I growl against her lips, my hands going straight to her ass for a tight squeeze. "I missed you, baby doll."

Tennessee grins up at me, and damn, what a sight. "Same," she gushes, cupping my jaw. "I don't know why, but it's almost as if last night was a fairy tale or something from a movie."

"Was it the dragons or the stepping on a condom this morning that did it for you?"

She snorts against my lips as she strokes her hands over the small of my back. "Or maybe it's because I am deliriously happy."

Good God, I can't get enough of that grin.

"Mmm, I love hearing that," I mutter, kissing her again. I pull back as her thumb glides along my jaw, and I notice she isn't wearing what I thought she'd be wearing. I hold her out in front of me to check her out, and she gives me a confused look. "I thought you'd wear your boots and a lot more orange."

She smacks me playfully in just a Vols shirt and jeans. I totally

TONI ALEO

thought she'd be decked out. She turns, showing me her butt that has TN patches on the pockets. "I even have my Vols socks on."

She may be speaking, but all I'm doing is looking at her thick ass in some tight jeans with the UT patches that are fraying at the edges. I have half a mind to nibble them off, but I know she'd fight me on that. "Sorry, I was distracted by your ass."

She leans into me, laughing as I kiss her temple. I look around the room, and it's not what I expected. The walls are a boring white, and I don't know, I thought she'd have orange furniture or at least something UT on the walls.

"You're being super judgy, D'Artagnan."

I laugh, but I have to ask, "I'm not, but is this your place?"

"Yeah?"

"Is this your stuff?" I glance at her, and I can see she doesn't know why I'm asking. "This isn't your stuff, right? None of this is yours."

"What do you mean?"

"I don't know. I just expected more orange and, like, girlie shit," I say, looking around at the dullness. I know she just moved here, but this stuff doesn't seem right. "This place isn't you."

"It's not mine. The company furnished it for me. I just haven't had time to decorate or anything. Not that I want to. I hate everything in here."

"Where is your stuff?"

"In my bedroom. I pushed it all in there, so I would look like I had my shit together somewhat."

I perk my brow at her. "You didn't have to. I don't care about that."

She kisses my jaw, her eyes so bright. "You're too good to me. Your Vols shirt is in the room. Come on."

She takes my hand, guiding me down a short hall. "If you're bringing me back here to seduce me, the floor in the living room would have been fine."

She snickers at that, lacing her fingers with mine as she pushes open the door. "It's boring in here too."

She isn't kidding. I look at the queen bed. "That bed is small."

"Compared to yours, yes, it is. So don't be surprised when I stay at

HAT TRICK

your house more. I love your bed," she laughs as she walks to the bathroom door.

"You look fucking good in it," I tell her as I glance around. She sure as hell doesn't look good here. This place is more suited to a boring dude than someone like Tennessee. She brings the shirt to me, and I take it, still looking around. I pull off my white tee and throw it on with ease.

"What do you think?"

She leans down on the bed, her eyes trailing along my body as a sneaky grin pulls at her lips. "I'm thinking I wasn't prepared to see that shirt on you, and now I'm regretting that my bed isn't big."

I lean down, my fingers brushing hers as our noses almost touch. "We've made it very clear we don't need a bed."

"You got that right," she whispers, and I nip at her bottom lip. Her eyes drift shut, but then they open once more and she looks down at my hand. "What happened?" she asks, moving her fingers along my busted knuckles. "This looks new."

I stopped to wash my hands free of blood. But I got that fucker pretty good, and two of my knuckles are split. As our eyes meet, I know that lying isn't an option. That she deserves the truth. "That guy you thought you wanted to date asked me to let him have you back."

Her brows come in, amusement taking over her features. "You're kidding."

"Nope. And when I told him no, he said something I didn't like, and I cracked his nose."

Her eyes narrow as color fills her cheeks. "What did he say?"

"The normal toxic dickhead kind of shit where I can get any girl I want and that I should leave the thick ones for ugly fucks like him."

I refuse to use "fat." I don't like that word—except when it's spelled with a PH.

She raises a brow. "He said 'thick'?"

Now my gaze is narrowing. "Did he call you anything but beautiful, baby doll? 'Cause I'll fuck him up."

She climbs onto the bed, wrapping her arms around me, and I stand up so our bodies are flush. "No," she promises. "But I never thought he liked the way I looked."

199

TONI ALEO

"Because he has a shrimp dick, and only a real man can handle all this lovin'," I say, cupping her ass in my hands. I kiss her lips softly, rubbing her butt as she pulls back, gazing up at me.

"Dart," she purrs, bringing my hand to her lips, kissing my knuckles.

"Yes, baby doll?"

Her lips curve around my knuckles. "Please don't entertain him anymore. He doesn't matter."

I nod. "I know. I think I hate him because he was able to touch you when I couldn't." I thread my fingers through hers as she trails kisses down the back of my hand. "Does it bother you that I was with other women?"

Heat flashes in her eyes. "I don't give a shit who you were with as long as you are here with me now."

I grin. "Are you saying that so I don't hit Shrimp Fuck again?"

She meets my gaze. "No, I mean it. For me, it's not the past. It's the future."

I swear she has me under her spell. "I like that future part."

"So do I," she says, leaning in and pressing her nose to mine. "The game is about to start."

"Then we better get in there." I'm rewarded with a wide grin as I help her off the bed, but before I can follow her out, something catches my eye on the side table. I stop and pick it up as the air rushes out of me in a whoosh. I hold it up as I call her name. She turns, and a blush creeps along those cheeks. "You framed it?"

She nods, crossing her legs and arms like she's embarrassed. "I told you, I never stopped thinking of you."

My heart sings as I put the photo down and pull out my phone . I open it and turn it so she can see. "I put that as my wallpaper in the car on my way to the airport."

Her eyes soften as she closes the distance between us, wrapping her arms around my neck. "See? No one matters but us."

I kiss her nose and then her lip, knowing she's right. Sometimes I have guilt about how I handled her ghosting me, but I know I was only surviving. I was trying to find my heart, when it was in Virginia. But now, it's in front of me.

HAT TRICK

"Can I ask you something?"

"Do I love you? The answer is still yes, dragons and all."

I feign like I can't breathe. "Thank God. I was worried." She beams up at me, squeezing me tightly, and I ask, "Do you even like this apartment?"

I can tell she wasn't expecting that. She shrugs as she looks around. "I mean, it's okay. It's close to the practice arena but far from you, which sucks. Why do you ask?"

Fuck, my impulses are riding hard right now. "It just feels cold here. Like, not homey."

"It's not my home," she explains. "I didn't get to stay in my apartment in Virginia for long. And since I don't know what the company is planning, like, if I'll be traveling or whatever they are thinking, I didn't want to decorate, make this a home and stuff."

Well, I don't like the sound of that.

She takes a deep breath when I set her with a look that I know tells her how I feel. "I don't know that for a fact. But when the time comes, I'll need to figure out my next move."

I rub my jaw as I hold her gaze. "Which means?"

She swallows. "I don't know, 'cause I'm sure they'll want this apartment for someone else. If I quit—" Her words are cut off when "Rocky Top" starts playing. She takes out her phone and sighs. "Pause this, okay? My dad is calling."

I'd rather not, but I hold that in as she answers. "Hey, Daddy!"

I follow her down the hall, feeling a little shitty. I just assumed she'd never leave, but that was stupid of me. She has a career. She doesn't like distance. She's good at her job and loves it. Damn it, why am I thinking I'm just the placeholder? Fuck no. That is not what's happening. She is figuring it out. We're good.

"Who's that there in the Vols shirt?" her dad asks, and I look from the TV to her. I make an uh-oh face, but she doesn't seem worried at all. "Is that Troy? I thought he was a Virginia fan."

"He wouldn't even wear a shirt for you?"

She gives me a pointed look and doesn't answer me. "No, Dad. It's not Troy." Her eyes cut to mine again as a slow smirk comes over her face. "Wanna meet my boyfriend?"

201

TONI ALEO

Warm spreads across my chest as she holds out her hand to me, and of course, I go to her. I might be a fool, but I hope that isn't the case. Before I can reach her, though, her dad says, "I thought I did. Goofy ginger dude who doesn't know good college football?" I snort at that as I take her hand, and her dad says, "That's not the goofy dude."

She threads her fingers through mine. "Nope. This is D'Artagnan Miklas."

I look at the screen and see a huge, burly guy with a long beard and a UT cap on his head. He looks me over, and I say, "Nice to meet you, sir. My friends call me Dart."

All of a sudden, a woman is in his lap. "Damn, darling! You got my balls!"

"Mom!" Tennessee cries, but her mom steadies the phone, and the little smirk that Tennessee gives me is on her face. "What are you doing?"

Her mom is trying to hold in her laughter. "So, um, this all changed very quickly. You've been there not even a week, Tennessee Lynn."

I chuckle as Tennessee turns bright red. "Yes, ma'am. And wasn't it you who told me to talk to him?"

Her dad's brows come together as I say, "Thank you for that. It obviously worked out for us."

"Obviously."

Then her dad lets out a loud whoop, "Hold up! Is this *him*?" he draws out, and more color fills Tennessee's face. "The *guy*," he says, making the word longer than it is, "from Nashville?"

"Momma, you told him!"

Her mom makes a face. "Yes, but only because Daddy has been bitching that Troy is trash. And I knew he'd be gone the moment you saw Dart."

"Wait, what did she tell him?" I ask, and Tennessee raises her brows at me.

"About how you two met," her dad sings. "I should kick your ass."

I press my lips together. "For buying her tequila shots at ten a.m.?"

Tennessee sputters with laughter, as does her mom. "Among other things," he says, giving us a look that tells me he knows we spent the night together.

HAT TRICK

"Wow. This is embarrassing," I mutter, looking away, and Tennessee just gawks at her mom. I clear my throat. "So, in my defense, it's all her fault. And then she ghosted me."

She smacks me, and I laugh along with her parents. I catch her hands, laughing as I bring her in, wrapping them around her back as I walk her out of view. "Thanks," she says through gritted teeth.

I grin down at her, kissing her nose. "Am I lying?"

"Yes. You came on to me."

I laugh at that. "Who was in whose bed?"

"D'Artagnan," she warns, and I can't help but kiss her nose once more.

"You're super-hot when you're having a fit," I tease in my best country drawl.

She isn't impressed. "I'mma beat you seven ways to Sunday!" she warns, and I laugh as she drags me back into the view of the camera.

"Tennessee Lynn, I haven't seen you smile like that in years," her mom says, and I cuddle my girl into my chest as that fills me with pride.

'Cause I know I make her happy.

"Neither have I," her dad says, "Listen, I want y'all to come up for a game. Just let me know when, and I'll make sure we have our box."

Tennessee lays her hand on my chest. "Daddy, Dart plays professional hockey. I don't know if he'll have time."

"We can look at my schedule," I tell her. "I'd love to come out."

She looks up at me with appreciation. "Really?"

"Yeah. Why wouldn't I?"

"You travel a lot, though," she says, and I can tell she's not the happiest about it.

"Yeah. But I'll do more if I'm going with you."

"Great!" her mom says. "Get us a date. 'Cause, boy, you look good in orange!"

"Mom, are you hitting on my boyfriend?" I laugh along with her parents as Tennessee adds, "But yeah, he does look mighty fine in orange."

I kiss her temple, unable to resist, as her mom says, "So, is Troy still gonna live there?"

TONI ALEO

I drag my lips from Tennessee's head. "I'm sorry?"

"Yeah. But I'm not the least bit worried about him."

"He lives *here*?" I ask, and she laughs as she shakes her head.

"No, in the building. His unit is upstairs."

I really don't fucking like that.

"Which, by the look on your face, you may have an issue with," she says, working her lip.

From the phone, her dad says, "Whoo-wee, Marcy baby. You may have started something."

Tennessee looks at them. "Ya think? Let me call y'all back." She hangs up her phone and looks over her shoulder at me. "I should have told you that, but I forgot."

"Between when I told you I kicked his ass and now? You totally forgot about him living in the same building as you?"

She holds up her palms to me. "I did because I don't care about him."

"Baby, he's got fucking stalker vibes. But I can't stay in this apartment. For one, I'm about to start road trips—"

"You are?"

My heart goes cold in my chest. "Yeah. I leave next week for a four-day trip."

She presses her lips together. "Well, that blows."

"I know," I agree, holding her anxious gaze. "But that's what I mean. I have to leave you, and you think I can do that when he's in your building?"

"I wouldn't cheat on you."

I laugh at that. "Baby doll," I say, taking her hips in my hands. "I'd never think that." I bring her in close. "For me, it's that I'm not here to protect you."

She leans into my chest, tracing the UT on my shirt. "You don't have to worry about him. He won't do anything."

I cup her jaw, squeezing her as I tip her face up to look at me. "I would kill for you. You don't know what you do to me, and we don't know what he is capable of."

Her eyes swirl with desire. "You really are passionate, huh?"

"Especially for the ones I love." I trail my thumb along her bottom

HAT TRICK

lip before dragging it down, loving how full her lip is. As much as I want to kiss her, get lost in these insanely plump, gorgeous lips, I have to say something. I can't hold it back. I won't. "Tennessee?"

"Yes, D'Artagnan?" she purrs, running her tongue along my thumb, sending chills down my spine.

As I gaze down at her, my heart pounding in my chest, I say what I've wanted to say since the moment I saw her in my bed. "Move in with me."

CHAPTER
Twenty-Eight

TENNESSEE

Lordy, he is so intense.

His jaw is taut.

His body is hard against mine, but it's those eyes that have me breathless. I know instantly he's not joking. He means what he is asking. He wants it. Needs it, maybe, and his gaze leaves me winded.

"With you looking at me like that, I'm having a hard time saying no."

"Then don't," he announces, snaking his arm around me so our bodies are flush. "Why fight what we both want?"

He's not wrong. "Are we crazy?"

A smirk comes over his lips. "Am I crazy for you? Yes, but I don't know if I'd say *we're* crazy."

"Dart, moving in together is a huge step in a relationship. We've been dating—"

"We're not dating."

"What?"

"Dating is trivial. What we are doing is building a life, because for me, there will be no one else but you. I don't just want to get my fill of

HAT TRICK

you and move on. I want to build a life. Us, Tennessee. What we want."

Come the hell on! He's basically laying it out for me. Offering me everything I've ever wanted. A man and a life I could love. The possibility of a future. Happiness. "You're killing me," I tell him, gazing up at him. "It just feels so right."

He nods. "Because it is. Tennessee, I've never lived with anyone but teammates. But before I even found out about that dickhead living here, I wanted you to live with me." My breath catches as he holds my gaze. "I love you in my kitchen, how you lie in my lap, how good you look in my bed, and I swear, we can hang up some orange shit if that's what you want. I just want my home to be yours."

Oh, heart be still, and brain shut the hell up. Those two never agree on shit! My heart is screaming, fuck yes! And my brain is saying, what if he gets bored with me? But even that doesn't feel right. Those are my insecurities talking. Because Dart does nothing that doesn't reflect his true intentions. His passion.

Still, I can't help but tell him, "I'm messy."

"So am I."

"I like to snack at night."

"We'll make sure we have enough for both of us."

"Sometimes even breathing is hard, and I just want to identify as a sloth."

"That sounds like a damn good time."

"You'll have to commit to the orange."

"No issue as long as you commit to me."

"Are you sure?"

He only nods, his eyes burning into mine. "I've never been as sure of something in my life until I fell in love with you."

I have to be insane. That's the only reason why my response comes so easily. "I'm yours, D'Artagnan."

"I know," he murmurs as his mouth drops to mine. "I've always known that."

Our lips barely touch as I whisper, "So have I."

"So, yes?" he asks, his eyes dancing with mine.

"Yes."

TONI ALEO

As our lips meet, I wait for the fear. The thoughts that the distance we'll have to deal with will break me or he'll find someone else.

But it never comes.

———

Lordy, my daddy is gonna have some words for me.

In my half-up hairdo, I've tied a black-and-red ribbon for the IceCats. On my body, I'm wearing a huge #11 Miklas black jersey with glittery red trim. Not a lick of orange is on my body, and while I know it's wrong in my mom's and dad's eyes, it feels right. This jersey feels like home. Like Dart's arms are around me, holding me tightly, and he's whispering sweet nothings in my ear. My ticket took me five rows up from the ice, and the game hasn't even started, but everyone is ready. The air is electric, loud, and truth be told, I may be a hockey fan. A giggle escapes my lips just knowing my daddy is gonna lose his mind.

Because I'm not an Assassins fan, but a fan of the IceCats.

Or better yet, number eleven's fan.

The crowd goes crazy when the jumbotron tells them to, and then the team is skating out onto the ice. I stand up to get a better look, and when Dart hits the ice, everything goes molten inside me. While I thought he was breathtaking on my ESPN app, nothing could have prepared me for seeing him live on that ice. He skates with such confidence and ownership. His stick is an extension of himself, and he takes a puck, bouncing it on his blade with ease.

That's my man.

Lordy.

I'm knocked from the thirst trap that is Dart when someone comes to stand beside me. I look over as she smiles at me, and I'm taken aback by her beauty. Long, darkish-blond hair with the cutest bangs ever. Her green eyes are mesmerizing and beautiful behind her dark-rimmed glasses. She has on an IceCats jersey too, and I swear I know her from somewhere. Or maybe I've seen her before.

"Hey. Sorry I'm late," she says happily, throwing her bag into the seat beside me.

HAT TRICK

I look around, confused. "Wait? Are you talking to me?"

She laughs. "Yes, silly! I'm Owen's wife—" she starts, but then she giggles loudly. "I love saying that! Which is crazy 'cause when we were younger, I hated him."

I just blink, utterly bewildered, then it dawns on me. "Owen, Dart's best friend. You're Angie! The bride to his dude of honor!"

"That's me," she says, tucking her hands into her pockets. "And you're Tennessee. Man, girl, you put my boy through hell!"

I inhale sharply, my eyes widening. "Owen told me y'all didn't hate me."

"I don't," she says, waving me off. "I get it, believe me. I wanted to ghost Owen, but I didn't have the distance you had to try to outrun him."

"I don't think there is any outrunning Dart," I tell her, knowing it's the truth. "Like my momma said, I was here a week and couldn't resist him from the moment our eyes met."

Angie snickers. "Yup, Dart called that."

"Did he?" I laugh and she nods.

"God yes, he intended on scooping you up when you guys went to the coffee shop."

My face burns. "I felt that, but he gave me space."

"He didn't want to. I can tell you that for sure."

"I know," I say softly. "I'm not a fan of space between him and me."

"Who would be? Do you know what it's like to be in a room with you two?"

I bring in my brows, and then I giggle. "I mean, I know what I feel... How do you know?"

Her eyes are bright. "Tennessee, I was at that party. A lot of people were."

I gawk at her as I feel my face burn with heat. "I don't even remember seeing anyone but Owen. Later..."

She laughs. "Exactly! You two are fire together," she tells me. "I'm not even the least bit surprised you two have moved in together already."

I press my lips together to keep from grinning like a fool. I don't

TONI ALEO

know why her approval of our choice to move in together means so much to me, but it does. "You don't think we're crazy?"

She scoffs, waving me off. "Not at all. When you know, you know."

"Exactly," I gush, turning to her. "I feel like I've known him forever."

Angie's eyes sparkle, or maybe it's the lights flashing. I don't know. "My girl Taylor Swift sang about twenty seconds and twenty years being the same thing," she says with a wink, and I laugh at that.

Because lordy me, I *feel* those lyrics. Deeply.

I didn't even hesitate when, after the Vols game, Dart packed up all my boxes and moved me out in a matter of minutes. Not that I had much to take. I really did sell a lot before I left Virginia, but I was ready. I wanted to leave that apartment; it held nothing I wanted. I want what his—I mean, our—home offers. Us, together.

Dart helped me clean the apartment and get it ready for whoever the company wants to have in it next. I sent the email that I moved out yesterday, and I haven't heard anything from the higher-ups. I'm not sure if that's a good thing or a bad one. Even so, my leads are coming in, and I have meetings out the ass for the next two weeks. I'll need them. Especially with Dart traveling. Something I'm not ready for at all, but I know is part of the deal with loving a hockey player.

"He makes it real easy to be completely crazy with," I admit, and her eyes are so kind and loving.

"That's Dart for you. His passion is intoxicating. And the way he tells you exactly what he is thinking…" She laughs a bit, shaking her head. "He's a mess for sure," she admits, and I hear a bit of Nashville twang.

I want to agree with her, gush over him, but then I realize something. "Are you and Owen from Tennessee? Is that why the wedding was there?"

"Yeah, both Owen and I grew up there. Our dads played hockey together for the Nashville Assassins."

"No way!" I exclaim, and she nods.

"Yeah. His dad is Shea Adler, and mine is Benji Paxton."

I gawk at her. "*The* Shea Adler?"

She grins. "*The* Shea Adler."

HAT TRICK

"So, no wonder Owen is so handsome. Shea is gorgeous." I quickly hold up my palm. "I mean that with all the respect in the world."

She's not the least bit offended. "Girl," she says, leaning in, "you should see Shea Adler in person—like, in your face, telling you you're the best thing for his son. I looked to the heavens and thanked the Lord that Shea Adler is my man's dad, 'cause Owen is only going to keep getting hotter with age."

"No shit," I agree, and we both laugh as we lean into each other. Wow. I like her. A lot. "That's crazy cool."

"Yeah, and like his dad, he's solid, wonderful, and makes me feel like the most gorgeous girl in the world. I hit the jackpot."

I wonder if I look like her when I speak about Dart. That awestruck look in my eyes, the parting of my lips, always waiting for Dart's to press against them. The heat burning my cheeks and every single inch of my insides. I know I do, because I feel what she is feeling right now. I did hit the jackpot, ten times over.

I look out at the ice, seeing as Dart shoots the puck and then skates around the net with ease. As I watch him, excitement burns in me, not only because he's gorgeous to watch, but that I'm almost done with his assessment. I can't wait to show him my findings. He's been asking, but I don't want to show him until I'm done and have a plan. Until I know he'll be impressed by what I have to say. Though, knowing him, I could show him a stick drawing on a sheet of paper, and he'd tell me it's the best thing he's ever seen.

Lordy, I'm so in love with him.

And hot diggity dog, he looks so damn good out there. The black of his jersey brings out his eyes and amplifies his neck tattoo, making him look really dangerous and sexy. The intensity in his eyes to make the shot reminds me of when I'm under him, screaming his name. The way he grips his hands along his stick, his ease of moving the puck, leaves me yearning and breathless. I watch as he skates toward the bench, and a trainer, a woman, throws him a water bottle. I'm sure she's watching him as closely as I am because this fine specimen of a man squirts his face, his hair, the back of his neck, and the front of his jersey, dousing himself with the water.

I've never wanted to identify as a water bottle so much in my life.

TONI ALEO

He shakes his head, water spraying everywhere, and my mouth goes dry. My heart slams into my ribs, and I pull my gaze away. If I keep watching him, I'm going to find my way onto that ice, and I'm not sure the rink people would appreciate us melting it.

Because we would. Ten times over.

I swallow, needing a distraction. "Have you and Owen been together for a long time?"

"We grew up together, but we didn't hook up until a couple years ago." Her eyes are on her husband, and I adore the tip of her lips. "I didn't like him growing up because he's cocky as all hell, but when we found ourselves in the same place—me, here for school, and him, here for hockey—I realized that I wasn't happy unless I was with him." She looks over at me and smiles. "Now, life has no meaning unless he's in it."

I look away, my heart slamming into my chest because her words describe how I feel about Dart. I haven't told my parents about my moving in with him yet, and I know they're gonna freak out. I've only known him a short time, but how can I deny what I am feeling? I dated Denis for ten years, and never once did I want the things I want with Dart. As much as reason tries to play in my head, my heart won't allow it.

It's his.

"Did Dart tell you he picked out my wedding dress?"

I shift my gaze back to Angie's. "No. Really?"

"Yes!" she gushes. "I had four, I think, and I hated them. All of them. Because I didn't think I looked good enough for Owen. But Dart comes along and picks out the most revealing dress and looks me right in my face and tells me that Owen has never made me feel anything other than wanted, so I should wear what makes me feel beautiful." Her eyes dust a bit with tears as she holds my gaze. She looks away, opening her phone and showing me a photo of her and Dart at her wedding. That suit looks real good on him, but it looked better on the floor of his hotel room. Angie, though, she is stunning, and the look of pure bliss on her face leaves me gasping.

"Oh Angie, you're perfect."

HAT TRICK

She nods. "I have never felt more beautiful in my life than I did that day, and I owe a lot of it to Dart."

In awe, I press my hand to my gut. "How incredible."

Her eyes are intoxicating. "You know, he told me about you that day."

"What? No way."

"Yeah," she insists, leaning into me. "Said it was one of the hardest things he ever did, choosing being my dude of honor over you."

I wave her off. "There was no choice. Please."

"For him, there was," she tells me, and I feel like we're the only ones here. Her words feed my soul and only make me love Dart more. "I think I knew then he had fallen in love. And believe me, I have watched him fool around for a long time, but he has never spoken about anyone the way he does you." I press my lips together as I inhale deeply through my nose. "Dart has my heart. Such a good dude, loyal to a fault, and so passionate."

"Very passionate," I agree as I look out on the ice, and my eyes instantly fall on him. He and Owen are passing the puck between them like it's a hacky sack. "I love him greatly."

"Not surprised." I feel her looking at me, and I look over to meet her gaze. "Not to sound like an overprotective best friend, but don't hurt him, okay?"

There is an edge to her voice, and I respect it. "I don't intend to."

She nods, her eyes searching mine. "I believe you wholeheartedly, and I know he can feel very scary and impulsive—he is—but from what he told me, you go with it."

"It's easy when I want the same things he wants."

Her lips curve. "Good. It's hard being a hockey player's girlfriend, and even a wife," she says, directing her gaze to where the guys are. I follow her eyes as she continues, "They're sought out, desirable, and tempted at every turn."

"I know he'd never step out on me," I tell her, and she nods.

"Good. But a bit of advice."

I look back at her.

"Don't believe a damn thing your brain tells you," she begs, her eyes holding mine. "Trust him, because he really does love you."

TONI ALEO

My heart skips a beat. "Dart must have told you I was nervous about the road trip," I say, my face burning a bit. "I've never dated an athlete before, but I trust him completely."

"I get it," she says with a nod. "Space is not ideal when it comes to someone you love, but please don't ever forget what you just told me."

"I won't."

"It's easy to say, but being away from Owen physically hurts, and of course, my trauma of being hurt left and right by assholes comes into play a lot. But know you're not alone, Tennessee. We'll exchange numbers. We can do things or even just lie around the house."

"You don't even know me!" I say, grinning at her.

"We'll get to know each other, because if Dart adores you, I know I will." She says it so confidently, just knowing I'll be worthy of her friendship. But it's hard to believe her when the women who were supposed to be my sisters basically treated me like dirt.

And they never rode as hard for me as she is.

"I appreciate that."

"Absolutely. And listen, it sucks being without them, but it only makes the homecoming that much better."

My lips tip up at that.

"Because I know Owen comes home ravenous, and I can't get enough."

"I have to admit, that part, I look forward to."

"It's the best," she says with a wink.

I grin at her. "Did we just become friends?"

"We totally did. And when you meet the other wives, you'll love them. We're a family, Tennessee. And again, you'll never be alone."

Her loyalty is overwhelming. Or maybe Lindy and Josie were never truly my friends. They never made me feel this included, and she just met me. In the short time I've been talking to Angie, I feel as if I've known her forever. It's odd but exciting at the same time. It seems that has been the theme of my life since meeting Dart. The instant connections, the faith that fate has me, and it's beyond anything I could have ever asked for. As my eyes fall to Dart once more, watching him do what he loves, I feel my heart slam into my chest just as hard as he slams his blade into the puck. He looks up, and our eyes meet, heat coursing through me. His lips curve into that easy, gorgeous grin, and he winks. It's a simple motion—silly, even. Just a smile for me, but I realize I want more.

I may have left home to find myself, and I did, but what I didn't realize was that I was meant to find the missing parts of my heart.

The parts I gave him.

My love.

Number 11, D'Artagnan Miklas.

CHAPTER
Twenty-Nine

Dart

My bag for my road trip is packed and by the front door, and that's where it'll wait until I get as much as I can of Tennessee.

I pull my jersey off her body, throwing it to the floor before the backs of her knees hit the bed and she sits that sweet ass down. She pulls off the shirt she has on underneath and unhooks her bra as I push her legs open, stepping between them. I take ahold of her left breast, squeezing it as I whisper, "I loved seeing you in my sweater, but I love you like this a hell of a lot more."

"You're entirely overdressed," she accuses, and I grin before I take her chin, tipping it up to meet my gaze. The red-and-black ribbon from her hair falls into her face, and I'm a goner. I drag my thumb along her plump bottom lip, and when she nips at the tip, my cock throbs at her naughtiness.

"I love you."

Her lips curve ever so slightly. "I love you."

Each time she says those three words, I feel like it's my first time hearing them.

She reaches out, her eyes locked with mine as her fingers make quick work of my belt buckle and then the button of my suit pants. They fall from the weight of my belt in the loops before I push down my boxers and step out of them, while she scoots up the bed, undoing her jeans. I grab the bottom of the legs, pulling the denim off her and to the floor before her panties follow. I move my eyes along her body, and I lick my lips when I get to her center, where she opens her legs for me. I start to unbutton my shirt. I want this to last, but I know it won't.

She shatters me.

Each button of my shirt is torture, and I almost rip it off. But instead, I drag my gaze back up to hers. "Touch yourself."

Her eyes widen. "What?"

"You heard me," I demand, my cock aching for attention. "Slide those fingers between those sweet thighs, Tennessee. Get yourself ready for me."

"I'd rather you touch me."

"I don't care. I want to make sure you can pleasure yourself when I'm unable to touch you and you only have my words."

Her breath catches as she lifts her hand from the bed, dragging it along her stomach. I throw off my shirt and put my knee on the bed, catching her wrist in my hand. I bring her fingers to my lips, sucking two into my mouth as she lets out a long, lusty sigh. Her eyes are dark, full of hunger, as I take her fingers from my mouth and guide them between her legs. I sit back as she slides her fingers between those slick lips, and a soft moan leaves her lips, causing every part of my body to go rigid.

"Fuck," I mutter, my heart pounding in my chest. "Find your clit, baby doll. Just like that. Mmm, I love that," I compliment as she swirls her fingers over her clit. She jerks against her hand, and a deep groan bursts from my chest as my own hands shake. I roll onto my stomach to keep from touching myself and move up the bed to where my mouth is right at her ear. She turns her head to kiss me, but I pull back, shaking my head. "Oh no. You only get my words, my greedy girl."

"Dart, please." Her words are strangled and dark, and I love how they make me feel.

"Begging won't work. Show me how badly you want me."

"I do," she cries, arching up as I trail my tongue along the shell of her ear, my body trembling everywhere. "Only you."

"God, your body is my heaven," I whisper in her ear, licking her lobe. "I want you so badly."

"Take me. Hard."

Fuck me.

"I will as soon as you come," I demand, sitting up on my elbow to watch her touch herself. The slickness of her desire is all over those sweet lips, her fingers, her thighs, and my mouth goes dry at the stunning sight that is her.

"Yes, Tennessee. Rock those hips. Think of my mouth right there, me flicking my tongue along that clit of yours, the raw need I have for you. Always have. My need to taste you, devour you. Fuck, baby, yes."

Her fingers move faster, her moans deep as her body flushes, making it real hard not to touch her. She takes her breast with her free hand as she fingers her slick center and her heels dig into the bed, and I've never seen anything as hot as her in my life.

"Do you know how gorgeous you are? How fucking hot you make me? I think of you constantly, Tennessee. Don't stop. You're almost there. I can see it. I can feel it. Aren't you, baby? Aren't you almost there?"

She turns her head, her teeth sinking into my shoulder, and I hiss out a breath, the pain so fucking good. That almost does me in. That almost has me taking over and being the one to bring her over the edge, but I can't move. I want to see her come.

"Come for me, baby. Come," I demand. "So I can go so deep into you, feel every inch of your sweet pussy. Come, Tennessee. Please. For me."

A choked sound leaves her lips as she seizes up, her thighs squeezing together, and I can't even think straight. She arches up, every inch of her body flushed red, and I can't keep myself still any longer.

"That's my good girl," I murmur as I move over her, trailing kisses along her chest, her stomach, before I lap at her center. She squirms under me, my name falling from her lips, begging me, and as much as I want to give in, I can't yet. I grab her wrist, taking her fingers into my

HAT TRICK

mouth, wanting to taste every bit of her desire as her eyes open to meet mine. I run my tongue along her wrist, her palm, then those fingers again, her desire doing a number on my body. "Fuck, you taste so fucking good."

"You make me crazy," she accuses, and I kiss her palm.

"Nothing compares to how you make me feel," I tell her before kissing her center, the jerk of her body such a reward. "I love looking at you like this."

She takes a deep breath, her eyes dark with desire as I cover her body with mine, taking that pouty mouth. She kisses with such urgency, and I feel the same since I know I'm leaving in a matter of hours. I didn't expect the pain that comes along with that fact. I have never thought twice about how much I travel until she came into my life. Until she became mine.

But I can't think of that now.

I tear my mouth from hers, licking and sucking on her jaw, her neck, and collarbone. I drag my tongue between her breasts before showing love to both of her taut nipples. I need to relish her and slow this down because I don't want it to end. As I suck her nipple into my mouth, I reach down, taking her by the back of her knee as I press my other hand into the bed, lifting myself up, pulling her nipple with my teeth as she hisses. I thought I was in control until she rubbed her slick center along my cock. I look down at her, and her lips curve just for me as she takes me by my cock and rubs it along her wetness.

"You feel that?" she asks, her eyes burning into mine. "You do this to me. You make me so wet, D'Artagnan. Always so wet. Only for you," she murmurs, and if she hadn't said my name, I would have forgotten it.

I'm lost in her.

She guides me to her entrance, but I catch her wrist. "Baby, I need a condom."

She shakes her head. "No, you don't."

I swallow past the lump in my throat, and a sane person would think this through, but I have no sane thoughts when it comes to her. I hook her leg around my hip as I move my hand to her chin, gripping it

TONI ALEO

between my thumb and forefinger. "Baby doll, take a deep breath for me."

Her eyes burn into mine as I slide my hand down her jaw to her neck, clutching it in desperation. She does as I ask, taking in the deepest of breaths, and I thrust into her as I squeeze her neck. She lengthens her neck, her eyes falling shut as she stretches around me, squeezing me and driving me wild. She tilts her hips, and I go deeper, every inch of me inside her. My grip on her tightens as I thrust into her, the thump of my thighs hitting her ass a sound I never want to forget. Music to my ears. Her pussy tightens around me, and she meets my hips with her own as I groan deeply just for her.

"I'm almost there," she somehow gets out, and I want her there. "Are you… Dart, are you almost there?"

"Fuck, baby, yes, I'm always there when I'm with you."

Our eyes meet, and the heat is all-consuming. She pushes her hands into my shoulders and rolls us over before she takes me to fill her once more. I hold her hips as she bounces on my cock, her tits jiggling with the motion before I slide my hands up her thighs, and then I sit up. I take her ass with one hand, squeezing her as I wrap my other arm around her waist. "I can't get enough of you," I mutter against her neck as she rides my cock, her fingers biting into my shoulders. "Ride me, Tennessee. Harder. Yes, my love. Fuck, you drive me crazy."

"Touch me please," she begs, and I do as she asks, unwrapping my hand from around her and pressing my thumb into her clit. "Oh God, yes!"

Her hips move faster as I circle my thumb along her clit, and I feel her tightening around me, driving me insane. "Faster, baby. Fuck yes."

"Come with me," she demands as she grinds into my thumb, my cock going deeper with each rock of her hips. "I want every ounce of your come, D'Artagnan. Now. Fucking come in me now!" she screams, and I don't know how or if this is actually real life, but I come so hard, I feel like I'm not even in my own body. Like she isn't real, but then I feel her squeezing me like a vise.

Her body trembles against mine as I drag my lips along her jaw,

HAT TRICK

and I gasp for breath. When my lips meet hers, I murmur, "You are unreal."

"I'm yours."

I wrap my arms around her as she does the same. Our mouths meet, and the world fades away, leaving just us.

Just our love.

———

I move Tennessee's wild hair out of her face as she gazes up into my eyes. Her arms are wrapped around my chest, while one of my hands holds the back of her neck, and I'm cupping her jaw with the other. We spent the night making love and I'm exhausted, but I figure I'll sleep on the plane. My bags are waiting for me, the suit I wear is tailored to my body, but my heart is right here, staring up at me. When a tear escapes down her cheek, I brush it away with my thumb as I spread my fingers beneath her ear, and my heart pounds in my chest. She lets out a choked laugh as she closes her eyes, the tears wetting her long lashes.

"It's stupid to cry. I know—"

"Tears aren't stupid. They're what happens when emotion takes over," I whisper, stroking my thumb along her cheek. "I love that you get emotional for me."

"But it's not like you're leaving for six months. It's only a couple days," she tries, and I know she's justifying her tears when she doesn't need to.

"For me, these couple days will feel like six months," I tell her, squeezing her to me.

Her lips part as she sighs deeply. "Exactly."

She rises on her toes, pressing her mouth to mine softly. She draws the kisses from me, slowly and with such tenderness. With each kiss, each swipe of our tongues, we clutch each other tighter as the kiss deepens, and when we part, we're both gasping for breath. I kiss her nose then the spot between her brows. "I'm going to miss you, Tennessee."

She swallows thickly. "Does that mean you gotta go?"

TONI ALEO

"I do," I say reluctantly, the clock on the stove taunting me. "I've heard Owen honk twice now."

She doesn't care; she doesn't want me to go just as badly as I don't want to go. Which isn't me. I love all aspects of being a professional hockey player. The different cities, different hotels, different food, but it doesn't hold the same appeal it used to, when I know my girl won't be with me. When I know she'll be alone.

"I'll miss you more," she tells me, kissing my lips once more. "But I'll be fine."

A grin pulls at my lips as I run my thumb along the brave pout of her lips. "I know you will," I agree, kissing the spot I just touched.

"I love you, D'Artagnan."

She makes me melt. "I love you too, baby doll. I'll text you."

Our lips meet once more for a quick kiss before I let her go, even though I'd rather not. She stands in only my shirt, Vols socks on her feet, as she watches me gather my things. I look back at her, and she forces herself to smile for me. "Till next time, D'Artagnan."

I give her a pointed look. "Last time you said that, I waited three months for you."

"That will never happen again," she promises as another tear falls. I almost go to wipe it away, but I know I'll never leave. I think she knows it too, because she wipes it away quickly. "I'll be here, the one waiting."

My heart catches in my chest, and nothing could have prepared me for the crushing love that hits me like a wave in the ocean. I welcome it, though. I crave it, just like I crave her. "Sooner rather than later, eh?"

She nods, swallowing as I turn. I can't look back as I go out the door, but before I even get to Owen's truck, my phone sounds with a notification. I throw my bag into the back and notice the notification is on Instagram.

I get in the truck, and Owen asks, "Tennessee okay?"

"Yeah, she's good," I say as I click it to see that I've been tagged in a status.

Tennessee's status.

I open it to see her at the arena, looking fucking delectable in my

HAT TRICK

jersey as she stands in front of the ice, making a heart with her hands. While the photo has my heart swelling, it's the caption that does me in.

I met somebody with blue eyes, who opens my door, and he makes me feel so damn loved. He isn't from where I am, but he sure feels like home to me. And he definitely has me doing things I've never imagined doing.

In Tennessee, they may call it a sin, and I still want the Nashville Assassins to win, but I'm wearing red and black for him. Rootin' for the IceCats. — Inspired by the lyrics by Megan Moroney but changed up for my #11, my heart, my soul. (Sorry, Daddy!)

I swallow past the lump in my throat and quickly type the only words I can even think at the moment.

I love you.

CHAPTER
Thirty

Dart

I line up for the face-off, my eye on the puck as the ref has the Blackhawk player move back a bit since he's a cheating bastard. "Back up. I'm not your momma's tit," I call to him around my mouth guard.

"Fuck you. I'll be looking for your mom after this, Miklas."

I laugh as the ref tries to get our attention, but I ignore him, calling to the dumbass, "Listen, I don't need another stepdaddy." I win the puck, throwing it back to Kirby, who skates with ease, carrying the puck as we forwards rush the goal. Kirby skates backward, moving the puck back and forth as he looks for an opening, but their defense is on it. He takes the shot, hoping for something, but it's blocked before it gets to the net. I fight a player for it before poking it out from underneath another player, and the puck flies to the boards, where luckily, Owen rushes for it. Once it's on his stick, he sends it up the boards, and it hits Chandler's blade, but he passes it quickly to Sawyer, who takes the shot, going wide. Kirby reaches out, catching the puck on his blade before it goes over the blue line.

While I'm thankful for another chance, I can't breathe and need the change, but I get back into position, watching as Chandler and Kirby

HAT TRICK

pass it back and forth, trying to draw someone toward them so we can get a clean shot. I skate back, fighting a defenseman and trying to block the goalie so that the puck can get past him. The defenseman doesn't let me get close and keeps knocking me in my side as we fight for the position. He wants me to move, but I want us to score, so I hold my own. I jab my elbow into the defenseman as Kirby lines up, faking the shot and passing it right to Owen.

I push into the dude, trying my best to be a distraction, but when Owen slaps his blade into the puck, it's not at the goalie, it's at me. We've practiced this a ton of times, and this is going to be sick if we pull it off. With my eyes on the puck, even though it's going at speeds unknown, I lift my stick, barely making sure not to go above the cross-bar, and deflect the puck into the back of the net.

The red light flicks on, and I throw my hand up as the goalie sinks into the goal. Owen comes for me, crashing into me as we celebrate the goal, shaking me violently. "That's why you're my best fucking friend!"

I laugh as he shakes me, and then we head to slap hands with the guys on the bench.

We've won, taking three of the four games for this trip. I didn't get any hat tricks, which is disappointing since Tennessee said she'd be wearing nothing but my hat for me when I got home if I did, but I did pretty well. Five goals and four assists. The feeling of scoring is one I'll never get used to, probably as much as I won't get over missing Tennessee for as long as she and I are apart on all the road trips to come. These last few days have been rough without being able to touch her or hold her when I drift off to sleep, especially after spending months yearning just for that. It was as if I got a bit of a taste before it was me leaving this time. But there is no ghosting whatsoever, and thankfully, FaceTime has been our savior. We talk every chance we get, and my baby doll follows directions very well. And watching her come is probably my favorite thing in the world. Who am I kidding? Everything about her is my favorite.

I come out of the shower, heading to my locker area, when I notice my phone is ringing. I reach for it to see it's Sabine. I grin as I sit down, answering her FaceTime.

225

TONI ALEO

"Great game!" she gushes, and I return her smile as I run the towel over my hair.

"Thank you, sunshine. Isn't it late? Shouldn't you be in bed?"

She shrugs. "Mom is out, so I'm just hanging out watching hockey."

I press my lips together and hold in my irritation. I had just sent my mom money earlier that morning. If she didn't have the money for groceries, how does she have money to go out? "Where is she?"

"I don't know. I heard her and Jasmine get into it about Jasmine staying late to watch me. I think she's going to quit nannying me," she says sadly. "Which is another reason I called."

Well, that's not good, but I try not to let that be known. I don't want Sabine to be worried. "I'm sure everything will be fine. Don't worry, okay?" She nods, but I know she is doing exactly what I just asked her not to do. She doesn't want to lose her nanny; Jasmine is the only consistent part of her life right now. Well, and me, but I'm not there. I'm a phone call away, but when I say I'm there, I am, and I take pride in that. "Listen, I got to get dressed and catch the bus. Let me let you go, and I'll call you in the morning before you go to school."

She agrees, even though I know she doesn't want to, and we say goodbye before I hang up and quickly get dressed, forgoing the tie so that I can get out of here faster. I grab my toiletry bag, stuffing it into my bag before getting up and heading out of the locker room. As I go through the door, I almost take someone out. I steady the person with a curse, and then I groan inwardly when my eyes meet her hazel ones.

"Audrina." My brows come in. "What are you doing here?"

Audrina Hawkins works for the IceCats as a trainer, but she doesn't travel with us. I haven't seen her all trip, so why is she here now? I have given her a wide berth, mostly out of respect for her best friend, who was my friend until I slept with her. "Hey, I stood in for Flex."

I nod in awareness. "Cool, I gotta—"

She stops me, her fingers wrapping around my bicep. She's a tall girl, very fit and very beautiful. "This is the first time I've been able to catch you. You stopped talking to us."

Us, meaning her and Thatcher. I press my lips together as our eyes meet. I used to run with Audrina and Thatcher. We had a blast and tore

HAT TRICK

up the town, and sometimes Owen came too. But when Owen stopped hanging out and I thought Sabine was moving in with me, I quit running around because I wanted to be home more. It didn't help that Thatcher didn't want anything to do with me when he'd discovered I had slept with Audrina. I should never have done it, and when Thatcher found out, he couldn't look at me. He may claim not to be in love with her as more than a best friend, but his actions say otherwise. He's madly in love with her, and if I had known, I wouldn't have slept with her. I honestly didn't know, and I was drunk that night we hooked up. It was nothing. Meant nothing.

Still means absolutely nothing.

Especially now, with Tennessee in my life.

"Rina, you know why," I say softly, holding her gaze. "I have to play with Thatcher, and I can't have bad blood between us on the ice."

"He's just being a stupid big brother. He doesn't want you to hurt me. It's cool. We've talked about it. He doesn't care."

That's not true, though, and I'm sure as hell not throwing Thatcher under the bus. I've already slept with the girl he loves—which makes me a dick, and he'll always hate me, just as I hate anyone who has touched Tennessee. I get it, and I know for a fact that he cares.

"I still think of you. Maybe we can catch up?" she suggests, but I shake my head.

I exhale. "Rina, it's been almost six months. I've moved on, and I'm very much in love with my girlfriend."

"Girlfriend? You made it clear you weren't interested in settling down."

"I hadn't met her yet," I say simply, holding her gaze. "Listen, I gotta call my mom. I'm gonna go—"

She laughs. "So, you're blowing me off again?"

"I'm not trying to be a dick," I say as I move past her. "But I never should have hooked up with you, and it won't happen again. Ever."

"Fuck you, Dart," she seethes, and I agree.

"I deserve that," I call back to her, and I do. The guilt of hurting Thatcher still burns in my gut sometimes, especially when I see him, but thankfully, I haven't had to lately. He did something to his knee and hasn't been traveling with us. I've apologized, but I know he

TONI ALEO

doesn't forgive me. Which sucks, but it happens. Not that I have the mental space to deal with that right now.

Not when I gotta deal with the incubator I'm supposed to call my mother.

I walk down the hall, dialing my mom's number. When she answers, though, I hear the sounds of a bar in the background, and my anger takes over.

"Dart, I can't hear you!"

"Then go outside," I demand as I head out into the chilly Chicago air. I lean on the wall so that I can see the bus and make sure it doesn't drive off without me. There is no way in hell I'm not going home tonight. I wait until I no longer hear loud voices in the background before I say, "What the hell, Mom? I send you money, and you're at a bar?"

"I came to unwind, Dart. You don't know how hard it is to work two jobs and take care of your sister. It's exhausting."

"Two jobs? You barely work either of them, and Sabine should be the only fucking job that matters," I fume, my voice low and dangerous. "What is wrong with you?"

"Who are you talking to? I am your mother."

"Hardly," I mock, shaking my head. "You did nothing for me. Grandpa did, and don't you forget it. Do right by me by taking care of Sabine."

"Whatever. I don't have to sit here and listen to you bitch at me for having a good time!"

"You are supposed to be taking care of my sister, and if you don't want to, sign the rights over. Give her to me because I will take care of her and love her the way she deserves!"

"I do love her!" she yells at me, and I laugh.

"You don't know how to love. And if you don't get it together, I'll take you to court."

She laughs at that. "You think they're gonna take a girl from her mother and give her to a hockey player who fucks his way through the week? Please."

Her words hit me like a freight train, exposing all my insecurities. "I'm in a relationship."

HAT TRICK

Her laughter is taunting. "Just until you get bored and find someone better to wet your dick! Face it, kid. You're me made over. We aren't ever satisfied with one person—"

"I am nothing like you!" I yell, my body shaking. "I am like my grandpa. I am a good man, a good person, and I love my sister. I will not give you a lick of money until I see that you are caring for Sabine."

"Ha! Then you'll never see her again."

My stomach drops. I fucking knew it. "Is that a threat?"

"Dart, you have no fucking claim to her. You are nothing to her—"

"I am *everything* to her."

"Because you buy her shit. That's all."

"No, I love her."

"Dart! You don't know how to love. You only know how to spend money and fuck, and that's it."

"The words of a mother," I spit out, disgusted by her. "You are trash."

"Takes one to know one, son. So, go fuck yourself, and if you withhold the funds, you'll see what happens."

She hangs up, and my hand shakes so badly it hurts as I stare at the bus, my vision clouding. I drop the phone to my side and lean my head into the brick of the arena. As the tears burn my eyes, her words taunt me. I know they're not true. I know she was trying to hurt me. And she did because I *was* like her; I was fucking my way through the week, but that changed the moment I met Tennessee. Or it did once we got together. Fuck. Am I like her? No. I'm not. Fuck me. I run my hand down my face, and I swear I'm not like her. I can't be.

Damn it. I don't have time to deal with that emotional baggage when I have no clue what I am going to do about Sabine. I can't not see my sister, I can't not be in her life, but I also can't keep throwing money at my mom for her to blow it on herself when she needs to be a mother to my sister instead. I close my eyes to keep the tears in, and damn it, I just want to go home.

I just want to see Tennessee.

CHAPTER
Thirty-One

TENNESSEE

I dislike being a hockey girlfriend, but my love for Dart outweighs my dislike a million times over.

I hate being away from him, but watching him play, score, and live his dreams fills me with such pride. I wish I had known this was how I would feel when I left him in Nashville. I wish I had known how much I could love him and that the time apart wouldn't be as devastating as I'd assumed it would. I wish I had known that being his would fill whatever void I felt. How his voice brings on waves of pleasure. How his smile always elicits such joy. How being apart with the promise of seeing each other again is better than living apart from him and trying not to love him.

Because I truly believe Dart's purpose on this earth is for me to love him.

With everything I am.

While I miss him, and I yearn for him like no other, I am okay. Mostly because I use work and Angie as a distraction. We are both workaholics and spend a lot of time together so we aren't alone. I can't get into the plants that she talks about more than I care for, but I sing

230

HAT TRICK

along to Taylor Swift with her as she tends to them. We go to lunch together, take turns cooking dinner, and we've gotten to know each other. It's easy with her, and I care for her a lot. I feel like she listens to me, cares what I have to say, and enjoys being my friend. It's been refreshing. At night, I sleep in Dart's shirt, on his side of the bed, just so I feel like I'm sleeping with him. But that won't be the case tonight.

I'll get to hold him tonight.

He said they'd be home around eleven, so Angie left a little while ago to shower and shave before Owen came home. I did all that this morning, and when she offered that I could water her plants while she got ready, I declined, but now I regret that. I should have gone and watered the damn plants. At least I would have been able to talk to Angie and I wouldn't be sitting here on edge. Just waiting and watching the clock.

Damn it.

I fold my legs beneath me and lie on my Vols couch pillow as I scroll through Instagram. I look around the room, at the little Vols stuff that mingles with his hockey stuff. I thought he would get annoyed by it, but he only made me feel as if my things belonged with his. God, he is a dream. I focus on my phone, and even though there are plenty of posts to look at, I find myself going back to my own post and the three words Dart left for me. *I love you.* God, they utterly wreck me. No one has ever commented that. Denis would like my posts and Troy had put hearts, but Dart, he says the words as a promise. And each time is better than the last. I can't wait to kiss him, hold him, tell him how much I love him.

When my phone sounds for my work email, I ignore it since I'm not working right now. I made a rule that I don't work after hours. Since I am a workaholic, it makes me nervous that I'll get burned out. So, I ignore it, even though I wonder if it's from the company I work for. Nope, ignoring it, and thankfully, a text comes through to distract me.

Mom: Hey, you up?

I bring in my brows as I glance at the time. It's late for her to be up, but I call her anyway. "Isn't it past your bedtime, young lady?"

She scoffs at that. "I could say the same for you, younger lady."

TONI ALEO

Our laughter collides. "I'm waiting for Dart to come home. He's coming off a road trip."

"Oh, that's who I was calling about, actually."

"Really? What about him?"

"Well, I haven't shown your daddy your Instagram post, but you know he won't be happy."

I snort. "Which is why I posted it on Instagram, so that y'all didn't see it. And that was, like, five days ago. Why are you just now saying something? Did you get Instagram and not tell me?"

"No," she says, and gone is the joking tone. "Josie actually sent it to me and then asked if you were bringing Dart to her wedding."

I'm unsure how to react to that, but I don't think laughing would be respectful. "Josie sent you my post?"

"Yes, and I've sat on it all day, trying to figure it out. I saw he said he loved you, and none of us is sure if he was just being silly or if he was seriously proclaiming his love."

I press my lips together. "Because a man like him would never be serious with me?"

"Tennessee Lynn, that is not what I mean," she bites out. "Don't be so defensive."

"Mom, you just said y'all were talking about my post, which I assume was you, Josie, Lindy, and their mommas. And then you asked if he was being silly or serious, after I've had issues with Josie saying things just like that to me. So why wouldn't I get defensive?"

"We weren't gossiping, Tennie. We were just surprised you'd not only wear his jersey, but go ahead and post your relationship like that. I didn't realize it was this serious already."

I hate how my old insecurities flood my common sense. "I love him," I say simply. "And he loves me. We're in love. It's serious."

"Oh, I didn't know. You didn't tell me."

"Because our love is for no one but each other," I say, my eyes burning with tears. "I should probably tell you, I moved in with him too."

"Lordy, Tennie!" she exclaims. "You've known him, what, a week total?"

HAT TRICK

"And I have never felt such love and support in my life. I am so unbelievably happy with him."

"Well, darling, of course you are. It's new and exciting—"

"No, this is real. This is us. He is honestly the best thing that has ever happened to me and has been the ultimate, most amazing person to fall in love with." I'm met with silence, and I wipe away a traitorous tear. "This is why I didn't tell you. I didn't want you to make me feel stupid for what I know is everything to me."

"Tennie, I don't want you to feel stupid. I only want you to be smart about this and not just fall so deeply for someone you hardly know."

"Mom, ten years with Denis, and he's marrying the person who was supposed to be my best friend. Then Troy is a crazy person, and I knew him for two months before I committed to a relationship with him."

"Those were bad choices, obviously, but you can't feel this strongly for someone you hardly know in such a short amount of time!"

"Time means nothing when it comes to what your soul wants," I say, getting up and starting to pace. "My soul is meant to be with his. His vibe, his heart, and his passion... He's incredible, Mom. Everything he is and everything I am are meant to be one."

"Lord Almighty, Tennie. Do you hear yourself? You're just infatuated," she accuses, and I shake my head. "I hate to say this, but this could very well be lust. And darling, I only say this because I don't want you to get hurt. Sex can only last for so long."

"It's not only the sex, Mom," I correct her, my face flushing. The sex is fantastic and everything I want, but I know it's not only that. "It's him. I never question if he loves me, cares for me, or anything like that. I am proud that he is mine, and Mom, he makes me feel like he is proud that I am his. I love him. Deeply."

"Tennessee, darling, please don't get caught up like that. Keep your wits."

"My wits have done nothing for me," I say, leaning on the counter, looking out at the ocean. "I've always been cautious, always stayed in the background—but not anymore, not when I know who I am and who I love."

233

TONI ALEO

"Jesus me. I pray to God for your sake that this isn't just a fling."

I press my lips together to hold in my sob. "It's not," I say. "I know it's not."

"Okay," she says, and I know she doesn't want to fight with me. She thinks she's right, and I know she's not. I squeeze my eyes shut to keep the tears at bay. I refuse to let my insecurities and her words convince me otherwise.

I love him.

"Denis and Josie want to have the wedding when y'all come at the end of the month."

My eyes fly open, and I squint at the door. "What do you mean?"

"They want you there. We all want you there. You, Lindy, and Josie are supposed to be dressed in orange and standing together for one another's weddings."

"I can promise you this, Momma, when I marry Dart, Lindy and Josie will not be standing beside me."

She groans. "Now you're marrying him?"

"He hasn't asked, but the answer would be yes."

"Tennessee Lynn, you sound crazy."

"Maybe I am," I admit, shrugging. "Because if being crazy is believing I am deserving of his love, then yeah, I am."

"Lordy me, Tennie. I can't with all that. I need you to be at this wedding. My best friends are asking, and we are all family."

"No," I say, shaking my head. "I haven't heard from Josie's and Lindy's mommas. They are nothing to me. You are my momma, and Daddy is my daddy, and Dart is my love, but that's where my family ends."

"Baby, you don't mean that. Y'all had a spat. Move on and be supportive of your friend at her wedding."

"To my ex!" I yell, completely unable to grasp how she thinks this is okay. "She has never been supportive of me. Hell, she told me to settle for him, Momma, and then she turns around and gets engaged to him? Explain to me how you are okay with this!"

"Honey, her momma said it was a one-night stand and she got knocked up."

HAT TRICK

I laugh at that. "Man, karma is a bitch, huh? She does know she doesn't have to marry him? She can just raise her baby on her own."

"You know she's not strong enough for that, and she's scared what her parents would say," she tells me, and I shrug, even though she can't see me.

"Sucks to suck, eh?"

"Tennessee, you don't mean that."

"I'm not going. When Dart and I come, we're coming to go to the game with you and Daddy, and that's it."

"Please don't be hardheaded. Think about it."

"I'm good. But I do love you, and I'll talk to you later."

"Tennessee Lynn—"

"Bye, Momma."

I hang up and shake my head once more in disbelief. I think my momma has lost it. If she truly thinks I'm gonna support Josie and Denis, she has another think coming. I refuse. I can't. I won't. Jesus. I set my phone on the counter and go to get myself a drink of water. But before I can even reach for a cup, his low voice runs down my spine.

"Hey there, baby doll."

I whip around, my heart flying up into my throat at the sight of him. I know every word I said to my mom was the truth as his eyes burn into mine. A sob almost escapes as I run around the counter, and he drops his bag just to catch me. The force of my body slams him into the door, but that doesn't stop him from capturing my mouth with his. He wraps his arms around me tightly as my legs and arms do the same, placing me right where I belong. The hum I swear I feel between us is back, and gone is the conversation with my mom. Gone are the four days of missing him. Everything is a distant memory, and I can remember only him. Just Dart's lips on mine as we hold each other with all the love we have in our bodies.

Dart carries me to the bedroom, laying me down before he sinks his body into mine. Our lips move together, and I can feel his heart slamming into his chest, just as mine is. I glide my fingers up his back, spreading them over the nape of his neck as I cup his strong jaw with my other hand. I pull him back, and just as I'm about to tell him I love him, something in his eyes makes me crush my brows together.

TONI ALEO

"Baby, what's wrong?" I see such sorrow in his blue depths. His jaw is tight, and this isn't my normal, exuberant man. He tries to shake his head, bringing his lips to mine, but I stop him. "Dart, I can tell something is wrong. What is it?"

He pauses, his eyes looking everywhere but into mine. He drops his head to my chest, inhaling deeply as I lie there, waiting. I stroke my fingers along his scalp, and I press my lips to his temple, kissing him softly as he breathes in and out.

"Dart," I whisper, caressing his neck. "My love, you're scaring me. I promise I did nothing but watch Angie plant stuff. I haven't even seen Troy—"

His eyes meet mine, confused, but a bit of annoyance is there too. "Do you really think I'm upset because I think you stepped out on me?"

"I don't know…? I'm freaking out."

"Do you trust me, Tennie?"

"With everything," I answer without hesitation.

"Exactly," he says, his voice low. "I trust you completely."

"Then what is it?"

His throat works, his Adam's apple bobbing before he lets out a long breath. "Sabine called me upset because the nanny and my mom got into it about my mom going out. I had just sent her five hundred dollars for groceries for the month, and she went out to the bar with it." I continue to caress his neck, watching his face as the stress of the situation with his mother and sister fills his features. "I talked Sabine down and then called my mom. She said some real fucked-up shit to me, telling me that Sabine only loves me for the money, that I'm not meant to be loved, only to be fucked, because I'm just like her—"

I've tried really hard not to hate his mom, but this might be the breaking point for me. "You are nothing like her, Dart. You know that, right?"

"I don't know. I've wanted so badly for her to love me. But what if I am, and that's why she'll never love me?"

"That's not true," I insist.

"I don't know. I mean, I couldn't even keep it in my pants when we were apart."

HAT TRICK

"Because we weren't together," I tell him, running my fingers along his jaw. "You weren't mine."

"But I was," he says, his eyes meeting mine. "And still, I tried to lose myself in someone else."

"Did it work?"

"No."

"Exactly," I say, my heart beating hard. "I don't know your momma, but I feel it would have worked for her. That she never would allow herself to fall for someone the way you have for me."

He closes his eyes, pressing his nose into mine. "I don't even want to think of being with anyone else. I only want you."

"I know."

"I love only you. Greatly." His words are once more a promise.

"I know, D'Artagnan." I clutch his jaw, bringing it up so he can look me in my eyes. "Am I with you for your money?"

He scoffs. "No, you have your own. You bitch when I buy you food."

"Yes. So why am I with you?"

"Raw sex appeal? You actually do want to break my nose by riding my face?" he jokes, but I don't laugh; I hold his gaze.

"I'm not joking, Dart," I warn him, and he looks down, exhaling. "You don't have to put a façade on with me. I know you. I know this hurts you, that you love your sister very much, want to care for her. And Dart, listen to me," I say, angling his face up with my thumb. "Even if there were no flashy, hot hockey superstar, no money, no beautiful house, no ocean, or even your fantastic cock—"

"Serious note, don't take my cock out of the equation. I need it. We need it. It's a huge player for our team." I try not to snort at his ridiculousness as he apologizes with a shrug. "Just saying."

"Dart, I would love you because of how passionately you love me."

His eyes search mine. "I do love you, with all of myself."

"I am going to be yours until forever falls apart and we're worm food."

His lips curve as he runs his fingers along my chin. "Can we be cremated? I'm not a fan of worms eating me."

"It's romantic," I tell him, and he grins. "'I'm going to be yours

TONI ALEO

until forever falls apart and we're burned to a crisp' doesn't sound as good."

"It doesn't, but worms aren't my jam."

"Lordy, Dart! You drive me crazy." His eyes burn into mine. "But I'm yours forever and then some, just know that. I love you, and I don't have to know your momma to know you aren't a lick of her, but your granddaddy instead."

His grin fades a bit as he trails his fingers over my lips. "You're so fucking country." My face brightens as he whispers, "I love you, Tennessee." I kiss his fingers when his eyes meet mine. "If I could get my mom to give me custody of Sabine, would you be okay with that?"

"Absolutely," I say, and I know I should think that through. We're still learning each other, still building our life together, but I know he won't be fully happy until he knows his sister is safe. His heart is so big, so beautiful, and I want nothing more than to never see him as upset as he was when he came into the house. Our home.

I roll him over with ease since I caught him off guard. I straddle his hips as he grins up at me. "What are you doing? I was memorizing your face."

I shake my head as I start to undo the buttons of his shirt. "You have already done that, many times over," I tell him, my eyes cutting to his. "I want to take care of you," I whisper, opening his shirt and placing a kiss along his sternum. "You always take care of everyone else. Let me take care of you." I sink my teeth into his nipple, and he hisses out a breath. "Give me control," I whisper against his scalding skin. "Can you do that?"

I rake my teeth over the ripples of muscles along his chest, and he says tightly, "I can do anything for you."

I've never believed any words more than those.

CHAPTER
Thirty-Two

Dart

I knew the moment I met Tennessee that a lifetime would never be enough time for us.

I'll need more.

I *want* more.

The feel of her lips is a high I don't ever want to come down from. I'm addicted to the way she looks at me, the sweet touch of her lips along my skin, and I'm obsessed with every breath she sucks in. Her promises, the way she thinks, how she talks me off the ledge. Her. Just her. That's all I want. She makes me feel safe, loved, and like nothing matters but us. But that's not true. My issues are her issues; her fears are my fears. She's the ultimate teammate. Even when my mom makes me feel like I'm not worthy of love, it only takes one look in Tennessee's eyes to know that isn't true.

Her love for me… Fuck, it's a drug.

And I'm totally hooked.

I watch as she trails her lips and teeth down my chest, my stomach, before she licks along my abs and belly button, her fingers working at my pants. She pulls out my belt and looks up at me through her lashes. "Think I could use this to tie your hands?"

I chuckle as I hold her gaze. "I love that belt, and I'll break it to get to you."

"Naughty, naughty," she says, tapping the end of the belt on my thigh, sending chills up my leg. She throws it to the side, thankfully, as she slides off the edge of the bed to her feet. She tugs on the laces of my dress shoes, untying them before pulling off the shoes and throwing them to the floor. I help push my pants down and off, along with my boxers. Her eyes are dark, desire burning in them as she pulls her shirt up and over her head, deliciously and completely naked for me. Her body is a treasure map, and between those thighs is my prize.

My mouth waters, and the slyest grin comes over her face. "You said I could have control."

Fuck. "I don't know if I'm the same guy I was ten minutes ago, baby doll, 'cause now I want to swallow you whole."

Her cheeks dust with color, but she tsks me. "Promise me."

"That's not fair."

"Do it," she demands as she takes my wrist in her hands. "It'll be worth it, I swear."

Excitement courses through my body, and I'm unsure if I'll regret this or thoroughly enjoy it, but I nod. "I promise."

The most beautiful grin takes over her cherub-like cheeks as she takes my hands in hers, pulling me to her, and my face comes into her chest willingly. "Can I taste you?" I ask, nuzzling my nose along the soft spot between her heavy breasts.

"Yes." She barely gets the word out before I run my tongue along the curves of her breasts as she pushes my jacket and shirt off me before letting the floor swallow them along with the rest of our clothes. I watch as her head falls back, her fingers biting into my shoulders when I swirl my tongue along her pink nubs.

"I missed you," I mutter against her skin. "I'd get so hard, just imagining these perfect tits in my mouth."

"Hey, I'm in control," she reminds me before taking my face in her hands and tipping my head up. She bends down, that sweet ass full as she leans in, running her tongue from the base of my neck, up along

HAT TRICK

the coarse hair, to my jaw, and then my lips before she whispers, "I would watch you play, and slowly, I would part my legs." Another swipe of her tongue, and my cock stands so tall and hard, I can't see straight. "Slide my fingers between my lips, so wet for you, so fucking desperate for your touch, and when you scored, I'd come, screaming your name."

My breath catches as she takes my bottom lip between her teeth, her eyes burning into mine. In that second, I know scoring will never be the same, not with that image in my head. She licks the spot she bit and whispers, "I came five times for you, your name falling from my lips as I exploded with pleasure and pride."

I groan loudly. "You're killing me, baby doll." My voice is not my own, and she only gives me that sneaky grin I want to kiss off her dirty mouth. "Can I kiss you?"

"Nope," she says, licking my bottom lip. "Behave."

"Absolutely impossible with you."

Her eyes dance with mine as she drags her mouth along my jaw, my throat, my chest before she falls to her knees before me. I look down at her, those thighs thick and that ass even thicker as she gazes up at me, her fingernails digging into my thighs. I hiss out a breath when she takes me in her hand, squeezing my throbbing cock in her warm palm. She rubs her thumb along the head of my cock, her eyes burning into mine as I jerk into her hand, but she doesn't let up. She traces the dips and curves of the tip with her fingernail, her eyes daring and fucking hot. I lick my lips, my gaze following the swipe of her tongue as she rubs her thumb over my tip, the sensation making me tremble everywhere.

"Goddamn it, you're so fucking hot."

"Do you want me to touch you?" she asks, squeezing me.

"Yes, please."

Her lips tip, and I notice her thighs squeeze together, driving me absolutely wild. I hold my breath as she moves toward me. Gone is all coherent thought as she runs her tongue along the bottom of my shaft, drawing the deepest moans from me. I force my eyes to stay open so I don't miss a fucking thing she does to me. Her mouth covers only the head, and she swirls her tongue along every inch of me as she squeezes my base with her palm. I fist the sheets, watching, in awe of this beauty in front of me. Her skin is flushed, and her eyes are dark. I want to wrap my arms around her; I want to lose myself in her.

But I know she won't let me.

The thrill has me on edge.

She moves off me, her eyes meeting mine before she sits back on her haunches. "Look what you do to me," she calls, opening her legs to her center glistening for me.

I can't breathe. I swallow. "Touch yourself."

"No, this isn't about me. It's about you," she tells me, but as she tries to get up, my hand to her throat stops her.

"I don't think you realize how fucking hot it makes me when you get yourself off. When you come undone, it's more pleasurable than my own release."

Her lips curve as she comes to her knees, leaning into my palm, and my grip tightens around her burning flesh. "Like this?" she asks, her fingers gliding down her body. My toes curl into the hardwood as I watch her fingers disappear inside her wet lips. I'm burning everywhere and completely taken with her.

"I've never been jealous of two gorgeous fingers in my life," I say, watching as she pumps her pussy with her fingers, her eyes not leaving mine, her lips parting as I shake with want. "I don't know if I'm able to just sit here, my greedy, gorgeous girl."

"No?" she draws out, her fingers digging into the flesh of her boob. "I thought I had the control here?"

I can only shake my head. "You do, but I need you to let me between those legs."

"Mmm," she moans as she moves her fingers faster. "Maybe I want to watch you squirm."

My mouth is dry, my heart is going wild in my chest, and I swear there are two of her, my eyes are crossing so bad. "Please, baby doll," I beg, tightening my fist around the sheets. "Let me be those fingers. Let me taste you. Let me consume you."

She moves to me, and I catch her by her waist, unable to control myself. Her eyes widen as she crawls into my lap, the tip of me grazing her wetness. I groan loudly as I look up at her, spellbound. She

HAT TRICK

pushes me back into the bed, and I go eagerly as she crawls up my body, such confidence and determination in those different-colored depths. She slides her center up my chest, and when she hovers over my mouth, I run my tongue the length of her, loving her taste.

"I could live on the taste of you," I murmur against her lips, but then she rotates her body, and her hands come to my thighs as she glides her pussy along my lips. "Oh, my greedy girl, what are you planning?"

"To fuck your mouth while you fuck mine," she says desperately.

She doesn't have to tell me twice. I take her ass in my hands and bury my mouth into her pussy just as she takes me deep to the back of her throat. I arch my hips, unable to sit still as she sucks me. She rides my face, yet I know she's being careful. She doesn't want to suffocate me, and honestly, that's all I want.

"If I can breathe, you aren't fucking my face hard enough," I insist against her lips before I slap the fuck out of her ass. "Harder. Tennessee. Faster. Now."

Her moan hums around my cock, and she lowers herself completely to my mouth before she does exactly what I want. She fucks my mouth, hard, with no restraint whatsoever. Her body quivers underneath my hands as I suck and lick, while she continues to suck me into her hot mouth. She squeezes her thighs against my cheeks as a roar leaves her mouth around my cock. I grip her ass, slamming her body against my face and losing myself in her release. I almost come, right there, deep in her mouth, but I want to be inside her.

I push her off me as she trembles, her body jerking while I get up on my knees, smacking those legs open. I move between them, and I thrust into her with ease. I press her legs back into the bed, and I fuck her so hard, I can't see straight. Her moans are loud, desperate, and I feel the absolute same. With each thrust, she squeezes me, draining me of all my senses. All I feel, hear, and need is her. Only her.

"Fuck me harder, Dart. Faster," she demands, and I can't help but do what she asks. "I love when you fuck me. Fill me, baby. Harder." Her words are like fire, and I slam into her warm body until my balls tighten, and I explode inside her with a choked moan. I shake as the vibrations of my release run through me before I fall onto her, her legs

TONI ALEO

wrapping around me, and I go deeper into her. I capture her mouth with mine, and our kisses are slow and lazy, our breathing erratic. I move my nose along hers as my hands stroke up and down her sexy body—the heat of her, the dips and rolls, the fullness of her—and I'm lost.

"This body was made for me," I whisper against her lips, and she nips at my bottom lip as her fingers graze my collarbone.

"You were made for me," she whispers back, her eyes full of love.

Just for me.

Our eyes stay locked for a long moment, only our lips brushing as I fall even more deeply in love with her.

"Hey," I whisper, and her nose presses into the top of mine.

"Hey."

My breath catches at how beautiful she is. How stunned I am under her gaze.

"When we're worm food, Tennessee—"

"I thought we were going to be cremated," she corrects, her eyes dancing with mine.

"Fine, I was trying to be romantic."

"Told you being eatin' by worms is way romantic."

"So romantic," I say dryly, rewarded with the most gorgeous grin. "When this lifetime is over…"

"Yeah?"

"I'll find you in heaven. And I promise, we'll fall in love all over again."

Her breath catches as she gazes into my eyes. "I'll be waiting."

I kiss her nose. "Make sure that orange dildo makes it up there."

Her laughter is quick, and beautiful bliss fills her face. My own laughter meets hers as our eyes lock in unadulterated love. "I'm stuck on your heart, D'Artagnan—" She pauses. "Wait, what is your middle name? How do I not know your middle name? You know mine."

Instantly, I feel embarrassed. "Okay, don't laugh."

She's already snickering. I have to look away so I don't laugh with her. God, my mom is an idiot. "D'Artagnan Athos Porthos Aramis Miklas."

"So, you're named after all the Musketeers," she says, and I nod.

HAT TRICK

Her lips curve, and she sputters with laughter. "God, I feel for five-year-old Dart. As if just trying to spell your first name wasn't hard enough."

"It was always the apostrophe. I never knew where to put it." Her laughter mingles with mine as I shake my head, holding her closer. "That's probably why my mom split. She regretted her choices and had no desire to teach me to spell all those fucking names."

Tennessee's laughter is gone instantly as her face turns dark. "She split because she wasn't, and still isn't, worthy of your love."

I lean my nose into hers.

"But I am. And I am truly stuck on your heart, D'Artagnan—" she kisses my nose "—Athos—" my cheek "—Porthos—" she takes in a deep, exaggerated breath before kissing my other cheek, and I grin wildly at her "—Aramis."

I gather her in my arms, my lips almost touching hers. "I love you, Tennessee Lynn."

Her smile falls, and she whines, "Do I really have to say it all again? I just love you, okay? All of you."

With that, we crack up, our limbs tangling as our foreheads come together, the bed shaking from our laughter.

And as her beautiful eyes fall on me, I know, God, I know, she is worthy of my love.

I'm worthy of hers.

And nothing can touch what we have.

CHAPTER
Thirty-Three

TENNESSEE

I've seen Dart in many ways.

On my ESPN app, on TV, and—my favorite—in person. The smell of the ice, the roar of the crowd, and a beer in my hand amplifying how awesome of a hockey star he really is. I've seen him as a friend, a dude of honor, and my lover before he was truly mine.

But nothing, and I mean not a damn thing, could have prepared me for seeing him with children.

Celeste, his teammate Kirby's daughter, sits on his shoulders, laughing loudly, while the baby, Raine, rides on his leg, the same laughter filling the living room with such joy as he walks around like a "monster." The girls are adorable and so sweet, but my heart is swelling at Dart's laughter. He falls to the floor, protecting Celeste's head before she gets up to jump on him, Raine following suit. My heart, well, I don't think it can handle the scene before us. My ovaries sure as hell can't.

When I was younger, my mom used to say I had childbearing hips, and I always believed that meant I'd have a ton of kids. My mom only wanted one because she knew she'd have her best friends' kids around

HAT TRICK

her and wanted to be able to give me everything I could ever dream of. While I did have Lindy and Josie, when I was home, I was alone, and I wished I had siblings. So, with my childbearing hips, I figured I'd have a lot of kids, but that changed when Josie and Lindy told me that I shouldn't because I'd just get bigger. That my husband wouldn't want a super-big wife. That we'd have to keep up appearances. It was the main reason I went on birth control, to make sure I'd never get big for the husband I couldn't keep if I were overweight.

I hadn't even really thought about any of that until this moment. Until Dart grabbed the girls and covered them in kisses. As I watch him, I can't believe I allowed my friends—and I use that term loosely —to ruin the idea of children for me. Or maybe it was fate.

I had to have that idea ruined for me, so that when Dart came along, the excitement of the possibility of children with him would hit me like a ton of ice. Or maybe I'm crazy as hell, like my momma has said, because I don't even know if he wants kids.

But surely he does.

Because I do now.

I want his baby dragons.

Freaking nerd.

He looks back at me, and I grin widely at him as he tosses Celeste over his shoulder as Raine chases them through the living room. I hadn't expected to leave the bed this morning since Dart didn't have practice until this afternoon to prepare for tomorrow's game.

But when he couldn't get ahold of Sabine this morning, he called Kirby's wife, Jaylin, who is a lawyer, for guidance. She asked him to come over, and since we're attached at the hip, here I am, hoping like hell she has an answer for him. I know his mind is on his sister, worried, and even though I haven't met her yet, I am too. I want her to be safe and cared for the way she needs to be.

"They love him," Jaylin says, pulling my gaze from Dart and the girls to her.

"He is wonderful with them."

"You should see him with Amelia's kids. All the kiddos love Dart. He is a big ol' kid."

I can't argue with her on that. Especially when he does a front roll

TONI ALEO

on the floor with Raine, their laughter intoxicating. "Raine! Are you going to be a gymnastics star like Amelia?"

She throws up her hands, bouncing, and Celeste laughs. "Yes! We both are! See, Dart? See?" Celeste bounces for him, her hands up, and I can't stop smiling.

"They're beautiful."

"They are," Jaylin agrees. "He's the same with Sabine."

I meet her gaze. "I haven't had the pleasure of meeting her yet."

"You'll love her. She's a doll baby." She leans on her hand, holding my gaze. "It would be a lot to take on a child who isn't yours, but Dart told me you were fine with it."

"I am. I want her to be safe. I sure as hell don't know how to raise a kid, but I know how to love."

Her eyes shine such a beautiful dark brown. "That's all you need, in my opinion," she says with a small smile. "Which is why it's killing me I can't find a loophole to get him custody of Sabine."

I swallow, and I notice Dart sits down, bringing the girls into his lap. "So, I wouldn't be able to get her?"

Sadly, Jaylin shakes her head. "You have no legal rights to her whatsoever, and your mom doesn't have to let you have contact with her."

Dart leans his lips into Celeste's hair as Raine cuddles into his side. His face is so sullen, it breaks my heart.

"I can send a letter, and maybe she'll get scared of my letterhead," Jaylin says. "But as much as I dislike her, I don't think she's dumb enough to fall for it."

I shrug. "It's worth a shot."

Dart nods. "Yeah, but Jaylin is right. She'll see right through it." My stomach hurts as I watch the sadness move across his gorgeous face. "But I think we should try it, just for shits and giggles, I guess."

"I already have it drafted. I can email it now, and we can see what happens," Jaylin says, and when he nods, she turns to her computer. "I'll have it sent certified mail, too, just to make sure she gets it."

"Thanks, Jaylin," he says, and the note of sadness in his voice has my heart aching. "Maybe I could offer to buy her off?" he asks after a moment. "She loves money."

HAT TRICK

"That's highly illegal," she tells him, and the disappointment on his face kills me.

"But could you make it legal?" I ask, and she holds my gaze.

"Let's try this and see what happens. Okay?"

I'm not hopeful, and one look at Dart tells me he's not either. I don't think Jaylin feels good about our options either, but she sends the letter. After watching a couple of episodes of *Paw Patrol* with the girls since Dart promised Celeste he would, we head out. The girls protest, but Dart has afternoon skate, and I have meetings with a couple of the players today to go over their assessments.

In the truck, Dart asks me, "When is my assessment?"

I blow out a breath, not sure why doing his makes me so nervous. "I'm done, just a little hesitant to go over it with you."

He brings in his brows. "Why?"

"I don't know. I've spent hours watching you play, and the only thing I can come up with is something so small, it's almost not worth it."

"So, you're saying I'm perfect," he says, giving me a cheeky grin.

"Yes, but also, I think you have some weakness in your left wrist that, if you did some extra rehab, would enable you to increase your miles per hour by at least eight."

He nods, seeming impressed. "That sounds awesome. Will you do my rehab?"

"I'd do your plan, but I'd pass it off to the trainer. I think her name is Audrina?" I notice he scrunches up his face, and I bring in my brows. "What? Do you not care for her? She seems nice and efficient."

He sighs deeply. "Well, just so we're crystal clear here, I hooked up with her like six months ago. Big mistake."

Now I'm scrunching my face. "Really? Audrina the trainer?"

"Yeah, she's a cool chick. But again, big mistake. I lost a really good friend. Which is her best friend, but even though I knew him before her, I didn't know he was in love with her."

"How did you discover he was in love with her?"

"When he found out we hooked up after a drunken night, he cussed me out and told me I was dead to him. She says it's because he's like a big brother to her and doesn't want me to hurt her, but he

249

TONI ALEO

never said anything like that. He just kept asking how I could sleep with her with how much she meant to him."

"Oh my."

"Yeah," he says slowly, sighing hard. "Huge mistake. And she just told me to fuck myself last night when she tried to get me to hang out and I told her no."

I blink. "She came on to you?"

He shrugs. "I guess, but I told her I didn't want anything to do with her. And she told me to fuck myself, so I'm sure she'll be excited to help me train."

"That's a lot," I say, and he nods in agreement. "I'll talk to Flex."

"Okay."

"For your sake, not mine. I don't want you to be tempted," I tease, and he gives me a dark look.

"Take it back."

"Nope."

"I'll pull this truck over and tickle the shit out of you. Right between your thighs, with my tongue."

I snort as heat flushes through me. "Is that supposed to make me take it back?" I challenge, and his face breaks into a grin. "Okay, fine. I take it back. I'll talk to Flex for me because I don't want to be jealous of you and her."

"There is no me and her." His face is so stricken over it, and I feel bad for teasing him, but I don't think it's the teasing but the memory of losing his friend.

"Have you tried talking to your friend?"

"Yeah, but he won't talk to me. Ignores me at practice and won't return any texts."

"That sucks. I'm sorry."

"Eh, it is what it is."

I know I shouldn't because it doesn't matter, but I say, "I didn't think she'd be your type. She's very thin."

He nods. "Before you, I didn't really have a type. I just liked women. Though, yeah, usually on the thicker side." I watch as his jaw clenches. He looks over at me, such sorrow on his face. "Now, my type

HAT TRICK

is you." He sends me a cheeky grin, and I roll my eyes. "Are you mad?"

"Why would I be mad?" I ask, holding his gaze. "I've told you before, your past is just that—a past that didn't include me."

"I know, but I feel bad," he laughs, shaking his head. "It's weird. I don't want you to think they matter, because no one has until you."

"Dart, you don't have to tell me that. I know."

"Fine, but I still hate every guy who has touched you."

I snort at that. He's so silly, but I can't bring myself to feel the way about his past that he does about mine. I don't care because he isn't with any of them; he's with me. And like with me, for the guys I've been with, none of them has ever made me feel what he does. I have never been in love the way I am with him. I don't give a shit about any guy or girl, because they aren't us. Together. The women from his past didn't do what I do, because at the end of the day, he is committed to me. He loves me. Only me.

"How many guys have you been with?"

"Nine," I answer, and he nods slowly. "You make ten."

"At night, I will curse them all, even if I don't know their names."

"You're insane," I accuse, and I stare at the side of his face. "Should I even ask how many you've been with?"

"Men? Zero," he answers, giving me another cheeky grin, and I laugh, shaking my head. "Women, well...even though your judgy eyes tell me you think I've been with a lot, it's actually only eighteen."

"Only eighteen," I tease, laughing. "But you're right. I was ready to say almost one hundred."

Now he laughs. "Jesus! You think I was a manwhore?" he jokes, and I grin at him.

"You weren't?"

He shrugs. "Maybe a bit, because those are the girls I've slept with, not the total number of who have gotten me off."

"Lordy me," I exhale. And I wait to feel inadequate or even jealous, but those feelings don't come. I know that no one can come close to what we have. We're fire together, and I know he loves only me. "And you call me greedy."

251

TONI ALEO

He reaches for my hand, kissing the back of it. "You are."

"Only for you," I say, and he grins against the back of my hand.

"Just know, you are the only one who matters, baby doll," he tells me, and I know he means it.

"I know," I say with a wink, and he kisses my hand again.

"Thanks for being so supportive about this shit with Sabine."

I squeeze his hand. "It's gonna work out. I know it is."

He nods, though his eyes are hollow. "I want it to, but if the letter from Jaylin doesn't work, I might have to offer her money and see what she says."

I swallow hard, my stomach twisting. "I wish she'd just recognize how wonderful you'd be for Sabine."

"How wonderful we'd be," he corrects, running his lips along the back of my hand. "She knows of you, so does Sabine. They knew before we even got back together."

"I can't wait to meet her."

"Me either," he says softly, sighing against my hand.

I watch him for a moment, and then I find myself asking, "Do you want dragon babies?" His laughter is quick and fills his face as he stops at a light. He drags his lips along my fingers, his eyes meeting mine as he chuckles against the back of my hand. "You're great with Celeste and Raine, and Jaylin said you're like that with all kids."

His Adam's apple bobs as his gaze stays locked with mine. "Yeah, do you?"

"I do," I answer, and I'm surprised by how confident I am. "Maybe not with wings, though," I tease, and he grins.

"I'll do my best to stay in human form when we start mating," he jokes, and Lord above, help me with this nerdy man.

On a serious note, I say, "Though, I'll probably gain weight."

He shrugs. "So? That's what happens when you have a baby. Works great for me because it just gives me more to hold on to when I'm making more of them." His lips curve in a sinister grin before he winks, blasting heat between my legs.

"Just so sure, huh?" I ask, astounded by his confidence in us.

"Yeah. Aren't you?"

HAT TRICK

I realize that, lost in his eyes, I am. "Yes."

He leans toward me, and I meet him halfway for our lips to press together. It's only for a second before the car behind us honks, but I don't get upset.

Because I have forever and a day for kisses like that.

CHAPTER
Thirty-Four

Dart

After going home and getting ready to head to the rink, which consisted of a lot of touching and more, we're back in my truck. Tennessee huffs a breath beside me.

"What's wrong?" I ask when I notice she is typing violently on her phone. "Who are you wanting to hit instead of text?"

That gets me a grin as she slams her phone down on her lap. "My momma is being unreasonable. We got into it last night—"

"I know. I heard." She looks at me with disbelief. "Yeah, I was standing there for like ten minutes before I finally spoke."

"Are you serious?"

"Yeah. I didn't say anything because I was in awe of you, but then you were going off and I was just stunned."

"You heard me?"

"Oh yeah," I say with a chuckle, and just like it did last night, my heart swells in my chest. Full of wild love just for her. "I was super in my feelings, but hearing you defend us, man, it did a number on me."

"I meant every word I said."

"Baby doll, I felt every word," I say simply, and even without her

HAT TRICK

telling me, I'd known she did. She was red-faced, stomping around and ready to fight for us. For our love. And I couldn't stop myself from falling in love with her all over again. Which is becoming a daily occurrence, really. "I heard it in your voice. Is she still not convinced?"

"It's not that." She rolls her eyes. "So, you remember my ex-best friends, Josie and Lindy?"

"The girls at the hotel, the ones who put you down and whom I dislike greatly."

Her eyes sparkle. "Yes. Well, Josie got knocked up by Denis, and now she wants me at the wedding."

My whole face scrunches up in confusion. "Wait. Isn't Denis your ex? The one she told you to settle for?"

"Yes."

"Man, I don't know what's going on in Tennessee, the state, because in Canada, there'd be a beatdown."

She laughs at that. "I'd have to care to want to beat her up. But can you believe my mom wants me to go to their wedding?"

"Eh…" I draw out. "Your family is intertwined with hers, so I get it."

"Really? You think I should go?"

"Fuck no," I laugh, and I feel her gaze on my face. "Why would you go to a wedding of a person who has put in your head that you don't deserve a man because of your weight, when she's marrying the dude she told you to settle for. Like, come on."

"That's what I said!"

"But," I say, trying to be the voice of reason, "if you did, to please your mom or be the bigger person—"

"Man, screw being the bigger person. I should slash their tires for this, especially with them wanting me to stand up for them."

"You're not wrong," I agree, and she throws a grin my way. "But I'd go with you, decked out in an orange suit. To the wedding and/or the slashing of the tires."

She sighs. "My ride-or-die."

"Damn right," I agree, covering her thigh with my palm. "Have you talked to Josie?"

"No. I have her blocked."

TONI ALEO

Man, don't cross this girl. "Okay, so you're done, done with her."

"Yeah," she says, taking a deep breath as I pull into my parking space at the practice arena. "I refuse not to be loved the way I deserve. Not anymore."

I squeeze her thigh, and she looks over at me. "I love you."

Her eyes burn with mine as she threads our fingers together. "I love you." I almost kiss her, but then her face scrunches up. "What in the ever-loving hell is he doing here?"

I whip my gaze to where she's looking, to find Troy getting out of his car. He has a brace on his nose, which I know makes me a dick for laughing at him, but that dude is a tittybaby. I go to get out of the car to find out what he is doing, but her hand comes to my chest, stopping me.

"Don't."

"I was just going to stand there and see if he ran into my fist again," I tell her, and she scoffs.

"Let it be," she urges me just as she looks down at her phone. "Oh, he texted me. He's going to meet me here to go over scans with the players, and then we have a meeting with his uncle." I grumble, and she sets me with a look. "I told you I had to work with him."

"Doesn't mean I have to like it."

"How you feel about Audrina is how I feel about him. One big-ass mistake that I unfortunately have to work with."

God, she's incredible. I capture her jaw, and I hope to God he is watching us as I take her mouth with mine, and she parts those lips instantly for me. Our tongues play, her hands coming up to cup my jaw as I drink from her lips, unable to get enough. We're both panting once we part, and her eyes burn with desire. "You're evil."

"You're mine," I tell her, and she kisses my nose.

"Not gonna argue with that, 'cause it's true," she says, throwing her door open as I do. I try not to let the fact that he is here piss me off, but it's hard when I hate the guy. She's right, though. Just as Audrina means nothing to me, I know that bench-rider means nothing to her. We gather her things, and I help her inside. We head into the conference room where she is going to be meeting with everyone, and I set

HAT TRICK

her bags on the table. Buttface sits at the table on his phone, trying to avoid eye contact, which only makes me think less of him.

"Go," she mutters to me.

I take her hand then and kiss her palm. "I love you, Tennessee."

Her cheeks warm as she pulls me to her, pressing her lips to mine. She gives me a sweet kiss, and then, against my lips, she says, "Text me when you're done."

"I will."

"I love you." I kiss her top lip and then her nose.

I pull away from her and wink before SirJackOff meets my gaze. "Nice nose brace."

He only glares as I walk out of the room, chuckling. I chance a look back to find Tennessee shaking her head, but that grin still sits on those lips.

The lips that belong to me.

———

I sit on the bench, downing a bottle of Gatorade as our third and fourth lines do the drills the first and second just did. Owen sits beside me, gasping for breath between sucking down his own Gatorade.

"I should have slept today instead of doing Angie all morning."

I almost choke on a mouthful from my second bottle. "You lie," I accuse once I swallow.

"I know. But God, I'm drained."

"I hear you," I agree, and we tap our bottles together before we both take long pulls. Out of the tunnel comes Sawyer, all fresh-faced and not the least bit sweaty. "Missed the hard shit."

He snaps his fingers before he puts on his gloves. "Oh darn. Instead of looking like you two, I was getting help with my speed. Did you know I turn my knee in when I skate?"

"'Cause you suck," I call to him, and Owen nods.

"Yeah. You're slow."

He scoffs, knowing we're just messing with him as he sits beside us. "Also, Ms. Dent is pretty impressive, while that pelican with the

TONI ALEO

nose brace is a dumbass. He kept trying to talk over her, and she finally looked at him and told him to let her do her job."

"That's my girl," I say proudly, wanting to re-break that fucker's nose.

"Yeah, she's pretty badass. Let me know if you decide to move on," Sawyer says, and Owen lets his head drop. "I'll jump on her in a second."

"Bro, come on. Don't piss him off."

Sawyer flashes me a teasing grin, and I flip him the bird with my glove, which is a feat. "No way. She's it for me."

"I figured. When are we going ring shopping?" Sawyer continues to tease, and Owen snorts.

"I wouldn't be surprised if he's already got the ring picked out."

"I don't. Thank you, jackasses," I say to them, but then we're called onto the ice for more torture that I love. As I do the drills and dig in, I can't help but wonder what kind of ring I want to get her. It'll probably have to be orange if I want her to say yes.

Even through the torture, I'm grinning.

Like a love-sick fool.

But my grin is gone when I get back to the locker room after my shower and see the multiple missed calls from Sabine and my mom. I exhale heavily as I quickly get dressed, and I head out of the locker room, even when all the guys are trying to talk to me. I walk into the lounge, and when I see there are people around to hear me, I go toward the side door, the crisp fall air hitting me in the face. I wish I had grabbed a hoodie, but the urgency of getting ahold of my sister is more important.

I dial Sabine's number, but she isn't the one who answers; it's my mom.

"You think you're slick?" she accuses, her voice harsh. "You think I didn't look up this lawyer and see she is the wife of your teammate?"

"It doesn't matter who she is married to. She handles a lot of child custody cases, and she is my lawyer."

"Well, you need a new lawyer if she's feeding you the idea she can get your sister for you. You have no claim to her."

"You aren't caring for her," I explain, trying to keep my cool like

HAT TRICK

Jaylin and Tennessee advised me to. "I have all my bank statements, all my texts from you asking for money for Sabine. I have been financially supporting both of you for the last two years. If I look at Grandpa's stuff, I bet I'll see where he was doing it before me."

"She is my daughter."

"Mom, I'm not disputing that, but you can't care for her."

"And you can?" she throws back at me. "You play half the year and are on road trips constantly. How are you a better option?"

"Because even with my traveling, I know she'll be safe and taken care of. She won't be with a nanny twenty-four seven. She'll be cared for by me or my girlfriend."

She laughs maliciously at that. "Dart, are you nuts? This girlfriend of yours wants you, not some eight-year-old getting in the way."

"That's not true. We've discussed it. She wants what I want, and that's for Sabine to be loved and cared for."

"How many times have you hit your head? No girl wants to be tied down to a kid who's not even hers. She wants your time and your dick, two things she won't get when your sister is there in the damn way." Her words drip with venom.

"Tennessee is with me because she loves me, all of me, and since Sabine is an extension of me, she loves her."

"First, Tennessee? What the fuck?" she laughs. "Is her middle name Muffin? Jesus, you know how to pick them. And second, listen to yourself. This is the same girl who ghosted you. She doesn't want to take care of your sister for you. She'll get overwhelmed and ghost you again."

Anger boils in my chest. "Talk about me all you want, but don't talk about her, okay?" I warn, clenching my fist at my thigh. "You don't know shit about her—or even me, for that matter. Hell, I bet you don't even really know Sabine. Just do what's right. Let me take custody, because she won't ever be in the way for us like she is for you."

"Us?" she laughs. "You sound ridiculous."

"Says the person who has said her daughter, a person she made, is always in her way."

"I should hang up on you," she warns, and I press my lips together,

259

TONI ALEO

wishing I had kept my cool. "But I need to know if you are going to take me to court, because I don't have the money for a lawyer."

"So, I should win," I say simply, and she blows out an angry breath.

"I'll draw it out, and you won't speak to her," she warns. "I'll lie about you left and right, son."

"Don't call me that, Kris," I caution, unable to call her my mom any longer. This woman is just the person who gave birth to me. She doesn't know how to love or even care for anyone but herself. "I need you to put your selfishness to the side for five seconds and realize how you're not only hurting me, you're also hurting Sabine. Your children." I'm met with silence. "Let me have custody. Let me raise her and love her. You can see her when you want, and I'll never not allow you to speak to her. You can live the life you want, and I'll raise Sabine."

"Dart, you're a baby. You don't want to raise any damn kids."

"You don't know me," I say, my heart in my throat. "Sabine is the sunshine of my life. Please do what's right. Not for me, but for her."

I almost think she'll just agree, until she says, "I'll need some money." I close my eyes, and a tear leaks out. It shatters me that she only cares about the money and not how amazing my sister is. "I want to leave here and start over somewhere new."

"I can do that as soon as you sign the papers and I'm given custody."

"That could take months."

"You're right, but I won't have you fuck me over," I sneer. "I'm not giving you a cent until it goes through the courts."

"Then what am I supposed to do with her now?"

"Take care of her, love her, spend time with her," I suggest, my anger taking over. "Or fuck, put her on a plane, and I'll take her now."

Her laughter is like acid on my skin. I close my eyes, not realizing until now just how much I hate her. How she could have ruined me if it weren't for the love my grandpa showered me with. "Mark my words, D'Artagnan, you may be gaining your sister, but I hope you're ready to lose that girl of yours. No one should be saddled with the burden of a child who isn't theirs. No matter how much they claim to love someone. She may think you're worth it now, but that'll change."

HAT TRICK

I want to cuss at her. I want to call her out. But instead, I press my lips together as I wipe away the tears that are falling.

"Get her a plane ticket and the paperwork going so this can be done," she bites out.

A sob tries to escape at the relief I feel, but I hold it in. I bend over at my hip, my hand biting into my thigh. Sabine will be safe. She'll be with us. She'll be safe.

I almost hang up, but then Kris stops me. "Hold on. She wants to talk to you."

I don't answer her, but then Sabine's voice fills the line. "Dart! Is it true? I can come live with you?"

I swallow my sob at her excitement. "Were you eavesdropping?"

"No, Mom just told me!" she says, and I can almost see her bouncing on her toes. "I am so excited. We're gonna have so much fun."

"We will, and you'll get to meet Tennessee, finally."

I'm meant with a loaded silence. "Tennessee? Your friend?"

"My girlfriend. We live together. She's really excited to get to know you."

I hear hesitation in Sabine's voice as she asks, "What if she doesn't like me?"

"Sabine, she will. She'll love you. You're awesome just like me, and she loves me."

"I'm sure you're right. Though, I wish it were just us. I miss being with you, but I'm excited to get to know her," she says, but I don't know if I believe her.

"I promise you'll love her. She's great."

"I'm sure she is," she says softly. "She doesn't know me, though."

"But she will," I urge, and I know she'll love my sister as I do.

Right?

This is the same girl who ghosted you. She doesn't want to take care of your sister for you. She'll ghost you again.

The words from the woman who gave birth to me infect my happiness as I hang up and look up at the heavens. She can't be right. Sabine will love Tennessee. I just know it. Just as I know Tennessee will love Sabine and care for her. But if that is the case, why are Kris's words

TONI ALEO

playing over and over in my head. Is it wrong of me to ask this of Tennessee? Will she hate me and leave me when it becomes too much?

I slide down the side of the building and clutch my face with my hands.

I can't choose between my sister and the love of my life. I won't.

This has to work.

Fuck, what if it doesn't?

CHAPTER
Thirty-Five

TENNESSEE

I don't know what I ever saw in Troy.

Did I really think I could get over D'Artagnan with him?

I was an idiot.

Because Troy is annoying as all fuck.

I never noticed how he speaks over me until now. How he thinks he knows my formulas and my program better than I do. It's unbelievable, and I'm getting more and more annoyed with each passing moment.

"You designed this program?" Kirby asks me when the AI version of himself is on my computer and I'm pointing out the weak areas in his hips.

"I did," I say proudly. "I designed it for my master's program."

"Wow. This is impressive."

"Thank you—"

"Which is why we scooped her right up," Troy says from beside me. I shift to my left leg to put some space between us as I click on one of Kirby's weak spaces. "We are excited to have such a program in our company. It'll help a lot of athletes."

TONI ALEO

My hand pauses on my mouth as I side-eye him. "I'm sure you mean *me* since the program is mine and I use it for our athletes."

Troy looks at me and shrugs. "Same thing."

"Not really," Kirby says before I can. "Lose her, you lose the program."

"Exactly," I murmur, and I don't appreciate Troy's comments or his tone. Like he owns me. Ooh, my daddy would lose his mind, and Dart...well, he'd beat Troy's ass for sure. I exhale as I bring Kirby's attention to the weak spot in his pelvic bone. "This is an old break. We can't fix it and your body already healed on its own, but look at the scar tissue around it. It's so thick that your nerves are being pressed on, and I believe that's what is causing the pain when you go into your stride."

He looks closer. "Shit. Is that fixable? 'Cause this pain is rough and constant when we have long road trips."

"Not really fixable," Troy says, and he tries to reach for the mouse, but I don't move my hand. "Tenn—"

"Excuse me," I snap, cutting my eyes to his. "This is my client, my assessment. Can you let me do my job?"

Kirby covers his mouth to hide his smile as Troy lifts his hand and steps back.

"Thank you." I clear my throat and explain the treatment plan for Kirby. I give him a folder of my notes and the scans for him to take to the doctor with him. "We'll try PT before we try surgery—which, if you're consistent with PT, I am confident you won't need the surgery."

He nods. "Will I come back for more scans to track my progress with *you*?"

Oh, I adore this guy. My smile is wide as I promise, "I'll repeat them every three months. I'll also take extra scans when you practice and at games, just to make sure I'm not missing anything."

Troy makes a face. "That isn't included in the IceCats contract."

"Not yet," I say simply. "But after my meeting with the coach about his son, he is wanting more for his players, and I offered."

"That's not your decision," he says in a low voice, his eyes narrowing as they hold mine. "Doing all that will pull you away from other teams."

HAT TRICK

"Maybe for you. But I am able to do all that for the IceCats and the coach's son's team, and I also got through most of my scans for the baseball team in the last week. I am very capable."

His eyes narrow to slits. "I'm in control of what we do, contract-wise."

I hold his gaze. "For now."

Kirby chuckles before he grips my shoulder. "Dart has his hands full with you."

With a wink, I say, "More so than he even realizes."

"Good," he says, patting my back. "Thank you, Tennessee. I look forward to working with you."

"As do I. Have a good day."

When the door shuts, I save and close my program before I look over at Troy since I can feel him watching me. "Yes?"

"I feel like there is a divide between us."

"No? You think?" I ask, my words dripping with sarcasm. "Could it be that you consistently talk over me, talk about my program as if it's yours…oh, and that you told my boyfriend you can only pull big girls to like you, so he should allow you to have me? Like I'm an object and not a person with feelings?"

Color drains from his face.

"So yes, there is a wedge, a divide, whatever you want to call it. It's big, thick, and fat right there between us. Where it belongs."

"We have to work together, Tennie. I am sorry for what I said. I did it out of love."

I laugh at that. "You don't know how to love. You know how to control, and guess what? The only time I'm controllable is in bed with my boyfriend."

He winces. "I know how to love you."

I push my hair off my shoulders as I gather my things.

"You just didn't give me a chance."

"Because the chance wasn't yours. It was Dart's." His eyes burn with frustration as I sit down, crossing my legs and putting my hands in my lap. "I have no issue working with you if you can let me do my job and not manage me like you're my boss and not my colleague."

TONI ALEO

"I asked you many times for us to live together here, and you told me no. But then you move in with him?"

I look up at him, unfazed. "Because I didn't want to live with you."

"But you want to live with him? Someone you don't know."

"My living arrangements are none of your concern."

"Do your parents know? Because they sure never seemed welcoming to me."

I snort, shaking my head. "My parents were very kind to you when Lord knows you didn't deserve it, and yes, they do know and support us. They love him."

"You let them meet him?"

"Yes, showed him off like the prized stallion he is." I'm being petty, but I refuse to let him tear down my choice. I am happy, and that's all that matters. "Now, if you're done, can we get this meeting over with? I'm sure Dart will be finished soon, and I don't want him waiting on me."

"Don't we have his scans to do?" he asks incredulously, and my lips turn up in the most devilish of grins I can muster. My level of petty is at an all-time high.

"Dart and I already went over his scans in our home, thoroughly."

Troy scoffs, looking away, annoyed. "We could have had a great life."

"No. We'd have a mediocre life," I say to him, my shoulders back and the confidence flowing off me in waves. Confidence Dart has helped cultivate in me. "With Dart, I'll have a great life. A strong, well-loved, protected, and satisfying life."

"You're delusional. He'll end up—"

"Before you say anything out of line about my boyfriend, remember he is not the only one who can break your nose. I'd hate to mess up my manicure, but you will not speak ill of the man I love."

"You've changed."

"No. I stepped out of the shadows and found myself."

His tablet on the table rings, and I'm thankful for the interruption. I know for a fact that if Dart were to come by and see the look on Troy's face and mine, he'd be in the room faster than he could put a puck in the back of an empty net. Troy huffs as he moves to the side of the

HAT TRICK

table and answers the call on the tablet. It's his uncle, for our meeting that I have no desire to deal with at this moment. My crossed leg bounces as I open my phone to see that I have no messages from Dart, which is odd. He always texts me, and I expected him to be done before me. I glance at the clock, and as I assumed, he should be done. I text him quickly.

Me: I've got another twenty minutes probably.

Dart: I'll be in the truck.

I purse my lips at his response, and something doesn't feel right.

Me: You good?

When he doesn't answer right away, my stomach feels sour. I set my phone down when I hear my name from the tablet, and I look up to see Mr. Richardson, Troy's uncle. "Good to see you, Tennessee. How are you?"

"I am well, thank you."

"Wonderful. Let's jump right in. Were you not happy with the apartment? When I got the email that you no longer needed it, I meant to get ahold of you right away. But you know how it goes sometimes."

"Absolutely. And the apartment was fine, but I had the opportunity to move in with my boyfriend, and I took it."

He makes a face, almost a confused but also rehearsed one, that I don't trust for shit. "Okay, so it's none of my business, but you didn't move in with Troy when you moved to South Carolina. So, of course, you can understand my confusion."

I only smile. "Yes, it is none of your business." His gaze is displeased, but I hold my ground. "As much as I appreciated the living arrangements, per my email, I will no longer be in need of them."

I can feel Troy's eyes on me as Mr. Richardson says, "Okay, moving on." He threads his fingers together and puts them on the desk as he holds my gaze. I am thankful for the computer because this man is scary. But I refuse to be bullied into giving him information he wants. "We'd like to buy your program."

"It's not for sale," I say without hesitation.

He doesn't like that one bit. "But when you were hired, we discussed it as an option to further your position in the company. So, you can be a shareholder."

267

TONI ALEO

"Things change," I explain. "I don't know if that's the route I want to go anymore. I believe a lot of details need to be discussed regarding my position in the company. I'm no longer confident that it's me y'all want, rather than just my program."

His brows furrow. "We want both."

"Which is refreshing, but at this time, I am not ready to discuss any purchase options for my program. I also don't want to relocate."

I see his jaw tick, and I can feel how uncomfortable Troy is. "When you signed on, you were fine with relocating."

"Once more, that has changed for me. I want to put down roots here."

He nods slowly. "That could pose a problem for us."

"I am aware, which is another reason why I'm not sure I want to discuss selling my program anymore."

He runs his hand down his mouth, obviously flustered. "Okay, we can discuss this again at a later time. But for now, I do need to tell you that your contract states you can't be romantically involved with an athlete you work with through CapitalCare."

I take a deep breath and hold up my finger to stop him. "If you check my logged-in time and D'Artagnan Miklas's files, you will see that my hours on the clock will not include him. I did all his scans on my time."

"Yes, but you used our cameras, didn't you?"

Oh, he thought he had me. "I didn't. Troy has your set, and I have a set that I purchased four months ago when Troy and I would split up to get more work done."

Mr. Richardson's throat works as he holds my gaze. "It is unprofessional to be sleeping—"

"Mr. Richardson, let me stop you there," I say, sitting up so my back is straight. "Who I sleep with and who I don't is not the concern of this company. You don't get to decide it's okay for me to sleep with your nephew but not the man I love. If my relationship with D'Artagnan Miklas is an issue for you and yours, I have no problem ending our relationship."

His eyes dance with his perceived victory. "It would be best if you did end the relationship."

HAT TRICK

"Fine," I say, standing up. "I quit."

Troy's eyes widen as I look at him. I could cuss him out, I could even throw the tablet at him, but he doesn't deserve any more emotion from me. Mr. Richardson is trying to stop me and is calling my name, but I ignore him as I gather my things and take off my long-sleeved CapitalCare work shirt, leaving me in Dart's IceCats player tee.

I didn't wear his shirt on purpose; it was honestly the first thing I saw when I got out of the shower, but now, as I walk away from Troy and this company, Dart's name across my back, it's the pièce de résistance. A huge fuck you, just the way it should be. Like I'd choose this job over Dart. Please. With each step I take, I only feel more confident in my choice and I get closer to the only person I would choose over and over again.

Dart.

CHAPTER
Thirty-Six

Dart

I get out of the truck when I see her coming down the stairs of the practice facility.

The smile on her face when our eyes meet takes my breath away, but when I see she is wearing my IceCats tee, I'm wrecked to my core as tears burn my eyes. I don't want to lose her, but I also don't want to trap her. I swallow thickly as I take her bags, and without control, I lean in for a kiss from her. I can't *not* kiss her when I'm near her. I need her as much as I need the next breath of air in my body.

"So, get this shit," she says all animatedly and beautifully. "Troy was being a douche canoe the whole time, and I was getting so pissed. He said the company was lucky to have a program that did so much for the athletes. Ugh. Excuse me, the program doesn't work without me!"

I only nod as I open her door and then the back to put her things in.

"So, then we have a meeting with his uncle, the CEO, and he brings up that I'm living with you."

My stomach twists as I nod. "That's none of his fucking business."

HAT TRICK

I shut the back door and wait for her to put her legs in the truck as she says, "Exactly!"

I shut the door, the dread heavy in my stomach as I move around the truck, getting in, and she continues. "He was so arrogant and thinking he had me under his thumb. And let me tell you, my daddy raised me to always stay five steps ahead of anyone I work for. He's been telling me not to sell my program for anything, that I'm sitting on a gold mine. Everyone at UT and Vandy knows that, and I didn't listen. But then, it's okay that I didn't, because if I had stayed in Nashville, I wouldn't have linked back up with you, and I wouldn't be as happy as I am now, ya know?"

"Yeah," I agree, my voice low.

Her voice gets louder as she retells what happened, and I can feel her passion, her love for me coming off her in waves that are slamming against my body. Her confidence is mind-blowing, beautiful, and I know, I fucking know deep in my heart, I'll never love anyone like her. No amount of pussy could ever make me forget her. Make me not love her. Nothing. I am hers, and I love her. Fuck, I love her.

"Any work I did for your assessment was done on my own time. I never charged them a lick because I didn't trust Troy. I had to protect my career. But now, forget that. I'm going to start my own company."

My hands shake against the wheel as I turn onto our road, and then I notice she has gone quiet. I can't look at her. I fight the urge as I pull up into my yard in case she wants to leave. She should want to leave; she has to, or I'll crumble and allow her to be put in a situation she didn't sign up for. She signed up for me. And while I know she said she wants my sister with us, the more I think about it, the more my mom's words play in my head, the more the fear builds that I wouldn't be giving Tennessee everything she needs.

"Dart."

I press my lips together, swallowing hard past this boulder-sized lump in my throat.

"D'Artagnan. Look at me."

"Tennessee—"

"I said, look at me," she demands, and my lips quiver as I do as she says. She reaches out, taking my sunglasses off my face, and her lips turn down as her eyes widen. Tears fill her eyes almost immediately as she climbs across the seat and into my lap. "D'Artagnan, what is wrong? What happened?" She straddles my hips, her hands coming to my face to hold me in place, so I can't look away. "Is it Sabine? What's wrong? Is she okay?"

God, she feels so good in my lap. I wrap my arms around her waist, not willing to say a word, the fear of the future threatening to consume me whole. I try to swallow again, but the sob that wants to escape is choking me. She moves her fingers along my jaw, her sweet eyes searching mine as I take a deep breath.

"I talked to my mom, and she is going to sign over custody of Sabine."

Elation fills her face as she squeezes my cheek, kissing me hard on the lips. I lean into the kiss, unsure if it will be my last, before she says excitedly, "Thank sweet Jesus! And God bless Jaylin. She is such a queen!"

I couldn't agree more, but the weight of everything else is crushing my chest.

"Baby, this is great news, but I'm super confused by your demeanor. I thought this was what we wanted?"

We. Us. Her and I. A unit. A team.

Tennessee and D'Artagnan.

That's what I offered her, that's what I want, yet…

I stare into her eyes, my heart racing in my chest. I feel as unsteady as my voice is as I whisper, "Tennessee." It's all I can get out as her eyes bore into mine for the answers I'm unable to provide.

"What the hell is going on?" she demands, her voice breaking.

"Tenn—"

"Stop saying my name. You don't say my name like that. I'm your baby doll," she snaps, and tears roll down her face.

My eyes fall shut as I press my lips together, trying to keep all the emotion in.

"Dart, tell me what's going on. You're scaring me."

"As much as I don't want to say this, maybe you should call CapitalCare and see if you can get your job and apartment back."

Her brows slam together as her eyes narrow to slits. "I think the

HAT TRICK

fuck I won't," she says with so much vengeance, I only love her more. "What the hell is going on? Does your mom think I won't be good for Sabine? Because at this point, an iPad would be a better parent than her."

I almost laugh at the truth of that statement. "I can't lock you down like this, have you care for my sister when she's not your blood or your child." Her eyes challenge mine as I whisper, "I love you too much to trap you."

"So, you think you're gonna break up with me, and I'm gonna go back to a job that I just chose you over?"

"It would be for the best," I tell her, urging her with my eyes. "You shouldn't be burdened with my family drama."

Silence stretches between us as she searches my gaze.

"You dumbass," she accuses, surprising the hell out of me. "Your drama is my drama because I love you. Your bullshit is my bullshit. Your love is my love. D'Artagnan, come on, dude. You're not stupid."

"I'm trying to protect you."

"By putting space between us?" she asks, her eyes wild and incredulous. "How'd that work for us the first time? You fucked around, and I got into a relationship with someone who couldn't even make me the least bit happy. Is that what you want for us?"

"Tenn—" My words are cut short by the look in her eyes. I can't help but chuckle at her. "Fucking hell, baby. You are scary-hot when you're pissed."

Her eyes are devastating. Her blue eye is the color of a hurricane, and her green one is giving me promises of lush lands. With a huff, she says, "I'm unsure if I want to fuck you right now or hit you upside the head for being so dumb."

I want to laugh at her because I know she means every word, but I'm sure she packs a hell of a punch and I'm already rattled as it is. "You deserve more."

"Are you serious?"

"Yes."

"So, what do I deserve?"

"Everything," I say softly, our eyes locking.

She pokes me in the chest. "You're everything." She pokes again,

TONI ALEO

harder. "Everything I have ever wanted." Once more, her fingernail bites into my chest. "And everything I have dreamed my future to be."

"Tennessee."

"No, D'Artagnan. It's you. I have never in my life loved anyone the way I love you. You scared me so badly at first, I tried to run. Dart, I'm not fucking running. I'm right here. I'm yours."

My lips start to quiver, and she leans in. "I'm not going anywhere. You're not breaking up with me, because we were made for each other." My hands shake at her hips, holding her to me as her lips dust mine. "You don't want me to leave, do you?"

I squeeze my eyes shut, our noses colliding as I shake my head.

"Then what the fuck are you even saying?"

"I love you, baby. I love you so much, and I don't want to trap you."

"It wouldn't be a trap if I am with you and the person you love, your baby sister. Dart, my love, I want all of you."

It's almost like the unsteadiness starts to even out with each promise from her lips. I hold on to her, needing her for that stable ground her words and body give me. Her trust and love that give me such hope. Where was she when my mom called? "I love you. So fucking much."

"I know you do," she whispers against my lips, catching my tears and wiping them away.

"I don't want to hurt you or ruin your life, Tennessee."

"Baby, you add to my life," she urges, her lips moving against mine. "What or who brought you to this way of thinking? I know I didn't. I want to have Sabine. I want to help raise her—and love her the way you do. I want to be that woman she can look up to. I want these things because she is a part of you."

"My mom…" I say, squeezing her body with my arms. "She told me you wouldn't stay once the burden of Sabine became real."

"Because she's a toxic bitch," she says, like the mention of my mom leaves a bad taste in her mouth. "First, Sabine isn't a burden. She's a gift. And second, fuck her. I'm not going anywhere because I'm not her and my love isn't conditional like hers. My love is yours, Dart."

I know this. I felt this from the first time I touched my lips to

HAT TRICK

hers. Tennessee was different. *Is* different. She is mine, just as I am hers. As I open my eyes and they collide with hers, I know her words are true. I don't want to be a broken heart left in her wake, and that's what I'll be if I force her to walk away. I won't ever find joy again because she makes everything so much better just by existing.

"I don't want to lose you. Ever."

She strokes her thumb along my bottom lip. "How can you when I'm not going anywhere without you?" When she presses her nose to my cheek, I feel her tears falling along my skin. "Or Sabine," she adds, solidifying her truth to me. My heart swells in my chest, my stomach dropping, and slowly, I open my eyes to find her in my arms and completely mine.

Her tears spill over her cheeks, and I wipe them away, holding her gaze as our love and devotion to each other envelops us. "I don't like when you cry."

"Then don't be stupid," she suggests, her eyes playful and fucking beautiful. "Once we have custody of Sabine, don't talk to your mom unless it has to do with Sabine, okay? We have to protect your peace."

We.

I grip her hips, unable to let her go.

"Do you understand me? Do you believe me, Dart? I'm not going anywhere. I promise you that."

I tighten my grip as her eyes capture mine. "I wouldn't let you if you tried."

She grins at that. "There is my man," she purrs, running her thumb along my lips. "Don't ever forget who you are, who I am, and who we are together."

"A team."

"A winning team," she corrects. "Now, take me inside and make love to me."

My face breaks into a grin.

"You've done stressed me out, and I need to come on your cock. Like, right now."

I slide my hands down to her ass, my body shaking with want for her. "My cock works just fine right here, ya know."

TONI ALEO

"Then what are you waiting for?" she challenges as heat coils in my gut, and said cock comes to life just for her.

"One thing," I tell her, holding her close.

"Which is?"

"For a moment to admire the woman I get to love for the rest of my life."

She leans in, her lips brushing mine as her eyes sparkle. "Worm food."

My lips curve against hers as I brush her hair off her shoulders, falling even more in love with her. "And we'll do it all over again in our next life."

"I can't wait."

"Neither can I."

Our lips crash together, and I realize that even if I'd tried to put space between us, it wouldn't have worked. It didn't before, and it wouldn't now. Or ever.

Because this love we have isn't a one-lifetime thing.

It's a multiple-lifetimes thing.

I will always find her.

Just as she will find me.

All we'll need is three rounds of tequila before ten a.m., an orange dildo, and each other to set the world on fire.

Epilogue

TENNESSEE

"Are you sure orange is my color, Tennie?"

I look over to where Sabine stands between my parents. She's wearing a pair of wide-leg white jeans with sparkly orange shoes and an oversize Tennessee hoodie. Her hair is up in a high ponytail with an orange ribbon tied in a bow. Her blue eyes are shining bright, and I love how much her face has filled out. When she came to us, she was skinnier than I liked, though I never brought it up because I knew Dart would lose it. Now, only a month from the day we got her, she looks healthy. And God, is she happy.

We all are.

My daddy's gaze moves from the game to set Sabine with a look, grinning from ear to ear as his booming voice fills our suite. "Darling, I don't think I've ever seen anyone look better in orange than you do right now!"

Sabine beams as she wiggles, and she smiles proudly up at me. I wrap an arm around her, holding her as we cheer on my—I mean, our —Vols. What used to be just my Saturday ritual has turned into

TONI ALEO

Sabine's and Dart's too. Even when he's not home, he keeps up with the game, and it pleases me to no end.

I still haven't gotten used to him being gone. I miss him like crazy, but when he is gone, it gives Sabine and me time to get to know each other. And lordy, I love her. She is her brother's sister, for sure. Passionate, kind, and so damn loving. I honestly don't even know what Dart's birthing unit was running her mouth about. I'm not trapped, not even in the slightest. Every day, I'm rewarded with the love of two people my life would have no meaning without. Is it easy? Not always. There have been some growing pains. Sabine missed her mom at first, but once we got her into school and violin classes, she started to find her footing. I know she's where she is supposed to be, and the fact that her mother hasn't called or checked in since the moment Sabine got to us only reinforces how I feel.

She's worthless, and Sabine is better off.

"Did that loan come through?" Daddy asks, pulling me from the gameplay and all my thoughts. Like I wanted, I have started my own company to rival CapitalCare. It's been a rough start since I offered to pay the fee to break the contract between the teams that wanted to work with me instead of CapitalCare, but it hasn't discouraged me. I'm excited. I just needed the capital, and even though my daddy was ready to invest, he would have to take out a loan to do so, and I wasn't okay with that.

"So…" I start, holding up my hand, "don't get mad."

"Jesus Christ," he mutters. "He talked you into letting him put up the money."

Him, being Dart. "Yes, but he is going to be a silent partner, and we still want you on board."

Daddy scoffs. "There ain't nothing silent about that boy."

"This is true," Dart says, slapping my daddy on the back respectfully. He wears a full Vols suit that he special-ordered and looks absolutely delicious in. I wish I had time to take him back to the hotel tonight and peel it off him, but he has to fly out to rejoin the team in California. He didn't have the days off he would have had if we had come earlier, but we pushed our trip back so that Sabine had time to

HAT TRICK

adjust before we brought her to meet my parents. It worked out too because I missed Josie and Denis's wedding. Much to my mother's dismay. "But my lawyer is drawing up the papers, and I promise Tennessee will be protected, as will I. We truly want you to be a part of Rocky Top Athletics."

Pride fills my daddy's gaze, but his eyes are still sharp as they hold Dart's. "I'm trusting you, boy."

His words are very weighted, and I know Dart feels every single ounce of it. A lesser man would cower to my dad, but not my man. With so much confidence and assurance, he says, "I know. And I promise you, I will never hurt her or do anything to put her in a position where she is not succeeding. Trust me, I want what you do—for her to be happy and flourishing. For all of us to succeed."

He doesn't say it, but I know in his heart, he sees us all as a family.

And for me, we are.

I can tell my dad wants to say more, probably scare him a bit, but Mom steps between them. "Thomas, don't be like that," she says, patting his chest. She turns to Dart. "He was watching your game the other night and said he needed himself a Miklas jersey to support you. He knows you've got our baby's back. We aren't worried, darling."

My face breaks into a grin as a flush moves across Dart's face. Daddy sputters as he sets Momma with a look. "You got a big mouth, woman."

"I do. It's your favorite thing about me," she says with a wink, and I promptly gag as Dart snorts with laughter. She cups Sabine's cheeks. "Darling girl, you want some ice cream?"

Sabine nods excitedly, and together they go to the ice cream bar in the suite as Dart says, "I'll ship that jersey, Mr. Dent."

"Thomas," Daddy says, meeting Dart's gaze. "I don't see you going anywhere, so might as well be on first-name basis with each other since apparently we're going to be business partners."

They shake hands, and my heart flutters in my chest. "Like I said the first time we met, my friends call me Dart."

Dad nods, a little tip to his lips. "Sounds good to me, Dart."

Excitement radiates through me as love shines in Dart's eyes. He

TONI ALEO

leans into me, kissing my lips as I tighten my arms around him. I still can't believe this is my life. That I get to wake up every day, kiss this man, raise his sister, and help athletes. Dart drags his lips along mine and then kisses my nose. "You look radiantly orange today, baby doll."

And I do. I go all out when I come to games. My orange glitter bell bottoms with my UT boots and oversize, long-sleeved UT jersey don't leave any question as to where my loyalty lies. I am a proud UT fan and live right on up to my namesake. "Rocky Top is my home sweet home," I say, and he grins.

"God, you're gorgeous."

He kisses me again as Daddy leans in. "Don't look now, but Josie and Denis are here."

I turn to where he is looking to see my childhood friend holding hands with my ex. Her hand is on her belly, and if I were a shitty bitch, I'd laugh at her for gaining weight, all of it in her face. But I don't have to. Karma is a bitch, and by the look on her face, I can tell she isn't happy. She is faking it. I would have assumed that would make me happy. But being in Dart's arms, knowing I never have to fake this, I feel nothing but sadness for her.

She'll never know what true love is.

"I heard a rumor," Daddy says, waggling his brows. "Josie has already stepped out on him."

My eyes widen. "I mean, she can't get pregnant again," I observe, and both the men in my life laugh at that. "It's sad, though. For both of them."

Daddy shrugs. "Like you said, darling, karma is a bitch."

Dart nods as I lean into him, just as Josie's eyes meet mine. Her face fills with a flush as I stare into her eyes, not reacting to seeing her. I'd wondered if seeing her would make me miss her, but it doesn't. Not even a bit. I have my family and a life I love. One I had to leave home for, and I don't regret that at all.

I look away just as Sabine comes crashing into us. "Dart, Tennie, look!" she gushes, holding up an orange violin that my parents have given her. "They said I can only play 'Rocky Top' on it, but it's orange! It's gonna go great with my blue and my black one."

"I wanted to get her a fiddle, but Tennie said no."

"Because it's not the same thing as a violin, Daddy!"

He laughs as Dart shakes his head. "You guys are set on making us Vols fans, huh?"

Momma laughs at that. "Making y'all? Boy, you've been a Vols fan since you met her," Mom says, hooking her thumb to me, and Dart doesn't deny it.

"I don't think you gave me much choice in the matter."

"I sure didn't," I say, clutching the lapels of his jacket. "Not that you're complaining."

He cups my face. "Nothing to complain about when I got you."

Lordy, just when I thought I couldn't love him any more, his words tickle my soul. Forever is looking pretty damn good for us.

But then the fight song comes on, and when my dad wraps his arm around Dart, I take Sabine in mine, and all together, we sing for our Vols.

As a family.

While nothing could make me happier than being at the game with my family, the Vols winning really is the cherry on top. As the stadium clears out, we all stay in the box eating dinner like we've done since I was a kid. My parents hate the traffic, and since we've always had a suite, we stay and eat so that nothing goes to waste.

When Daddy stands, wiping his mouth, he explains, "I'm gonna take Dart and Sabine around, show them the stadium before y'all gotta head out."

"Cool!" Sabine gushes, and I send her a smile.

"Don't be surprised when you decide this is the school you want to go to," I warn her as Dart kisses my temple.

"Like you'd let her go anywhere else?" he says against my skin before kissing me again.

I grin up at him. "I mean, are there other options? It's the best school ever."

He chuckles as he kisses my lips and then rushes to catch up to my dad and Sabine. Once they are out the door, I look across to where my mom is watching me, her lips curved up in a pleased smile. "He makes you so happy."

Breathless, I nod. "He does. I love him very much."

TONI ALEO

"I can tell," she says, exhaling. "I owe you an apology for questioning y'all. If I had spent even a second around you two, I would have known never to doubt you."

She holds my gaze, her eyes full of guilt. "I am sorry, darling." I shrug, and she adds, "For everything. I guess since I'd have a hard time living without my best friends, I thought the same of you. But darling, you don't need anyone."

"I need him," I say, my heart swelling in my chest.

She gets up as I do, and we hug tightly. No matter how much she gets on my nerves and always butts in, I love her deeply. "I am so proud of you."

I hold her closer. "Thanks, Momma."

She takes my hands in hers. "Come on. Let's catch up with everyone."

We walk hand in hand out the door and through the stadium. Memories of running through this place as a child hit me, each one including Josie and Lindy. Some good and some bad, but now that I know Dart and Sabine are here, we're making new memories. Better ones that will forever live in my heart. When Mom turns toward the tunnel that leads to the field, I glance over at her.

"Did Daddy get clearance to show them the field?"

"Yes, from my understanding," she says. "You know he likes to show off."

"True," I laugh as we head down the tunnel to the field, but my laughter falls off when my eyes meet his.

Dart stands in the middle of the field, surrounded by orange and white flowers, the bright lights of Neyland Stadium illuminating his gorgeous face. To his left, Sabine has her new orange violin to her cheek as she runs her bow across it, the melody of "Tennessee Orange" filling the space around him as she gets lost in the music. My heart basically comes out of my chest before I look at my momma.

Tears spill down her cheeks as pride fills her gaze. She tips her head toward Dart and whispers, "Go on, darling. Your forever is waiting."

She kisses the back of my hand and then lets it go as my eyes meet his once more. A small grin pulls at his lips, and the world falls away.

HAT TRICK

A feeling I still haven't gotten used to, even though it happens a lot when it comes to him. I will myself to move, closing the distance between us, his smirk growing as Sabine plays in all her glory.

Sabine's eyes land on me, and my heart shatters when she mouths, "I love you."

As she gets to the chorus of the song, I stop right in front of him. My tears tumble over my cheeks as our eyes lock, excitement and love coursing through my body. "I was wondering how long you were going to make me wait to be your wife."

His face breaks into a grin. "What are you talking about? I just wanted to have a nice song played in the middle of a field with flowers —just to see you smile."

"Lies," I accuse, and his eyes burn into mine.

"Yeah, but what's not a lie is that I would have married you the day I met you, Tennessee Lynn." My breath catches as my tears fall faster, my love so damn great for this beautiful man. "I have and always will love you with every single ounce of my body and soul. I know for a fact that our souls are meant to be one and that my life isn't worth a damn unless you are in it."

He starts to lower to one knee, his eyes never leaving mine. "Everything about you makes me happy. Your smile, your laugh, the purse of your lips, the passion you have for me, and every bit of how *greedy* you are." He sends me a knowing wink that leaves me breathless. "You rattle me, baby doll, to the core. But you also steady me."

I swallow past my sob as I whisper, "I love you."

His breath catches before he reaches into his pocket and brings out a red box. He opens it to reveal the most stunning orange diamond engagement ring I've ever seen. It's huge, surrounded by smaller diamonds encrusted on a platinum band. My hand comes over my mouth in shock, my heart slamming in my chest as our eyes meet once more. "When I asked your dad if I could marry you, he laughed and asked if I was even sure you'd say yes," he tells me, and I shake my head. My daddy is a riot. "I'm not scared you'll say no, Tennessee. I know you'll say yes because I know that you love me, that nothing can come between us as long as we have each other."

TONI ALEO

I wipe my face, unable to look anywhere but into his blue eyes.

"You are not only good to me, but to Sabine, and I can't thank you enough for that. For making our home hers."

"I love you both."

"And I love you more for that," he says, not only making that promise with his words, but his eyes too. I'm lost in them. "Put me out of my misery, Tennessee Lynn. Be mine forever. Be my baby doll, my greedy girl, my dragon queen," he teases, and laughter bubbles from me as I fall to my knees in front of him. I cup his face as our foreheads press together, our noses colliding just as hard as our loving gazes. He sucks in a deep breath and then lets it out in a whoosh before he says to me, "Be my wife, Tennessee."

I run my fingers along his jaw, my heart a jackhammer in my chest as I stare into his eyes. "As if I have any choice in the matter," I tease as his lips curve. "Because I've been yours since that second round of tequila shots." Light shines deeply in those blue depths as he holds me close. "So yes, D'Artagnan Athos Porthos Aramis Miklas, I want nothing more than to be your wife."

His lips capture mine, and we wrap our arms around each other as my heart sings for him. Our kiss is long, drawn-out, and has my heart exploding in my chest for this passionate, strong-willed man. When we part, both gasping for breath, he slides his nose along mine as he whispers, "I'm gonna love you forever, baby doll."

"And then some," I add, and his eyes sparkle for me.

"And when that's not enough, I know I'll find you again, Tennessee."

My body tingles under his gaze, his words, his heart. "I'll always be waiting, and I won't ghost you again. Promise."

Dart's eyes dance with mine. "I won't make that mistake again."

"I won't either."

I press my lips to his top one, and he whispers, "I love you."

Oh, those three words. If I weren't already on my knees, I'd fall to them once more. My favorite words to hear from his naughty lips and the same words that are just as easy as breathing to say back to him.

With my lips brushing his, I whisper back, "I love you."

HAT TRICK

Our lips move together again, and just like the moment in that hotel room all those months ago, I know I'll never be the same.

Not when my soul belongs to this man.

My everything, my nerdy dragon king—but most of all, my forever.

Acknowledgments

This is a big year for me. *2023*. My son turned eighteen and went off to WKU, where he is becoming an incredible young man. I am so proud.

Michael and I have been married for twenty years this year. He is, and always will be, my favorite hockey player.

Alyssa will turn sixteen by the time this book comes out, and each day she is growing into such a beautiful person. She is going to do such big things.

This year also marks the end of Michael's and my thirties. It's insane how time is so fleeting, and while I wish it would slow down, I am proud of the fact that I keep fighting. I don't give up or quit.

This year also marks ten years without my mom, and I miss her daily. She gave me the gift of loving books. It was her and Michael who pushed me to write and publish. I couldn't be more thankful for the woman she raised me to be; I just wish I weren't so mentally ill. Still, though, even if I am mentally ill, I am not mentally weak. I just have to fight for myself more than others, which is okay. I was made for this, and I will continue fighting.

When I went off my meds and wrote two books in a matter of weeks, it was a gift. It reminded me who I am, and while I love *Heavy Shot*, *Hat Trick* is by far my favorite. I started reading romantasy and found my inner smutty slut. LOL. I love her, and I want to explore her more and more. I am proud of this book—and myself. And my inner smutty slut.

Now, my life wouldn't be complete without Lisa. I love her. Deeply. She supports me, she cares for me, and I know she has my back, no matter what. She gives me space when I go on my silent bouts, she pushes me to be better, and she is always there for me. I love her.

Franci, Heather, Jessica, Stacie, Jill, Jeanette, Christine, my girls. My betas. I adore y'all. Thank you for helping me make Dart and Tennessee who they are.

To Bobbie Jo, my life would have no meaning without you.

Michael, Mikey, Alyssa, and Phoebe, each day I wake up and I fight, for you. I love you.

While the people above are a huge part of my life, I wouldn't be who I am without YOU. The person who reads my books, who likes my posts, who reviews my books, who always supports and loves me. Thank you. I am forever grateful for you.

Love,
Toni

Also by Toni Aleo

NASHVILLE ASSASSINS

Breaking Away

Laces and Lace

A Very Merry Hockey Holiday

Wanting to Forget

Overtime

Rushing the Goal

Puck, Sticks, and Diapers

Face-off at the Altar

Delayed Call

Twenty-Two

In the Crease

One Timer

Nashville Assassins: Next Generation

Dump & Chase

Power Play

Bring It Home

Blades of Glory

The Chase is Over

Dirty Toe Drag

Bellevue Bullies Series

Boarded by Love

Clipped by Love

Hooked by Love

End Game

Spiked by Love

Saved by Love

IceCats Series

Juicy Rebound

Wild Tendy

Hard Hit

All the Sauce

Taking Risks

Whiskey Prince

Becoming the Whiskey Princess

Whiskey Rebellion

Patchwork Series

(Paranormal)

Pieces

Broken Pieces

Spring Grove Novels

(Small-town romances)

Not the One

Small-Town Sweetheart

Standalones

Let it be Me

Two-Man Advantage

Misadventures

(Standalones)

Misadventures with a Rookie

Misadventures of a Manny

Assassins Series

Taking Shots

Trying to Score

Empty Net

Falling for the Backup

Blue Lines

About Toni Aleo

WALL STREET JOURNAL, NEW YORK TIMES AND USA TODAY BEST SELLING AUTHOR TONI ALEO IS AN AUTHOR YOU CAN'T MISS!

make sure to Join my Mailing List: https://www.subscribepage.com/tonialeonewsletter

My name is Toni aleo and I'm a #PredHead, #sherrio, #potterhead, and part of the #familybusiness!
I am also a wife to my amazing husband, mother of a WKU Hilltopper and a gymnast, and also a fur momma to Phoebe, Gaston el Papillon & Winston.
You can usually find me hollering for the whole Nashville Predators since I'll never give my heart to one player again. When I'm not in the gym getting swole, I'm usually writing, trying to make my dreams a reality or being a taxi for my kids. I'm obsessed with Harry Potter, Supernatural, Disney and anything that sparkles! I'm pretty sure I was Belle in a past life and if I could be on any show it would be supernatural so I can hunt with Sam and Dean.
Also, could I LOVE hockey anymore?

www.tonialeo.com
toni@tonialeo.com

Made in the USA
Coppell, TX
06 October 2023